"BY ANY OTHER NAME"
being the first book of
THE SAUDER DIARIES

◆

a true account of
airship pirate and gentleman

Hans Sauder

aboard the infamous airship
"THE BLOODY ROSE"

MICHEL VAILLANCOURT

The Sauder Diaries
"By Any Other Name"

By Michel R Vaillancourt

~~~***~~~

"Lazarus Edition"
Independently Published by Avenger Press Services
At Amazon.com CreateSpace
Copyright 2010 – 2012 Michel R Vaillancourt
All Rights Reserved

~~~***~~~

DEDICATION

To my parents for instilling in me a love of literature that has stayed with me and inspired me to write.

To my wife Christine, for challenging me to prove that Hans Sauder's world would work, and for supporting me while I did so.

To my dear friend Tracey, for complaining there were no good airship pirate stories to be read and for introducing me to Steampunk in the first place.

To Abney Park, for being the original Airship Pirates.

To the fans, for understanding why it was important that this be the "Lazarus Edition" and who patiently waited for the pirates & friends of the Bloody Rose to get back under sail.

Thank-you.

~~~***~~~
~~~

"I Have Become A Pirate"

Diary Entry for April 3rd, 1888

My name is Hans Sauder, of Bremen, Germany. I was born in August of 1866. My family immigrated to England when the Crimean war threatened to destroy everything my father and grandfather had struggled to build.

Today I became an airship pirate. It can be rather unfortunate where life leads you.

As a result of this unexpected turn of events, I have decided to start a diary so that I can document my journeys. When I am eventually captured and brought to justice, this log will serve as my primary recourse of law.

I wish it understood from the outset that I am being coerced into cooperation by threats of murder and hardship. I have no choice but to comply until we are apprehended by either the Allied or Russian Air Navies. It is my sincere hope that this document will serve to exonerate me from blame of wrong doing.

*****

Hans woke to an unpleasant triumvirate of sensations. His skull still rung from the blow across its back that had sent him plunging into starred darkness. His ears were filled with a gruff, guttural voice that seemed directed at him. His nose was filled with the harsh Stygian stench of smelling salts. His eyes opened and slowly focused on the thin-bearded and goggled man leaning over him.

He was in irons and shackled to the bed he was stretched out upon. He noted with some relief that the man looming over him wore the accoutrements of a doctor of medicine. That dramatically reduced the odds Hans was part of a madman's post-doctorate research program.

"Ah, *Pan* Sauder, you are awake. Excellent. It would seem that *Panna* Annika's enthusiasm has not done permanent damage," the doctor said with a very amused note in his voice. He had a deep, rough Slavic accent that marked him as likely from the Russian areas; this was potentially bad news.

"How ... how do you know my name?" Hans asked cautiously, looking around slowly. The medical room was small. There were three beds including his, all with occupants in various states of ill health. Examination lighting was mounted on a ceiling track that could be moved over any of the beds. Shelves and cabinets painted white with red crosses covered almost every inch of wall. A door was at the corner of the room farthest from his bed. The doctor pulled the goggles up from his eyes to his brow and then wordlessly held up the leather folder that Hans recognized as containing his travel papers for his trip.

"Where... where am I?"

"The sickbay of *HMAFS Bloody Rose*," the doctor replied.

"Captain Blackheart's ship!?" Hans blurted in near terror. Suddenly, the idea of being an item of research did not sound nearly so bad.

The doctor nodded as he ground a couple of items together with a mortar and pestle. "The same. You will note, however, *Pan* Sauder, that you are on a bed in the sickbay and not a table in the galley. So long as you do not prove foolish, short-sighted, or suicidal, you are quite likely to live to see your next birthday," the doctor chortled.

"*Kapitän* O'Raedy is a harsh man, but his legend is partly fiction," the doctor continued more sombrely. "I am Doctor Alexi Koblinski; I have been the ship's doctor for two years now. You will note I am in reasonably good health, beyond a damaged liver; that is the curse of life as a pirate."

Hans was silent as the doctor tended to the other two patients in the room. They made no sound. He presumed they were sedated against the pain of the chest wounds they both seemed to have suffered.

His mind raced. He was shackled aboard one of the most feared pirate ships in both Europe and Russia. Perhaps they intended to ransom him? While his family was not royalty, they were wealthy. Thus, the pirates would wish him in good condition for the future exchange. He was certain his family would not hesitate at whatever sum Captain Blackheart demanded.

He recalled the fright of waking up in pre-dawn to sounds of cannon fire, shattering glass and cries of "Pirate" from the crew of the passenger merchant he had been aboard. He had gotten caught up in the fray, armed with a broken chair leg and his smallsword. The details blurred at that point, memories left in a fog from his first life-or-death fight and a blunt instrument to the back of the head.

Doctor Koblinski came back over to where Hans was and checked his pulse wordlessly and wrote the results down on a piece of paper. He was a tall man, possibly a bit more than six feet in height. He was gaunt of face from a combination of low mass, age and fatigue. His thin beard traced his jaw and connected to his side burns, more salt than pepper.

"I must thank you, *Pan* Sauder, you are a very kind man," Doctor Koblinski commented apparently at random as he finished updating his record.

"Um... pardon, *Herr Döktor*?" he replied, somewhat confused.

"You are a most precise swordsman. Your injuries to Kevin and Jacques, while painful and very effective at producing shock, are away from vital organs and arteries. They will both survive with stories to tell," he said waving his fountain pen in his hand as he spoke. "Very restrained of you for a man confronted by pirates while wearing his pyjamas."

*****

Captain Blackheart was unmistakable when he entered the sickbay some time later. While Hans was only an inch or so shorter than Doctor Koblinski, Blackheart was even shorter than that by at least a full two inches. However, what the Captain lacked in physical height was made up in shoulders, chest and aura.

He was a big man, in every aspect of how he stood, moved, looked and even spoke. He was easily twice Hans' measurements in chest, arm, and leg girth. Shoulder length coal black hair ended in a gentleman's curls, while his likewise coloured beard was tightly trimmed. Two long scars traced his left cheek to his ear, remnants of near misses with sword blades. His skin was deeply toned from a combination of sun and wind. The eyes were dark, heavy browed and piercing; Hans felt he was being wordlessly interrogated at some unknown level when that gaze came to rest on him where he now sat up in his bed.

Blackheart wore a black overcoat with gold braid and trim along its edges. The coat was left open, showing a battered leather vest, sword and utility belts, a flying scarf and white silk shirt. A couple of pistols were thrust into hangers on the sword belt.

The Captain's voice was a dull growl that hinted at an iron menace as well as careful measure of both what he spoke and what he heard. "So, you would be the Germanic chair thug that felled three of my crew? Yes?"

"Ah... Chair thug?" Hans stammered. He was acutely aware that the Doctor was intently occupying himself on the far side of the sickbay suddenly.

"Aye," Blackheart chortled, "you brained Emily with a chair leg, and used it to put a drubbing on Kevin and Jacques."

"I... I am sorry.. I did not realize that..."

"Oh, stop sniveling," Blackheart barked and Hans instantly fell silent. "You did better than the rest of that boat load of rats. You were almost the only real resistance we had. Now... who the blazes are you?"

"I'm Hans Sau..."

"No, you dolt. I know your name. I even know your father's name. I could not care less about that. Who are you?"

Hans blinked and hesitated, completely uncertain what to do with the question. Blackheart stared back at him and Hans was very aware of a dwindling amount of patience left in the Captain's eyes.

"I ... I am not sure what you mean, *Herr Kapitän*," Hans said in a forcedly level tone.

"Where did you learn to fight?"

"The University of Heidelberg Sabre team ... silver medalist, three years in a row ... and a Judo symposium in Berlin ... and several pubs in Heidelberg, Prague and London."

"Ah. There. You see ... your name... well, that can be anything. Where you have been, what you have done, where you are going, what you are doing ... *that* is what makes you who you are. Now ... your papers ... you are travelling from London to Stockholm ... why?" Blackheart leaned forward from where he now sat at the foot of the bed, apparently very interested in the upcoming answer.

"Aeronautics engineering ... I ... I am learning to design engines for my father's airships..."

"And outside of Daimler-Benz, the finest airship engine design school is, of course, the *Kungliga Tekniska högskolan* in Stockholm. You are a very bright man, then, as well as a very dangerous one."

Blackheart leaned back and rested his chin in one hand as he considered Hans for a few long and wordless moments. He seemed to come to a decision, giving a slight nod to his inner dialogue before speaking aloud to Hans.

"Well," said the captain, "the way I see it is you have got two choices. You can either join my crew or we can throw you overboard."

"What?!" Hans blurted, going pale.

"Oh, now please," Blackheart said with a dismissive wave of his hand. "We are a civilized group so we would give you a gliderchute. You will have to walk from where ever you land to somewhere safe, but I am quite sure you would be fine."

"Of course, you are good enough fighter and with your education and talents we could use you as an engineer for my ship. She is a good vessel, but getting a little old. I am sure a bright man like you working with Arietta and Visivald could do amazing things."

"But... you are pirates! I would become an outlaw! A man without a home or country!" Hans exclaimed.

Blackheart sighed. "You say that as though it were a bad thing. Mister Sauder, please consider ... while I had to rifle your papers to determine your name, you knew my name without introduction. We are hardly homeless gypsies here, we pirates. We live a grand life of adventure and travel. This ship has flown the north and south of Europe, into the reaches of Africa and beyond the Easts and Wests of the Mediterranean sea.

"No one here is poor, sick, restricted by class, birth status or even gender. Tell me, what does wrapping yourself in the flag of a country give you?"

"You are murderers! Thieves! Scoundrels reviled in every civilized place you travel!"

"*Kapitän* O'Raedy you will *not* strike a patient under my care!" Doctor Koblinski thundered, waking the two other patients with a start and arresting Blackheart's heavy open hand halfway through its arc to Hans' face.

"As for you, *Pan* Sauder, I will remind you that your current doctor is one of the thieves, scoundrels and murderers you decry. I take the Hippocratic Oath I swore nearly a decade ago very seriously. But," he shrugged expressively and then gestured at the sickbay around him, "... you are the company you keep." He turned back to the two patients that were now awake and making utterances of pain.

Hans turned back to meet Blackheart's glare. Blackheart lowered his hand without comment, his dark eyes unwavering from Hans' own.

"Thieves we are," Blackheart said in an incongruously conversational tone. "But we steal far, far less than the governments waste in needless 'improvements' to Dragons, Chimera, Galvanotaurs and the like to feed the ravenous maw their own debased 'national pride' and 'national interests'."

"The Crimean war ended years ago, but still the governments of Europe, the Baltic, and North Africa waste time, money, materials, and lives building better engines of destruction. I can assure you, Mister Sauder, that while some of my crew are indeed killers, none are nearly the murderers as the scientists, politicians and nobles you so highly respect."

"And as for being reviled," Blackheart laughed aloud. "For an educated man, you seem to miss important topics from your understanding."

"Oh?" Hans replied coldly. "Such as 'Aeronautical Banditry for the Aspiring Gentleman'?"

Blackheart guffawed and shook his head. "'Economics and the Need of Distribution'," he countered. "For example... the ship you were a passenger aboard this very morning. We took a gentleman's sum of 200 Marks from the safe, another 200 Marks in vanities like jewelry from the passengers, and an amusing assortment of choice goods such as 200 bottles of port, ten dozen pairs of garments by Levi Strauss of America, nearly a ton of fine Caribbean sugar, plus some mundanities such as coal, kerosene, food and drink for ourselves."

Hans blinked in open mouthed astonishment. "But ... what ... "

"... are we going to do with a ton of sugar and enough denim to outfit an army?" Blackheart grinned at him. "Sell them, Mister Sauder. We are going to sell them."

Blackheart made an expansive gesture with both hands as he continued. "There are dozens of merchants around Europe alone that operate entirely on the economy of selling expensive stolen goods cheaply. Take the denim garments, for example. The whole stack is likely worth around 130 Marks sold to individuals. We will sell the stack to a merchant outside of Brussels for perhaps 40 or 50 Marks. He will likely resell them for a total around 80 Marks to his customers. We benefit, he benefits and his customers have access to fine goods imported from America that they could not even get or otherwise afford."

"But...! The merchantman! The passengers! They have lost every..."

Blackheart silenced Hans with a gesture. "They are insured. They will have the price of their lost goods and cargo paid to them in full. No one in their right mind operates these days without it. Over 500 ships travel the region around the Mediterranean alone every month. You double that if you extend your watch from Norway to south of Ethiopia. Almost every one of them is paying insurance."

"In total, the *Bloody Rose* takes one victim a month during the summer and half that in the winter. It is very rare that the entire ship is taken or lost... we do not have the room aboard or the crew so we only take the cream of the crop. That is less than a tenth of a percent of the traffic, Mister Sauder."

"Your fancy newspapers and *kaffehaus* press sheets have deceived you, Mister Sauder," Blackheart said with a hand over his heart in an act of mock despair. "The mighty scourge of the skies, Captain Blackheart and the incarnate evil crew of the *Bloody Rose* are doing nothing at all that the governments themselves do not do. We are a very thin tax on the cost of doing business, and we bring goods-wealth of the rich to those that would otherwise not have it."

Hans stared at Blackheart, stunned. He could not believe his ears. The *Bloody Rose* was known across Europe as a murderous pirate ship that took few prisoners, left few survivors and pillaged entire shipping companies to bankruptcy. Her reign of terror had run almost four years and was well documented in credible newspapers. Even naval cutters had fallen prey to the infamous pirate ship.

"You ... you are a lying madman..." Hans began in a low voice, laden with denial of what he had just heard.

"Actually, *Pan* Sauder," the doctor interrupted from where he was tending to one of the other patients, "I can attest that *Kapitän* O'Raedy is in fine mental health. While I have known him to indulge in inebriated hyperbole when trying to impress a woman, I have yet to catch him in an outright lie."

Hans turned back from Doctor Koblinski to meet the shark-like grin of the amused Blackheart.

"So Mister Sauder, what will it be? Do you want to take your chances with a mile-high gliderchute jump and a Dragon? Or will you become an engineer on a pirate ship? Do understand that this is a special, limited time offer. Hesitate too long or reply too belligerently, and I may be forced to ... ah ... terminate our new relationship."

From Hans' perspective there was no choice at all. Jumping in this area of Europe was madness. Even if he did survive the descent and landing, he was very sure it was almost impossible to survive on the ground long enough for him to get anywhere meaningful. He would die down there. His only hope was to go along with Blackheart and the rest of the villains of the *Bloody Rose* until he could either jump ship at a port or the ship was finally captured by the Allied Air Navy.

There was a long moment of silence in the sick bay, brightened only by the mechanical sounds of the ship and the sound of the doctor's movements at a medicine cabinet. Hans dropped his head in defeat as he spoke.

"I will be your new engineer. But hear me clearly, *Herr Kapitän*: I will not kill anyone for you. I will not be a murderer no matter what you say," Hans said in a firm voice.

"You keep telling yourself that, Mister Sauder. Just keep telling yourself that. Mark my words... you will be a killer within a year, at your own desire. I know your kind all too well ... a taste of power, adventure and a pretty girl, and suddenly it is a bit easier than you thought." Blackheart gave him an ugly grin.

"But that is of no consequence. Welcome to the crew of the *Bloody Rose*. As soon as the good Doctor tells me you can assume duties, we will get you a bunk, some clothes and a watch to stand. I am quite sure you are going to be a fine addition to our crew."

"Right Of Passage"

Diary Entry for April 5th, 1888

After having been deemed fit enough to stand duties aboard the Bloody Rose, I was introduced to the Chief Engineer Arietta Itala, an Italian woman of Ethiopian heritage. She has made it eminently clear to me that while she respects my knowledge and accepts Kapitän Blackheart's addition of myself to her staff, she is in charge without question in the Propulsion Room.

In addition, I made the acquaintance of several of the crew and was obligated to convince them I would be able to carry my own weight in both duties and battles. While I will not kill anyone, I must confess that my love of both sword play and grappling fights does lend itself well to life in this particular arena. I suspect they were rather unaccustomed to a man of education also being able to manage himself in a physical contest.

During my first watch I was astounded to learn that the Bloody Rose is fitted with an EMIPALE ...this would explain much about her successes against military airships and even experimental aeroplanes.

*****

"Well, *Pan* Sauder, you would seem to be in good health and state of mind," Doctor Koblinski said after his morning examination. "I see no reason you should be occupying one of my beds any further."

"*Dankeschön, Herr Döktor.* You are a most pleasant conversationalist, but I also know you have better things to do than cure me of acute boredom," Hans chuckled. He had discovered that, amongst other things, the good doctor Koblinski was a ruthless chess player.

The doctor passed him a set of clothes which he explained would be suitable for work and life aboard the ship. They were likely to be a size or so too large, but they were better than nothing, and the previous owner had no use for them.

"Previous owner? Why did he give them to me?" Hans asked, puzzled as he pulled the brown cotton pants on and tied the front closed.

"Because a fifty-eight calibre musket ball laterally through the fore-brain allowed few other options than for him to pursue a voyage to the afterlife," Koblinski replied blandly.

Hans froze, with only his head and one arm in the white shirt he was pulling on. "He is dead?"

"Indeed. That diagnosis would be a ... ah ... 'no-brainer', as the gunners would say," the Doctor deadpanned. He frowned, studying the expression on Hans' face and then spoke again. "Please, *Pan* Sauder, you may as well put the clothes to use. He is a dead man. Whether you are clothed or not will not change that, and Alexandru was a good man. I think he would prefer his clothing go towards getting a new crewman off on a good footing."

Hans nodded slowly, finished pulling the shirt on, and then the richly embroidered vest. He was still somewhat discomfited at wearing the clothes of a dead man. It somehow seemed wrong, in spite of the evidence presented. He suspected his life for the next few weeks would be a constant balance of this kind. He pulled the blue-grey flight coat over top and fastened two of the buttons. The flight goggles were shoved in a coat pocket.

The doctor shook his hand and explained to him which way to go to get to the upper deck. From there, he would be introduced to the chief engineer. He paused a moment before opening the sickbay door for Hans.

"I should warn you of a couple of pirate traditions, *Pan* Sauder.   The first is that you will be expected to demonstrate that you are not going to be an undue burden or liability in both daily life and in combat. Do not be bashful or reluctant. Show off, in fact. Seeming weak or lacking confidence will simply result in the crew victimizing you for the duration of your life on the ship."

Hans lofted a brow and looked squarely at the Doctor. "Pardon?"

"You have to sleep some time, Sauder. If breaking a rib or bruising an eye or two ensures that you do so without fear, I suggest you take that opportunity."

"Secondly, an earring or two are considered badges of honour amongst pirates; usually to mark important things in their career, such as joining a crew, their first kill, a promotion, or the like. I would encourage you to allow me to do the piercing work should you choose that ritualistic route; I will assure you my equipment is at least clean."

The idea of having his ear or ears pierced as some record of villainy really did not agree with Hans at all. It seemed rather preposterous for a gentleman of any upbringing to even consider it. Certainly, his family would not approve of the idea.

"Um... well, thank-you for the advice, *Herr Döktor.* I will keep these things in mind," Hans said with a slight bow and nod. He stepped out into the narrow corridor, made his way along it, and then up a ladder into the bright light and chill air of the main deck of the *Bloody Rose.*

The sky was a brilliant blue, with the heights of what he thought to be the Pyrenees Mountains off the right side of the ship. He paused after closing the hatch, somewhat dazzled at the sight.

He was given a rough shove from behind, which nearly set him off balance. He turned to see three of the crew standing directly behind him with very unpleasant grins on their faces.

"I am MacIssac," said the closest. He had a sizable and well-worn oak belaying pin in his left hand, resting on his shoulder. He was dressed in rough clothes, including a tired vest, stained kilt and battered jack boots. "The short mutt here is Blauchuk. The one-eye is Cemil."

"Sauder," Hans said with a nod, eyeing the trio warily. He was aware that activity on the deck had come to a halt, and there was a great deal of attention focused on the nascent confrontation.

"So you think you are going to join the crew, do you?" the Scotsman asked with ridicule heavy in his voice.

"That is what the *Kapitän* has said, *ja*. I trust that will be sufficient for the likes of you?"

MacIssac spat at Hans' feet. "The 'likes of me' and me two chums here thinks you haven't got the spine or guts to last ten minutes around here. You aren't going to eat our food, cut into our shares and cause us grief, do you understand?"

Hans' eyes narrowed. This was likely partly what the doctor had been referring to earlier. "I understand that you need to speak to a hygienist, and possibly a psychologist. Particularly if you think that your worries are of any concern to me. If you press your luck, you will need to add a dentist to the list."

The three other men looked back and forth between themselves, obviously baffled. Hans sighed. "I said that you stink like goats and if you think strutting like roosters will get you anywhere with me, you are also barking mad. If you continue your threats, I will leave you spitting teeth on the deck. Do I need to speak to you dullards like addled children?"

The crew that had gathered around burst into laughter and it was quite plain that MacIssac was seeing red. "Blauchuk, teach this son of a bitch some manners. Let's see how his fancy words work for him," the Scotsman spluttered.

The man called Blauchuk stepped forward, lip curled in a sneer, and fists balled tight. He was a brick of a man; a touch short, but easily of more mass than Hans. "I am going to beat you like a cheap whore, Sauder," Blauchuk growled in a heavy Slavic voice, "and the only way I'll stop is when you promise me ten percent of your shares."

"I am going to throw you around like a bag of potatoes... and you are about to wind up mashed," Hans retorted. Blauchuk moved far faster than Hans would have given any man his size credit for and struck with such force that he slammed Hans' blocking arm aside. The blow struck him squarely in the jaw and sent him sprawling backwards. The crew laughed at Hans and cheered for the Slav.

Blauchuk took two steps forward, obviously meaning to attack him even as he was on the deck. Hans' left leg came up fast and squarely into the other man's groin, buckling him over with a bark of surprise. The right foot followed, bracing onto his gut and then Hans reached up, grabbed him by the shoulders and rolled him straight up and over, using both feet to lift and propel the heavier man. Blauchuk slammed shoulders and back onto the deck of the *Bloody Rose*.

More cheers, jeers and noise erupted from the crew. As Hans sprung to his feet, he glanced around swiftly. The other two had not joined the fray, but were standing back, watching the fight between Blauchuk and himself. It seemed that most of the crew was now around to watch the fight. Even Blackheart was on the quarterdeck railing, looking down at him with visible interest.

He and Blauchuk, who was apparently unimpeded by the fair amount of pain he should have been in, circled each other warily.   Hans' brutal opponent twice stepped forward trying to engulf Hans in a rib-crushing bear hug; Hans scarcely dodged aside each time. In the back of his mind, he marvelled at the speed with which the other man moved. Hans had never seen the likes of it.

Blauchuk lunged forward with a roar and a swinging punch. Hans stepped ahead and aside, blocking the man's leg with his own, grabbing his wrist and shoving the other shoulder. Suddenly off balance and spinning, the Slav's feet left the deck almost to his own waist height as Hans torqued him around. He fell heavily to the deck with a smash.

Hans leapt on him like a revenant. Both knees landed squarely across the base of Blauchuk's ribs and the downed man cried out in a choked bellow. Hans back handed him left-right-left in a windmill flurry and then rolled off him and rose.

"Are you done being slapped around like that whore you spoke of?" Hans challenged. The crew cheered in approval.

Blauchuk started to rise and Hans simply swept the bracing arm out from under him. He grabbed a flailing arm, jammed his foot into the connected armpit and pulled with all his might. The Slav cried out as the joint pulled free and then as Hans pulled again.

"Done? *Ja oder nein*?" The Slav seemed to hesitate and Hans pulled again, eliciting a full-throated scream this time.

"Done! Done!" Blauchuk choked. Hans let his arm fall to the deck under its own weight and Blauchuk cried out again in pain. Hoots and hollers from the crew surrounded him and he was sure he saw money changing hands; betting.

Hans turned towards MacIssac, only to find Cemil advancing on him in a hand-splayed and predatory gait. "I am Jabbar Cemil of Arabia, son of the desert jackals. I will crush your bones to sand, and you will beg for mercy. You shall only have that mercy for the cost of ten percent of your shares."

Hans realized there was more to this rite of passage or acceptance than merely a beating. There seemed to be some formula the two men were using. At the heart of it was owing to another man, but there was more to it than just that.

"I am Hans Sauder ... my father owns a kennel and you, son of a jackal, will make a fine addition to it unless you pay me ten percent of your shares." Approving noise rose from the crowd at Hans' bravado and demands.

The two traded blows and blocks for several passes, achieving very little. The one-eyed Arab fought some mixture of fisticuffs and wrestling that seemed to thwart Hans' every move and repeatedly rewarded his efforts with a punch to the body. Hans took and dodged a few more blows before he saw an opportunity he could exploit. He blocked, grabbed and spun Cemil around and then swept the Arab's feet out from under him, driving him face down into the deck.

Under other conditions, Hans would have allowed the other man to regain his footing and a chance to disengage. However, he was already beaten, bloodied, winded, and coming to the realization that he would likely have to fight the Scotsman as soon as the Arab was finished. He had no option for kindness; he drove the toe of his boots into the fallen man's ribs three times in rapid succession. Cemil coughed blood and lay still.

More noise from the crew. More money changed hands. MacIssac stepped forward.

Hans wiped the blood from his nose and gave MacIssac a cool look. "Let me guess, Scot... If I do not give you ten percent of my shares, you will rape some Welshman's sheep?"

"Oh, I've no need for sheep, Kraut. Your mother is always available and willing when a man like me is in town."

Hans nearly walked straight into the left-handed stroke of the belaying pin to the side of the skull that would have laid him out with one blow. He barely ducked out of the way of the back swing. It was only after a third near miss in as many swings that Hans realized he had been baited and nearly paid for it at the hands of an expert fighter. He intentionally dove and shoulder rolled aside and away from MacIssac. He needed distance.

An icy calmness descended over him. The cheering and howling of the crew was slowly reduced to a dull buzz. The pain of the bruises from the fighting faded into a warm and hazy wash.

The two fighters danced around each other, judging and pressing. A fist slammed into Hans' arm as he again narrowly avoided the pin. Hans sprung forward like a leaping mastiff and slammed his forehead into the centre of MacIssac's chest, staggering him. He grabbed the reeling Scotsman by the front of his shirt and shoved him backwards and then jerked him forwards, pulling him completely off-balance. His hands changed positions, one in MacIssac's hair and one at the back of his trousers, shoving him along. Without a break in the moment, Hans started running the two of them across the width of the deck towards the oncoming guardrail.

The crew parted before them and Hans ran the other man straight into the railing with all the force he could manage. The Scotsman's feet left the deck, and he lurched forward with a scream at the yawning void beneath his face. The German's two hands were now the only things keeping him from falling to his death far below.

"Pay or fly... your choice..." Hans gasped.

"Pay! Pay!"

"Be happy I am agreeing with you," Hans said in ragged breaths. He pulled the other man back and then shoved him to the deck.

Silence had fallen over the ship. All eyes were on him. Hans noted that the Captain was passing the Doctor a fist-full of money with an amused look.

"Well?" Blackheart bellowed. "Do we keep him?" The crew thundered its approval. "A pirate needs a sword. Give that pirate a sword to fight with," Blackheart commanded.

A tall, lean, walnut-haired woman stepped beside the Captain. She had a slight enough figure to have been taken for a man at this distance but for her bare midriff and the shape of her face. "He can use his own sword... if he can go get it." She pointed out over the railing behind Hans.

He turned to see one of the crew crawling back along the horizontally-rigged starboard-side mainmast of the ship. Beyond the crewman, hanging by a rope over the void below, was his smallsword.

His eyes narrowed. The sword had been a gift from his father and uncle the year he turned sixteen. It made no difference to Hans then or now that it was a very average blade. It was a cherished gift that marked his arrival as a man of the Sauder house. With it, came the responsibility of defending his honour and that of his family, as the Sauder men had for generations. He had travelled all over Allied Europe with that sword. Now, there it was, swinging by a string at the end of a mast over the Pyrenees.

He squared his shoulders. He was simply going to have to go get it. He wordlessly walked over to the very railing he had nearly run the Scotsman over and looked at the rigging. He spent a moment trying to suppress the fear of going out there with nothing but air on all sides and the ground a thousand or more feet below.

The hundred pirate crew shouted cheers and encouragement at him; it seemed to Hans they wanted him to succeed. It was as though, by besting the three men, he was already a member of the crew. This was just the icing on the cake.

"*Show off*," the Doctor had said to him. He nodded to himself and ran his eyes over the triangle structure of the ropes, masts and cross members. He backed up five steps, steeled himself against his fear, sprinted forward, and dove.

There was a frozen moment in time as his belt-line cleared the guardrail. In his mind flashed the image of sailing past the rigging and starting the long fall to the ground below. He utterly rejected it. He had *never* failed catastrophically at anything in his life. He would *not* now. He *would* land in the rigging net, he *would* reclaim his sword, he *would* win his freedom and he *would* return home in triumph to his family. In that crystalline instant of surety, there was not a force in the Universe capable of stopping him.

He landed in the rigging net chest first, grabbing the half-inch thick ropes that comprised it with all the strength left in his hands. The crew cheered. He stood in the rigging, turned to face the ship and its crew. He thrust a triumphant fist into the air with a bellow of raw will. Like a single savage animal, the crew roared in reply. He turned and went to get his sword.

*****

Hans carefully climbed down the nearly vertical ladder into the Propulsion Room of the *Bloody Rose*. He had spent the bulk of the afternoon walking the ship, learning her layout. The morning had been spent in the sickbay with Doctor Koblinski getting a few stitches and otherwise cleaned up from the beating he had taken. He would likely ache for days. Which was better than the first two would manage.

The *Bloody Rose* was unabashedly a gunboat by design, mounting sixteen guns of three different calibres and carrying the guns crews to support them. She was 110 feet long, 28 feet at her widest and from weather deck to keel was 24 feet. Typical of her day, her gas bags and rigging were mounted along the sides of her hull, almost increasing her total width by a factor of five, and giving her a hexagonal profile as seen from the nose or stern.

However, this gave her a clean, open "weather deck" and lifted forecastle and quarterdecks that allowed military operations of any kind. The guns were set in three rows per side; one set was above and one set below the bags and rigging. The third set was comprised of the lightest guns and was mounted on the weather deck itself.

While she had sails, they were not for combat. The cloth she rigged was for looking like a merchantman, or for conserving fuel. She mounted a trio of retractable propeller pods that, when under full steam, would drive her at a very aggressive 80 knots.

Arietta Itala, to whom he had already been introduced, was the Chief Engineer. She was forceful woman of Ethiopian heritage that had been bred, born and raised in Italy. Hans found it curious that either a Negro or a woman would somehow become the head of engineering on a pirate ship, let alone both, but he was not about to ask any questions just yet. He wondered just how much she actually knew about engines and aeronautics, or if she was merely an attractive face for the Captain at the upper deck mess table.

"What took you so damn long, Sauder?" she demanded imperiously.

"This check list of spaces and items you wanted me to find and become familiar with is both lengthy and diabolical. The 'prop wash dispenser', 'crate shadow cleaner', 'long weight manager' and 'forecastle roof crank' were particularly uncalled for," he scowled at her as he passed the task book back to her.

She laughed at him. "Well, at least you are not still wandering around cluelessly," she said with an almost astonishing richness in her voice. He imagined she would have been quite a singer with the proper training. "Now that you know the ship overall, we will get to the meat of the matter. Come with me."

She led him to the front of the cramped Propulsion Room, up and down quarter-height ladders and along a suspended walkway. "The *Bloody Rose* has a hybrid propulsion system. We have dual steam boilers driving Roper-Ludstrom pistons," she said pointing as she spoke, "as well as the much higher performance kerosene motors. In all cases, the power does not go directly to the propellers."

"No? Why not?" Hans asked, clearly puzzled.

"The motors are electric. The boilers and the engines are used to create electricity for the ship's use and drive the propeller pods. The balance ballast of the ship is entirely made of Plante chemical batteries, allowing us to keep a reserve of power. This allows us both tremendous torque and control when using the electric propeller pods. Do you understand?"

Any questions Hans may have had about her competence were cast aside. He bombarded her with questions about efficiency, design quirks, safety, voltage controls and anything else. She led him around, over, through and beside nearly every part of the equipment as she explained and illustrated. She was obviously pleased that he actually knew something about the matters of airship engines and hulls at all.

He noted she had no feminine fear of the usual grime that went with the job of coal/ oil slurry boilers and engineering in general. By the time an hour had gone past, the two were in dire need of bathing. Not that either of them noticed.

A blonde, balding Norwegian fellow named Visivald Aron joined them shortly thereafter, and Chief Itala introduced them. Visivald was also an engineer, and was sufficiently qualified that he could run the Propulsion Room alone outside of battles or emergencies. Hans learned that for the next while, he would be training and standing watches with Arietta. During battle or emergency, all three would be in the Propulsion Room. Eventually, and with enough hard work, he would get his own watch, making everyone's life much easier.

The notion of having his own watch-keeping ticket as a *bona-fide* airship engineer appealed to him momentarily. He dismissed the notion as quickly as it came. He would not be staying around the *Bloody Rose* long enough for it to come to pass.

As the Norwegian went about the process of doing his pre-watch take over, Itala took Hans over to a very sophisticated piece of equipment. It was marked with an embossed brass plate that read "EMIPALE", and sported all manner of gauges, dormant tubes, and dials. In the centre of the console was what looked to be the top half of a clock face. It was numbered from -3 on the left to +3 on the right-hand side. A pair of watch hands rested both on the zero position, straight up.

"Do you know what this is?" she asked him, watching him carefully. He shook his head. "It certainly looks very advanced ... there are indicators for current flow, and many Tesla tubes, so it obviously governs electricity for some purpose ... and those look like Gauss-Faraday meters of some kind ..." he trailed off and then shook his head.

She tapped the embossed brass plate and touched each of the letters as she spoke, "Electro-Magnetic Inductive Polar Aerostat Lift Engine." She paused. "Now do you understand?"

"You have got a WHAT?" he blurted, his eyes wide.

She laughed at him in that musical tone of hers and then settled on an amused smile. "You see? I am not just pretty."

"But ... but I never said ..." he stammered.

"You did not have to. Every man I have met has presumed it is my smile, voice and walk that keep me alive. While they are useful assets as a trophy woman in my native country, they are of limited value as a pirate. I put my brains and my hands to good use." She clapped her hands together once as illustration of the point. "Now, you seem to know this machine is of great value. Can you tell me what it is, and how it works?"

He opened his mouth, feeling rather ridiculous at his earlier presumption of her role as the Captain's eye-candy. Negro or not, woman or not, she was clearly an intellect to be reckoned with and an accomplished engineer. He vowed to never make such a mistake again.

"Do you intend to speak, or merely catch coal dust?" she queried politely. He closed his mouth, recomposed himself and answered her as respectfully as he could. "No. Teach me."

The EMIPALE system used three large steel drums built into the hull to create a local resistance to the Earth's natural magnetic field. Much as placing the like poles of two magnets together causes them to push themselves away from each other, the EMIPALE generated lift. This required significant quantities of electrical current and some method of ensuring that the magnetic repulsion generated by the system was of the correct intensity and polarity to the exact point on the Earth's surface they were over. This in turn required a differential analyzer to rapidly and repeatedly recalculate the settings for the system, while a human operator oversaw and applied corrections manually. Done correctly, the EMIPALE system could easily increase the lift of an airship by half while it operated. A mistake on the part of the human operator could suddenly result in half of the lift of the ship being violently taken away.

Hans had heard about the theory of how such systems would work, but neither he nor his father had ever seen one. Rumours were that the largest battle platforms in the Russian and Allied Air Navies had them, but they were hush-hushed secrets. Yet, here he was, sitting at the controls of one. His father would never believe him.

"I must ask ... how did you get one of these?" Hans said after she had finished explaining the entire system to him and led him around the ship twice more in an hour and a half.

She flashed her perfect pearl-white smile at him from beneath the grime and dirt on her already dark face. "The original chief engineer built it from parts he had stolen upon his departure from a Russian war laboratory. Since then, the Captain has been very careful to keep it in good working order, so we keep ears and eyes on the black markets of Europe and Russia for pieces we may need. Now, are you ready to try your hand at operating it?"

Hans nearly clapped like a school boy.

"I thought so," she laughed. She walked to a voicepipe and spoke into it. "Steering, this is Propulsion. We are going to be testing the EMIPALE for about a quarter hour."

"Thank-you, very good," came the muffled reply. A series of whistles and bells sounded throughout the ship.

"*Signore* Aron, flash up the kerosene engines and channel the batteries for the EMIPALE, please," she ordered. Hans watched her carefully as she went through the start-up sequence for the system with him until the entire machine was giving a warm electrical hum and its tubes and dials were all aglow with power.

Managing the EMIPALE was deceptively simple. A series of gauges would disagree with each other as to the total value and polarity of repulsion needed. He would then move the two clock hands on the hemisphere dial to set the correction. This, in turn, would change the electromagnetic environment around the ship, resulting in a new set of disagreeing gauge values, and he would repeat the process.

She closed a knife switch and said "That is it, you have the board".

The ship fell nearly a foot and a half from beneath his backside. "I would strongly recommend a correction of some kind, *Signore* Sauder, before the magnetic drums tear themselves from the hull. That would greatly upset me," Itala said sternly. She was braced, both hands solidly grasping a piece of over-head piping, but otherwise apparently unconcerned about the implied doom about to befall them. Aron had simply clipped his work belt to rings on his watch-keeping chair.

Hans flailed, over compensating in the opposite direction, resulting in the ship surging upwards almost a yard. The wood and metal of the ship moaned in protest. He corrected again, almost evening out the lift and quite nearly deadening the next drop.

After fifteen minutes of fighting with the system he had gotten to the point where he was beginning to see the pattern of error and required correction and anticipating what to do next. About half way through the process, she ordered Aron to take twenty percent of the gas from the bags and then another twenty percent, leaving more and more of the lift-load of the ship with the sweat-covered Hans.

Finally, they re-inflated the gas bags to full pressure for the altitude they were at, and shut the EMIPALE down. "That is harrowing work," he said as he wiped his brow and shook his head.

"Not bad, *Signore* Sauder. You learn quickly and have a good mind for mathematics. Now, take this list of tasks, do them to the best of your ability and report back to me. Then you will be done for eight hours until it is again my watch."

He nodded and took the task book from her and skimmed it over. He margin-noted a couple of items and stood to go.

"One more thing, *Signore* Sauder. You are a welcome member of my crew here. You only answer to me, and the Captain. However, if you wilfully disobey me in any way, you will discover the reason I do not owe anyone a tenth of my wages. Do you understand me?"

He involuntarily ran his eyes over her very obviously female frame and thought about that. He had a very sudden disinterest in finding out directly how she would have dealt with the likes of Blauchuk.

"Understood, *Frau* Itala. *Dankeschön*."

"Blood, Splinters and Iron"

Diary Entry for April 8th, 1888

It has been three days now that I have been working as an engineer aboard the Bloody Rose, with Chief Itala as my supervisor. The work is interesting and satisfying. I have certainly come to enjoy working with her as a person as well. She and the Doctor will be two people I miss when I leave the ship.

Over the past three days, I have begun to settle into the routine of life aboard the Bloody Rose. Like so many things in life, I must guard against the complacency that a comfortable routine brings. I cannot lose sight of my objective of gaining my freedom and returning home.

I thought that today might well be the day when I would be liberated from my forced role as a pirate. We were surprised by a French Frigate, the Triomphe. There was a bloody battle, including a boarding action. Unfortunately my attempt to win my freedom did not go as planned and the Bloody Rose continues to be my captive home.

Regardless of what else I may think of him, I must acknowledge that Kapitän Blackheart is a keen judge of men and character. I must remember this for future dealings with him.

*****

"Good morning, *Signore* Sauder," Itala greeted him from her position in the watch-keeping chair. "You found a few hours of sleep, I trust?"

"*Ja, Frau* Itala," he answered as he arrived beside her. He sipped at the insulated metal flask of coffee he carried and gave her a polite nod. "Sleeping in a hammock with eight others in the room with me is taking getting some used to, but it is fine."

He picked up the task book and got started with the work that needed to be done for this watch. Only one of the two coal/oil slurry boilers was lit, and it was running at the lowest setting on its throttle, keeping the noise in the Propulsion Room to a minimum. With all four engines at full power, the propeller pods streamed and the blades turning, the noise was sufficient to drown out anything less than a shout.

Normally as they worked, Arietta lectured. For example, yesterday the discussion was on the start-up and shutdown process of the kerosene engines. This was how they spent the time on watch; each doing their required duties, and at the same time keeping up a constant dialogue on whatever topic it was she had decided to educate Hans. From Hans' perspective it was like trying to juggle and drink under a waterfall at the same time. He routinely surprised her with the depth of his own knowledge, but at the same time, she understood the power and propulsion systems on the *Bloody Rose* like no one else. Today however, she seemed content with a companionable silence.

The Propulsion Room was a full two decks high, from the bottom of the ship up. It also occupied almost the entire aft quarter of the ship in length. It was a maze of tarnished brass and copper pipework and tanks; brightly coloured control cables and electrical wires; worn valves and gears; and all other manner of mechanical apparatus that was associated with the job of moving the ship and providing the power to do it.

Hans climbed up an access ladder that took him to a series of reservoir tanks. He used a dip stick at each tank, noting how full it was in his task book and which ones would need to be refilled. From his vantage point above and somewhat behind her, he could look downwards to where Arietta sat in the watch-keeper's chair. She leaned back in the chair with the calves of her long legs kicked up over a nearby brass pipe that ran past horizontally. Her eyes drifted over the assortment of gauges that detailed the engineering health of the complex Propulsion Room as it operated.

She sipped from a metal flask identical to his; like him, she was a coffee drinker. While he preferred his with sugar and milk – a point she had teased him about, claiming he drank his coffee like English tea – hers was tar black and unsweetened in any way. They had sampled each others' flasks a couple of nights past and had been rather hurried in returning to their respective normals.

He took his time at the job of dipping the tanks. The truth be told, this secretive view of the Engineering Chief was one of the more pleasant parts of his job. While he was not the sort to sow wild oats as his father had cautioned him against, he certainly did enjoy the sight of an attractive woman. Negro or not, Arietta was a very attractive woman.

One of the things that Hans found most interesting about her was her height. She was likely the tallest woman aboard, nearly the height of the doctor. That would have placed her at nearly six feet tall. Nature had given her the sort of figure that women from London to Lisbon and from Brussels to Berlin tried to force upon themselves with a corset and bustle. While she was wasp-waisted, her shoulders and hips were proportioned to her height, making her a formidable presence when she was displeased. From his vantage point above her lazily reclining profile, she was a very pleasing sight.

His eyes took a slow tour of her shape below him. Her skin, eyes and hair were all the colour of fresh-ground coffee and the flash of her pearl-white teeth when she smiled or laughed was almost jarring. Her attire rarely varied, which he found interesting. She usually wore men's riding boots on her feet, which were matte black and swept back at the knee. Her pants were almost loose, but still tapered to the line of her leg in alternating dark charcoal and sooty-red vertical stripes. Her shirt was a jaunty red and white lace-up with a pocket-laden leather vest over top. She wore two crisscrossed belts at all times, each one loaded with a selection of tools and tins; she always seemed to have just what she needed at hand when working.

She shifted slightly and adjusted her shirt collar, exposing some of the dark skin of her breasts to his gaze, and he felt himself flush slightly. He quickly finished dipping the last two reservoirs and came back down the ladder. She gave him an amused smile as he went over to the pump and valve station.

He cranked a pump arm to transfer kerosene from a tank in the forward-bottom of the ship to one of the smaller "ready to use" gravity-feed reservoirs, above the engines, which he had noticed was very low. As he worked, he reflected that he was in a real danger aboard the *Bloody Rose*. An intellectual danger, not a physical one he mused; he had taken the Doctor's advice to heart. He had no hesitation at all in using a judo throw into a bulkhead to blacken the eye of any pirate that so much as clenched a fist around him.

No, the real danger here was being seduced into the easy idea that the real-world education he was getting from Chief Itala on the engines and systems of the *Bloody*

Rose made it worth staying for. She was a charming woman, a formidable intellect, and a tremendously well rounded engineer. She was also easy to speak to, easy to look at, and easy to work with.

She had told him last watch that next week they would be dismantling the port-side kerosene engine to give it a complete cleaning and maintenance. She would ensure he knew that engine – a genuine Spitsbergen Foundries 656 – inside and out before they were done. This was a far more interesting approach to learning than books and classrooms, even at a prestigious place like the Royal Institute of Technology in Stockholm.

Of course, at the "KTH", he would wind up with an actual degree that could be displayed on the design documents of his father's future airships. He could not say the same for any engineering ticket or other education he fancied he might earn from Arietta.

Life aboard the pirate vessel was not exactly as he would have imagined. It was, by far, more mundane than he would have believed. The crew totalled 100 or so souls, half of those gunner-marines. The men aboard outnumbered the women 11 to 1, but he had already learned that every last one of the 'ladies' aboard were murderesses and not to be trifled with. Notably his Chief Arietta Itala and the Marine Captain Annika Nadezhda had intentionally killed during at least one of their three "Right of Passage" fights.

The daily routine aboard the *Bloody Rose* was quiet and predictable. He worked in the Propulsion Room for eight hours and then had eight hours to himself. Hearty meals were served four times a day; 7am, 11am, 4pm and 8pm. Beer or strong drink was allowed with meals so long as you could do your job. If you were not sleeping and not already working at an assigned task, then you were fair game for whatever work detail needed man power. Hans considered this reasonable. It was obvious to him that a ship this size needed constant care and attention. However, many of his shipmates grumbled at every lift of the Boatswain's Call.

Quarters were cramped and personal space at a premium. He had a space for his hammock, his upright locker box and his locked boot box to himself. The maximum ceiling height was nine feet; in many places up to a third less than that. As he had said to Arietta, eight other men slept in the 100 square foot room with him. If you were not in your hammock, you were expected to keep it rolled up and stowed it away so the place was less cramped. The sleeping bays were grouped by trade and by rank, save for the women, who all shared one bay. Blackheart, of course, had his own cabin space.

The noise was a nearly constant unpleasantness. At any time of day or night, 30 pirates were up and about, working, living and moving within the ship. The steam plant and generators thrummed. The wind whistled and sang in the rigging. Pipes, drums and bells sounded irregularly to pass communications around the ship. Mornings were loudest, particularly just after breakfast as more than two thirds of the ship's crew was up, about and working through the tasks and training of the day. Often, the guns were run out and back a dozen times or more at this hour, as the crews practised their skills. This had the same tonal quality as a stampede of demented wild boar to Hans in his hammock.

The odour was also something he was having a difficult time getting used to. Gunpowder, steam, oil, sweat, food, spruce, coal, and a myriad of other scents combined to produce an atmosphere in the below decks areas that was sometimes sickening to Hans. Among other things, he was used to well ventilated manors and dormitories, as well as the company of people who considered only bathing weekly as an unpleasantly stretched minimum instead of an optional luxury. Of course, water was a hoarded resource aboard the ship; to replenish meant hovering, vulnerable, over a lake at low altitude while pumps were run. However, there were limits to austerity in Hans' mind.

A series of whistle blasts rang out followed by a ringing bell. Hans turned and looked over at Chief Itala; he did not yet recognize that combination. He saw that she was inexplicably pulling her flight coat back on.

"We are under attack! Tie back your tails, and put on your goggles and breather!" she barked at him.

"Under attack? But …"

"That was the action alarm … but we have not been told to run up the engines or furl the masts and sails … which means that we are the prey! Get dressed, damn you, Sauder!"

He ran to where his coat hung and grabbed it. The ship rolled sharply and the shouts and cries of the crew racing for their battle positions rang throughout the ship. The roaring howl of what sounded like a steam locomotive gone feral filled the air and then faded.

"Cannon fire… and a near miss. Below us, I think. PUT YOUR GOGGLES DOWN," she bellowed at him.

"What…? *Ja!*" He pulled his down to match hers and pulled on his leather breathing mask. It was normally only worn on the upper deck to cut the chill wind from making breathing impossible. He had never put it on below decks before. Itala reached over and flipped up the collar of his coat.

"Bring the port boiler to full steam, and then start flashing up the starboard. Move, man!" she shouted at him as she turned to answer the calls of the Steering House voicepipe. Hans struggled to keep his balance as the ship rolled and pitched as he moved. The terrible roaring howl again filled the air, but instead of fading away this time it was cut short with a tremendous crash and the sounds of splintering planks and tearing timber. The *Bloody Rose* lurched and heaved, nearly knocking Hans to the deck.

"We took a hit! Heavy balls, from the feel of it … military. This could be a real fight," Itala shouted over the noise. She seemed almost gleeful at the prospect. "Did you hear the sound of the wood?"

"Of course," he shouted back as he furiously cranked valves, fear fuelling him with adrenaline, speeding his movements.

"When the planks splinter from the strike of a cannon ball, they turn into dozens of flying arrows … if you wish to keep your vision and your looks, you keep your goggles down, your mask on, and your collar up. Use the ties on the inside of your coat to pull the sides back, to free your legs as you move. The coat is thick enough to protect your body from the ricocheting splinters. How is that boiler?"

"All valves open, coming to full pressure and flow!" He paused for a moment. "Ricocheting? What about direct?"

"Are you a pious man, *Signore* Sauder?" she asked in an apparent *non sequitur* as she worked quickly at a set of levers, valves and dials.

"Um … not really, no, Chief," he replied.

"Then I will see you in Hell," she laughed. "Now, quickly, start up the next boiler … we will need all the power we can manage for the propellers and the EMIPALE … Steering this is Propulsion … Roger, aye, power to the furlers and stream the propeller pods … we will need two minutes for the EMIPALE … Yes, two minutes! We got caught with our knickers down … Aye, Sir, fast as we can!"

She glanced over at Hans and then back over her shoulder as the Norwegian came sliding down the ladder from the upper deck, landing heavily. "Aron, get the starboard kerosene motor flashed up and then take the EMIPALE ... Sauder! Take the watch chair so I can manage the electrical transmission board."

"*Ja!*" Hans shouted, banging himself hard against some pipework as the ship lurched again when he tried to move towards her position. The sound of thunder filled the air and the ship shuddered. He tumbled against Itala as they traded places, and she reflexively braced herself to steady him.

"*Divertente, sì?*" she laughed. "At least we are shooting back now!"

"What?" he asked as he reached from where he sat to spin a valve to balance a climbing pressure gauge.

"Huh? Oh! I asked if it you thought it was fun!" She was grinning like a mad woman, deftly moving with each lurch, plunge, swerve and shudder of the ship. By now the sounds of cannon fire, both incoming and return, were nearly constant. The two kerosene engines roared with the throttles opened wide and the two boilers carried the deep, bassy thrum of a ten-ton kettlepot.

The sound of rushing wind became louder as Arietta worked the controls to lower the three propeller pods, with the sounds of large electric clockworks and pulleys churning away.

"EMIPALE is powered ... I have the board!" Visivald bellowed over the cacophony of battle.

"Sauder! Tell Steering they have propellers and lifters!"

Hans nodded and called up the voicepipe as she told him. The din above meant he had to repeat himself twice, shouting to be heard.

The feel of the ship's motion changed. Her turns became sharper, her climbs and dives became more aggressive. No longer constrained by the wind, she moved like the predator of the sky she was renowned to be. The sound of the middle-calibre cannons joined in on the next chorus of fire and smoke. They had more treble in their thunderous report than bass.

Aron was working furiously at the controls of the EMIPALE, making Hans' first efforts look truly amateur. Chief Itala was nearly swinging from pipe to strut as she moved around the Propulsion Room, timing her motions against some unseen metronome of battle that allowed her footing to always be true. Hans was more than busy, balancing the steam pressures, generator revolutions, and propeller speeds of one of the most aggressively built power plants he had ever seen. The power of two thousand charging horses was at his fingers. He was nearly light headed with adrenaline at the sounds and feel of the battle raging around him between the *Bloody Rose* and her assailant.

There was a howling crash that reduced time to a crawl for a long moment of terror. He glanced over his shoulder in time to watch a square yard of the port hull explode inwards. The wood tore itself apart into a scything hail of splinters that murderously filled the air with their hissing flight. Each of the deadly splinters and shards ricocheted two or three times before coming to a halt. He threw his arm In front of his face in an automatic reaction, feeling dozens of sharp impacts over his arms, chest, goggles and breather mask.

Hans' masked scream of fear was completely occluded by the sound of 12 pounds of iron tearing through the hull, air, pipework and then port boiler at 600 feet per second. There was a tremendous second burst of sound as the water in the boiler "flashed" under the rapid loss of pressure. The entire Propulsion Room was filled, in a matter of seconds, with a cloud of steam.

The only thing that stopped them all from being scalded to death was that the geyser of exhausting steam was faced away from them. Most of the initial gout of super-heated vapour went out the ragged hole in the hull which the ball had made on the way in. As it was, Hans was desperately thankful for the breather mask covering his mouth and nose, preventing him from painfully breathing the steam.

Hans brushed foot-long splinters off his arms. He rapidly threw levers and turned valves to "choke" the fires out in the wrecked boiler. With no water in its tank to cool it, the entire thing could turn into a cherry-hot heap of slag that would burn straight through the hull.

Itala was suddenly beside him in the hot fog. Red blood seeped between the dark skin of her fingers where she had her hand clamped over a wound in her left upper arm. The piece of metal that caused the injury still jutted cruelly out from between her fingers.

"A real fight," she grinned weakly and leaned heavily against him. She shouted up the voicepipe to inform them of the loss of the boiler and that the EMIPALE would drain the batteries in less than two minutes. Blackheart's voice came back down saying two minutes would be enough.

There was another roar and crash, and the *Bloody Rose* lurched and screamed. An over-speed alarm sounded on a propeller pod. Itala weaved her way to the electrical control panel and opened a series of knife switches as fast as she could. She looked over at her two crew with a grim look in her goggled eyes.

"*Un motore morto*, two to go. I hope the Captain ends this soon, or we are in trouble," she shouted over the sounds of even more cannons, tearing wood and screaming men.

What sounded to Hans like a series of balloons exploding reached his ears. Visivald looked relieved.

"Harpoon grapples," Arietta explained as she rejoined him. Her normally bright eyes were narrow with pain behind her goggles. The cannon fire suddenly stopped. "The two ships are tied together now ... The attacker cannot risk shooting us down without taking themselves with us. *Cavi di metallo* ... sorry ... metal cables ... launched by compressed air and rocket motors ... They cannot cut them fast enough to save themselves. The Captain has forced a boarding."

Another series of whistles and bells sounded. Itala looked at herself and then at Visivald. Hans could clearly see where the steam had scalded part of the Norwegian's face and one of his hands and forearm. He must have been in tremendous pain, but he wilfully stayed at his post, working the controls with everything he had.

"You are the most fit of all of us, *Signore* Sauder. You will go," she said, moving to a locked chest on the deck beside the watch-keeping panel.

"Go? Where?" he asked, drawing a complete blank at what she might mean.

"To the main deck. To fight in the boarding battle. I wish I could join you, but not like this," she said as she unlocked the box. "Now, listen to me. The French and the Spanish will show no mercy to pirates. To be captured by them just means jail and public execution. You will fight like the devil you are, or you will die. Take this," she passed him a long, sleek-looking firearm in a leather holster on a belt.

"It is a bolt gun. It is powered by air. You grab the ring on the butt of it like this, and then pull and push twice." She demonstrated. From above, the sounds of battle had faded and now the air was rapidly filling with what seemed to be cheering and cat calls.

"You then put the projectile in the muzzle, like this. It is thirty-eight calibre, and made of a steel shaft with aluminium fins. At any distance within the length of the ship, the dart will break ribs or tear holes in limbs," she said with a nasty but forced smile. "Do not hesitate to use it. Tell me, what is my first name?"

He looked at her blankly.

"Do not be dull, Sauder, what is my first name?" she barked at him.

"Arietta!"

"*Bene*. Now," she took a pair of leather bracers out of the lock box. Each of them had a long, stiletto-like blade jutting out past the length of her hand. She strapped one onto the uninjured arm. She passed Visivald a crossbow, which she loaded for him with a lever device.

"When you come back down ... if you do not call my name, Visivald will shoot you in the back. That will be nicer than I will be to anyone who makes it to the bottom of the ladder alive without calling my name. Do you understand, Hans?"

"Yes, Chi ... Arietta," he stammered. He strapped on the belt she had given him and holstered the gun.

There was a tremendous crash of wood against wood and a groan that shook the ship. The noise above turned from cheering to the primal scream of some monster. She grinned at him. "Go. Kill a couple of the bastards for me. You will have stories to tell me of what I missed on our next watch together."

*****

Hans opened the hatch to the upper decks to find his path blocked by the back of a uniformed man. Without warning or comment, Hans clubbed him across the back of the head with the wrench he carried in his free hand. The man fell like a stone to the deck beside the hatch. Hans clambered out and looked around.

The upper deck was some Faustian Hell. Smoke swirled and fires burned, while the wounded and fallen lay in pools of blood and bile. The air was saturated with the stench and sound of pitched battle unlike anything he had ever seen. He steeled himself against his reaction to flee back down the ladder.

He looked up, praying to see a German or English flag on the other ship. His heart sank at the sight of the red, white and blue bars of France. The battle was clearly between the pirates and the easily identified French marines and sailors. The other ship was only slightly bigger than the *Bloody Rose*, and the numbers seemed even. The current tide of the battle had carried onto the deck of the pirate ship, and its crew was on the defensive.

Hans looked around, trying to figure out some way he could surrender to the French; to prove his innocence. On the quarterdeck, he saw a desperate hope.

Captain Blackheart was in a pitched battle with two Frenchman, wielding his single cutlass against the two men. As skilled a swordsman as he was, they were still keeping his efforts neutralized. The victor would be the last to make a mistake or tire.

Hans set his jaw. Perhaps he would become a killer today. Chief Itala had said it was an air-powered gun with enough force for breaking ribs. He reasoned it would be unlikely to deliver an immediately fatal wound. He was of a desperate mind. If the French would give no quarter to pirates, he had to do something that would make it clear that he was not one of them. Otherwise, the French Marines would quite likely kill him.

He rapidly charged and loaded the bolt gun and took aim ... on the Captain. He had never really fired a pistol at range before, but he had seen it done. He held the gun in a two-handed grip to steady it, and stared fixedly into the glass targeting lens, placed precisely on Blackheart's face.

The battle swirled around him as though a dream happening to someone else. He felt as though he stood in a tunnel of destiny, with nothing between him and the man who had tried to make him a pirate.

He pulled the trigger and everything went horribly wrong. One of the two French marines stepped sideways while trying to feint for an opening and walked directly into the line of fire. The dart slammed into the back of his head, shattering his skull with a cry. The shot man staggered and then dropped like a puppet with cut strings. The other marine looked over to see what had happened and Blackheart's heavy cutlass split his skull to the shoulders.

"Well done, Mister Sauder! Good shot!" Blackheart bellowed. The tunnel between them collapsed and suddenly Hans was in the middle of the pitched melee. A Frenchman came at him, with sword swinging. Hans slammed him face-first into the deck and broke his ribs with his boot. He pulled out his smallsword and was immediately engaged by another assailant. The attacker fell, slashed from shoulder to hip.

The battle became a colourless blur. It was a timeless, mechanical affair to Hans, in a place devoid of emotion. He tried to surrender two or three, perhaps four times, shouting in French at whoever attacked him, but they paid him no heed. "Pirate," they shouted back at him. Some, he cut. Others, he threw. A few, he shot. At some point, he registered he was bleeding, but had no idea how he had been wounded.

Finally, it was over. The pirates had won.

The decks of both ships looked like what they were: war zones. This had not been some simple battle between trained pirates and untrained merchants where a few stubborn souls met their end and the others struck their colours immediately for fear of their own lives. Both crews had been trained fighters and none of the injured had sold their wounds cheaply.

Captain Blackheart strode over to him, with a wretched grin on his face. "Well, well, Mister Sauder. It seems I was right about you, aye, my boy? When push came to shove, you did it. And a handy shot it was, too. Chief Itala gave you that did she?"

Hans looked at him, wordlessly. He pushed his goggles up and pulled the leather breathing mask down. Grime, char and blood stained his face. Anger suffused his features. His eyes had a terrible darkness in them and he felt sick to his soul.

Blackheart cocked his head, studying him with the same look he had given him in the sickbay, when they first met. He lofted a brow at what he found.

"Well, well, Mister Sauder. That is not the look of a man pleased with his accomplishments. Those eyes ... those belong to man that missed his intentions," Blackheart gave him an amused smile. "I see. Well ... I supposed we have *both* learned something today, then, have we not? You should return to the Propulsion Room right away, Mister Sauder ... I do believe you should return Chief Itala her little assassin's gun before someone else is harmed by it."

"This is not over, *Herr Kapitän*," Hans whispered.

"Oh, no, Mister Sauder. Oh, no, it most certainly is not. I expect you and I shall be keeping each other on our guard for a long time," Blackheart chuckled in some macabre amusement.

*****

The next hour or so was barely organized chaos. Hans had lifted the hatch into the Propulsion Room to find two dead Frenchmen at the bottom of the ladder. After a moment of shock he immediately shouted Arietta's name two or three times until she acknowledged him. One of the

French had died with a crossbow bolt in his back. The other had four narrow punctures in his chest; each kidney and each lung.

Itala and Aron had already begun repairs before Hans had arrived. Hans was immediately put to the job of cataloguing the damage and estimating the number of hours for each item. He was happy to immerse himself in the work, insulating himself from the nightmare he had participated in on the upper decks.

After a time, he passed the list to Itala. "Thirty-six hours, presuming we have all the parts. And that does not touch the boiler … it is likely irreparable, even with a dock and time to cut a hole in the hull," he said grimly. He did not have any faith they had thirty-six hours to avoid another fight.

She nodded and reviewed the list. "We do not have all the parts with us," she said with a heavy sigh after a period of staring at the page. "I want you and *Signore* Aron to go scavenge from the French frigate. Specifically look for what you have on this list, but take everything you can pry loose. We are short one boiler, one kerosene motor and 30 percent of our lifting gas. That means that to make any headway without the French ship tied to us, we will need to run on the EMIPALE almost constantly. We will need the second Spitz running for that."

The next fourteen or so hours were a back-breaking job of salvaging everything possible from the French ship, the *Triomphe*. The crew of the *Bloody Rose* were like ants, feeding from the corpse of the animal that had tried to harm them. Everything of value that could be taken was brought back to the pirate ship. Stores, provisions, ammunition, parts, cargo, water, fuel and anything else that could be easily moved by groups of four to six gunner-marines under the direction of the stewards and engineers was looted. Some was stowed for future use or sale while some was used immediately in the repairs.

At one point, Doctor Koblinski stopped him on the upper deck of the *Bloody Rose*. "Ah, *Pan* Sauder. I am very pleased to see you alive," he said with a genuine smile. Hans wiped a filth-covered hand on his pants and shook the doctor's hand.

"*Ja*, *Herr Döktor*. A couple of shallow cuts and many more bruises, but I am fine," he said with exhaustion heavy in his voice.

"Good! I was afraid you had perhaps not survived. It is the first fight you were in where you were not immediately in my sickbay afterwards!" Koblinski laughed.

For some reason he could not fathom, Hans laughed for a long time.

"The Moses Reverse"

Diary Entry for April 10th, 1888

The tenacity and ingenuity of the pirate crew amazes me. After the murderous battle against the French air-frigate 'Triomphe', the Bloody Rose has escaped south across the Mediterranean Ocean to an inland airship port known as al-Myāh Wālsmā'. Unfortunately, Captain Blackheart's clever strategy of a "Moses Reverse" has effectively prevented me from pursuing my bid for freedom.

However, it did give me a chance to see and experience the local culture in a way I otherwise would not have. I have two mementos of our visit here that I am looking forward to showing to my family upon my return home.

This, in turn, has resulted in an unexpected complication to my life aboard ship in the form of the Captain of the Gunner-Marines, Annika Nadezhda. As a result of recent actions on my part, she has taken an interest in my "career" as a pirate. I am sure that once the novelty wears off, she will forget about me.

*****

The morning sun burst over the eastern horizon. It transformed the pre-dawn gloom by bathing everything in its radiance of molten gold. The wind was light and the clouds high. At a scant hundred feet above the water cruised the *Bloody Rose,* running without lights but making no other attempt to conceal herself. Her masts and sails were still furled back and stowed and one propeller pod was streamed and spinning. She was still scorched and gouged from her battle of two days' past.

She had spent the previous day at high altitude, drifting in the chill air above five thousand feet, while her crew made repairs around the first clock after the battle. With sunset came her liberation from the hulk that her crew had torn apart to heal her wounds.

They left the *Triomphe* and her surviving crew behind. Her gas bags were bleeding slowly, her fuel tanks had been drained and her cannons spiked. There was nothing the crippled ship could do but slowly drift in the wind and sink to the ground below. Surprisingly enough to Hans, he heard that four of the Frenchmen had opted to join the pirate crew of the *Bloody Rose*.

They had fled steadily southwards through the night at forty knots. The rising sun did not change her course nor her speed. Once again, she would cheat the hunters and make good her escape.

Hans stood at the bow of the weather deck of the *Bloody Rose*, staring out at the azure water below. The air smelt very different than he was used to in either London or Berlin. He had not slept well last night and after his last watch in the Propulsion Room with the injured Arietta he had chosen to remain awake.

He eventually had found his way to his current location, leaning on the guardrail with just his coffee flask for company. Annika, the Gunner-Marine Captain, stopped beside him in the refuge of the wind brace that was sheltering him. He guessed she was on her mid-watch rounds.

He offered her his coffee flask absently. She sniffed at it, had a mouthful, and with a nod of thanks she passed it back to him.

He glanced her over as casually as he could manage. She was about two inches shorter than him, which put her somewhere around five foot eight. As he had noted when he first saw her, pointing at his smallsword out over the Pyrenees, her figure was slight enough to be mistakable for a man at a distance. In distinct contrast to Arietta, she was slight of breast, hip and *derriere*. Where the Italian Ethiope was lush, Annika was muscular. Where Itala was dark, the Russian Captain-Gunner was a very fashionable shade of pale, with icy blue eyes. Her hair was a walnut brown and kept in a short fighting cut.

She was currently dressed in her battle gear. Thigh-high leather boots in a flashy red stain, with two-inch square brass plates stitched over them covered black leather pants. The pants closed at each side, laced with bright red cording that started at mid-thigh and tied at the hip. A long line of her pale skin was left visible beneath the lacing. Red leather sabre gauntlets, which were covered in brass plates similar to her boots, dressed her to the elbows.

She wore two silk shirts, a white over a red. The white shirt had several slashes and tears in the sleeves and around the shoulders, which he guessed were from the battle with the *Triomphe*. In a defiantly *risque* fashion statement, she wore a purple, black and gold striped corset over-top the two shirts, fashionably shaping her figure from waist to above the fullest of her modest breasts. A brace of pistols was slung in a bandolier from a shoulder to the opposite hip, and a heavy cutlass was in a scabbard hanging from a waist belt. Her flight goggles were up, while her leather and brass breather mask was currently pulled down below her chin.

"Good morning, Captain-Gunner. Where are we, do you know?" he asked her politely.

"The middle of the Mediterranean or thereabouts," she replied, apparently doing the same thing he had just been. "With the Sun positioned as it is, I would say we are making a course for Egypt."

"Egypt," he exclaimed, "but why?"

Annika shrugged at him. "Oh, likely because the entire Allied Air Navy will be looking for us over Europe for the next two weeks or so. So, we will make port in central Egypt or Persia, enjoy ourselves, make needed repairs, resupply and such before heading back into European airspace. It is much easier to not be found if everyone is looking for you in the wrong place." She chuckled for a moment and then said "The Captain calls it the 'Moses Reverse'".

"The Moses Reverse?" Hans asked puzzled.

Annika grinned at him. "Yes, we are fleeing in to Egypt!"

Hans groaned and rolled his eyes. He turned to face her more fully as they talked. "Will the governments there not object to a pirate ship in their country and port?" he asked as he adjusted his collar against the wind.

Annika laughed at him. "Object? I must have hit you a lot harder than I thought when we first met. No, you dullard. We are very nearly celebrities. Or at least the men are," she said sourly. "There are almost two dozen pirate ships that call Egypt and Persia safe ports of refuge."

Hans blinked at her in stunned shock, a sensation and expression he was starting to get accustomed to. "Two ... dozen?"

She merely nodded at him. She took the coffee flask out of his unresisting fingers and had another mouthful. She gave the flask back to him and then resumed speaking.

"While the prices we fetch are not as good as in Europe, it is much easier to resupply the ship and enjoy life ashore. As long as you stay in Pirate Town you may do as you please, drink as you like and whore to your satisfaction. If you leave Pirate Town you are at the mercy of the local customs and officials, none of whom have a tolerance of foreigners or pirates."

Hans spluttered a heated denial that he was not the sort to solicit prostitutes. Annika merely laughed at him over her shoulder as she walked away.

*****

They made port late in the afternoon of the next day. They had followed the Nile south for nearly a hundred miles and then turned West for almost a similar distance. The port city was called al-Myāh Wālsmā'. It was built around a sizable oasis that provided the basis for daily life. In the Northern quarter of the town were almost 30 airship docks with another five under construction.

The docking towers were 25 feet tall of stone and mortar with another 25 foot high wooden platform atop the stone. The wooden structure was nearly as wide at the top as it was tall, which lent a bizarre, mushroom-like appearance to the towers. Half of the towers had ships docked, of which two were at least triple the size of the *Bloody Rose*. The idea of pirates with first- or even second-rate ships of the line left Hans somewhat unsettled.

The docking manoeuvring was done with the sails still furled and the rigging pulled in, using only the single propeller.   The *Bloody Rose* was soon secured tight alongside, both fore and aft. The next few hours until nearly sunset were spent with the hard and back-breaking task of unloading the captured spoils of the laden pirate ship.

From the height that they were moored, Hans could see beyond the edge of the port city. It was nothing but vast unbroken desert. Knowing how far they had travelled by air, he was certain that there was nowhere that it would be humanly possible to walk to outside of the city. He refused to give up hope that he could jump ship eventually, but he recognized it would not be at al-Myāh Wālsmā'.

In spite of the arduous work of the afternoon, Hans noted that the overall mood and demeanour of the crew became more light and excited. He asked a gunner named André Dubé, who was a Frenchman from British North America, what the occasion was.

"Oh right, you are new to all of this," Dubé said with a nod and a grin. "Pay and Party, *mon ami*, it is time for Pay and Party. Once all of this is aground, and the money men are done haggling with *Capitaine* Blackheart, then we will all get our shares," he explained as he passed another twenty-five pound bag of sugar for Hans to set on a crane pallet.

The two men had doffed their shirts early on in the process, choosing the comfort of working stripped to the waist in the hot, dry air. Two other crew would bring a wheeled cart stacked with bags, and Dubé would toss the bags to Hans to set three by three by three on a pallet. When the pallet was loaded, Hans would ring a bell for the steam crane to lower the loaded pallet to the ground below. An empty pallet would be brought up, and they would repeat. It would take three pallets to move the full load to the ground below. They were currently mid-way through pallet number two.

"Shares?   How is that sorted out?" Hans asked, curiously.

"Oh, easy enough, you get one share for every six months you have been with the crew, plus one share if you are you a lead gunner or an engineer, plus two more shares if you are Master or Chief, or five more if you are an officer."

"*Le Capitaine* works out how much we have made since the last pay-port, totals up the number of crew shares and then mathematics out what each share is worth. You get paid in equal amounts of Stirling and Marks."

Hans stowed two more bags of sugar in the time it took him to think about all of that. The notion of Blackheart as a pillaging homicidal accountant did nothing to amuse him. "If you do not mind the intrusion, what was your last pay?" he asked, with his curiosity finally overcoming his sense of decorum.

The Franco-Brit grinned at him. "Four shares for me," he said with a wink of his eye. "I managed a shadow less than a total of 20 Marks. Not bad for two months."

Hans managed to not drop the next bag to arrive in his hands. 20 Marks every two months was more than enough for his father to pay all the estate staff at their English country home a generous wage for a year. Four more bags of sugar came and went before Hans spoke again.

"So you have been doing this at least a year, which means you likely have been paid the entire economy of an English gentleman's manor for a year. Why are you still here?"

André did not answer immediately, passing two more bags during the silence. "Just so you are aware, several of the crew would not like that question. By which I mean, they would not like it enough to break your jaw to ensure they did not hear it again within a month or two." André paused to let that warning sink in. "We all have reasons for being here. Me, the answer is a pretty girl and two miles of sugar maple hills north of the city of Montréal in British North-America. She is a rich man's daughter; without lands and security to offer, I am nothing."

"So, I travelled in search of my fortune, three years ago. I joined the crew a year and a half ago. This fall, when the green hills of my home turn to the fiery gold of my love's hair, I will leave this life and return to claim her hand."

Hans quite nearly cheered at the Franco-Briton's conviction of the mastery of his own destiny.   He considered asking if the lady in question – or the father, for that matter – would be amendable to a pirate in the family, but decided against it. He rubbed absently at his bruised jaw and then stowed another bag of sugar.

*****

A handful of hours later, the entire crew gathered on the gas-lamp-lit deck of the *Bloody Rose*. Blackheart announced that even with the damage from the surprise battle with the *Triomphe*, a crew share would be a handsome five and a half Marks. The crew erupted with a deafening cheer.

Hans was very pleased to discover that his two shares – one for being a new crew plus one for being an engineer – netted him a total of eleven Marks, divided equally between British and German currencies. He recalled Captain Blackheart's initial words to him that there were no impoverished amongst Pirates.

Quite honestly, he was forced to admit that he had never seen such a sum in his own hands before. He could understand André's choices to help attain the hand of his desired. Still, Hans had no wish to grow accustomed to this brutal life of illicit gain. He stowed the money in his locked box, keeping a full two Stirling and full two Marks in his inside vest pocket. Perhaps he would see something in the port below to bring home to his family as proof of his adventure thus far.

He returned to the upper deck dressed in clothes suitable for the chill of the desert night air. Low-cut, brown leather boots, comfortable dark blue laced cotton pants and a white cotton laced shirt made his attire. He had a simple belt around his waist with a coin purse on it, and a dark blue bandana tied over his hair against the dust and chill. He did not bother wearing his blade with him. He wished no worries with the authorities, and he was more than capable of defending himself with his hands.

He unexpectedly found MacIsaac and the other two from their previous encounter again blocking his path.

"You and I, Sauder, we have unfinished business between us," MacIsaac announced, resting the belaying pin in his left hand on his left shoulder.

"What? One beating was not enough, MacIsaac? Do you need to be shown the railing again?" Hans snarled, immediately setting into his Judo defensive stance. He knew this brawl would be a much different and more difficult one. He would not have their overconfidence as his ally. On the other hand, all three of them had two or three bandages on them; the battle with the *Triomphe* had left few unmarked.

The three gunners laughed and visibly took ease. "You still have lots to learn, Sauder. We'll make a pirate out of you yet." Three men each held out small money sacks. "You beat us for your Right of Passage, so it's us that owe you 'Duties' as your crewmates. Ten percent, counted by the Captain himself."

Hans relaxed, but eyed the trio warily. "I do not ...", he started harshly and then stopped. He regarded the three for a long moment and then smiled. "Fine. If you owe it to me, then I can do with it as I please. Go give it to the gunner Dubé," he said with a nod.

"What?" MacIsaac blinked and shook his head as though to clear his hearing. "That is almost a full share you are giving away to that Frenchman. Are you mad?"

"Yes. As a Hatter. Now do as I say or I will add whatever I find in your unconscious pockets to what Dubé gets," Hans said coolly, lowering back into a fighting stance. Had he just been too bold, he wondered?

The German and the Scot stared at each other for a long moment. "I think, Mister Sauder, tha' y'really do mean business," MacIsaac said, faintly impressed. "Well, it's your money. Spend it as you please. Come on boys, let's go find the lucky Frenchman, and then go find ourselves some strong drink and willing women!"

Hans watched them warily as they filed past him and then turned to head below deck. He waited a long moment and then shook his head.   He made his way to the gangplank and whatever a night in "Pirate Town" might hold for him.

*****

In the early night hours, the Pirate Town district of al-Myāh Wālsmā' was a cacophony of sounds, a collision of smells and a collage of sights quite unlike anything he had ever experienced. A set of four sizable open air markets offered all manner of goods and services. Everything and anything for any taste, appetite, morality or vice was available. Hans was bewildered, shocked and amazed at some of the things he saw for sale. The stories he had heard about Bangkok and Montmartre held no candle to this. At one point in his explorations he had an ugly realization.   The only reason there were vendors was because there were buyers.

The rulers of the town were cunningly treading a lucrative line here. While their own customs and ways might forbid the sort of life style and vices that the visiting pirate crews indulged, it permitted a way for the money and goods they carried with them to be delivered into the local economy. If any given month saw fifteen ships, as at present, selling the loot of European trade and then buying local goods and materials for repair and resupply, then the small fortune of almost a quarter million pounds moved through Pirate Town every year.   The derivation was rather shocking to Hans.

Harsh justice awaited any pirate who strayed out of the trade zone and conducted themselves poorly. This ensured that there were no incidents where the drunken and debauched visitors caused injury, damage or unrest in the remainder of the town. The more Hans learned about the world that the ships and crews of piratedom lived in, the more fascinated he became.

He wandered around for over an hour, observing and exploring. After a while, he decided that perhaps a souvenir of the visit would be in order. After all, he wanted to be able to prove to his family the details of his extraordinary adventure on his way to school in Stockholm.

He bought two items which he felt would be iconic of the visit. The first purchase was for his younger sister. For her, he found a duo of finely carved alabaster statues. One was of "the ship of the desert", a camel, while the other statue was a very regal looking cat. He was very impressed with the workmanship, but taking his cue from other transactions he had witnessed in his exploration, got into a spirited argument with the merchant over the price. After a few polite minutes of that, they settled upon a price that Hans considered very fair and the merchant grudgingly admitted would not force him to close in destitution.

The second item cost the entire contents of his pockets. He had stopped in a bladesmith's store thinking to buy a small locally-styled knife or such which his father could use as a letter opener for his office desk. That plan went over the side as soon as he laid eyes upon the weapon hanging proudly on the back wall of the shop.

He fell into a swordsman's lust with the blade as soon as he saw it. It was a glorious work of precision art in gold wire, wrought silver and Damascus steel. The merchant explained to him that the sword had been owned by the adventurous son of a Sultan. When the young man took the throne after his father's death, he bade his servant sell the blade in the market here, so its adventures would never cease. The merchant, being the most renowned and honest bladesmith in the town, was the obvious choice for the man-servant to discharge his duty. Hans was quite astounded at the very notion.

The weapon nearly felt alive in his hand. Called a scimitar, it was similar to the cutlasses and sabres he knew well, but yet with an entirely different progress to the curve and balance. The merchant quite shockingly offered that if the dread pirate and skilled swordsman Hans Sauder wished to ensure the functionality of the weapon, he could test it on a slave.

A six inch diameter bundle of reeds instead fell victim. It was cleft in a single stroke, and the standing bundle was almost perfectly smooth at the point of passage. The merchant showed Hans how to properly flick and roll his wrist so that he could strike with the blade even as he drew it from the cleverly designed scabbard.

The discussion about price was much shorter than the one concerning the alabaster statues. It was also much more clearly in the merchant's favour.

Not wishing to attract unsavoury attention, he had the merchant wrap the hilt and scabbard in strips of cloth. He could still easily draw the blade, but its value was nicely concealed. Since he was now very happy and his coin purse was now very empty, he made his way in the straightest line he could back to where the *Bloody Rose* was docked.

After he had gone about a third of what he guessed was the distance back to the *Bloody Rose*, he was caught by the sounds of an argument. This area was comparatively quiet, and the sounds of quarrel were unmistakable. He glanced into the alleyway that held the dispute, and did a double-take.

It looked like the Captain-Gunner Annika. She was lying in a heap, with four burly locals standing around her. She was dressed in what decidedly looked to be a man's clothes, instead of the usual compromise of attire for the ship. One of the men knelt beside her, holding a cap she must have been wearing in one hand. He unceremoniously pulled her shirt open and roughly ran a hand over her chest. He looked up with a toothy grin to his companions and said something in their language. All of them laughed in a tone that narrowed Hans' eyes.

"Ahoy there, gentleman. That is my shipmate you are manhandling. Leave her there and walk away, or they will find your cold corpses with the morning sun!" Hans threatened, trying very much to channel Captain Blackheart's commanding menace.

The two men closest to him laughed, drew curved knives from the belts, and ran at him. The first was hip-thrown into wall as he slashed at a Hans. He landed in an unmoving heap, his blade skittering aside. Hans deflected the second man's stabbing attack, forearm to forearm, while pulling him off balance. Hans finished the engagement by giving him a sharp blow across the back of the skull with his elbow. The burly man marked his length in the sandy alleyway.

Hans turned about to find the other two making ready for a hurried escape. One held a short straight sword and a lantern, and the other was picking up a giggling Annika over his shoulder like a potato sack. She seemed to bat playfully at her kidnapper's hands and chuckled something that Hans could not make out.

The lantern-carrying swordsman stepped directly towards Hans at a slow and deliberate pace. Hans knew an expert fighter when he saw one. The swarthy Egyptian smiled a slow and very ugly grin.

There was an almost musical tone in the sound of the scimitar leaving its scabbard. Hans levelled the blade at full arm's length towards the other swordsman. The other man's eyes went wide and in that instant, Hans struck. He whipped the tip of the sword across the Egyptian's forehead, in a long shallow cut. Within a second, the other man could not see, blinded by his own blood running into his eyes.

Hans stepped forward and knocked the sword out of the blinded man's hand with his own. He wordlessly grabbed the lantern out of the other hand and set it on an abandoned crate that had been left in the alley. He unceremoniously grabbed the screaming and flailing Egyptian by the hair at the back of his head and slammed him face-first into the alley wall. The man fell and was silent. Hans sheathed his blade and then leaned down to pluck the man's knife from his belt. He looked up and spied his quarry jogging down the alley with Annika thrown over his shoulder. She now seemed to be complaining in Russian about the bumpy ride.

Hans shook his head, rolled his eyes and took a low aim. With a side-armed throw he hurled the knife squarely into the seat of the fleeing man's pants. The man screeched and howled as he fell, with Annika tumbling like a giddily protesting Russian rag-doll.

Hans strode over and used the sheathed scimitar to club the downed man senseless and twitching with two blows to the head. Annika was giggling while trying to sit up, but apparently unable to manage the coordination required to do so. Hans had no idea what was wrong with her, but highly doubted that remaining at the scene of a fight would be good for either of them.

He tucked his sword and scabbard back into his belt and picked her up, one arm under her shoulders and one under her knees. She was heavier than he would have guessed, but he could manage. He was vaguely surprised she did not smell of alcohol at all. He had expected that with her antics and incapacitation, she would have reeked.

He looked around, trying to sort out what to do. The obvious answer was to make due haste back to the ship. However, he expected that if he seemed to be carrying a man's body over his shoulder through Pirate Town, then he might well get unwanted attention from either authorities or vultures. He looked down at the barely conscious Captain-Gunner and a slight sigh escaped his lips.

He carried her back just inside the alleyway and set her down. He quickly cast about the spot, found an old bottle, and broke it. He'd have used the knife sticking out of the downed man's backside for this, but he didn't want him to accidentally bleed to death. So, a shard of glass would be his scalpel for this operation.

He slashed off her sleeves half-way up the arms. Her shirt bottom, he slashed from high-mid back to waist at front. He then tied the two sides of her shirt together snug below her breasts. This showed a lot of her slender back, a modest bit of cleavage and left her midriff bare, but actually also left her reasonably covered. The amount of bare skin was scandalous by the standards of Queen Victoria's England, but he did not take Annika as the sort for petticoats anyway.

Her pants he slashed just above the knee on the inside to mid-thigh on the outside, making them into rakish-looking shorts or knickers. He noted she was a surprisingly attractive woman for her slight figure, when she was not trying to look like a man.

He had the vague idea she would likely beat him senseless for this in the morning when she regained her faculties and saw herself. However, it was the only plan he could come up with. He tossed the glass aside and carefully picked her up and set off towards the airship towers. Hans Sauder, airship pirate of renown with his dishevelled dockside wench, was heading back to the ship with his conquest. Or, at least, that's what he hoped it looked like to anyone that might be inclined to wonder.

Annika suddenly rather forcefully poked him in the shoulder. He stopped and looked down at her with a frown. She had a very serious look on her face, and was looking at the new cut of her shirt. She looked up at Hans, working to focus her eyes on him.

"But Hans," she slurred and giggled, "I am not that kind of girl." She nodded once, tugged at the cut of her shirt to expose a bit more cleavage, blew him a kiss and then passed out without further comment.

Had he been a man of a different morality, he might well have been tempted to take advantage of the situation, he mused. However, his parents had raised him as a proper gentleman. Hans gave a much-suffering sigh, looked Heavenwards for strength, and set off towards the *Bloody Rose*.

*****

"Well, *Pan* Sauder, while I will not give you high marks for fashion design; I will say that you did the right thing in getting me out of bed," Doctor Koblinski said. He had given Annika a quick exam, a pair of injections, and forced a few cupfuls of a solution down her throat. He had then arranged the bed she was in and pulled a blanket over shoulders, leaving her dressed as Hans had brought her. He ushered Hans out into the hall where they now spoke.

"What is wrong with her? She is not drunk."

"Opium," the Doctor replied with a sigh. "She does this to herself from time to time. However, this is the first time she has risked herself in these areas. A drugged, sleepy and attractive woman is fairly an invitation for problems in this port. She really must know better than this. Normally she indulges her vice when we are in Europe and there is much less risk of this sort of thing."

"She is an opium addict? But … how does she remain in her position?" Hans questioned.

"Oh, she is normally a sound sleeper, and does not roll about, even when under the liberating effects of opiates," the Doctor dead panned.

"*Döktor* …" Hans began crossly.

"Why do you not ask her yourself when she is sober? I am sure you would find any response from her very educational, *Pan* Sauder," Koblinski suggested politely.

"Pardon? I am sure you are aware of her reputation as a murdering, ill-tempered and violent woman, *Herr Döktor*. She would be just as inclined to send me head-first to your…" Hans trailed off.

"You see, *Pan* Sauder? You are a very clever man … you knew the answer to your question already. Think more and perhaps react less hastily," he replied with a polite demi-bow and smile.

*****

The first shafts of dawn found Hans on the bow of the *Bloody Rose*, dispatching imaginary foes with his new sword. He paused, panting somewhat from his exertions. He took a mouthful from his coffee flask and recapped it, tucking it into the carrier on his belt pouch.

He slid the blade back into its scabbard with a sigh. Sleep had been unpleasant again for the second night in a row. He leaned against the guardrail of the ship, and stared out over the lightening desert sands beyond the town. He watched the golds, oranges and tans of the vast sea of sands take on a breath-taking hue as the sun climbed lazily over the horizon of its nightly containment.

"*Dobroe utro, Gospodin* Sauder" came the raw voice of the Captain-Gunner. She moved to stand beside him just out of his personal space at the railing. She, too, looked out over the oasis town and desert sands.

"I am very sorry, *Frau* Nadezhda, I do not speak Russian. German, English, and very poor French are my limits," he replied. She was dressed in a loose white cotton shirt, buttoned high. She also sported light wool pants that had been dyed a flat red, and low cut brown boots. She wore her sword belt as well, canted from waist to hip.

"I said, 'Good morning, Mister Sauder'," she repeated. He glanced at her, meeting her gaze. Her bright blue eyes were dull and bloodshot. It was obvious she had tried to clean herself up, but her level of success was dubious. "Thank-you" she said quietly.

He shook his head in dismissal of her thanks. "It is quite alright. We are both crewmates and it was the right thing to do."

"I suppose you will want either sex or money from me to keep your mouth shut about this?" she said, her voice and bearing suddenly hostile.

Hans turned to face her fully, and lofted a brow. "*Nein*," he said. "I do not do the right thing because I expect to be paid. I do the right thing because it is the right thing. You owe me nothing, Captain-Gunner."

What ever she was about to say suddenly departed her, clearly leaving her with no wind in her sails. Her shoulders nearly sagged for a moment before she regained her composure. "Are you sure, Hans?" she asked suspiciously.

He found it rather odd that she would use his first name. He had learned very quickly that most addresses were by last name alone. First names were for personal and non-professional discussions, which were rare. "*Ja*, Annika, I am quite certain. Regardless of the company I keep these days, I am not a pirate who would rescue someone just to hold them ransom at some later date. I tell you again, *Fräulein*, you owe me nothing."

He turned back towards the vista beyond the guardrail. He saw people moving in the streets below already. The smell of roasting and smoking meats and wood fires reached his nose. His stomach rumbled.

"Hungry?" she asked.

"*Ja*. I have been up most of the night, and was practising my sword work for about half an hour before you arrived. In all honestly, I am quite nearly starved. I should go to the mess and get something to eat."

"Let me buy you breakfast in the town. It is the least I can do for you by way of thanks," she suggested.

His initial reaction was to decline. Firstly, he was not terribly interested in her company. As he had told the doctor, her reputation for being an ill-tempered and violent woman was nearly legendary within the crew. Secondly, she was an officer. There was an unwritten rule that the officers and crew kept a distance from each other. Having breakfast with her at dawn in some Egyptian oasis town would certainly not be keeping distance. Third, he was learning that pirates gossiped like milk-girls. The last thing he needed was some of the crew seeing them having breakfast together at this hour and deciding he had bedded the Russian woman on some roof top in the town. Of course, with pirates, there was no telling if such a rumour would elevate his standing amongst them, or result in a fight.

*****

"You have quite an appetite, *Fräulein*," he observed. They were sitting in a small bistro-like establishment which was directly beside the acre or so of open water of the oasis. It had the visual flavor of something he would have expected in Milan or Toulon, but with influences of the local culture married to it. They were sitting beside an open window, still shaded from the early morning sun by an awning. The morning breeze carried with it the smell of palm trees and dates in the desert air.

They were enjoying a fare of skewers composed of meats, vegetables, dates, figs and breads, all glazed in a honey and spice mixture. The wooden skewer was then set to cook over a rosy bed of coals until the glaze began to turn a golden caramel. With each skewer being nearly a foot long, there was substantial fare to be had in two or three of them. She was working on her fourth.

He took a mouthful of the honey-mint-vinegar drink in his glass. It was known locally as *sekanjabin*. She had told him it was essentially the same as Greek oxymel. He had no idea what that meant. However, given its ingredient list, it was surprisingly tasty and refreshing. He was on his second glass.

She swallowed her current mouthful and nodded. "I am a busy woman. I have a crew of cut-throats, scoundrels and brigands to stay one step ahead of. And those are the ones I trust at my back the most."

"Thank-you for breakfast. This is quite tasty. I will have to remember this for when I return to England," he said with a slight gesture of his hand towards the skewer remaining on his plate.

"Thank-you for preventing me from waking chained to a wall in some Beirut brothel," she replied with a shrug. "I am sure several of the crew would have thought you had done them quite a favour had you just continued on your way. However, I am not yet ready to retire to a life of leisure," she laughed.

Hans nearly choked on the mouthful of drink he had just taken. "You have a very peculiar sense of humour, *Fräulein*."

"We are in private here, Hans. Just call me Annika. And you have a very peculiar sense of stubborn self-denial," she said with an amused note.

"What do you mean?" Hans asked as he picked up the third skewer from his plate and took a mouthful to chew.

"You are a remarkable fighter, a talented engineer ... you could be a very rich man within a year or two of life aboard the *Bloody Rose*. You are reasonably handsome – possessed of a nice backside and shoulders, if I do say so myself. You could have been with almost any woman you wanted in Pirate Town last night, but instead involved yourself in saving a fellow pirate's behind." She waved her half-cleaned skewer in a circle as she spoke.

"And yet, you have implied you do not consider yourself a pirate. This, in spite of the trail of fallen you left behind you on the decks of the *Bloody Rose* and the *Triomphe*. And in spite of the extra hours you have put in working with dear Arietta on the repairs in the Propulsion Room to ensure our escape. You took your shares without hesitation when you were paid yesterday. You just suggested you would be returning to England, but you bought a most magnificently lethal sword."

She poked him in the nose with the end of her skewer, much to his surprise. "You, Hans, are a pirate. You may continue to resist the notion, but mark my ..."

The sound of the slap rang out through the bistro. Much to both of their surprise, he had backhanded her with considerable force. He ground his teeth to contain his temper. The look in Annika's eyes had nothing to do with anger or violence. He stood without a word, and strode out of the bistro, leaving Annika absently rubbing the side of her face, looking after him.

"Nineteen and One Pirate Nights"

Diary Entry for May 2nd, 1888

About three weeks have passed by since my last diary entry. Largely, this is because there has been precious little to write about, and I could not see a point to filling this text with irritated rantings about the boredom I am enduring.

Finally, at this time, the crew are almost fully recovered from our encounter with the French frigate Triomphe. Everyone is out of their hammocks and on their feet. The hammocks that were left empty by the cost of battle have been refilled by recruiting from the pirates who are between ships at this port.

The good Döktor Koblinski now has a much needed assistant who has proved invaluable in the recovery of the crew. One of the French crew who opted to join us was a Gwendoline Coline, a professional nurse. As Fate would have it, she is a spirited woman of approximately the good Döktor's age.

I have also found that ports of call make for strange bedfellows, both literally and figuratively. It has been amusing observing how the various members of the crew conduct themselves in their idle time.

My last comment in this entry is that for the first time since I was sixteen, I was accosted by a bout of homesickness. I still miss my parents, brother and sister terribly. However, we sail again tomorrow and I expect the routine activities of being a working engineer will occupy me sufficiently to remove this pain.

****

The more time he spent aboard the *Bloody Rose*, the more enigmatic a figure Michael O'Raedy, the feared Captain Blackheart, proved to be in Hans' eyes. A current demonstration involved "Auntie Coline" as she had been dubbed by the male members of the crew. She was one of the four French sailors that had "jumped the gunwale" after the battle with the *Triomphe* and joined the crew of pirates.

She was a professional nurse, and used to working on a predominantly male ship for a male doctor. She was not an unattractive woman, but certainly on in her years, comparable to Alexi Koblinski, the ship's doctor and her new boss. Why someone's grandmother would have taken on the life of the nurse to a shipload of pirates was quite beyond Hans' capacity to comprehend, but that was for her to reconcile.

However, a fortyish year-old woman in her twilight years was not going to have very good luck with any Right of Passage, regardless of any oath to do no harm. Even if the fight was with three of the women crew, all of them were murderesses and in many cases far meaner in a fight than their male crewmates. Hans had actually been prepared to step in to simply and forcefully end her fights for her.

Blackheart, however, precluded that. He made the announcement loud and clear that Pirate Traditions allowed the Captain to opt to fight for a new crew member in a Right of Passage. As he had done for Doctor Koblinski, he would stand for Nurse Coline. He then pointedly asked if anyone had objection to the lady in question joining the crew. Not a single person moved or spoke and that firmly ended that. The Captain also made it quite clear that anyone making her life difficult in any way would be presumed to have too much free time on their hands and he would resolve that issue personally.

She had rapidly endeared herself to the crew simply by her delightful bedside manner and a complete fearlessness in visiting the injured and ill in their hammocks. No matter what the ailment was, nor the temper of the patient, she seemed to be possessed of an inherently disarming charm that reduced the grumpiest and most pained of the pirates to at least a temporarily contented hound. Someone cheerfully greeted her one morning as "Auntie Coline" and the affectionate moniker stuck.

Alexi had grumbled during a chess match with Hans that he was now the second choice physician aboard his own ship. Even with his grumbling, it was rather plain to Hans that the good Doctor was not immune to his new Nurse's personal charm and grace. He opted not to point that out, however.

In spite of the fact that the *Bloody Rose* had been the victor in the battle with the French air-frigate *Triomphe*, it had not been bought without cost. Two dozen of her Gunner-Marines had died during the battle and in its aftermath. Half of those had died in the initial exchange of cannon fire between the two ships. The French gunners had been targeting the gun decks in an attempt to defang the *Bloody Rose* as quickly as possible.

Using Koblinski's definition of wounded – any battle injury that caused a crewman to be unable to stand at least one watch in the day – almost 80% of the surviving crew had been wounded to some degree. Both Annika and Arietta were technically wounded, but insisted on remaining on their feet and doing their jobs. Hans considered himself tremendously lucky to have escaped the murderous fight essentially unscathed.

*****

Hans had been spending a significant amount of his waking hours in the Propulsion Room with Chief Itala since the morning after "Pay and Party" day. There was a tremendous amount of work to be done and in his eyes, the sooner it was done, the sooner they would be returning to Europe. The sooner the return to the skies of Europe, by extension, meant the sooner there would be a chance to regain his freedom.

Thus, enlightened self-interest suggested that doing the best work possible on the repairs to the Propulsion Room systems was a wise choice. It also meant he would remain out of the path of the Gunner-Marine Captain Annika Nadezhda. He suspected this was a good health investment.

There were three significant projects that needed to be undertaken, and Arietta involved him in all of them. Visivald helped as well, but was prone to being gone for a day or two at a time into the vice houses of Pirate Town.

Over the twenty or so days the *Bloody Rose* was moored, they averaged twelve hour days working together six days of the week. The starboard propeller pod had taken the bulk of a four pound load of grapeshot. The hit had shredded the nearly four miles of wire used in the electrical motor windings. The entire fairing and enclosure had to be dismantled and then all of the wire and remaining shot pulled out. The wire was sold to a smelter and a full spool of new wire brought in from Cairo. Then, the entire motor had to be rewound by hand, the bushings and brushes rebuilt and the other associated electrical systems redone. The motor was then tested and the pod reassembled. It took them three tries to get everything working to Chief Itala's satisfaction.

The destroyed boiler was a minor nightmare. A hole had to be cut in the hull, as Hans had guessed. The wrecked unit was removed by cutting saws as well as breaking hammers and then sold as scrap. The new boiler and piping assembly was purchased from another vessel that had a spare in their storage hangar here in the port city.

Of course, it did not remotely fit onto the crane pallet or cargo net while fully assembled. It first had to be carefully disassembled into a total of eleven pieces. Each piece was then individually brought up with the crane, and then man-handled with block and tackle through the hole in the hull. As each piece went in, it was then carefully put into place and the entire unit slowly reassembled.

That painstaking process was hardly the end of the affair. The new boiler and pipe system then had to be completely tested. It was lit, brought to full power and pressure and let to run for hours at a time to ensure there were no leaks, weak joins or bad valves which would fail during the stresses of heavy operations. Such a failure could potentially kill someone.

Hans noted that Arietta also seemed to be far more relaxed in her dealings with Hans when it was just him and her. When the Norwegian – or anyone else – was around, she was "Chief Itala" and he was "*Signore* Sauder". When it was just them, they were simply "Arietta" and "Hans".

He considered it wishful thinking that perhaps he had caught the older woman's eye and she fancied him to some degree. He had found out in their work-chatter that she was nearly a decade his senior. If age had cost her some of her beauty over the years then it was likely just as well, he had decided. Hans very much doubted he would have gotten anything of material value done had he met her in her early twenties, as he currently was.

While they had been running steam pressure tests and boiler temperature ceiling tests, he had certainly not objected to her choice of minimal attire. The Propulsion Room had been unbearably hot, lacking the natural cooling effect of flight. All she wore were her striped pants and pocket vest. He had nearly stabbed himself in the back of the hand with a screwdriver from male inattention, the first time she had walked past him dressed like that. He also noticed that she tended to work within line of sight of him anytime his shirt was off under those sweat-soaked conditions. On the other hand, a woman of her looks could have her pick of the town, and he had to admit there was very little reason she would be attracted to him beyond an intellectual friendship.

Repairing the out of service Spitz 656 was less of a chore, simply because the damage to it was comparatively minor. However, given that they "had the time", Itala insisted that she and Hans tear down both engines completely and do the upcoming planned cleaning, tune-up and rebuilds now. Working with Arietta was an amazingly valuable educational experience. Essentially, she did the first engine as a lecture piece and then had him do the second alone as she watched and answered his questions or provided guidance. The two 656 engines were veritable works of art and very well crafted, Hans discovered. He made a note to himself to mention the Foundries to his father when they next spoke.

*****

It was the third Saturday morning that they had been docked at the port city. In a handful of days, they would be setting sail north for the skies of Europe in search of fresh prey. Uncharacteristic clouds hung in the sky, muting the normal glory of a desert dawn. Hans was up once again before the sun, having passed another night of fitful sleep.

The dreams and sometimes nightmares varied, but all revolved around either the terrible moment where Hans had shot the wrong man, or the horror of the ensuing battle and all he had witnessed. Hans was fairly certain that, other than the French marine he had shot in the back of the head, he had not killed anyone in the fight. However, he certainly felt he had blood on his hands from the two that had been fighting Blackheart. That did not sit well with his conscience at all.

Alternately, the dreams were a less frightening expression of unreasonable fears that he was some modern-day Ulysses. He was perpetually unable to leave the *Bloody Rose* and return to his family for reasons and events completely beyond his understanding or control.

So, yet again, he was standing at his habitual spot on the bow of the ship, with his coffee flask, staring out at the oasis town and the desert beyond it. Chief Itala would not be in the Propulsion Room before 9am, he guessed, for the start of their next long haul of work together. He was surprisingly starting to feel a bit groggy in contradiction to the coffee he drank. Thinking he might take advantage of that, he started heading towards the aft end of the ship, for the hatch that would take him down towards his sleeping bay and his awaiting hammock. Another couple of hours of sleep would be welcome.

He was rather unprepared for the sight that met his eyes as he approached the mid-ship gangplank on his way aft. Captain Blackheart and Chief Itala were coming back aboard, leaning against each other heavily and laughing like fools. He did not need the mostly empty bottle of wine in Arietta's hand to suggest to him they were drunk. Their state of severe inebriation was fairly apparent in their movement and their voices. To use the popular Gunner phrasing, they were both "smashed with a bottle, and reeling from the impact".

The two of them looked like a couple of truant children trying to sneak back into their house before their parents noticed them. The fact that Hans was standing a dozen paces away apparently failed to register with them. Based on their attire, he guessed they had been out at a costume party for the various in-port vessel captains and guests. Hans presumed the Captain was supposed to be dressed as

Julius Caesar, and the Engineering Chief was dressed as a dark-skinned and striking Cleopatra. They made a rather amusing pair at first glance; she was more than four inches taller than he was.

They giggled, "shushed" each other, then wobbled and teetered over to the door of the Captain's cabin, where it opened up onto the mid-deck. There was some more laughter and they finished off the bottle between them in a couple of mouthfuls each. Blackheart had to stand on his toes to whisper something to her. Her hand flew to the top of her dark breast in a dramatic bit of mock modesty and then she said "Oh, Michael ... after a night like that, you most certainly do have permission to lay alongside!"

Hans watched the two of them disappear into the Captain's cabin and the door close with a clattering drunken attempt at discretion. He contemplated the toes of his boots for a few long seconds and shook his head.

"Right," he said aloud.

He decided to perhaps go for a walk about the Pirate Town to clear his head and get away from the confines of the ship. If Chief Itala and the Captain were indulging in a lover's dalliance at this early time of the morning, he very much doubted she would be at the bottom of the Propulsion Room ladder by 9am.

He glanced around to find the Captain-Gunner Annika Nadezhda wordlessly watching him from within the morning shadows, where she leaned against the far gunwale. Her arms and legs were crossed, and her head tilted to a side in a gesture of speculation. He had no idea how long she had been there, or if she had seen the Captain and Chief Engineer come aboard. The Russian and the German both looked at each other for several seconds without words or actions passing between them.

Hans turned on his heel, and headed down the gangway. He rather hoped she would not follow him. He was in no mood to deal with her temper or accusations about his nature, he decided. When he reached the bottom of the docking tower and he was sure she had not actually followed him, he was surprised to discover he felt disappointed and annoyed. That only served to confuse him. He picked a random direction and set off at a brisk walk.

After a few minutes of irritable travel, he felt almost obliged to ask himself what the issue was. He was behaving quite irrationally, really. He slowed his stride and gave the matter some thought.

Firstly, he had to contend with the notion he was quite clearly infatuated with his boss. That was, in a word, daft. Worse, it was unprofessional; his father had told him that personal affairs and professional spaces are horrible combinations. Someone always winds up hurt or feeling taken advantage of. He knew better. So, while Arietta was definitely an attractive woman, he needed to stop acting like a mid-teen schoolboy and return to a more professional stance.

In addition to all of that was the matter that he was leaving the *Bloody Rose*. It would be cruel and unkind to encourage or pursue a personal relationship with her. He was not staying around to continue it. He frowned at that thought, but swept the reaction aside. He had responsibilities to his family that precluded him "skylarking" around on pirate ship.

Second to the initial chain of thought was the fact that while he had chosen to conduct himself in a fashion befitting an English gentleman, he really couldn't expect that from a bunch of pirates. Annika – Captain-Gunner Nadezhda, he corrected himself – had broadly implied that the norm among pirates was to conduct themselves with as little morals in sexual matters as they displayed in any other aspect of their lives. At least, they had very few morals beyond their very odd sense of "Pirate's Tradition and Code", of which he infrequently heard reference.

He had seen the various women of the ship returning at all hours with either a different male crewmate than the night before, or gossiping with another lass about the talents of the "paid company" available, or not returning at all for a couple of nights. He really ought not to be shocked that Chief Itala had opted to pass a night with the Captain, regardless of Hans' opinion of the man. They were both officers in function, and that made any liaison between them far less problematic than across lower-deck lines. There was some sensible safety in choosing each other as party-partners and lovers.

He watched a shop keeper raising the sun-shade awning over his store front as he walked past. The man used a simple block and tackle arrangement with a clockwork to furl it at the end of the day. Winding up the clockwork unfurled the awning in the morning. A clever man, Hans mused. He did the hard work in the morning, and let the machinery do the work when he was ready to go home.

Annika – Captain-Gunner Nadezhda, he corrected himself, again – had called him attractive. That thought produced a certain dissatisfaction within him. Not that the Russian found him attractive, but rather he had little idea what that meant in life. He found a quarter-ton piece of sandstone near the edge of the oasis' central lake, and sat down on it. The stone had the advantage of being shaded by several date-laden palm trees. It had the disadvantage of being directly opposite the bistro he had tried to have breakfast with An ... the Captain-Gunner.

While he was German by both birth and blood, he had been raised in the conservative culture of the English upper middle class. Even during his travels through some of the more libertine-minded parts of Europe in his late teen years, he had remained true to his upbringing. He was careful of his drink, his language and avoided unseemly relationships. He'd had a few ladies express an interest in him over that period, and was not entirely unused to the taste of a woman's lips, but had never let anything ever go any further than that. He distinctly recalled his Uncle Orel pointedly remarking that the last thing Hans' mother needed from him was an embarrassed explanation about an Austrian girl and having to sort out how to relocate a bastard child from Prague to the country home in English Cotswolds.

Hans deftly and absently skipped a rock across the placid waters of the oasis, its surface quiet and gray under the still clouded sky. He paused for a moment, and let himself consider the charms of the ladies of the *Bloody Rose*. Piracy either exclusively attracted pretty girls, or ruthlessly disposed of the less so, he mused. There was not a plain one amongst the lot. And while Annika – yes, Annika for the purposes of this exercise – and Arietta were easily the most attractive, the rest were not terribly far behind. With each of them, it was something different from the prior woman that defined her unique beauty to Hans.

With the Ethiopian Arietta, beyond a doubt, it was her statuesque figure and musical voice. For the Russian Annika, it was the feline grace of her slight curves and her aura of risk. The French Yvette was characterized by her nearly-numbing smile and bawdy wink. The Spanish Dolores smoldered with her dark eyes and smoky voice. Greek Marianna stood out with the remarkable length and shapeliness of her legs, and her relaxed nature. Irish Onora was a pale-skinned and red-headed spitfire. For English Doretta, it was the shape of her face and the fullness of her lips. Each one was a pretty lass in her own right, with some defining thing he could say caught his attention.

And so, what would he say if, for example, Greek Marianna offered to show him her lovely legs in greater detail and in closer proximity? Why was his first reaction to going further than a kiss or a press of the hand to a cheek, that it was some sort of moral crime?

Unbidden, the image of Arietta in her Cleopatra attire came to his mind. He frowned. He wondered what bedding a woman like her would be like. Or in opposition, Annika? What would the similarities be? The differences?

While he understood the mechanical aspects of human sexuality – both from discussions in University classrooms and dorm-yards – it was otherwise quite unknown territory to him. Given the screwdriver in the back of his hand of last week, it was self-apparent that at some Darwinian level, the reaction for a man's desire of an attractive woman was wired like a switch, battery and light. It just took the right combination of look or charms to throw the switch, even temporarily. If that metaphor was correct ... then were the Calvanists or the Libertines in the right? The Inquisitors, or Casanova?

Philosophizing brought him no peace. Beyond more base discussions of masculinity and pecking order within the male pirates he knew, there was obviously something about bedding a woman that was remarkable. From what he had observed, most of his crewmates at the very least felt it was an experience worth paying for. Of course, he thought ruefully, they also felt the same way about alcohol and some drugs.

*****

The bar had the visual flair of a circus having run headlong into a distillery. An assortment of 400 or so pirates, scoundrels, and harlots of both sexes were at tables of three to five, or wandering around. Games of dice and cards were played, and money passed back and forth. Trays laden with beer, rum, whiskey and other alcohols were carried high by attractive and risqué-dressed serving staff, both men and women. Given that the male to female representation of the *Bloody Rose* seemed to hold for other pirate ships, there was shrewdly similar inverse balance in the wait staff.

Electric lights shimmered overhead while candles were set in trios on each round wooden table. Thirty-foot lengths of six-foot wide tri-color fabric were draped from ceiling beam to ceiling beam, and then from beam to half-way down the wall. No drape seemed to have the same colour combination repeated. A trio of musicians on a side stage played bright music of a variety of countries at apparent random. Exotic-looking belly-dancers moved through the crowd with hulking, bare-chested and tanned bodyguards immediately behind them. A pair of beautiful women led a black-furred panther around on a jewelled leash. A similarly handsome pair of men led a magnificently maned lion.

In spite of appearances of the place, it was Monday evening, mid-way to midnight. Several ships were departing over the week and several new had come in over the weekend, resulting in a heady mix of relief, abandon and hedonism. Money, drink, drugs and sex were the menu of choice for the evening.

At one of the side tables away from the bandstand, sat Hans. A remarkably slight and pretty red-headed lass was curled up on his lap. Her arms were around his neck, her head on his shoulder and she was functionally wearing little more than her tea-toned bloomers, chemise and a black velvet corset. An amber, velvet and lace choker adorned her neck, and a bright red sash was tied about her waist. Hans was dressed in his usual attire, save that these were not a dead-man's hand-me-downs. A pair of spectacles with cobalt-blue lenses for respite against the sun covered his eyes, and his hair was somewhat tousled by the lass in his lap.

A cigar and a glass of drink were setting on the table in front of him, with a row of cards splayed. A few more were in held in his left hand; his right hand was on his company's hip. He whispered something to her, and she reached out, and lazily tossed a few of the coins from the modest pile in front of him into the centre of the table as he announced "Raise... 5 shillings, gentleman. I am feeling lucky tonight." He gave a comfortably hazy sigh and leaned back into his chair as the red-head nuzzled at his neck.

He had spent most of Sunday miserable. He woke in a terrible mood from a hideous dream where, as he tried to return home, he had been clapped in irons, branded across the forehead with a skull and cross-bones, and his mother and sister cried, wept and wailed as the county judge sentenced him to Dartmoor Prison. He had prowled the ship for an hour afterwards, trying to get the image out of his mind. His head had played cruel games with him for most of the day. Guilt, images and happy memories of his brother Karl, his sister Valeria, his father, his mother, and his Uncle Orel announced themselves to him in an irregular parade.

He had rather thought he might go mad at the torment he seemed hell-bent for leather to inflict upon himself. He wallowed through the day, resorting to a tincture from Doctor Koblinski to ensure he slept soundly. He did not even ask what was in it; he simply downed it and went to his hammock.

When he awoke this morning, his mind was much more at ease. He realized it was the first solid night of sleep he had gotten in nearly three weeks. Yet, there was still a lingering sensation of homesickness for his quiet and predictable life with his family. This in turn led to a distinct and remarkable sensation of dissatisfaction. He had recalled his first meeting with Chief Itala, where he had casually dismissed her out of hand for her gender and her skin colour He distinctly recalled his vow to never make that mistake – one of allowing pre-taught notions – to inhibit rational thought and scientific scepticism as it concerned his dealings with individuals.

Which is what had him at a tailor's shop outside of Pirate Town later that morning. He had paid Cemil to come along with him and translate. The deal was simple; Hans was buying new clothes. If Cemil acted as his agent, Hans would cover a new set of clothes for him at the store and a bottle of rum besides at the tavern of Cemil's choice that night. The Arab could hardly believe his good fortune.

They were careful in their comportment, walked in the bright and open, politely asked for directions, and found what Hans was after. Hans had Cemil explain what he and Cemil each wanted, and then fixed the price. He then paid double to have the full resources of the tailor shop put to having it done for sunset.

“Are you sure you understand how much money you just paid for four sets of shirts, pants plus three vests?” Cemil asked as they walked back.

“Yes. Three pounds Stirling. A full quarter what I would have paid for it in London from a much less talented tailor, and it would have taken a week to get it,” Hans replied as they walked back towards Pirate Town.

Cemil blinked his good eye in disbelief. “A ... quarter? Where the bag-bleeding hell do you buy clothes? That much money would nearly keep a family alive for a season where I am from!”

“Money,” Hans explained, “has a warping effect on the economy around it. The more a group of people can pay, the more they will pay. And in my case, I could care less about if I had paid six pounds Stirling. I have the money;

we are going to sail in two days and then we get paid again. It is not like there is much to spend it on aboard the *Bloody Rose*."

Cemil studied him for a few moments as they walked. "You really are the son of a rich man, are you not, Sauder?"

"Cemil, my father owns his own airship construction yard, design company and is thinking about building an engine foundry. He owns two houses, including a country estate. I have never wanted for anything until I joined the crew of the *Bloody Rose*." He stopped and looked squarely at Cemil just inside the perimeter of Pirate Town. "The worst thing that happened to me when I joined the crew, Cemil, Son of the Desert Jackals, was that I beat you."

Cemil looked askance at Hans. "Are you sun-struck, by chance, Sauder? You are making no sense to me, even though you sound like you are actually speaking English."

Hans laughed and then turned to resume walking. He glanced at the one-eyed Arab walking beside him and then clapped him on the shoulder. "Just trust me when I tell you it meant I missed a tremendous opportunity to try on a dead-man's clothes properly."

He had gotten a shave and a haircut at a reasonable barber and had sprung for a like indulgence for Cemil. They had parted ways at that point, and then rejoined late in the afternoon. Hans had found the English spectacles with the sun-tinted lenses in the meantime. The tailor had everything exactly as Hans had wanted it and he happily paid the balance. He conveyed his thanks and appreciation to the man through Cemil and then they returned to the ship.

After they had gotten food from the mess and then prepared for the balance of the evening, Cemil took Hans to the "Desert Bizaare". Cemil had explained that any woman – or man – wearing a red silk sash and red leather wrist cuffs was for hire. Hans bought him his bottle from the bar and they parted ways for the balance of the evening.

Hans had decided this morning that, in the name of rational decision making, a bit of experimentation was called for. Now that the apparatus and environment for the experiment was prepared, it was time to engage the process.

He had simply strolled around for a time, soaking in the sense of desperate euphoria that permeated the place. He watched the women of all types and figures move around him. He sipped at his first beer since he had left Germany in his late teens. At one point, a petite red-head had boldly walked over to him, brazenly ran her hands down over his chest to the top of his belt and asked him if he was interested in company. She wore a red silk sash and leather wrist cuffs.

He beckoned to her to follow him, and led her off to a side. "And what are the Devil's details in having your company?" he asked.

"Six shillings on my back, eight on my knees and twelve on my stomach. I am a girl of many talents, and you look to be a man of many demands," she said, stepping closer and moving her hips and chest against him with a lascivious lick of her lips.

He leaned over and whispered in her ear. "And if I pay you ten times that, do I have decorative company at my side for the night?"

She gave him a shrewd look and nibbled on an earlobe before answering, nearly crossing Hans' eyes. "For a pound-and-twenty Stirling, G'uvnor, you can tie me, whip me, bugger me and have me beg you for seconds and thirds," she said in a low and husky voice. Hans turned scarlet at the image in his mind.

A short while later, he was involved in a game of "American Riverboat-Style Poker". The red-headed lass, who he simply referred to as "Wench", was in his lap contentedly amusing herself with keeping him in a mild state of arousal. She also fetched him drinks, assisted him with his gambling and was otherwise doing a fine job of being his professional escort.

His brother Karl, free of irritating obligations of family duty such as studying how the business was run, had spent a good amount of his school time as leisure time. He was unsurpassedly good at billiards, had five different sorts of card games memorized, threw darts well and had backgammon and baccarat down cold. During idle winters, he had taught Hans how to play poker.

Hans, given his memory and intellect, was declared by Karl to be a hazard to gambling halls. Hans had analyzed the number theory behind the game, reduced it to a set of card-counted probabilities, and then had Karl teach him the nuances of different ploys.

He was currently enjoying the progress of the evening's experimentation in spades. He was, he estimated, half drunk; alternating between glasses of rum and whiskey. He was amused at the physiological contradiction caused by simultaneously smoking and drinking. His speech was somewhat slowed, as was his eye-hand coordination. On the other hand, he was mentally more sharpened than he could ever recall.

He was currently playing cards to lose. His strategy for the evening was to lose no more than a full Mark. So, he had begun with a few poor plays to establish himself as a beginner with more money than brains. He had then settled in, winning some and losing others, until he had established a pile worth about a pound or pound and a half in winnings. The congratulations about "beginners luck" had started to fade and sour, and since then, Hans had been losing far more than he won. The mood of everyone else at the table was improving steadily.

He was not yet prepared to cross the moral Rubicon of bedding a woman that he had no emotional interest in. However, he had to admit that the woman currently running her fingers through his hair and tracing her tongue along a bit of the side of his neck was certainly generating significant physical interest. She was skillfully keeping him in a simmering state of arousal which was an entirely new source of physical enjoyment for him.   He could understand why someone might wish to pay for this sort of pleasure.

He gestured towards his whiskey glass and the wench leaned forward and picked it up. She had a sip for herself and then fed him a mouthful, and returned the glass to the table.

He whispered in her ear, and she kissed him full on the mouth for a long moment. They both considered the cards in his hand and she tapped two of them ... he nodded and she threw two more coins on the table for him as he again verbally raised the stakes.

He quite clearly heard Blauchuk's Slavic gravel loudly demand "What did you say, bilge rat?"

The area around Hans fell silent. He looked over to see the powerful Slav holding another man by his collar off the floor. He sighed and whispered to his wench, and she disengaged herself with a pout. "She will hold my interest, gentlemen. I will be right back," he told the other players at the table. She smiled with shark-like sweetness at them as she took his seat and picked up his cards.

"Mister Blauchuk, do you care to tell me why you are throttling this poor sod, and why you are standing surrounded by his crewmates?" Even in his drunken state, Hans could smell a fight in the air. The tension was rapidly spreading throughout the bar, and everything was slowly coming to a halt.

"Hello, Sauder," Blauchuk grunted, not taking his eyes off the other man. "He called Miss Annika a cheap Russian whore."

Hans could feel his lip curl involuntarily. "He did? I see. Put him down, please, Blauchuk."

"But ..."

"Blauchuk. Now."

Blauchuk growled, but did as he was told. He took a step backwards and Hans stepped forwards.

The other man was likely Irish, Hans guessed. He was about the same height and build as Hans with a violently stubborn look in his eyes.

"I am going to strongly suggest that you apologize, sir," Hans suggested with an evidently forced smile. "The Gunner-Marine Captain Nadezhda is very respected by the boys of the *Bloody Rose* ... and I am sure you do not want to waste the rest of your week healing from whatever my friend here was thinking of doing to you."

"I'm going to strongly suggest you mind your own dog-shagging business, you pompous ass," the other man spat back in a thick brogue. "Your 'Annika' is a drug-swilling, Blackheart-balling whore with the leg-spread of a mainyard and the only reason she's in charge of you bunch on the *Pink Pansy* is that you all live up to the ship's name." He puffed his chest out in a challenge.

"Ah, I see," said Hans with a nod and a reasonable tone, amidst snickers and laughs. "Blauchuk?"

"Yes, Sauder?"

"You get the three behind you. This son of a bitch is mine," he snarled, and slammed his fist straight and gracelessly into the Irishman's nose. There was an ugly crunch, the Irishman flailed for balance, a splat of blood hit the floor and the entire bar went berserk.

The next few minutes were the same sort of hazy blur that he had sunk into during his "Right of Passage" and the boarding battle. The only difference was that this was not some lifeless, mechanical affair.

Perhaps it was the tobacco. Perhaps it was the drink. Perhaps it was the gambling. Perhaps it was the simmering state of arousal he had been in for the past hour. Perhaps it was a combination. He was not sure he cared. He just knew had never felt more alive.

The details were a jumble. He took a beating, and gave as well as he got. He recalled Cemil sand-bagging someone that had him in a choke-hold. He clearly remembered MacIssac bellowing "That's the spirit, lad!" to Hans as he downed another man. Blauchuk just seemed to be picking up anyone he did not recognize, lifting them over his head, and lobbing them at anyone else he did not recognize that was nearby.

The only other thing he would clearly remember in later years was three dozen beaten and battered pirates from the *Bloody Rose* stumbling home in a mostly victorious state. They were caterwauling bawdy airshipman's shanties at the top of their lungs with bruised ribs and blackened eyes as they made way back to the ship, with Hans in their midst.

"All Quiet in the Eastern Skies"

Diary Entry for May 11th, 1888

Another week has passed in my life aboard the Bloody Rose. We ran north by north east for the first day on propellers alone. Once we had crossed into the region of the Black Sea, we then unfurled our masts and sails, resuming our guise of a wind-blown merchantman.

We have since been cruising through Bulgaria, Rumania and we are now following the Carpathian Mountains to the north-west. I would guess that should we remain on this course, we would enter the airspace of my homeland within a week.

One of the crew that I have grown to know well is a brick of a man named Blauchuk. After explaining some of his unfortunate background to me, he has asked if I would mentor him in a few matters where he finds his education lacking depth. This should prove to be an interesting relationship.

I am again noticing the ease at which I find myself slipping into the daily routine of life aboard the Bloody Rose. I am less ill at ease with it, but must still remain committed to my plan of taking leave of the ship as soon as Fate permits.

Of last note to my diary was the amusing evening I passed with the ship's officers, mid-week. Apparently each member of the crew takes a turn at being the "duty steward" for supper. It was an enlightening evening, to say the least. I gleaned some fascinating insights into the personalities of the ship's officers.

*****

The desert sun had been clear of the horizon for only a few hours before the *Bloody Rose* cast free her last line. A warm, dusty desert wind challenged her authority in these skies. Her centre-line propeller-pod had been lowered from its hiding place in the Propulsion Room. Its powerful electric motor droned with steady purpose as the helmsman expertly turned her to the chosen course.

On her decks, the crew worked to finish the task of making the ship ready for powered flight. They moved carefully, hunkered down against the gale-force winds now sweeping over the ship as she drove through the skies at forty knots. Leather tethers and steel clips kept every man secure against a moment of turbulence throwing them overboard.

The *Bloody Rose* climbed rapidly with her gas bags inflated to maximum lift and the EMIPALE heaving her upwards. As well, her two sets of Bernoulli foils, one forward and one aft, were canted at an upwards angle, using her forward speed to also push her upwards through the air. Within a few minutes, she was levelling out at a thousand feet above sea level.

Within the Propulsion Room, the engineering crew was busy. Chief Itala was in the watch-keeper's chair, Hans was working on a vibrating mechanical linkage and Aron was in the process of shutting down the EMIPALE.

Arietta called up the voicepipe to confirm that they were running only on "bags and planes" and the EMIPALE was "secured". A call of confirmation came back down the pipe. She turned back to look at where Hans and Visivald now were both puzzling over the misbehaving linkage.

"How many men does it take to fix a pin arm?" she quipped. Both Hans and Visivald wordlessly shot her a black look, and then turned back to their work. She laughed her musical lilt and focused her attention back to the bank of dials, gauges and controls that displayed the condition of the complex systems of the Propulsion Room. After a few more minutes of work and head-scratching on the part of the two men, the difficulty was repaired.

"Very good, gentlemen," Chief Itala smiled. "*Signore* Aron, you will have the next watch. We will see you in six hours. *Signore* Sauder, you have this watch."

Both Hans and Visivald looked at each other and then at Arietta. "Um, Chief ... I do not yet have a watch-keeping ticket," Hans reminded her politely.

"Correct. Which is why I will be sitting over there on the fire-blanket chest," she said, gesturing towards the hefty, brass-bound oak and cedar trunk. "I will be reading and doing assorted irritating Chief Engineer-type paperwork. If you have questions, you will ask me. If you get into trouble, I will be over to help. After three weeks of tearing apart and rebuilding the entire Propulsion Room, I would guess you may have accidentally learned something. If you prove my suspicion correct, you will have your Ticket by early next week."

The Norwegian clapped Hans on the shoulder and grinned. "That is very good news for everyone, Sauder. We all get a bit more sleep that way."

Hans grinned back. "Well, let us see if I can make a week without burning a boiler out, first," he laughed.

*****

The next morning, Hans was on the upper decks to watch the dawn. He had slept well enough, but had woken early when the sound of the ship had changed significantly. They had gotten far enough north that they had shut down and stowed the centre-line propeller-pod and then unfurled the masts and sails. So, this morning, the wind across the decks was a very pleasant twenty miles per hour.

He was doing some simple practice routines for his Judo and sword work, before the morning routine of gunnery drills and sail maintenance began. He would later give himself the excuse that he was so completely caught up in the focus on his form that, while he did hear the Gunner-Marine Captain approach, he did not expect her actions. The truth was he had no idea where she came from. One moment he was alone on the forecastle, the next moment the Russian brunette was swinging her cutlass at his head.

He dove to a side, and was immediately forced to roll away as she tried to slam her booted foot into the middle of his chest. He came up sweeping and swinging with his legs and forearms. She side-stepped or blocked each one, and he only narrowly escaped having her bloody his nose; she renewed the bruise on his jaw instead.

The scimitar cleared its scabbard in time to block the next two solid chops from her cutlass. They traded a few more stalemated blows as they circled, darted, leaped and dodged around the bow area and its assorted winch assemblies and mechanisms.

"Captain-Gunner ... if I might be so bold ..." he said as he traded a series of attacks and parries with her.

"Yes?"

"Why are you trying to kill me?"

"Oh, *Gospodin* Sauder, I am not trying to kill you. If ... oh, very nice attack ... If I was trying to kill you, I would have just drawn my pistol and shot you in the back at the start of this," she laughed, her ice blue eyes flashing in the golden rays of morning sunlight.

"Ah. I see. Well ... that is somewhat comforting to know ..." He paused momentarily as she forced him to use a shoulder-roll to avoid having his ribs bruised by her armoured knee. "So … what exactly is this beating about?"

"You are impressively agile, Sauder … Hmm? Oh … Well, firstly, I am curious about just how good a fighter you actually are. Secondly, it is much more interesting than having breakfast with you … at least here, I am swinging as well," she laughed again. Her mirth was cut short by his fist striking her in the bicep of her sword arm.

Much to his dismay, she did not drop the sword, which was the effect the attack was supposed to produce. Instead, she opened the distance between them with a bound and glanced at the point of impact with a lick of her lips.

"You are a clever man, Sauder. It is a good thing I am more stubborn than most, *nyet*?" She switched the sword to her other hand and sprang forward. He stepped to meet her, their swords ringing out in the morning air. "The other reason I am here is that I am told you started a rather impressive bar-brawl in my name. Why?"

He tried not to look too embarrassed at her question. "Partly because I was drunk," he said as he circled her warily. "But mostly because it seemed to be the right thing to do at the time."

"How very Pirate of you, *Gospodin* Sauder." Her observation was delivered as a taunt.

"Perhaps," he said as he delivered a combination of sword blows, sweeps and grapple-attempts that forced her into a dozen-step retreat. "You may call it what you wish. *Döktor* Koblinski's assertions about the company I keep notwithstanding, I must live and work with the rest of the crew. It was the right thing to do."

"Stop. Enough," she said after she had driven him backwards a few steps with a flurry of attacks. She retreated a few steps from him to disengage. She pulled her breather mask down from her face. Hans was somewhat satisfied that she was at least flushed and panting to some degree. He held his guard against her for a moment until he was certain she was actually done.

"*Spasibo*," she said with a wink. "Again tomorrow?"

"*Du bist willkommen*," he said with a shake of his head. "Unlikely. I believe I will be on watch at this time tomorrow."

"Perhaps another time, then, Hans. I must go ... work begins," she said as she sheathed her cutlass. She gave him a half-bow, turned on her heel and strode off, pulling her mask up and her goggles down. Hans stood there panting, left with the vaguely uncomfortable sensation he was missing some vital piece of information.

*****

The next watch, Arietta tried to burn a boiler out on him. He had just returned to the watch-keeping chair at "very dark in the morning" from his visual inspection rounds when he realized that the water level for the one currently lit boiler was nearly empty. Each boiler had a foot-long glass tube that was at the watch-keeper's station. Gravity and pressure kept the water level in the tube at the same proportionate level as in the boiler tank. A low "glass" meant the boiler was low as well. If the boiler went dry, the firebox temperature could rise fast enough to eventually cause the tank to melt. That would, in turn, cause a terrible fire in the Propulsion Room. In the worst of nightmares, the actual metal of the boiler would begin to burn, creating an unstoppable blaze.

A rapid glance showed him that the feed and tank pressures were dropping slowly but steadily, and the fire box temperature was rising in direct proportion. He glanced over to where Arietta was reading a book.

"Chief! Port-side boiler water is almost out!" he called to her.

"So fix it," she said disinterestedly. She did not even look up at him.

He frowned and shook his head. Without further comment, he cranked the levers and valves to choke the firebox to a bare simmer. He left the chair, went to the electrical panel and opened and closed the knife switches there to the combination required to have the ship running on battery alone. He then went back to the watch-keeping chair, and completely choked the firebox.

"Steering, this is Propulsion ... we are running on battery only and with both fires out," he called up the voicepipe.

"Thank-you, Propulsion. Mister Sauder, is that you?" came Blackheart's voice.

"*Ja, Herr Kapitän,*" he replied, suppressing a sigh. Marvellous; he is trying not to have the ship burn to the keel around his ears, and the Captain is on duty.

"Why are we running without fires?"

"Water feed issue. I am working on finding the problem right now," Hans replied.

"Very well. Hurry up with it, Mister Sauder ... Batteries only last so long," Blackheart growled.

"Aye-aye, *Herr Kapitän.*" He grumbled under his breath and then considered the problem. "Chief, can you give me a hand finding out what is going on here?"

"No. Busy," she replied absently, making a side-margin note in the book she was reading.

He thought a few uncharitable things about the nature of officers and shook his head in irritation. He went over to the boiler, started at the point where the cold water return pipe entered the boiler, and began working backwards along the pipeline. In short order, he found the problem. A lever valve clearly marked "do not close" was closed, preventing water from flowing to the boiler.

His eyes narrowed and he said something uncharacteristically coarse in German and opened the value. He could hear water pour through the piping. He walked past Arietta, still engrossed in her book, and went over to the watch-keeping station. Already the water level in the starved boiler's glass was rising. He waited until the water level was back to normal, and then restarted the firebox.

"*Herr Kapitän*, this is Propulsion. Starboard fire is relit, but we are still running on batteries. There is ... 60% capacity remaining. I will cut the generator back into the circuit within two minutes, after I am sure we have no other issues."

"Very good. Thank-you," came the reply.

He made sure that the boiler pressure and temperature were in the safe zones for operation and then he undid his changes at the electrical panel. He resumed his position in the chair and frowned, wondering how the valve had gotten closed. He turned in the chair and looked over at Arietta. She was holding up a man's pocket watch and giving him that lovely smile of hers.

"Seven minutes, Hans. Good job. You did very well. You kept Steering informed, removed the immediate danger and then were smart about finding the problem," she said, looking very pleased.

"Oh, for Heaven's sake. That was a test?" he said, exasperation clear in his voice. She nodded at him.

"Get used to it. I need to know that you can deal with the 'usual' stuff which goes wrong outside of battle without losing your head. As I said, you did well. Better than I expected, actually. You dealt with me ignoring you much better than I thought you would."

"*Dankeschön*, Chief. I think," he said wryly.

She laughed at him.

*****

"Sauder, I need your help," Blauchuk declared as they left the mess area after the evening meal. Hans looked at the burly Slav with a lofted eyebrow.

"Oh? With what?"

"Can we go talk somewhere less busy?" the Slav said uncomfortably. Hans was a bit sceptical about this, but nodded.

"Follow me," he said. They went forward and down into the "Tank Hold". All of the liquid storage tanks were in this area, with ladders and access walks around them. As well, the two coal bunkers were here, with the horizontal bucket hoist back to the Propulsion Room. The ship thrummed and sang around them dully.

Blauchuk was dressed in a dark and somewhat beaten and patched bib-and-brace overall dungaree with a heavily stained gray shirt. A gray cap, similar to the ones worn by the Confederates in the American Civil War, was on his head. A hefty, hand-made red wool scarf was around his neck. Hans had noted that, generally, Blauchuk's apparel was a stack of hand-me-downs or took-from-thems. However, under any and all conditions, the red wool scarf was a constant. He presumed it was sentimental to the Slav; probably made by family.

"What is on your mind, Blauchuk?"

Blauchuk suddenly looked rather lost. He opened his mouth and closed it three times before he managed to say "Chess."

"Chess?" Hans queried, puzzled.

"Chess!" Blauchuk nodded enthusiastically, as though Hans now possessed all the information required.

Hans sighed and scratched at his forehead patiently. "What about it?"

"Could you teach me? How to play, I mean?" Blauchuk asked quietly.

"Well ... yes, I suppose I could, but ... why?" Hans answered carefully. He distinctly recalled the brick-like Slav's performance at the "Desert Bizaare" during the bar fight there.

"I want to be smart. Not just strong and dumb. I'm tired of being dumb," he said morosely. "You ... well, you're smart enough that you don't need to be strong. You can do stuff just because you can think of doing it!" Blauchuk gushed, waving his arms as he spoke. "I can't think of stuff like you do. So all I can do is be strong and take orders."

"And you think if I teach you chess, it will help?" Hans asked.

"Yes. You see, Miss Annika is going to be able to get her own ship someday. I want to be her Gunner-Marine Captain. But I can't do it right now. I'm not smart enough," the Slav said with his brow furrowed in determination.

"She's like you; it doesn't matter that she's not a big and strong guy. She thinks all the time and does smart stuff. That's why *she's* the Gunner-Marine Captain; she's out-smarted everyone that has ever fought her," Blauchuk said, with obvious reverence in his voice for the Russian woman.

Hans was rather surprised at the Slav's forethought and planning in the matter. He knew where he wanted to go and what was blocking him from getting there. To Hans, the irony here was that Blauchuk was quite obviously not stupid, or he would not have thought to ask Hans for help to achieve his goal. The problem was education, not intelligence.

"Well ... okay. If it means that much to you, then I will be happy to help. I think the best place to start is a book on the basics."

Blauchuk shook his head glumly. "I ... I can't read," he admitted.

"You cannot..." Hans began.

"Don't laugh! It's not my fault. No one ever taught me." Blauchuk rather looked like he might explode into either rage or tears.

"I was not going to laugh," Hans said encouragingly. "Okay. Well, I think you would be much better served by learning to read first."

"Why?" the burly Slav asked, puzzled.

"Well ... being able to read is like unlocking a door to all the things you want to be able to do. You can learn almost anything you want, anytime you want. You just get the right book to get you started," Hans explained, with a kind smile.

"Oh," Blauchuk said. He thought very carefully about that.

"Now, I apologize for my curiosity, but where are you from that you were never taught how to read?"

Blauchuk lapsed into a sullen silence that lasted long enough that Hans was starting to wonder if he was going to get an answer. "A laboratory in Nizhny Novgorod," he replied quietly, with a hint of shame in his voice.

"A laboratory ..." Hans trailed off.

"Promise me you won't laugh or scream if I show you a secret," the Slav said with a sudden child-like intensity.

Hans nodded and then said "I promise, Blauchuk." He had no idea what the other man was about, but he could tell that it was of great importance. It had the feel of a burden, and for whatever reason, Hans felt the least he could do was share a bit of whatever it was that bothered the Slav so deeply.

Blauchuk nodded in solemn affirmation and wordlessly pulled his shoulder-length hair aside and pulled his habitual scarf from around his neck. An inch down and an inch back from the jaw joint, on either side, was a bolt sticking out of his neck.

The two men looked at each other for a few very long moments.

"You are a Galvanotaur, correct?" Hans asked carefully, breaking the thick silence. Blauchuk nodded. "How old are you? Do you know?"

"Eleven," Blauchuk replied.

A decade after the Crimean War fizzled to its barely settled conclusion, an Italian scientist succeeded in using electricity to animate a hand-constructed creature from the cadavers of a group of different species of dogs. The resulting creature was essentially a clean slate with minimal fundamental behaviours. In other words, it barely knew how to be a dog, but at the same time demonstrated characteristics of each of the different breeds it had been built from.

In pursuit of a "super soldier" project, the Allied Empires rapidly stopped experimenting with animal parts and began assembling human constructs. Dubbed "Galvanotaurs", after the principle of Galvanism that was used in their creation, it was not long before the Russian Empire also began developing their own.

In essence, Galvanotaurs were hand-built human war machines. They had a tremendous tolerance to pain, shock and environmental extremes. Their strength and endurance were the stuff of modern legend. They were largely fearless and had a distinct tendency towards reverent loyalty to authority figures.

Like so many other creations that stemmed from the Crimean War, however, the Galvanotaurs were dangerously flawed. They were, effectively, super-powered children. The temper tantrum of a child capable of throwing a regular man across a room using only one arm, while being able to ignore the first and sometimes second gun shots to the chest, was not to be underestimated.

Generally speaking, both sides of the Truce of Paris had given up on them for general purpose infantry. However, there were always rumours of elite shock-troop units or specialized bodyguards available to be "built to order".

"Eleven," Hans repeated. "From my limited understanding, that is quite impressive." Hans paused and thought for a moment. "Who else knows this about you? On the *Bloody Rose*, I mean."

"The Captain, I think. The Doctor. Miss Annika, too." The Slav seemed concerned by something. "Are you still going to want to help me?" he finally asked.

"Oh, yes," Hans nodded. "More so than ever, Blauchuk. Your secret is safe with me. And, just so it has been said, I have a tremendous respect for the fact that you have managed to find a home. From what I understand of others of your origin, that is rather unusual. That your place is amongst pirates does not take away from that."

Hans smiled encouragingly and continued. "I think, *Herrn* Blauchuk, that once we teach you how to read, there will be very little to stop you from achieving anything you put your mind towards."

"Really?" Blauchuk asked in surprise.

Hans clapped him on the shoulder. "Really. Now, we have a lot of work to do. Depending on which watches I have, it is up to you to meet me after either the gun-run practice or after supper. One hour a day, and I am sure we can make good progress. Okay?"

Blauchuk nodded with the expression on his face of a child given his first gift at Christmas. Perhaps, Hans mused, he was.

*****

The next three days passed rather pleasantly. Dangerously so, Hans thought. There was a solid physical routine coupled with some kind of daily challenge to his intellect or his character. They forced him to look at everything around him with a sense of sharpness in a way he had not done since his early days at the University in Heidelberg. He also had to admit that day-to-day living with the pirate crew of the *Bloody Rose* was no worse than life in the Dormitories. Beyond the part where his Dormitory-mates were not known to spend time murdering merchantmen with axes and cap-and-ball revolvers, of course.

The Russian Captain-Gunner had apparently decided her day was not complete without either an evening or morning sparring practice with him. She was, he fully understood by now, a better warrior than he was. Perhaps he was a better sword fighter in terms of technique than she was. Perhaps he was, indeed, better at hand-to-hand from the perspective of Judo versus Russian-style Fist Fighting. Those were both moot points in reality. There was a line he would never cross in their fights, and they both knew it.

He always held back, trying to minimize injury or risk of a terrible accident. Annika, on the other hand, would cheerfully beat him senseless if he made a serious mistake. He was fairly sure she would not actually send him to Sickbay on purpose; it was also rather clear she was also not too terribly concerned about any accident that might arrive at the same result.

They talked both casually and seriously as he avoided her merry attempts to murder him. She was an intriguing woman, and beyond her looks there was something about her that Hans had to admit held his attention anytime she was around. Then again, that might simply be his sense of self-preservation.

Blauchuk proved to be devoted in his one hour per day of reading work with Hans. The young German had decided that while perhaps the Slav Galvanotaur was not the most formidable intellect aboard the *Bloody Rose*, his firm determination to succeed would certainly carry him far. There was simply no discouraging him at all. Everything was just an obstacle to be overcome, and Blauchuk had little fear of trying and trying again.

Hans was using a simple system of discussing the day's events with him as a learning mechanism. Blauchuk would tell him something, and Hans would write it down on a wax tablet and read it back, pointing at each of the words. Then Hans would write down his reply, and read it aloud, pointing at the words. It made for slow discourse, but everything was immediately meaningful.

In the Propulsion Room, Chief Itala seemed to invent a new calamity hidden under a carpet for him to solve every other after-dark watch. So far, she had yet to completely confound him, but she was certainly stretching his skills as an engineer, his powers of perception as well as his abilities of analysis and reason to meet her challenges. He nearly did not care if he ever got the Watch-Keeping Ticket or not at this point. He would be damned if he was going to let her best him in a game of "What Did Arietta Break Today?", even if she was the one making up the rules to the game.

"Good job, *Signore* Sauder. I thought I had you that time," she said with a musical laugh.

"Cross wiring the generator voltage repeaters on the Watch Keeper's station panel was diabolical, Chief," he growled at her good naturedly.

"It was terribly amusing watching you crawling the entire length of the wiring bridge three times," she said with a grin. "Well, Visivald will be here in a few minutes; I will turn the watch over to him. Go get some sleep. I will see you at supper tonight."

"Pardon? At supper?" Hans asked, puzzled.

"Oh! I forgot to tell you. You are the Duty Assistant Steward for tonight. You will be helping serve the Officer's table in the Captain's mess this evening. *Signore* Bridges will be expecting you thirty minutes before the evening meal bell. Make sure you are clean shaven, with a fresh haircut and tidied up, with clean clothes. You will be serving the table, and besides, the ship's ladies prefer the look of you when you do not appear to have just crawled out of the slurry grinder," Arietta said with a grin and a wink. Hans flushed and mentally stalled at the implication in her words. Arietta burst into laughter and he beat a hasty retreat up the ladder to the main deck.

*****

James Bridges was, arguably, the most unappreciated man aboard the *Bloody Rose*, Hans decided. As the Chief Steward, he was in charge of the team that ensured that every man and woman aboard the ship was fed, warm, and had a hammock to sleep in, no matter what happened. In addition, he was the *aide-de-camp* for Captain Blackheart, ensuring that the bureaucratic parts of a successful pirate ship were running smoothly at all times.

"So, you are the famous Hans Sauder, hmm?" Chief Bridges said, peering up at him. He was a short, stout and portly man with the start of a balding palette and stove-pipes for arms. He had an auburn befrazzled beard that simply ignored attempts to bring it to heel with a comb. He dressed smartly in a white jacket, shirt and pants; Hans had no clue how the man kept the ensemble clean.

"I do not know if I would use the term 'famous', Chief," Hans replied carefully. "Chief Itala tells me I am to assist you this evening. I have no clue what to do, but I am happy to learn."

"That is an excellent attitude, Mister Sauder, an excellent attitude indeed. Now, first … the officers speak freely and openly at the table. Anything you see and hear is in confidence. If Captain Blackheart is given any reason to believe you are going to repeat what you see or hear, he will shoot you in the back at the end of the night. Please be clear and understand I am not joking; I have seen him do it three times in the two years I have been with the ship."

Hans digested this information. "I trust that if I decide this is an unacceptable risk that I am allowed to decline to serve?"

Bridges laughed. "I am starting to like you already, Mister Sauder. You are one of a handful smart enough to ask that question. The answer is yes. Do you intend to exercise that option?"

"Oh no, not at all, Chief. I was merely curious. I am quite capable of keeping my mouth shut," Hans said with a nod.

"A fine virtue in a gentleman, Mister Sauder. The routine is very simple … you will stand by the service window over there," the Steward said, pointing a finger towards the spot. "As the meal comes to the window, you bring the plates to the table. You do not speak unless spoken to. You do not attempt to attract attention; you simply wait. The Captain is served first, then the ladies at the table, and then the gentlemen. Seating is pre-managed, and you serve those seated closest to the Captain first."

"Once they all have their plates, I will pass you your plate. You eat at the window. Roast duck with sides of asparagus in creamed cheese on fresh bread and rice is the table for the night," Bridges said with a grin.

"You are also to keep your eye on the wine glasses at the table," the Chief Steward continued. "If you see a glass less than half full, and the current plates are served, you stop what you are doing, get a decanter from the window and go fill the glasses. If they give you the glass, it means they are done with wine ... you may have whatever is left in it."

"Once the Captain and the ladies are done eating, then dessert and port will be served. The same protocols apply as before. You clear the table of plates, silver and glass, and then bring out fresh dishes and drink as I give it to you."

"Coffee and tea, cigars and cigarettes are the last of the evening, and then it gets very informal. Again, your job is to be quiet and unobtrusive unless you are directly addressed. Do you follow me so far?" the Englishman finished.

Hans nodded. "Exactly how my father expects his servants to behave at our two homes," he said bemusedly. "I have heard Beneton, our head butler, saying similar things a few times over the years. I must admit to never having expected to be the servant one day."

Bridges chortled and smiled. "A bit of service is good for the soul, Mister Sauder. It keeps a chap from gaining unnecessary airs and detachment from his fellow man."

Hans smiled and nodded. "An interesting lesson, Chief; I will likely give that notion considerable thought over the evening," he said wryly. "Now, once the meal is finished what is then left to be done?"

"Ah ... well, then you and I clean the whole place up, including dishes, while the Captain does his last rounds before bed, and we make ourselves absent by the time of his return. It is a busy two or three hours, but you will eat well, have a bit of wine and port, get to enjoy some gifted company and sleep well afterwards."

"Well enough then. Shall we get about the job of removing any of my unnecessary airs?" Hans said with a laugh.

The two men set about the task of preparing the Captain's Mess for the evening dinner. The table itself was stored in the floor under an oriental carpet. The carpet was rolled back and stowed aside, and then an electric system raised the table up. Chairs were stored under the table when it was lowered, and had to be taken out and set around. Simple table linens and chair covers were put in place, giving the entire thing an illusion of permanence.

Candles were set out and the initial placement of glass and silver was done. Translucent coloured shades were put over the windows, giving a cheery gold light to the room. A dumb waiter lift chimed and Bridges passed Hans a white jacket to pull over his vest and white cap to don. Shortly thereafter, Blackheart came in from the main deck.

He glanced at Hans without a word, passed him his coat, and then gave a flick of his hand towards a coat rack. Hans reminded himself of his role for the evening, and went to hang the coat up.

In total there were ten officers aboard the *Bloody Rose*, most of whom Hans already knew fairly well. At the head of the table was Captain Michael O'Raedy, the infamous Blackheart. To his right sat Chief Engineer Arietta Itala, and to his left was Gunner-Marine Captain Annika Nadezhda. The ship's doctor, Alexi Koblinski, sat beside Arietta, and beside Annika was the empty chair set for the Chief Steward, James Bridges. Next down the table from the Doctor was the Spanish Deck Officer, Amram Nando. After the empty chair were Watch Officers Doretta Tillie and Jeffery Wilton, both from England. After the Spaniard were two more Watch Officers, the Dutch Piet Adelbert and Donát Jani of Hungary.

Piet and Donát had joined the *Bloody Rose* at her last port of call. Their Right of Passage fights had each been spectacular, with two bloody wins apiece.

Everyone in attendance at the table was dressed in white shirts, dark pants, and low boots. Weapons were conspicuously absent, save for Blackheart, who had a pair of revolvers and his cutlass all slung on his weapon belt, hung off the back of his chair.

The first course of the meal was much more difficult for him than Hans would have guessed. He was sufficiently used to proper meal etiquette that his timing and deportment were as good or better than could have been expected of a non-professional servant. That was not the issue. He hated being invisible.

No one said a direct word to him. Arietta and Annika looked right through him, never acknowledging him, even with a smile or glance. Alexi and Blackheart likewise pointedly treated him like a ghost. He quietly ate his meal as Blackheart told some amusing anecdote about running a Russian blockade to drop supplies to an English army unit that had gotten cut off. The ladies laughed gaily at the portrayal of the incompetence of both sides, while the gentlemen applauded and approved of some of the tactics and heroics. Hans was obligated to remain staid and silent, over by the serving window, save for brief forays to refill wine glasses.

Hans had to admit that Blackheart was a capable storyteller. Even though he was playing at being distracted by the excellent repast before him, he was deft in how he orchestrated highs and lows and wove laughter in with sorrow to keep everyone in the room quite nearly spellbound. From what Hans could determine, O'Raedy had started his career with Her Majesty's Royal Navy. How he had wound up the infamous Captain Blackheart of an airship would likely be an interesting story of itself. It infuriated Hans that he was forbidden by protocol to ask the question; to be involved at least in passing with the social dinner.

He could, he supposed, be a boor and breach protocol. However, he had a personal pride in doing everything with a sense of excellence that precluded selfish spitefulness; at least most times, anyway. Which meant that he would be damned if he did not play his role with as little reproach as he could, no matter how much it grated him.

As he silently and swiftly cleared the table for dessert, he realized that this was exactly how he had treated innumerable servants and wait staff over the years of his life. He had always been so distant with the servants at his family's homes as well as those employed at the various places he had taken lodging over the years.

It was considered "normal" in this modern time; servants were to be treated as animated furniture. In some homes, the staff were expected to turn away and look to the floor as the master or lady of the house passed by them. Hans had never questioned how that might feel, to be functionally treated like some sort of ghost of housework's dispatch. Now he knew. He did not like it much at all.

"A bit of service is good for the soul, Mister Sauder. It keeps a man from gaining unnecessary airs and detachment from his fellow man," the Chief Steward had said.

Paid for their service or not, if Hans expected others to treat him with dignity, then he realized that he had best treat others with their due dignity. Did he even know the servants at his father's home as well as some of the crew of cutthroats and scoundrels he now lived with? Servants he had spent years of his life seeing at every supper time, or every summer day in the garden? Compared to pirates he had known for less than two months? He was internally horrified at his conclusion. "Detachment," indeed.

"Well, Mister Sauder, what did you think of the duck this evening?" Blackheart asked him, contemplating the young German over the rim of his port glass.

"Undoubtedly the best meal I have eaten in months, *Herr Kapitän*," Hans said with a nod and smile as he set a plate of white cake and fruits drizzled in a raspberry liqueur and hot chocolate sauce in front of a delighted Arietta.

"I am very glad you approved, Mister Sauder. I know you must be very well accustomed to eating better than the lower deck mess allows for," Blackheart said as he cut a piece of his cake and swirled it in the liqueur and chocolate.

"Actually, *Herr Kapitän*, the food from the mess is better most nights than what was available at the junior student's kitchen hall of the University," he chuckled.

"A bit more port, please, Hans? For both Arietta and I?" Annika requested with a light smile and a casual grace that seemed so very different than the woman who sparred with him with such deadly intensity. She had an almost aristocratic bearing about her, yet still with a soft charm.

"Of course, *Fräulein* Nadezhda. One moment, if you please," Hans replied with a smile. He returned with a decanter and quickly visited everyone's glasses as they permitted.

The next hour was a pleasant buzz of conversation. He was periodically directly included in the goings on. In one instance, Nando and Koblinski were in a spirited argument about the validity of Philosopher Friedrich Nietzsche's concept of "will to power". The Spanish officer suggested that since Sauder and Nietzsche were countrymen, perhaps Hans would have some insights. Hans politely demurred, offering that he was not much of a man of philosophy. The Captain laughed at him.

Once the plates, silver and glass had been cleared away, Hans set out cigars and cigarettes. The ladies and the Doctor all opted for cigarettes. The remaining gentlemen all lit cigars. Alexi told Hans to take one for himself. Hans glanced towards Blackheart who met his eye and nodded slightly. Hans thanked the doctor and lit a cigar. Chief Bridges took his chair and lit up as well.

Backgammon, checkers and cribbage boards shortly covered the table with everyone having broken from the organized seating plan to whatever more suited their mood in terms of a game. Hans quietly continued to ensure the coffee, tea and port were available, as well as bringing a bit more of the dessert out when requested. He kept to himself, over by the serving window. Simply having been spoken to directly and included in a bit of the social atmosphere had eased him significantly. He vowed he would remember this lesson for the future.

Twice he had gotten the direct impression that either Annika and Arietta or Annika and Doretta had been eyeing him and making him the subject of discussion. He had no clue what they were about, but he doubted any good would come from it.

At the end of the evening, before the eighth bell of the Dog Watches, everyone had departed, leaving just Sauder and Bridges. They rapidly cleaned and tidied. The table was lowered into the floor, and the Captain's double-bed was lowered from a wall. When the bed was pushed up and away, it looked like panelled wall with a picture on it.

"Well done, Mister Sauder," Chief Bridges said as they both stepped out onto the moonlit and cloud-covered main deck. "Excellent job. We'll see you in three months."

"Three months?"

"Aye, Mister Sauder. About every 90 days you will be back up here again. Please do not get killed in the mean time. I enjoyed working with you."

Hans chuckled and thanked the Chief Steward. As he walked towards the down-below hatch, he was very much hoping he would not be aboard the pirate ship long enough to serve another dinner to the officers of the *Bloody Rose*.

"Taking Prey"

Diary Entry for May 14th, 1888

I am repeatedly amused of late by the fickleness of the Fates. The trio of Spinsters seem to give little care at where and when the threads of the lives of a man and a woman join for a period of time.

For example, take Döktor Koblinski and Nurse Coline. While recent events have made it clear that I am hardly an expert on affairs of the heart, I am fairly certain that the two of them have extended their relationship aboard the Bloody Rose beyond a purely professional one. While perhaps others might find the notion of such a thing as unseemly, I am personally quite happy for the good Döktor. It seems rather storybook for two individuals of their age to find romance together so quickly as crewmates aboard a pirate ship, particularly in these harsh modern times.

The Captain-Gunner seems to be of the opinion that I am quite popular 'au-distance' with the ladies of the Bloody Rose. I am given to understand that my looks, physical abilities and strong personal code have made me the subject of some discussion amongst them. Annika herself has expressed a particular interest in me that has nothing to do with professionalism. I am somewhat uncertain of my opinions on her overtures.

The Kapitän has demonstrated both a good memory and a sense of humour in more operational matters. I was again reminded by his actions that he understands the motivations and emotional pressure points of key members of his crew. It must also be noted that he *demonstrates little remorse in exploiting those things to achieve his desired ends. In spite of this, the crew of the Bloody Rose are fiercely loyal to their anführer.*

In closing this entry, I am obligated to note that we "took prey" this afternoon. The Bloody Rose attacked and boarded the Spanish merchant ship "Suerte Bailarín". The fight was a far more lopsided affair than the battle with the Triomphe. A single volley of cannon fire and we were able to force a boarding. I was obligated to take part in the action and in securing the engineering space of the Spanish ship. I did my best to minimize the casualties that I caused as well as those caused by my crewmates. Two of the Spaniards voluntarily "jumped the gunwale" to join the crew of the Bloody Rose, including one Engineer.

*****

The pirate airship *Bloody Rose* was under full sail in the clear night sky, with the snow-capped bulk of the Carpathian Mountains off her starboard side. She was about halfway between Budapest and Prague, keeping a steady altitude of about 750 feet above the ground. A sharp storm line had forced her down below 200 feet for part of the afternoon, making everyone edgy. However, the evening sky had cleared and the winds had abated, allowing her to make back to good height again.

The watchman rang four bells to end the "mids" watch and shortly afterwards the hatch leading from the Propulsion Room opened, casting a faint shaft of dull red light into the air. Hans climbed up and out and then closed the door carefully. He dogged it shut with a yawn. He was bone-tired from the combination of the hour and the absolute quiet of the night.

However, the mid-watch upper-deck rounds needed to be done. So, armed with the fresh and mountain-chilled air of the night, as well as a recently filled coffee flask, he hoped he would feel rejuvenated enough to remain awake until the end of the watch. He had yet to doze off on watch, but he very much doubted he would enjoy Chief Itala's idea of a wake-up call.

Mostly the upper-deck rounds involved making his way around to the various powered systems on the deck such as the winches, mast and sail furlers, search lights and the like. At each spot, there was a small test lamp that, if lit, indicated the system had power available to it. It took him a total of about fifteen minutes to check each of the various points.

In the last quarter of his walking about he realized that Alexi and Gwendoline were standing on the tail of the ship together. He was about to call to them in greeting when he realized that would likely be unwise. They were standing close together, staring out at the retreating scenery, holding hands. She was leaning her head against the Doctor's shoulder and they were periodically exchanging quiet words.

Hans paused for a minute, looking at the winch beside them and then at his task book. They kissed lightly and briefly as he watched them in the star-lit darkness. He nodded to himself with a smile. He wrote "Sufficient Electricity" beside the position on the hull diagram for that winch and continued his rounds. Arietta would just have to trust him on all nuances of this point, he thought bemusedly, as he moved quietly on.

*****

It was early in the afternoon watch when the whistles and bells had begun ringing aboard the pirate ship, calling her crew to action. Hans' feet hit the deck at the bottom of the ladder with full force as he slid down. He took the shock into his legs and sprung forward even as the action alarm resumed its whistle and bell sequence.

Arietta had apparently somehow managed to beat him here by a handful of seconds. She was sliding into the Watch-Keeper's chair as Visivald moved to take his position at the EMPIALE control panel. She glanced back and grinned at him before she pulled up and buckled her breather mask.

"What is going on?" he asked as he rapidly made his way to where she was.

"Taking prey," she said with a wicked light in her eyes and nasty tone in her voice that inexplicably left Hans momentarily finding it very difficult to think of her professionally. He was rather startled by the reaction.

"This time we are the hunter, however. It is much safer for us this way, if not quite as exciting," she said with a musical laugh. She tapped the goggles covering her brown eyes as a reminder to Hans. He had a sudden memory flash through his mind of the sound of the air filled with flying splinters and his blood went cold. He hurriedly pulled his goggles down and breather-mask back up.

The ship was already running with all three propeller pods down and the sails and masts furled. Chief Itala directed Hans to bring the remaining cold engines to full power. He nodded and swiftly set about the tasks required to do so.

Arietta answered a call from Steering via the voicepipe. Hans could hear her request for the message to be repeated and then she acknowledged, sounding puzzled as she did. "*Signore* Sauder ... report to the Steering House. Bring your sword," she ordered, still sounding puzzled.

"The Steering House? Why, Chief?"

"No clue, *Signore* Sauder. *Capitano's* orders. Get a move on," she said with a shrug.

Hans climbed back up the ladder and made his way to the Steering House that sat on the front edge of the quarter-deck. It was mostly windows on the front, sides and top. Inside, things were busy. Captain Blackheart, Captain-Gunner Nadezhda, Watch Officer Wilton and two other regular crew were there. One crewman was at the rudder wheel, the other was at the levers that controlled the Bernoulli foils. The three officers looked at him as he came in. He thought Annika winked at him for some reason, but presumed he was mistaken.

"Ah, there you are, Mister Sauder," Blackheart said with a shark-like smile. "You, Mister Sauder, have inspired me," he chortled.

"I have, have I?" Hans asked dubiously.

"Oh, indeed. I have been so impressed by your on-going attempts to spare lives that I thought I might try it myself. Do you see that ship ahead and low of us?" Blackheart pointed at the blur of colour in the distance. Hans nodded, starting to feel uneasy about where this conversation was going.

"Well, normally, we would run up alongside her and put a few volleys from the twelve and eight pounders into her to slow her down. Then we move in closer with a figure-'S' pattern and fire a pair of broadsides of the fours, eights and twelves with grapeshot to clear her decks and shred her sides," Blackheart said. He illustrated as he spoke, using his two hands to represent the *Bloody Rose,* her victim and the movement of the vessels relative to each other. "Of course, Mister Sauder, the entire procedure from start to finish is a messy process that kills a lot of people."

"I would imagine it does, *Herr Kapitän.* Guns fired at people tend to do that," Hans said coldly.

"Aye, indeed they do, as I am sure you are very aware of. But, this is where you get to make a difference in being a civilizing influence around here," the pirate captain replied with note of amusement in his voice. Blackheart passed him his spyglass and pointed at the soon-to-be victim. "Take a look. Can you identify her?"

Hans took the spyglass and adjusted it to bring the other ship into sharp focus. He could see the Spanish colours flying from her stern staff. *"Suerte Bailarín"* was painted, gold on black, across her stern immediately below the flag staff. Her weather deck had a couple of rows of crates lashed down with nets. That was unusual; she must have been loaded very heavy. He could see a single large-diameter stern propeller spinning. He guessed it was almost fourteen feet across. A few guns were on the deck, enclosed in wind breaks. Like the *Bloody Rose*, her gas-bags were carried in rows along each of her sides.

He took the spyglass away from his eye and looked at Blackheart. *"Ja, Herr Kapitän.* That is a Dornier *Luftschiff* 129-B; a state-of-the-art airship freighter. If she alerts to us, you will have a merry time catching her ... her top speed is about 90 knots. That is very hard on her fuel, however. Her *Kapitän* will want to keep her around thirty to forty knots, because all of the newest generation of Dornier's carry no sails at all. They are powered flight only, which is going to be the way of the future. She will have a mild bite with an octet of eight pound guns."

Blackheart took back the spyglass and nodded, obviously impressed. "Excellent, Mister Sauder. Now ... Here is your big chance. You are to tell our good Captain-Gunner here where to put the first two 12 pound balls. If you can prevent her from running away with that impressive top speed, we will not need to tear her to ribbons with grapeshot. "

"You expect me to tell you how to cripple a civilian merchant ship so you can pillage it, *Herr Kapitän*? I think perhaps you have mistaken me."

"*Au contraire, Monsieur* Sauder," Blackheart said in an amused tone. "I know you very well. You will do as I ask, because if you do not ..." he trailed off and gave a shrug and a pause. "Well, I will just do this the old fashioned way and there will be many more dead Spaniards than there could have been."

There was a heavy silence in the Steering House. The German and the Englishman stared at each other, their gaze unwavering for several seconds. The two crewmen pointedly studied their gauges and controls. The other two officers watched; Annika was fascinated while Jeffery looked puzzled about the confrontation.

Hans kept what he thought was a cold and impassive expression on his face, even as his heart sank. He was in no position to deny the captain. No matter what he did, unless the *Suerte Bailarín* saw the *Bloody Rose* in time, the ultimate outcome would be the same. The only question was how many innocent lives ended. He certainly did not wish to spend the rest of his life knowing that he could have prevented a massacre, but did not out of spiteful stubbornness directed at the pirate captain he was staring at.

Without taking his eyes off of the captain, Hans finally asked "Captain-Gunner, how accurate are your best crews?"

"They can hit a man-sized target on the traverse at a thousand yards," she replied, with an odd quality in her voice.

"The target point is about half the diameter of the propeller ahead of the point where the shaft enters the hull. That is about where the mechanism for adjusting the blade angles will be. A strike there will cripple them with almost no risk of injury to anyone," he said in a voice devoid of emotion.

Blackheart smiled. "Thank-you Mister Sauder. I appreciate your contribution to our success." He turned and looked at Annika. "Fire at Mister Sauder's target, Captain-Gunner, as soon as we are inside 900 yards. We will make the shot with our port guns. Your crews are Dubé's and Cortez's, yes?"

"Yes, *Kaptan*. My two best," the Captain-Gunner replied with a nod.

"Good. Helmsman, bring us to course three-three-four. Planesman, set twelve degrees up angle. Engineering, set all propellers to full power ... I need 80 knots. Make bells and whistles for preparation for an attack dive." Confirmations returned to Blackheart from around the Steering House.

"May I go, *Herr Kapitän*?"

"Oh, no, Mister Sauder. I would like you to remain here so you can see the value of your knowledge. And then Captain-Gunner Nadezhda will have need of your talents."

Hans looked at Annika who grinned at him and then gestured at him to stand off to a side. She walked over to a da Vinci range finder and trained it on the *Suerte Bailarín*, who they were now climbing away from. She spoke into the voicepipe beside her.

The *Bloody Rose* soared high with the sound of her powerful electric propellers thrumming through the ship and the sound of the wind roaring past. Blackheart looked up and over his shoulder and then back towards where the hunted ship was about to disappear from view under the pirate ship's bow. Hans looked up as as well, and blinked against the glare of the sun, high and behind them, through the windows.

"They will never see us, Mister Sauder. They will be blinded by the sun until it is too late," Blackheart commented. "It is a tremendous advantage to us. We will be able to fire the first shot with relatively little peril to ourselves."

"Eight thousand yards, Captain," Annika reported.

"Helmsman, take course three three five. Planesman, set your foils to twenty five degrees down angle and stand by to execute a forty-five degree starboard roll on my order. Engineering, cut the lifters and stand-by for over-speed alarms. Captain-Gunner, you have the shot," Blackheart ordered.

Everyone held on as the nose of the ship dropped. The thrum and roar turned into a hollow wail that filled the air. "Airspeed eighty-four knots and climbing," the helmsman reported.

"Crossing four thousand feet, Sir. Target deck is at one thousand two hundred," the Planesman called out, a note of excitement in his voice.

The *Bloody Rose* dove out of the afternoon sun upon the *Suerte Bailarín* like a hawk upon a witless dove. The Spanish merchant cruised along through the lightly clouded skies, blissfully unaware of the onrushing menace. Hans held on to a brace-handle with the fascinated sensation of someone watching a train-wreck in progress.

"Helm, touch port 3 degrees," Annika ordered.

"Aye, ma'am ... 3 degrees port helm on!"

"Gun deck, make ready ... steady ... steady ... port twelves, as she clears, FIRE!" Annika shouted into the voicepipe. The *Bloody Rose* rocketed past the *Suerte Bailarín* at nearly one hundred knots. The air was filled with the sound of the wind howling past the joints of the airship.

"Planesman! Forty-five degree starboard roll NOW!" Blackheart bellowed.

Two thunderous rapports filled the air, one after the other, as the aiming point on the *Suerte Bailarín* came into the view of the two twelve pound cannons on the pirate's port side. They were mounted one over the other, with the bulk of the gas bags separating them. The high gun fired first and then as the ship rapidly rolled over, the second gun fired.

The two arcing acts of ballistic violence slammed into the merchant's hull with in a yard of each other. Hans was stunned at the accuracy of the shots, given the severity of the dive and roll. Oil-black smoke poured out of the gash in the target's side.

"Planesman, cancel roll and bring us to level! Set thirty degrees up angle! Engineering, maximum lifters! Helmsman, 15 degrees starboard turn!" Blackheart shouted, his eyes fixed on the rapidly on-rushing tree-tops below them.

"Crossing six hundred feet! Thirty degrees up angle on!" the planesman cried back.

The *Bloody Rose* shrieked like a tortured beast in every strut, spar and spacer in her hull as she flared out of her dive. Hans nearly lost his grip on the handle he was hanging onto for dear life. His eyes registered the needle of the altimeter in front of the planesman dipping momentarily below two hundred and fifty feet before it began to climb. He swore he could smell spruce sap in the air. Another second or so and they would have been pulling boughs out of the ship's battery ribs, Hans thought somberly.

The pirate ship climbed in a long, curving turn that placed the merchantman in the arc of her loaded starboard eight pound and twelve pound cannon. Blackheart, Nadezhda and Wilton surveyed the targeted vessel with their spyglasses. Blackheart lowered his first with a pleased nod.

"Two perfect hits, Captain-Gunner … Well done to your men. Well done to you as well, Mister Sauder … she is losing way rapidly and coming to a stop. It looks like her propeller is just freewheeling at this point. As long as none of the crew aboard are fools, we might be in danger of ruining our reputation," he said with a laugh.

Hans scowled but said nothing. Blackheart opened a drawer in the chart table and pulled out a chair leg and passed it to Hans. Hans took it with a puzzled look on his face.

"You did more than well enough with that the first time you took part in a boarding action, Mister Sauder. It is likely a better choice for you than a pistol. After all, you never know what sorts of accidents happen with firearms," the Captain said pleasantly.

Annika bit her lip to suppress a laugh and then gestured at Hans to follow her. "Come on, *Gospodin* Sauder, we have an engine room to secure."

*****

The initial boarding was swift and simple. The two ships were brought together by the steel cables and steam-belching winches of the boarding harpoons. The entire contingent of gunner-marines swarmed over the gunwale as soon as the grappling-claws had grabbed onto the Spanish ship. They split up into teams with at least one Spanish-speaking member in each group yelling that anyone holding a weapon would be killed without question. Annika and Hans made straight to the engineering area.

They came in through the hatch door and Hans found himself staring at a dark-browed and burly man pointing a Coach Gun at him. Hans froze in fear. There was a deafening blast beside his right ear and the man's face was smashed in, throwing a grey-red splatter behind him. The shot man tumbled and flailed, the short shotgun firing into the deckhead. There was a loud mechanical click beside his left ear and Annika shouted something in broken Spanish. She paused a moment and then repeated herself. Two other frightened men stepped into view with their hands raised.

Hans looked left and right to find Annika holding a tri-barreled pistol in each hand, one beside each of his ears. She had fired the right one; that ear was still ringing from the rapport. However, there was no way the two men could know which gun had fired.

"Duck under the right hand pistol, Sauder, and go check them for weapons. Then tie their hands. Do not step directly between us at any time. I would rather not shoot you," the Captain-Gunner hissed at him. Hans drew his scimitar and moved as she had instructed, keeping his sword at the ready. He relieved each man of a belt knife and tried to ignore the mess on the floor and wall. He tied their hands with cord and pointed at chairs. They sat, pale with fear.

Hans looked at Annika in disgust. "You killed him."

"Of course. Its a rule of survival, Hans ... 'do unto others before they do unto you'. Another moment and he would have spilled your guts on the deck with that thing. It was either you and him, or just him. I chose to ensure you lived."

"You could have just ..."

"Oh, shut up, Hans," the Russian snarled at him. "If I had just wounded him, he would have shot you and then I would have killed him. Get this through your thick head, Hans ... Mercy is what you give after you have won. Not before. You are amongst pirates and you will be treated that way by everyone you meet. Either play by our rules, or die. Get off your Imperial British Morality Horse and learn how the world really works. Now, keep your mouth shut and ensure that nothing is amiss with the engine systems. He would not be the first engineer that would try to scuttle the ship that was just boarded by pirates."

They glared at each other for a moment, then Hans nodded and did as she had ordered. Annika holstered the emptied tri-barrel and transferred the loaded one to her right hand. One of the two men watched Annika intently.

"*¿Qué ves?*" she challenged him him in her broken Spanish.

"*Usted. Pirata Señora, quiero ser un pirata también,*" he replied. The other, older, Spaniard looked at him as though he had gone mad.

Hans peered around a section of piping and valves. "What did he say?" he asked.

Annika gave an amused smirk. "He said he wants to be a pirate, too."

It took about fifteen minutes for Hans to be sure nothing was amiss within the engineering area. He walked over to where Annika was instructing another gunner-marine to take the two Spaniards up to the weather deck. The three men left, leaving Annika and Hans in the engineering room.

"Go close the hatch, Hans," she said quietly. He lofted an eyebrow at her, but nodded wordlessly and did as she said. He returned and stood in front of her. When she backhanded him, he did not even try to avoid it. He gritted his teeth and rubbed the side of his face.

She pulled her armoured leather gauntlet back on while they stared at each other. "Are you really that naive, Hans? Did you really think he was just going to threaten you, then you would put down your sword and then it would all end well? He would have just shot me instead. Did you consider that?"

"Annika ... I froze. I saw the gun and I stopped thinking. I did not have time to move before you killed him," he said quietly while avoiding her gaze. He paused for a moment and then looked directly at her. "Thank-you for saving my life, Captain-Gunner and I apologize for my words afterwards"

Annika looked at him with a rather surprised expression. "You are unused to real battle, are you, Hans? For all your skill at play fighting, that is the first time you had really looked Death in the face, yes?"

He nodded. He suddenly felt rather inadequate. He had an unreasonable feeling that he had just been tested by the Cosmos in some way and had failed.

She nodded at him. "You did better than some then, Sauder. It gets easier with practice. If you remain with us beyond Brussels, I would expect you will get more practice," she said encouragingly.

Suddenly, she was all business. "Do an inventory of what engineering supplies there are aboard that are worth taking and then go discuss it with Chief Itala. We have work to do."

They carefully raised the two entwined ships up over three thousand feet, where few airships tended to fly or look. The crew were kept under vigilance while the crew of the *Bloody Rose* took inventory of the potential spoils. The engineers and stewards replenished the ship's stores while the gunner-marines occupied themselves with taking on saleable cargo.

It took them from mid-afternoon until after dark to finish the process. When the *Bloody Rose* left the side of the *Bailarín*, the merchantman was in the same condition as the *Triomphe*. Her bags were bleeding, her guns had been spiked, and her tanks and powder emptied. The sinking Spaniard would come to the ground somewhere in the Carpathian foothills, and then her Captain and crew would have the job of trying to make their way to a safe town.

Two of the Spanish sailors had jumped the gunwale as the dusk had fallen. One was the young engineer that had expressed his interest to Annika. The other was a hullwright by training that had been working as a cargo handler. They brought nothing with them but the clothes on their backs, a weapon of preference, and one or two important personal effects. Otherwise, they completely left their old lives behind to start anew as a pirate of the crew of the infamous *Bloody Rose*.

*****

Annika was waiting for him as he climbed out of the hatch that led down into the Propulsion Room. Chief Itala had given him leave to go twenty minutes before the end of the watch, volunteering to do the turn-over with the Norwegian and Jimeno Salvador, the new Engineer. The Spaniard was very junior in his knowledge, but Arietta felt that with some training he could at least serve to be a spare set of capable hands during battle and for repairs. He spoke little English, but that was unlikely to be much of a barrier since Visivald spoke enough Spanish to get the point across.

Hans closed the hatch, eyeing the Captain-Gunner warily. It was very early in the morning, with the sun not yet risen, making it unlikely she was expecting to spar with him.

"Good morning, Captain-Gunner. Difficulty sleeping?" he asked politely. He was not sure if he actually cared about the answer, but it was at least a way to find out what was on her mind at this hour.

"*Da,*" she replied, adjusting the cuff of her left hand gauntlet.

"Oh? What is keeping you awake?" he said as he adjusted his breather-mask and raised his collar against the cold morning air. He could see his breath emerging in puffs from the brass mesh-covered holes in his mask only to be swept away by the wind.

She tilted her head to a side slightly, as though internally debating her answer to him. She hesitated for a moment and then spoke. "You. Care to come forward with me, drink some coffee and talk for a little while?" Her question nearly sounded like a challenge to him.

Hans blinked at her, not quite sure he had heard correctly. "Pardon?"

"Do not make me repeat myself, Sauder. *Da ili nyet*? Yes or no?"

He nodded to her and she waved to him to follow. They went forward into the forecastle, up to the very bow of the ship into the "Rope Locker". The compartment held the various coils and rolls of ropes that were either spares or currently not in use. As well, bales of canvas, heavy cotton and silk were also stored here for repairing or making sails. A work bench was to the starboard side wall, and a parts locker and cloth rollers occupied the port wall. The rest of the place was coiled-rope pallets on the deck and rope bundles and spools hanging from the ceiling.

She unhooked her sword and gun belts and seated herself on the edge of the workbench, letting her legs dangle. She pulled her goggles, mask and gauntlets off and dropped them in a pile atop the weapons. Hans sat on a crate facing her after likewise putting the sword and club on the deck beside it. He put his mask and goggles on the little space left beside him on the crate.

"So what about me, *Fräulein*?" he asked bluntly.

"Are you staying past Brussels, or not?" she demanded.

He blinked at her, surprise clear in his features. "What? What do you mean?"

"We have four Engineers now, Hans. You could leave the ship with a clean conscience from Brussels and return home to your fiancée. Is that what you intend to do?" She crossed her arms, and her entire bearing was at once hostile and dismissive.

"Fiancée? Brussels? What are you talking about, *Fräulein*?"

"Call me Annika, please, Hans," she said sharply. "And you know very well what I mean. We will be ending this leg of our cruise at our usual contact outside the city of Brussels. Everyone knows you have a lady you are pining for and that you are planning on leaving the ship to return to. She must be very special to you, Hans, given your dedication to her," she gestured with an irritable wave of her hand.

"So my question to you," she continued, "is if you are planning on leaving in Brussels and making your way back to England from there, or if you are going to wait until we are cruising southward again until we are more towards the Channel coast of France?"

Hans glanced at the closed hatch door and then quickly around the space they were in. Annika rolled her eyes.

"No one is going to stumble in on us or overhear us, Hans," she said with a slightly exasperated note in her voice. "The rest of the girls know I will be up here for the morning. Nor did I tell them with who, so you do not have to worry about your reputation for dedication to your fiancée."

Hans started drumming the fingers of one hand on the crate frame irritably. "Annika, what in a wet-powder Hell are you talking about? I was not aware we were going to Brussels. I was certainly not aware I could leave the ship in Brussels. I do not have a fiancée. And do I understand correctly you can reserve this space like a meeting room?"

She blinked at him, surprise clear in her features. "What? What do you mean?"

The two of them stared at each other for a few moments and then both burst into laughter for a few heady minutes. They laughed hard enough that they had to regain their breaths before the conversation resumed.

"So ... you are not leaving in Brussels?" she asked, shaking her head and chuckling.

"I did not know I could! Do you mean I can just walk off the ship any time I choose?" Hans said incredulously.

"Oh, Hans, of course you can! Being an airship pirate is about freedom! You are not shackled to some oar, here. You earn your Right of Passage, and after that, you do your job, do it well, stay as long as you want and live as you please. What did you think?" she said with and expressive gesture of her hands.

"I thought I was a prisoner or something," he replied in great seriousness. "I thought I was trapped aboard. I have been trying to figure out how to jump ship or win my freedom. Now you are sitting there telling me I can leave any time I choose?"

"Well, I would suggest you do it at low altitude," she said with a laugh. "But yes. You pack your bags and walk off. It is considered courtesy to give the Captain and your senior master each about a third of your last pay, as a thank-you for having taught you what it takes to live long enough to be able to leave. That would be Arietta, in your case. So you pack your bags, say your good-byes, 'Pay Your Respects', and walk off the gangway. You can even come back later on in the future, if you want. Its about freedom, Hans. It always has been. Why in God's name did you think you were a captive?"

"Annika ... I woke chained to a bed and then my options were to either join or get thrown overboard. What was I supposed to think?!" he said, throwing his hands in the air.

She covered her mouth with her hand in attempt to contain her laughter, and failed utterly. She laughed helplessly at the progressively souring expression on his face for a few moments and then got control of herself.

"Oh, good lord, man. You truly are clueless. You were chained so that when you woke up after that cutlass bell I applied to the back of your head, you would not try and assault poor *Döktor* Koblinski. He has been stabbed often enough by his own scalpels over the past two years that he restrains every new patient until he sure what their temperament is like," she chuckled.

"What sort of idiot attacks a *Döktor* trying to take care of him?"

"You would be surprised. Usually the military types; they just do not know when to stop. Alexi now keeps a spray bottle of ether in his pocket, just in case, most times," the Russian woman said with a grin. Hans shook his head and rolled his eyes.

"As for you being thrown overboard," she continued as she played with the gauntlets beside her, "I know that O'Raedy told you that you would get a gliderchute. Its not as if you were told you would have to go over in your underwear."

"Annika, you know as well as I do that no one in their right mind travels on foot in Europe. Offering me a gliderchute and a walk home is no choice at all!" he exclaimed crossly.

"Oh, please, Hans. You are an intelligent and well educated man. Arietta raves about how smart and capable you are. You cannot possibly believe that all of Europe is a blasted wasteland crawling with robber armies, automatons and Galvanotaurs gone mad, and that all of that charming host living in fear of rampaging Dragons!"

Hans lofted a brow. "Why would I not? That is *exactly* what the place is like, Annika. With the mess that the Crimean War made after it spilled into the rest of Europe, you cannot even travel safely by train in most areas. Airships are the only way to travel outside of the patrolled areas around cities. You know that," he said irritably, folding his arms over his chest.

She looked at him for a long moment in the thick silence. "You have been lied to, Hans," she said quietly. "Things have not been that bad on the ground in Allied Europe or in the Russian Empire for over a decade. Yes, there are places you must be careful, but there are many more where the robber-armies have built fiefdoms and now are just as interested in peace and quiet as anyone else collecting taxes from their citizens. There even many more areas than that where the governments of Europe have used their military might to exterminate anything less than a Dragon."

"Annika, why would the newspapers and *kaffehaus* press sheets lie? These are organizations with reputations to protect ... reputations that enable them to do business."

The Russian brunette shrugged. "You do not need to believe me, Hans. I had hoped you trusted me more, but so be it. You will see what the area north of Brussels looks like with your own eyes in a week or so. The point of the matter is that you are not some sort of prisoner of war aboard the *Bloody Rose* in the servitude of *Kaptan* Blackheart." She paused and sighed, looking somewhat glum for a fleeting moment. She continued speaking, in a conversational tone. "So, from Brussels back to England then? To your awaiting lover?"

"Yes, back to England ... but why are you so convinced I am returning to a woman, Annika? I have no one like that in my life. That is not the way a gentleman conducts himself," Hans said curtly.

"Oh! You are of Visivald's tastes, then?" she asked.

"What? What do you mean?"

"Visivald Aron, your colleague, the Norwegian engineer. He finds no pleasure in a woman. He prefers a man's strength and form in his relationships," she said with an accepting gesture.

It took Hans a moment to understand what she was saying. He nearly physically recoiled at the very notion. "Oh, for ... Good heavens, no! What do you take me for, Annika?" He shuddered in disgust. "No, no ... I am a man who finds his attraction in women, trust me. What ever gave you the idea otherwise?"

She laughed. "Well ... you are a three-time topic of Cat's Call in the time you have been here, and you have yet to even try to charm the pants off of any of the Ladies of the Rose..."

"'Cat's Call'?" he queried, raising a hand to pause her discourse.

"An English country 'hen' game, according to Doretta. We usually play it when we are trying to get to sleep and one of you roosters has one of us in a bit of a state. Who ever it is that is feeling lusty says 'The Cat Calls' and then the name of whomever it is that has 'inspired' them. Then, the rest of the girls either say something they do not like about that fellow, or a one line fantasy about how they would like to be had by that fellow. It spreads the misery around," she said with a dirty grin.

Hans turned scarlet red.

"Three times, Hans," she said holding aloft the appropriate tally of fingers and giggling at his deepening rouge. "On top of that, you have half-hacked me out of my clothes when I was drugged, silly and easily persuaded and then did nothing with it. I bold-face offered you sex and you declined. Arietta spent a week wandering around the engineering area half-dressed when you two were alone, with the place as hot as a Turkish sauna, and you did not even so much as lay a hand on her. We spent three weeks in Pirate Town, Egypt, and you did nothing but work. We have all just been presuming you have some woman you were promised to back in England that you were completely devoted to."

"Um ... no. I have something called a moral upbringing. I do apologize for shocking you all with it," he scowled. "I do not just 'sleep around', as they say. I certainly do not rape a drugged woman. I certainly do not take payment of any kind for doing the right thing for someone I know. Chief Itala is the *Kapitän's* woman, and so I am not going anywhere near her, no matter her looks or my interest. Besides, she is my boss and that would be unprofessional of me. I told you I am not the sort who solicits prostitutes; syphilis is no way to conclude a man's life story," he stated flatly, gesturing as he spoke.

"And again, no, I am not a homosexual," he continued. "I am very aware that the *Bloody Rose* has a complement of beautiful and fascinating women aboard. I do not need to take any of them to my hammock to prove my manhood to anyone. When I marry, then my wife will be my lover, and I am quite content that way, thank-you."

"So why are you so Hell-bent for leather upon returning to England, then? If you do not have the arms of a lover to speed back to, why the rush to return to stodgy old England? If you spend a year on the *Bloody Rose*, you could learn, earn and do so much! I would guess that life aboard as a pirate is a bit more interesting than as a school boy."

"I have responsibilities to my family, Annika. I am the eldest son and heir to the Sauder Industries name that my grandfather and my father have built since before the start of the Crimean War," he explained patiently. "It is my duty and obligation to return to my family in England. I am training to take up the mantle of being the third of the Sauder line to build our family's fortune."

"While, yes, as you say, this a much more exciting life to lead, I cannot stay," he said, suddenly sounding weary. "My brother is a *bon vivant* with no ambition in his body. He has never once spoken of an interest in taking up the Sauder mantle. Honestly, I think it is some sort of cruel joke that I am the one on the *Bloody Rose*. I think he would be thrilled to have the chance to live some sort of grand adventure of sword fighting, drinking, gambling and pretty ladies."

"My sister is a darling and sweet piece of fluff," he continued. "She will make a fine housewife to some lucky Englishman and mother to his children. But she will never be given the reins of the Sauder machine. That is the job of the men of the family. I know you may well find that offensive, Annika ... in truth, now, so do I ... but that is how it is. Perhaps when the time comes, my daughter will be a woman like you, that power and leadership will not be alien ideals. But, right now ... I am the first son of the Sauders and my place is with my family. Not skylarking around Europe on a pirate ship."

"How very tragic, Hans," she said softly with a note of pity in her voice. "You seem to be trying to escape from freedom into servitude. Well ... do as you feel as you must." She slipped off the edge of the workbench and then silently pulled her gauntlets back on. Hans watched her as she then donned the pistol and sword belts.

She walked to the hatch door leading back towards the main deck. She opened the door partially and paused with her hand still on the handle. She looked over her shoulder towards where he remained seated. "Do I infer that you are a virgin, then, Hans?"

"Yes," he said simply.

"Well," she said impishly, "if you would like to change that before you take leave of your life as a pirate, feel free to seek Yvette, Arietta or I when when we reach Brussels. The ship usually spends at least two nights there and most of us spend some time aground. Arietta and I are only mostly like black widows ..." She gave him a bawdy wink, stepped through the hatch and closed it behind her.

Hans just sat there on the crate, staring at the hatch, trying to make sense of everything he had just heard and said. He unscrewed the top to his coffee flask and realized it was empty.

In a sudden flash of anger, he hurled it against a wall. The flask rebounded from the wall and onto the deck, spinning for a few moments before finally coming to a rest. Hans scowled at it.

"The Letter From London"

Diary Entry for May 20th, 1888

With this morning's first light, we left an Allied airbase which was hidden a scant thirty-four miles north-east of Brussels. Everything has changed since I have last written.

Our course took us past Prague, then on to the area around Hamburg and Bremen. I was frankly astounded that we would be so bold as to sail straight into Imperial German airspace in such a fashion, but we have attracted little attention. Between Hamburg and Brussels we attacked and captured another merchantman, this one of Swedish flag. Weather conditions made things challenging, but Blackheart is a shrewd tactician and we once again "took prey".

From there, we sailed high and south-west towards Brussels and arrived with full cargo holds at a small lake town not far from the city. We set down at a camouflaged airship dock to meet a trio of merchants that specialize in buying and reselling the gains of the pirate trade.

The town knows how its bread is buttered, as it were, and does not mind pirate crews visiting to make merry and spend money. While we were there, a message was delivered to Kapitän Blackheart from London.

The Bloody Rose has been given a Letter of Marque. Tensions have been running high between the Russian and Allied Empires and limited exchanges across the Scorchlands have been taking place. In essence, we are being hired to exclusively practice our trade in Russian airspace for a while.

In exchange for doing so we have been paid a hefty sum, the bounty on the Bloody Rose has been removed, and we have been given a few interesting pieces of new technology. Thus our departure from the secret airbase this morning. We are now heading east by north-east towards the area around Warsaw. Everyone aboard seems pleased by this turn of events.

I close this entry on a more personal note. Annika Nadezhda, the Captain of the Gunner-Marines, has convinced me to remain aboard until the end of our raids into Russian airspace. It seems that after the end of our month of these operations we will be flying directly back to London, England.

Given that I will be unable to attend classes at the KTH until next semester at this point, another month aboard the Bloody Rose will change little on that front. However, I will undoubtedly gain valuable first-hand knowledge of more military-style operations that will benefit the family business in the future, if the Cold War is about to go Hot once again.

※※※※※

"Well, there you are, *Pan* Sauder. Just leave the hand taped for a day or so until the swelling goes down. The ground mixture I soaked the inside wrapping with will help with the pain and bruising. The good news is that it is your left hand and you did not actually break anything, so you should still be mostly functional," Doctor Koblinski said. He scribbled a few things down on his notepad with his fountain pen.

"I am somewhat compelled to ask, however, *Pan* Sauder. What ever possessed you to punch *Panna* Nadezhda in the stomach? That corset is not for looks, as I am sure you now realize," he said in a highly amused tone.

Hans rubbed at the taped hand and replied in a clearly irritated voice. "I told you already, I did not know that her corset was, in fact, body armour Whoever came up with the idea of fabricating a corset with a saddle-leather backing, airship-grade duraluminum for boning, and hiding it under a silk covering is diabolical," he grumbled. "We were sparring and she was teasing me about being afraid to hurt her, so I thought that a bruised set of ribs would be enough to silence her prattle for a while. Good lord, that hurt."

Koblinski looked somewhat embarrassed and uncomfortable.

"What now?" Hans said with a scowl.

"It is my design," he said sheepishly. "It was her birthday present from last year. It will stop a revolver round quite nicely," he said helpfully.

Whatever Hans was about to say was lost in the initial cacophony of the action bell suddenly cutting through the ship. He simply rolled his eyes in disgust and then left, heading for the Propulsion Room.

*****

"Rough date with Annika this morning, Hans?" Arietta teased when she saw his bandaged hand. She sat in the Watch-Keeper's chair, well into the preparations for what ever was to be demanded of the engines.

"We were SPARRING," he growled.

"Ooooh, touchy!" she laughed at him. "Visivald and Jimeno should be here in a couple of moments; they probably just got to sleep. Let us get started on preparing for the action to come."

Hans nodded and made his way over to one of the pair of Spitz 656's to begin its "flash up" sequence. "Any idea what is going on, Chief?" he called out from where he was.

"Taking prey," she replied as she expertly worked the levers, dials and switches in front of her. "O'Raedy must have lost a few hands of poker back in Pirate Town. It is a bit unusual for us to hit two ships within a week of each other like this," she laughed.

The Norwegian and the Spaniard came down the ladder shortly thereafter. The sails and masts had been furled, and the centre-line propeller pod was lowered and running by this time. Visivald took the chair at the EMIPALE control panel, Hans took the Watch-Keeper's chair, and Chief Itala and Salvador moved together around the Propulsion Room as she showed him what needed to be done as part of the lead-up to battle.

Hans was given the order from the Steering House to bring the next two pods into operation. He flipped the switches and pulled the levers that lowered the two remaining pods from inside the hull of the *Bloody Rose*. The sounds of venting steam, turning gears and spinning clockworks added themselves to the other engineering noises that filled the air.

The ship began to lurch and bounce in a fashion that Hans had learned was related to weather, not war. Bells and whistles rang out.

"Chief! Message from Steering ... we are chasing a Swiss 'octopus' that has seen us coming up on her. She is making for a squall line so *Herr Kapitän* says things are about to get rough."

"Thank-you, *Signore* Sauder. Do you know what an 'Octopus' is?"

"*Ja* ... a so-called 'Bernoulli Barge' that uses a combination of foils and eight tiltable propeller pods to augment the lift from its minimal gas-bags."

"Correct again, *Signore* Sauder. Tell the Steering House that the message is received and understood. Gentlemen, it is tethers and clips time."

The next fifteen minutes were a gut-churning nightmare as the two ships played cat-and-mouse in the roiling storm. Rain beat against the deck above and the hull beside them in a pulsing roar. Gusts of wind sounded like singing gales.

The pirate ship was tossed around with the constant violence from the elements. Visivald was now not only fighting the magnetic topography of the region, but also the sudden down and up drafts of wind that shoved the *Bloody Rose* around.

Chief Itala stopped beside Hans at one point and winked at him from behind her goggles. "If Blackheart has a fault, *Signore* Sauder, its that once he smells prey to be taken, he will not give up. I hope we either catch that Swiss bitch soon, or that she gets away from us ... it is hard to do a boarding with half of your crew airsick." Hans nodded at her wordlessly. He was feeling positively green. Salvador had already been sick once.

Within a few more minutes the *Bloody Rose* shuddered and thundered as she fired a broadside. She heeled over into a tight turn to bring her other side guns to bear. Within moments, they spat black-powder anger at her prey.

The sound of the rain and wind abated sharply. The sounds of small-bore incoming cannon fire were heard and then abruptly cut off by the pirate's own guns firing again. The sounds of exploding balloons and hissing rocket motors cut through the din.

Hans looked over at Visivald and the big Norwegian gave him a thumbs up. "I have learned to love that sound, Sauder. It means I get to relax."

"Not today, *Signore* Aron. The Chair Thug has a bad hand and our Spaniard needs to see the other end of the job. So, you and Salvador are heading up for boarding crew. Usual duty ... securing and cleaning engineering. Do not forget to check the individual motor pods on this bird."

Visivald gave a long suffering sigh as he finished the stand-by routine for the EMIPALE. The boarding alarm went off, followed by the sounds of the two ships' gunwales meeting. As the pair of men went up the ladder, Hans and Arietta pulled down their masks and raised their goggles.

"So, what did you do to your hand, anyway?" Arietta asked, standing beside him.

"I forcibly discovered that the Captain-Gunner's corset is body armour," he grumbled.

"Try unbuckling it first next time, Hans. You would get further," she quipped. The Italian-Ethiopian laughed so hard at his wordless glare that she had to hold herself up with the back of his chair.

*****

The minimal resistance that the boarding force was met with was rapidly and ruthlessly crushed. In short order the two tethered ships were climbing for the chill air of five thousand feet. The altitude was likely a concession to their location, Hans guessed. The higher you went, the less likely you were to meet anyone else up there.

"A bit of a ride, was it not, Mister Sauder?" Blackheart asked him as they met in passing on the upper deck.

"*Ja, Herr Kapitän.* Rather uncomfortable," Hans replied, trying to be as polite as possible. They had taken the Swiss merchantman "the old fashioned way" and there were dead and wounded everywhere aboard her. Koblinski, Coline and two other crew had been busy providing as much first-aid as they could since the Swiss ship had been secured. Hans had been cursing Michael O'Raedy's name under his breath for two hours now.

"We cut the storm," the Captain replied. "The Swiss tried to just go around the outside edge ... deep enough to hide from us, but a longer route. I took us straight through. As hard on the crew as it was, when the Swiss came around, we were already there and waiting for her. She flew right into our arms. Keep that in mind for the future, Mister Sauder. Sometimes being unkind to your crew is the only way to assure victory. At the end of the day, all that matters is who gets to sail away with a story to tell."

*****

Once the Swiss merchantman was left behind them, the *Bloody Rose* stayed high, and took her course towards the south-west. The pirate ship left her masts and sails furled, and ran on her centre line propeller pod. By sunset of the next day, they were descending at a small picturesque town north of Brussels. From a mile above the town, the lights of the neighbour city were dimly visible in the distance.

The solitary airship dock was disguised to look like a barn beyond the edge of the town proper. As they approached, part of the roof opened in two huge doors and a platform of metal struts and wood decking raised upwards. Steam gouted irregularly and electric lights flashed from various points around the rising structure. The sounds of heavy gears and cog-bars under a stressful load reached the ears of those on the deck of the pirate ship. When the whole apparatus was ready for the incoming ship, it had doubled the height of the barn.

The *Bloody Rose* made fast alongside the platform and three businessmen appeared on a mechanically elevated section that rose on the east side. Blackheart strode out to meet them with Chief Bridges and Captain-Gunner Nadezhda behind him, and the mercantile business of airship piracy began.

An hour later, the crew of the pirate airship were fully occupied as their own stevedores. It would take them until late tomorrow to unload everything, but the choicest goods were being moved aground immediately. The holds of the *Bloody Rose* were quite nearly full and there was little by way of supplies that needed to be brought aboard in exchange. The seized booty from the two victims of the past few days had been put to good use.

It was much later in the evening when the pirate crew assembled on the midships weather deck before their captain. An early morning rain storm had fled over the day, leaving behind it a cool dampness that made the night air still. A waxing moon was shining in a star-speckled and cloudless sky. The mechanical sounds of the airship and the docking platform obscured the noises of the natural world at night. Blackheart stood at the front railing of the quarter deck, flanked by his officers. The gas lamps flickered softly as everyone waited expectantly for the news.

"We have had a banner week, my lads and lasses," O'Raedy said with a grin. "Two plump birds down with no real damage to ourselves and both of them packed with choice morsels. The merchants here are a crafty bunch, but our name gives us some muscle and the goods we offer are in demand. Apparently there is a sudden shortage in a few types of commodities in this area ..." He gave an exaggerated "who knows" shrug as though to say he did not understand why that might be the case. The crew rippled with laughter.

"So ... a single crew share is a gentleman pirate's sum of ..." he trailed off, leaving everyone to hang for just a moment longer. "Six and a half pounds Stirling! One of our best yet!" He thrust his heavy fist into the air and the crew shouted its approval. They all knew that while there might be bigger pirate ships cruising the skies, few were anywhere as profitable for their crew as Captain Michael "Blackheart" O'Raedy's *Bloody Rose*.

*****

Hans' two shares totalled him thirteen Marks. He again told the three pirates that owed him "Duties" to pass that money onto the Franco-Brit Master Gunner. In less than two months, he had made enough money to pay for the wages of a house servant for a year and given away almost half that again. If Blackheart was to be believed it was not even money that anyone noticed moving around the economy.

It was another "Pay and Party" night, apparently. From where he stood on the bow of the ship, it seemed that most of the crew were heading aground to the local taverns and shops to make merry for the evening. Annika had said they would likely spend two nights here, which made some sense, Hans thought. Everyone would log a long and hard day of unloading the balance of the ship's holds into the waiting horse-drawn or steam-powered carts tomorrow. Afterwards, an evening of relaxation and party would again be on everyone's agenda. Departure would be with the sunrise after.

Hans was not terribly sure what he personally wanted to do with his spare time here. He supposed he could spend another evening in a mildly drunken haze with a paid escort in his lap. Certainly, he admitted to himself, that had not turned out to be a such a bad choice back in that Egyptian oasis town. He idly wondered what became of "Wench" after the bar fight had begun. He rather hoped she had the presence of mind to scoop the table of his winnings and make for a backdoor. He found a bit of delightful irony in the notion that a prostitute might have robbed a pirate of his loot in the chaos of a bar-fight in a brothel.

"And what is *her* name, Hans?" Annika asked him with a teasing tone.

"Hmm? What? What do you mean?" Hans started. Yet again, he had not heard her approach. She was preternaturally stealthy, it seemed.

"The only time a man gets that look on his face, Hans, is when he is dreaming of a woman that caught his manhood's fancy," she laughingly accused him.

"'Wench'," he said. "I have no idea what her name really was. Not that it matters. I very much doubt I will ever be in the same country with her again." He turned towards the Russian woman, while still leaning on the railing. "You are a very sharp woman, Captain-Gunner. I am unused to being read like a book."

The Russian brunette shrugged at him. "It comes with the job."

He nodded. "I suppose it would, given the job involves avoiding getting knifed in the back by your crew or shot in the chest by the enemies of your *kapitän*," he said with a smirk.

"You are always such a dramatic fellow, Hans," she said with a wink. "Any plans for the balance of your night?"

"None. Solid and restful sleep, Heavens be willing," he said casually.

"I am going swimming and then a bit of carousing. Care to join me?"

"Swimming?"

"Mmm-hmmm. The lake here is beautiful, and I love swimming by moonlight. I have a spot I know well and I have yet to see any evidence of another human being around it. It is a half-hour walk there and then I usually swim and relax for an hour. I then come back to the town to amuse myself until breakfast. Are you interested?" she asked as she re-shouldered a sizable carry bag.

"Annika, you are an officer. Spending time with you swimming by moonlight is a touch dubious, in terms of common sense. I really should decline ..."

"But I notice you have not actually *done* so. What exactly are you afraid of, Hans?" she questioned, with a challenging countenance in her bearing and voice.

*****

"Not so bad a walk, was it?" Annika asked as they came to a small, secluded cove at the south end of the lake. It was well away from both the town and the airship dock. The old willows which hung heavy over the lake waters were backed by even older oaks. Together, they lent an air of solitude and quiet to the place. Fireflies danced in the night air of late spring, their reflections lost in the rippled image of the starry heavens overhead. A splash noted the existence of at least one jumping lake fish. A small beach of tiny stones and heavy sand was in one corner of the cove. There was a crispness that came with the lake air that blended with the rich smells of the moss, ferns and forest.

A couple of old logs were a short distance from the water on the sand. She made her way over towards them. She set the shoulder bag down atop one and glanced at Hans.

"Sorry ... I was a bit caught up in the scenery. It is a rather beautiful place on a rather beautiful night. And no, as you say, not a bad walk at all. The path along the lakeside is remarkably scenic," he said as he stopped beside where she was. Of course, a few minutes of the scenery had involved quietly enjoying the sight of the athletic Russian brunette striding ahead of him on narrow sections of the path. He suddenly sighed and shook his head.

"Hmm? What is wrong, Hans?" Annika asked him.

"'Clueless', I believe is the phrase you gunners use to describe this sort of absence of planning. I do not have anything close to swimwear with me. I was so busy getting nagged off the ship, I did not think to bring swimming clothes or anything to dry off with afterwards"

"Hans Sauder! I did not nag you into coming," she scowled at him. Her expression further soured as soon as he burst into laughter and she realized that she had taken the bait offered to her. "If you can stop laughing like a demented child long enough, I would appreciate you unbuckling my corset in the back. I can do it myself; it is just faster with help." She turned around, presenting her back to him.

As Hans silently undid the eight brass buckles holding the two sides of her corset together, she continued speaking. "Do not fret about having formal swimwear, Hans. If we do go straight back to a town tavern from here, you are not going to want to have ten pounds of dripping wet clothes in a bag with you, anyway. Just pull everything off, put it over the logs here, and jump in."

"Pardon?" Hans blurted. She turned around and looked at him bemusedly as she doffed the corset and tossed it over a log. It landed with a heavy thunk of metal and leather.

"Get undressed and swim nude," she said. "It is just us here ... I have already seen you a couple of times in sweat-soaked cotton pants with your shirt off, so you will not be surprising me over much. I already know you have a good set of shoulders and a nice ass. Everything else is details."

She pulled her two shirts off over her head, only to find that in the time she had taken to do so, Hans had faced away from her. "What are you doing, Hans?"

"Annika," he began crossly, "it is hardly proper..."

"Oh, shut up, Hans. *I* am hardly proper. For a German, you are one of the most up-tight Englishmen I have ever met. You can sit here on the beach if you want, but I am going swimming. I swim in the same attire that the Almighty gifted us with at Creation. If that offends you, then you are going to spend the night offended while I swim," she growled at him.

He could tell by the sounds behind him that she had continued to disrobe. A few moments later, she gave an exasperated sigh and padded off. He waited until she had been splashing for a few moments before glancing over his shoulder.

"It is safe, Hans," she said with a roll of her eyes. "You are spared the ungentlemanly sight of an unattractive woman in the nude." She was off shore a short distance, up to her neck in water, treading slowly.

Her clothes were in a heap atop the armoured corset on the log beside him. He sat down on the log and looked at her. "For the record, Annika, I have never said you are unattractive. The problem is just the opposite. You are damnably attractive and I am leaving for England in three days."

She dove under the tranquil waters and disappeared from view for a moment. She surfaced a few yards off to the right of where she started, but still within hearing of him. "Hans, I am not asking you to fall in love with me and offer to take me back to stodgy old England as your terminally bored wife. I am having a swim and thought you might enjoy the exercise as much as I enjoy having some company. You are one of the only men on board I address to by first name on a regular basis. You are a wonderful change from the usual dolts in this life of mine."

"That is it?" he asked, rather surprised. She nodded, took a hearty breath and dove beneath the surface. She left a trail of bubbles for the fifteen yards or so she covered before resurfacing.

"That is it," she stated and then a paused for a moment. "Well, okay, that is not *entirely* it. If you decided you wanted me to be your lover for a night or two, I would not argue much with you. But you have made it plain you are not at all interested, so I will be content with a swim."

Hans was very glad she could not see the red tint to his cheeks at the suggestion of being her lover. He suddenly had a very clear vision of his younger brother Karl laughing hysterically at him as he tried to explain his fear of going swimming in the nude in a secluded glade with an attractive woman. He pursed his lips and then pulled his shirt off. She wolf-whistled at him and he sighed. She burst out laughing.

"I know you are uncomfortable, Hans, so I am going to go for a swim up the lake. I will be back in four minutes. You should be able to be safely up to your neck by then." She turned away from him, and dove under in a single motion. He caught a glimpse of her work-toned derriere in the star light as she went under. She surfaced and set off in a strong, rhythmic stroke that propelled her through the still lake water with surprising grace.

He watched her disappear from view while arguing with himself. He might as well have been sitting on sandstone beside an oasis instead of a log by a lake, given his mental state.

"Oh, to hell with it," he said quietly to himself. "A swim in the dark with a woman I will likely never see again from three days hence will not change anything." He pulled his clothes off and strode into the chill water with a wince. He started off in a steady front crawl in the same direction as the pretty Russian source of his moral confusion.

She was well on her way back when he saw her. He swam along side her, matching her stroke for stroke as they returned to the cove. "Oh ... Annika?"

"Yes?"

"Tag! You are it!" he shouted and then shoved her by the shoulder under the water. He immediately struck off at right angle to their original direction. She surfaced, spitting lake water and venom. While he spoke no Russian, he did not need a translator to understand that she was rather displeased.

While he was at first a faster swimmer, she simply ran him down by persistence. He ran out of steam, faltered in his stroke and she grabbed him by an ankle and pulled him backwards. His cry of surprise was cut short by what felt like a gallon of lake water. She mercilessly climbed on his back and tried to hold him under for a few seconds.

The ensuing utterly graceless melee was largely in her favour until he finally got his feet on solid lake bottom and his head above water. He copied Blauchuk's preferred melee tactic and used buoyancy to his advantage to pick up the squealing Russian and toss her with all his strength. She landed flat on her back in a tremendous splash of water. He swam and dove, grabbing her about the waist.

The splashing struggles continued for another minute or two until they had exhausted themselves and were now clinging to each other for support in the chest-deep water and giggling in fits. Their well of laughter suddenly ran dry as they realized their closeness.

Her arms were under his, gripping his shoulders, and her legs were twined about his waist. Her head rested lazily against his shoulder. His arms were around her, one at her waist and the other her mid-back. Her slight yet firm breasts were pressed against his chest. When she looked up at him, arousal sparkled in her eyes.

"Annika..." he faltered.

"Oh, shut up, Hans," she whispered. She tangled her right hand in his hair and pulled his mouth to hers.

Fire burned within their kiss and electricity was everywhere they touched. They hungrily devoured each others' mouths and necks for several heady, breathless moments, until Hans broke off their current frenzied kiss.

"Annika ..." he gasped, somewhat dazed at the intensity of their passion.

"Make a decision, Hans," she growled lustily into his ear. She untangled her legs from about his waist to stand against him in the water. Her palms traced down over his broad chest. "I know what I want ... you. I know when I want ... now. So either throw me over your shoulder, carry me up to the thick ferns under the trees and take me as your woman ... or go get dressed and get out of my sight for the rest of the night." She bit his ear. "You are driving me crazy," she whispered.

He stared down at her, wrestling with his physical desire and his emotional confusion. Her eyes burned with her search for his acquiescence. She saw the conflict in his features and greedily pulled him to her for another searing kiss. Her hands were blatant in their manipulation of his need.

He pushed her away from him and she lost her footing on the slippery bottom moss. She disappeared with a choked shriek under the lake waters for just a moment. When she surfaced spluttering, she found him swimming to shore.

"What? What are you doing? Where are you going?" she demanded in frustrated anger.

"I am getting out of your sight for the rest of the night, Annika. I knew you were a cunning and dangerous woman, Captain-Gunner. I apparently did not understand quite how much so. If I stay here you are going to convince me to cross a line that I do not clearly know that I am ready for."

"Dammit, Hans ... you want me! I want you! Why do you have to make it any more complicated than that?"

He pulled on his pants once he reached their clothes and then turned to look at her. She had swam a bit closer towards shore, but was still standing in the lake, waist-deep. He looked at her for a long moment, marvelling at the sight of her athletic body dotted with tiny jewels of lake water and bathed in a glow of moonlight.

"Yes, I lust for you, Annika. You are likely the most attractive and difficult to resist woman I have ever met in my life..."

"... but that is not good enough for you, Hans?" she accused.

He pulled his shirt on and fastened buttons as he answered her. "I am sorry Annika. Right now, at this stage in my life, no, it is not. I am not even sure I can tell you why. All I know is that it would be a mistake."

"Why? What is wrong with a man and woman sharing their pleasure? You are the only man worth me on that scow! Do you not understand, Hans?"

"I understand that I leave for England in two sunrises, Annika. The last thing either of us need is to fall in love. Good night, Captain-Gunner."

He left her standing in the water with her jaw agape.

*****

It was late in the next evening, well after nightfall, when the black and silver steam-carriage hissed to a halt outside of the town hall. There was a brief pause and then it rolled ahead to be more out of the way. Its electric lights went out, it gave a final burst of the sounds of steam, gears and pistons, and then fell silent. The left side door opened and a woman in widow's clothes stepped out. She was dressed in the style of a well-to-do Englishwoman, with the long gloves, narrowed waist, accented bustle and hoop skirts. She was black from head to toe, save for her pale skin, blue eyes and a hint of carefully coiffed blonde hair. A beaded black veil made a conceit of covering the beauty of her face.

She was a bit more than five and a half feet of height, and other than the influence of her clothes, was proportioned as a Raphaelite model. She carried a small purse in one hand. She reached into the steam-carriage to remove a blue leather-bound travel case, similar to those which bankers carried. She closed the carriage door, ensured it was locked, and started towards the Inn.

Four burly shadows stepped from the second darkened alleyway she crossed.

"'scuse me, missus..." said one of the men. She stopped and turned around, regarding them quietly.

"Yes, gentlemen? What can I do for you at this late hour?" she asked in a manicured English accent.

The four of them stood around her in a loose semi-circle. All were obviously woodsmen, with rough beards, features and clothes.

"Well, y'see we're all representin' the 'Donations t'impov'rished folks fellowship', an' seein' ye te be well heeled an' all, we were goin' te ask ye t'donate the contents o' yer purse an' travel case," the first of them said with a gap-toothed shark's grin.

She gave a prim smile and shook her head. "I am so very sorry, gentlemen, but the contents of my purse are the domain of a lady. Likewise, the contents of the travel case are not mine to give away. However, if you can assist me, there might be a small reward for your troubles."

"Oh? An wot would tha' be, missus?"

"I am looking for an officer of the crew of the pirate ship *Bloody Rose*, who I think we all know to be somewhere in this area. Can you take me to one of them?"

"Naw, don't know any of them," he said.

"A pity. Good evening, gentlemen," she nodded politely, gave an abbreviated curtsey and then turned to walk away.

The four men looked at each other somewhat confused. The leader nodded wordlessly, indicating her to the third man in the group. The thug immediately stepped forward and grabbed her by both shoulders. She sighed and with a surprising action, turned around kicked him with the spiked heel of her walking boots in the meat of his left calf. He squawked in surprise in time to have her knee him soundly in the crotch.

As he doubled over grasping himself with his eyes bulged, she swung her purse over-handed. There was a bang and a small flash as the bag crossed the top of the arc. It slammed down on the back of her assailants head like a maul, propelled by a shot-glass sized rocket motor concealed within. The impact drove him face-first into the ground with the grace of rag doll, crushing his nose with the landing. He did not stir.

Another of the men stepped forward with a suddenly brandished hatchet in his hand. She side stepped the downward chop and slapped him across the face. There was a white-blue electric flash, his eyes bulged, and he toppled over into a twitching heap.

She turned towards the leader while flicking her hand outwards towards him. The gesture deposited a tiny, silver barrelled pistol from wherever it had been concealed on her person into her hand. She blinked at what she saw, and held her fire.

"Hello, ma'am," said Blauchuk. "I do not think it is very nice that they tried to hurt you." He was holding both of the remaining men at arm's length to either side of him by the throat, off the ground. "Do you want me to take them away and hurt them for you?"

She smiled. "No, I do not think that will be required. I think they likely have learned their lesson. Let them go."

Blauchuk pulled the pair in front of him, their feet still not touching the ground. "You should say thank-you to the nice lady when I let go. I am really good at hurting people and I do not like cowards that pick on nice ladies. Got it, bilge rats?" The two men nodded frantically while continuing vainly to pry at the fingers around their throats. He put them down and once they had regained their breaths, they flapped for forgiveness, grabbed their fallen comrades and fled into the night.

"Excuse me, my brave hero ... what did you just call those poor louts?" she said sweetly.

"Oh. I am sorry, ma'am. I called them 'bilge rats'. I should not be using bad language around a nice lady," Blauchuk apologized.

She covered her mouth with a gloved hand and chuckled demurely. "Oh, that is quite alright. That sounds like a very nautical sort of term, though ... are you a sailor, by chance?"

Blauchuk nodded happily. "Oh, yes. I am a pirate! I am part of the crew of the *Bloody Rose*."

*****

Hans was seated off to a side in the relative quiet of the Inn's public room. He was sipping a reasonably tasty local beer and having a very early breakfast. It was somewhere after the turn of the day and most of the townspeople had long since called it a night. Even the visiting crew of the *Bloody Rose* had vacated by now; either having found local company for the night or returned to the ship. Thus, Hans was able to sit mostly alone with his thoughts and a reasonable meal in the dimly lit oakwood confines of the pub.

He was trying to decide if he should have given in to Annika the previous night or not. At a physical level, he had very much wanted to. However, he had to accept that doing so potentially would have made it very difficult to continue with his intended plan of returning to his family. Between Annika and Arietta, it would be far too easy to find a reason to stray from his responsibilities to his family.

On the other side of the shilling was the idea that he was not so weak-willed that a night of heady lust with any woman would change his mind about anything. He could have indulged himself in a dalliance with her, knowing full well that the entire affair would be nothing but memories from two mornings forward.

He was beginning to understand that he was a romantic at heart, with high ideals of love and courtship. He was attracted to Annika – that much he admitted – even though he was not entirely sure why, beyond her physical appearance. However, her apparent singular interest in bedding him with no real long term interest in a relationship between the two of them flipped almost all his emotional switches the wrong way. He sighed and then took a sip from the stein.

Given his state of mind, he nearly groaned aloud when Blauchuk entered the pub with a stunningly attractive widow, and pointed Hans out to her. Blauchuk left with a happy grin on his face and she made her way over to him. She stopped at the edge of his table and gave a polite tip of her head to him before she spoke.

"Excuse me, sir. Was that your Galvanotaur?" she asked in the same sort of voice one might expect to use to order tea and crumpets. Hans nearly snorted his beer.

"Pardon?"

"The rather short and stout fellow I entered the Public Room with. Is he your Galvanotaur?"

"No. He is his own man. A friend and a crewmate. Why?" Hans asked stiffly.

"Good. I believe we have business to discuss. May I join you?" she said in a disarmingly sweet tone.

Hans regarded her for a long moment and then gestured to the chair opposite him. She nodded with a flutter of her eyelashes and seated herself. She set her scorched purse on the table and the leather travel case she carried on the floor beside her.

"Who are you and what is this about? English widows do not go tromping about the wilds of Belgium unescorted. Nor do they consider the possession of a Galvanotaur a casual matter. Which means you are the sort of lady who does not need an escort. Which also means you are the sort of lady who is unlikely to actually dress as who she is."

"Camilla Williams, British Intelligence," she said quietly. Hans' hand dropped to his sword belt and then he froze. She had suddenly levelled a pistol at him. While he had no idea where she had kept it secreted on her person, it did not very much matter. It was small, made of silver and rosewood, had two barrels side-by-side, and was squarely aimed at his heart.

"Please do not be rash," she suggested pleasantly. "The last thing I want to do is hurt you, Pirate ... but please understand it is still on the list of options." Hans nodded and slowly took his hand off the hilt and placed it alongside the other on the table where it was clearly visible to her.

She nodded her approval. "A smart and deliberate man. I like that. What is your name, Pirate?" she asked, keeping her voice low and lowering her pistol hand below the table, out of sight.

"Hans Sauder. A pleasure to meet you, *Frau* Williams," he said dryly.

"Oh, and a sense of humour as well. What a pleasant surprise, Mister Sauder. I trust that, since you have not denied it, you are in fact a pirate? And a member of the *HMAFS Bloody Rose*?"

"Yes, I am. Would you like something to drink? Tea? The beer here is also quite good" he stated. It was obvious she was not here to kill him, or he would be dead already. She could have shot him as soon as she reached the table. Something else was afoot. Hostility toward her would only slow the process of finding out what it was.

"Oh, a gentleman? Another nice surprise", she said with a light smile and an air of genuine delight. "Yes, a glass of wine or a cup of tea would be very nice. I am in an adventuresome mood tonight, so I will let you choose."

He ordered her a glass of moderate white wine and once the serving girl had stepped away, he looked at the Englishwoman squarely. "So what is it you want of the *Bloody Rose*?"

"Straight to business is it, then? That is quite fine," she said after a sip of her wine. "Things are becoming openly unpleasant between the Allied Empires and the Russian Empire, if you have not been near a newspaper of late. The British Crown wishes to offer a Letter of Marque to the *Bloody Rose* for a period of forty-five days. Depending on how things go on the political front, that may be extended. Now, are you in a position to discuss this, or would you rather deliver a message to your Captain for me?" she said with an airy wave, as though explaining that the aforementioned crumpets were over-seasoned.

Hans struggled to remain impassive. A Letter of Marque was sanctioned piracy. The pirates would technically no longer be pirates so long as they only struck Russian targets. "I think it best if I was your messenger boy, *Frau* Williams. An engineer is hardly the sort to make those decisions on behalf of his *kapitän*," he said carefully.

She nodded. "How is it a fellow of such clarity and intelligence wound up a Pirate, Mister Sauder?"

"I was delayed on my way to school one day, and it has been downhill ever since," he said dryly.

She chuckled demurely behind her hand. "That sounds like quite a story you are not telling me. But that is fine. We all have our secrets and I have learned that some are best left covered. Now, I have a message tube for you and this travel case. The case contains a Marconi-Beacon Direction Finder. Just string out the wire antenna, turn it on, and it will lead you to the *rendezvous* point explained in the letter."

She passed him a black leather tube about eighteen inches long and two inches wide. It was bound in brass and sealed against the weather. She then gave him the travel case.

"You will have twenty-four hours from the point the *Bloody Rose* leaves this town to make the *rendezvous*. If you are late, the results will be rather unpleasant for everyone involved. I expect your Captain will be very interested in what that letter has to say, Mister Sauder."

"I am quite sure you are right, *Frau* Williams. You may rest assured that *Kapitän* Blackheart will be reading this within the hour of our parting ways."

"Wonderful. My superiors will be pleased about that. This is a rather delicate affair, Mister Sauder, as a man of your intelligence can likely immediately fathom. This is a fine wine, by the way. An excellent choice," she said offering a flutter of her eyelashes and smile to him as praise.

As they chatted socially for a few minutes while she finished the wine. She was exactly the sort of woman that his parents and uncle would have approved of, he thought to himself. Beyond being a spy, of course; his mother at least would have been scandalized at the very idea of a woman in such a role. She was possessed of impeccable manners, clever speech with a soft and feminine voice, an excellent sense of deportment, a sense of class in all of her actions, and she was exquisitely pretty without being excessive.

She was exactly the opposite of any of the "Ladies of the Rose". From Hans' perspective, the only interesting thing about her was she was a spy. The rest was not worth a broken spindle shaft to him. He needed to think about that, he realized.

"Well, Mister Sauder, it has been a pleasure chatting with you. However, it is hardly the sort of hour a lady of good upbringing should be out, so I shall take my leave. Do have a safe voyage." She left a small card on the table with an uncharacteristic wink at him, and gracefully departed out the door and into the night.

The cream-coloured calling card had her name, a London address and a telegraph exchange number on it. He lofted a brow, tucked the calling card into his vest pocket, then picked up the tube and case. He was soon striding through the darkness towards the airship-barn. He hoped he would not be interrupting Arietta and Blackheart.

*****

Blackheart dropped the letter on his desk, had a sip of coffee from the lidded mug, and regarded Hans skeptically. "So do I understand you correctly at this early hour, Mister Sauder? You were sitting alone in a pub and had an attractive woman claiming to be from British Intelligence deliver this letter to you? And she told you the travel case contained a Marconi-Beacon Direction Finder intended to allow us to find the *rendezvous* location mentioned in this letter?"

"*Ja, Herr Kapitän. Das ist correct*," Hans replied with a nod. He took a mouthful of fresh coffee from his flask and recapped it. Blackheart had been sound asleep and alone when Hans had started pounding on his door ten minutes ago.

"Did you read the letter, by chance?" Blackheart questioned.

"*Nein*. Specifically not. I will admit to curiosity, but I did not break the seal on the tube."

"And the case? Did you open it?"

Hans shook his head. "*Nein*. It occurred to me on the way here that the simplest way to remove the *Bloody Rose* from the sky, *Herr Kapitän*, would be to have a bomb in that case. They cannot best us in combat, but subterfuge would probably work well against pirates, I would guess."

Blackheart smiled. "You parallel my thoughts, Mister Sauder. You are a shrewd and clever man. Go get the Captain-Gunner out of her hammock. She will be able to open this and ensure it is not rigged to blow us all to Kingdom Come."

Hans tried to not look dismayed at the notion of going to get Annika from the women's sleeping bay. He apparently was unsuccessful.

"Had a bit of a falling out with the Russian, did you, Mister Sauder? Just tell her it is on the Captain's orders and that I am already considering her late," Blackheart chuckled. Hans nodded and left.

Marianna opened the door to the women's sleeping bay, wearing little more than a small towel wrapped around her. Thankfully she was sleepy enough that Hans' nearly futile attempts not to stare went unnoticed. Marianna nodded to him at the second repetition of his message and went back inside, leaving the door slightly ajar. He heard a brief discussion and a glaring Annika appeared at the door.

"Tell the Captain I will be there in ten minutes, *Gospodin* Sauder," she said coldly. She closed the door in his face without warning or further comment. Hans rolled his eyes and returned to the Captain's cabin.

Annika arrived almost exactly ten minutes later in her battle gear with a *portmanteau* in one hand and a small metal toolbox in the other. She took the travel case of questionable contents out onto the upper decks without comment and closed the door behind her. She returned about twenty minutes later and dropped it on Blackheart's desk.

"It is safe. It has got something that looks like a Marconi wireless in it. But nothing that explodes or electrocutes," she said, folding her arms. "What is this about?"

Blackheart glanced at Hans for a moment, apparently found something amusing, and turned back to Annika. "We have had a letter delivered to us from London. Whitehall, to be exact. They are offering us a Letter of Marque."

"So it is true, then, what I was told?" Hans broke in.

"That is quite correct, Mister Sauder ... a Letter of Marque. I am sure you have heard the old saying 'If you cannot beat them, hire them'," Blackheart chortled. He had a gulp of coffee and continued.

"The device in the case will lead us to a hidden Allied airbase. Once we arrive, we will have an interesting selection of new fittings for the ship, including air-to-air rockets. We will also get a challenge and reply book and the candles for it. A hefty sum of cash, as well. All we have to do is sail into Russian airspace, fill our holds, and come back here. Then we get a full pardon. And possibly another Letter of Marque."

"It is a trap," the Russian said irritably. "That device likely leads us right to a battery of anti-airship guns."

"Oh, possibly. Trust me; I will not be taking any of this at face-value until we get paid and sail away unscathed. However ... it is too good an opportunity to pass up." He paused, then picked up the folded letter again, and tapped a corner of it against his chin thoughtfully.

"Captain-Gunner, please have 'Sister Itala' present herself to the Captain's cabin in her 'Habit'. She has work to do," he said.

Annika nodded and left. Hans looked a question to Blackheart.

"You will see," he replied.

*****

Hans did not recognize the woman that stepped into the Captain's cabin behind the Captain-Gunner and the Deck Officer. She was dressed in a mixture of heavy cloth, leather and metal. Her features were obscured by a piece of studded leather armour that covered her from the point of her nose to the points of her jaw and down. A heavy cowl, with a hawk-beak like point, hid her eyes.

Her entire ensemble was pigmented with the disturbing colour of the purple-blue of venous blood with accents which were the red-black of dried blood. The heavy boots came to just below her armoured and spiked knees. They possessed almost a full inch of lift, increasing her height with dramatic and imposing effect.

The forearm guards looked familiar to him; a hand length spike extended from the point of each wrist, and formed a blade from that point back to each elbow. She adjusted an armoured glove and then looked at him. He recognized the eyes.

"Arietta?" he blinked.

"That would be either Chief Itala or Sister Itala to you, young Sauder," Blackheart reminded him. "But yes. Rather awesome to behold in her religious attire, is she not?"

Hans had a flash of memory from when he had first met Captain Michael O'Raedy. "*... your name ... well, that can be anything. Where you have been, what you have done, where you are going, what you are doing ... that is what makes you who you are ...*"

He suddenly realized he had no idea who Chief Itala was. Or Captain-Gunner Nadezhda. Or Doctor Koblinski. Or even, really, Captain Blackheart. He had been entirely living in the here and now with all of them, without really thinking about how any of them had wound up choosing this life.

"So, what is the occasion that you need me to live ten years in my past again, Michael? You know I do not like this," she said coolly.

"The agreement, Sister Itala, is twice per year. I did not call upon you at all last year," Blackheart stated with a severity in his voice. "We have a potentially dangerous location we need to fly into. We will either be very rich upon arrival, or blown out of the sky. You know as well as I do that the one thing airships do not do well is battle with ground artillery. So ... we will triangulate the location by doing a one hour long 'V' pattern from our departure point at ninety degrees to the initial bearing. Once we have the location pinned, we will climb to five thousand feet and you will take your leave of us. We will wait two hours and then start our approach."

"When you hear our motors – Mister Sauder, you will run two propeller pods ahead and one at 50 percent power astern to ensure we make enough noise to be heard for miles – you will launch your signal flares," Blackheart finished.

"Red for clear, yellow for caution, green for danger, and silence for I am dead, as usual?" Arietta asked casually. Blackheart nodded.

Arietta looked at Hans. "You have control of the Propulsion Room while I am gone. Salvador is too junior, and Aron is not a leader or critical thinker and has no desire for responsibility."

"Yes, Chief," Hans nodded.

Blackheart looked at Hans levelly. "Mister Sauder ... Can I trust you with my Propulsion Room and the lives of my crew? You once made it clear that you would not shed many tears if I came to an unplanned end. So I need you to look me in the eye and give me your word I can trust you with the lives of my crew."

Hans looked at his foot for a long time. He was aware everyone was watching him. He thought very carefully for a moment. He realized he had made a mistake in his reasoning just a few moments ago. He did know these people in the room with him now. He might not know who they were once, but he certainly did know who they were now. He might not like some of them. He might not like the things they did. But ultimately, if he was honest with himself, they had all earned his respect in one way or another in the past six weeks. Six weeks; it seemed like either forever or no time at all. All of these people had made an impact on his life that would shape how he lived to the end of his days.

He looked up at the man who was his captain, for better or worse. Hans met Blackheart's gaze without hesitation. "*Ja, Herr Kapitän. Sie haben mein Wort. Sie können mir vertrauen.*" He paused and repeated himself in English. "You have my word. You can trust me."

Blackheart smiled and nodded. "Welcome aboard, Mister Sauder. I am pleased to have you as my temporary Chief Engineer."

Arietta smiled at Hans. "Come on, *Signore* Sauder. We have a bit of preparation work to do before I jump overboard a mile above the earth with nothing but steam and canvas to save me."

*****

The glider launcher was a steam-driven system. A brass cylinder on the triangle-winged bi-plane glider was filled with steam under high pressure for the ten minutes before launch. The nose of the glider pointed towards the bow of the ship, so that even though it was clamped to the deck, it was effectively already "flying".

When the pilot pulled the release bar, the clamps would let go and the glider would immediately lift into the air. The pilot would then turn in the direction of intended flight, open the valve on the pressure tank and rocket through the sky for a minute or so until the tank ran dry. Then she would begin her gliding descent to her destination.

They worked together to check the glider, connect the steam delivery hoses and ensure the controls worked correctly. He periodically glanced at her; she was acting very much as Chief Itala, but looking so very unlike her.

Finally, he stopped, leaned against the launch frame and said "Who are you?"

"Arietta Itala, of the Sanguine Sisterhood, Hans. Consider it sort of a Sorority of Guardian Angels of Death.

The easiest way to reach an untouchably corrupt man has always been a pretty woman. It is not really a religious order, contrary to the Captain's commentary. He has a sense of humour; it is a Sisterhood, thus I must be a Nun, thus my armour must be a Habit."

"So you are not really a Nun?"

"Oh, hell no, Hans. I am a once a night kind of woman," she said with a laugh.

"What?" he said, clearly not getting her jest.

"You know what they say about Nuns, Hans... None in the morning, none in the afternoon and none at night!" she grinned. Hans rolled his eyes and went back to adjusting a pressure regulator.

"So – and excuse me for asking, I mean no offence – the Sanguine Sisterhood are a league of assassins?" Hans asked carefully after a moment.

"None taken, Hans. It is a fair question," she said, gesturing at the bladed and spiked bracers she wore. "After a fashion, yes. The purpose of the order, ostensibly, is to ensure that no tyrant in Italy lasts long enough to threaten the greater good of its people. We are trained to hide, steal, infiltrate, spy, and kill. We use our looks, our gender, and our brains to do our jobs from the shadows and fringes. However ... like anything that is built and managed by humans ... the current actions of the Order are at odds with its original intent. So I left."

Hans nodded. "I think you are ready to fly, Chief. We will double-check the steam-thrust tank once we start charging it. But that will be a while from now."

She nodded. "I am going to be in the Tank Hold for a while ... I need to prepare myself mentally and practice wearing my armour again ... accidentally stabbing myself to death with my knee spikes would be a lousy way to finish my life," she laughed.

Hans laughed and nodded. "Well, we will speak again in two hours then, Chief."

*****

"So, Hans? What did you decide?" Annika asked him as he stood at the bow of the *Bloody Rose*. They were heading back to the lakeside town to meet Arietta. In a few hours, the Privateers of the *Bloody Rose* would be heading north west into the airspace of the Russian Empire.

"I ... I have not yet decided, Captain-Gunner. The situation is rather confusing."

Six hours ago, they had made the approach to the hidden airbase, with every nerve on edge every cannon and post manned and ready for action. They spotted two red flares as they approached. Everything had been exactly as described in the letter to Captain Blackheart.

There was a dock-load of materials waiting for them. Amongst the heap was an upgraded differential analyzer for the EMIPALE that was ten times more accurate than the current model, twenty "Sargasso" balloon mines, a dozen "Cudahawk" wire-steered rockets, enough hi-velocity gunpowder to fight a war, a challenge and authentication system using smoke rockets and a code book. Almost 4000 pounds Stirling – the equivalent of two banner months of raiding – was brought aboard in cases. The Pirates were now Privateers.

They had loaded everything aboard and left as quickly as they could. The Allied Military did not come aboard, instead simply loading things onto the electric crane and hoist, and the pirates unloaded everything on their side. Everything was inspected for unpleasant surprises. However, it all turned out to be exactly as promised.

As soon as they had departed at full power, Hans had been called to the Captain's cabin from his post in the Propulsion Room. He had not known quite what to expect when he arrived, but the ensuing conversation between the German and the Englishman was even beyond that.

"The *Bloody Rose* is now armed with some of the most advanced weapons available anywhere, Mister Sauder," Blackheart said as he paced slowly about the cabin. "One of those Cudahawks would cripple a vessel our size at over a mile. The balloon mines require a mind with a keen sense of analytical thinking and a skill for mathematics to deploy properly."

"They are, in a word, useless. The first choice I have to be my Advanced Weapons Officer is currently my Chief Engineer, and she does not wish to leave her cherished domain. My Captain-Gunner is a lousy shot with a cannon, and thus I certainly do not wish to give her a rocket or a mine. Even if she could use the systems, I cannot replace her in terms of her abilities in a boarding or in leading the men. They love to hate her and at the same time worship the deck upon which she walks."

"I am taking this ship into airspace aggressively patrolled by some of the best airship crews in the world," he continued. He was still pacing and gesturing with one hand while the other was now tucked behind his back as though standing at ease. "Once we are seen, they will not be passive about their hunt for us, nor in their attempts to destroy us. I need those weapons to be available to me."

He turned and faced Hans, who was beginning to understand why he was standing in the Captain's cabin. The Englishman stabbed a finger at the German.

"You, Mister Sauder, are exactly the man I need for the job. Do not answer me right away. We have to meet Arietta back at town first before we depart. That will be around sundown. I am offering you the position of becoming my Advanced Weapons Officer for the duration of this cruise. We are covered with challenge-and-reply codes for forty-five days. I intend to spend one month in

Russian airspace and then return so we have plenty of time to travel to London to report our results."

Hans was stunned. *"Herr Kapitän ..."*

Blackheart raised a hand to silence him. "We are privateers now, Mister Sauder. This entire endeavour is sanctioned by the governments and nobles you hold so dear as beacons of order and civilization. You will be receiving a commission aboard a vessel acting under the authority of the British Air Force. You would be paid shares of the profit based on your new rank. And when we reach London, you can return to your family empire with a clean and honourable ending to your little distraction from your schoolwork. Give it some thought. Dismissed."

Thus was it that Annika found him at the bow of the ship a couple of hours later. The privateering vessel was wasting time in the skies over Belgium before heading to the town to pick up its Chief Engineer. The Russian woman had quietly joined him and had said nothing for several minutes as she stood beside him, staring out into the distance. When she had asked him her first question, he had been completely honest. He was at an *impasse*. Part of him begged to stay and pursue this new great adventure. Part of him could not wait to 'Pay his Respects' and flee back to the peace and sanity of life with his upper middle class family.

"May I intrude in your personal affairs, Hans?" she said, turning to face him.

He turned his head towards her and replied. "You did that, Annika, when you invited me out for a swim. Possibly as early as when I rescued you from an early retirement in Beirut."

The sound of her laughter was muffled by her breather mask and the wind blowing past them. "Fair enough. You have missed six weeks of your semester at the KTH. By the time you make it to England, spend time with your family, get turned around, and head to the *Kungliga Tekniska högskolan* in Stockholm, you will have missed so much of the current semester that it will be impossible to catch up, no matter how clever you are."

"Stay with us. Please," she said, with a soft look in her blue eyes behind her goggles. "The *Bloody Rose* needs you," she said and then hesitated. "So do I. I am sorry for my childish fit at the lake, Hans. I am unused to being turned down. I think you would be the first man, ever, in my life to do so. I do not even know why you did ... I know, you have told me of your responsibilities and such ... but I do not understand. I want to ... try it your way, I suppose. You spoke of falling in love, Hans ... and well, I am not sure I even know what that means ..." she trailed off, sounding increasingly embarrassed and uncomfortable as she spoke. There was no way to be quiet in this discussion with the sound of the wind and the engines engulfing them. The only mercy was that no one was near them.

"So, stay for the cruise, and leave in London," she finally finished with a brusque nod. "Everything you see and do would be valuable for your family business."

Hans looked at her for a long moment. He thought about everything she had said and what some of it implied. He thought back to his reaction to the conversation with the widow-spy. He nodded. "I will stay. I think it will be a far better education than I am likely to find anywhere else right now."

"A Quiet Little Town"

Diary Entry for June 5th, 1888

I said farewell at dawn today to a more unlikely friend than I will ever again have in this charmed life of mine. His departure from the lives of myself and the rest of the crew of the Bloody Rose was the most heroic thing I think any of us will ever see, no matter to what age we live.

Few can claim in their lives to have even seen a Dragon. Fewer of those can then be said to have been within its aura of destruction and walked without fear. I know of no tales of a single man who had the courage to stand his ground alone against one and successfully kill it. He did exactly that, by keeping a clear head and an analytical mind, while a town was torn apart around him.

We have been in the airspace of the Russian Empire for two weeks now. In that time we have destroyed a merchantman, a frigate, and took prey of a second merchantman. We are now men and women at war, we the crew of the Bloody Rose.

If the English government has thought to kill two birds with one stone, they might well be on the right track. Everyone's nerves have been on edge and lookout watches have been doubled. We are out of our element, and upon the home ground of the enemy. This is not how pirates operate.

We simply destroyed the first two targets, as much out of caution as anything else. The pirates-turned-privateers were unsure of how often or frequently other ships cruised through these areas, and so Kapitän O'Raedy did not wish to risk being caught vulnerable while looting.

Damage sustained in the battle with the frigate gashed some of our water tanks, and so we made our way back across the Scorchlands to an Allied border town to repair and take on water. It was there that the Dragon attacked. Based on its behaviour, it was obviously "rogue". The nearby abandoned train station likely attracted it, but once it started attacking the town, it began firing upon everything and everyone that moved.

The injuries inflicted to the crew of the Bloody Rose were on par with those taken during the battle with the Triomphe. The town's graveyard now counts privateers amongst its occupants. They fought and died with a selfless gallantry that is the stuff of sagas.

I believe it is the only time I have ever seen Annika either afraid, or weep. In all fairness to the Captain-Gunner, I cannot claim to have fared any better.

With repairs made, supplies loaded, and friends buried, we have returned to Russian airspace. Hopefully our luck will improve after this calamity.

In closing, I must note that I have accepted a commission aboard the Privateer HMAFS Bloody Rose. I am the "Advanced Weapons Officer", giving me the equivalent rank of a Lieutenant.

This position makes me directly responsible for the deaths of at least 250 Russian airmen so far. French or Russian, it really does not matter much to my conscience at this time. As Kapitän O'Raedy told me at *supper one evening, all I can cling to is that had it not been them, it would surely have been us. At the time of this writing, I am not really convinced how stable that moral precipice truly is.*

*****

"How is it, Mister Sauder," Blackheart queried bemusedly, "that as a man who intends to be responsible for the design of the most modern of future airships, you know nothing about how they move from place to place beyond the guts of an engine room?"

Hans shot O'Raedy a black look and turned back to the sighting compass. He noted the compass bearing and vertical angle of deflection of the object he had in the cross hairs. He then rapidly copied those numbers down on a notepad with him. He repeated the process twice more for two other objects ahead of the ship. He went to the chart table and began working out the position of the ship on the chart and then its altitude above the ground.

In theory, what was supposed to happen was that by extending a pencil backwards from each of the landmarks on the map along each of the associated recorded bearings, the lines would converge on a single point. That point was the position of the ship. Sometimes, a small error would create a small triangle, known as a "cocked hat". A quarter-mile was not a problem.

Two miles – the current width of error of his last set of "fixes" – was a problem. A similar process for altitude yielded a margin of error greater than their actual expected altitude. Hans sighed. Three "bad fixes" in as many tries. The good news was that at three thousand feet above the ground, the odds of running into something were fairly slim, even if he was unable to prove exactly where they were.

"The problem, Mister Sauder, is two-fold," Blackheart said. He tapped the map. "Your landmarks are too close together, and too close to our expected position. Thus, small errors are magnified rapidly. Secondly, when you use the ruler, you are sliding it along the chart to extend your line; it is too short for the job. As you are moving it, the ruler is not sliding straight. That compounds any error. Watch me again," he told the German.

Hans watched and listened as Blackheart walked him through the entire process again. O'Raedy explained to him why he chose the landmarks he did and the relative merits of each. He then took the fixing bearings, and went to the chart table. He chose a wheeled ruler nearly twice the length of the one Hans had been using and quickly laid down the fix lines. The cocked hat was, at best, an eighth of a mile in size.

There was more to being an officer than Hans had expected, and it was taking some getting used to. Firstly, Hans had changed sleeping areas. The male officers all slept in the same set of bays, three to a bay. He had double the space to himself as before, and there was a small folding desk with an electric light to go with it. It had felt very strange to him to be packing his things to move, but not to leave.

Next, he no longer stood engineering watches. Instead, he stood bridge watches with Blackheart. The pirate captain insisted that Hans learn how to navigate and at least understand basic combat manoeuvring concepts. Bridge watches were always stood in pairs, he discovered. No matter what, there was always one officer on the bridge, regardless of the time of day.

The change in schedule and station had complicated his teaching periods with Blauchuk. Originally, the burly Slav had been concerned that his German friend and mentor's promotion would mean an end to their arrangement. Hans had assured him that this was not the case and they had continued with their once-a-day lessons, after the officer's mess dinner. Blauchuk was learning surprisingly fast, and was already reading simple texts by himself. Both Hans and Blauchuk were very pleased with the progress.

The look-out alarm went off, indicating one of the watchmen had spotted something. A flashing lamp indicated which post. A call via voicepipe got the details. "Merchantman, ahead and high, *Herr Kapitän*," Hans reported.

Blackheart grabbed his spyglass and Hans took a spare from a rack and they scanned the area indicated.

"There she is," Blackheart said with a nod. "Mister Sauder, bring the ship to readiness. Our first catch of the cruise awaits."

Within a handful of minutes, the *Bloody Rose* was ready to begin stalking her prey. There was no need to furl the sails and masts. They had been making no pretence of their purpose here, and had been running on all propellers since leaving the hidden airbase near the city of Brussels.

"Orders, *Kaptan*?" Annika asked as she joined them in the Steering House.

"Burn her down, Captain-Gunner. We will not be risking looting this time around. She is unusually high for what I consider normal. So the question in my mind is if the high air is not normally empty air on this side of the border. I do not wish to be caught pillaging at five thousand feet only to discover that it is a traffic lane in current-day Russia."

Annika nodded. "We will start firing as soon as we are in range of the twelves. Can you give us an 'S'-figure advance to get off all four of the heavy guns as soon as we can?"

"If an 'S' advance is what you need, Captain-Gunner, then that is what we will do. Pay attention, Mister Sauder, you are about to learn something new in ship handling," Blackheart ordered.

The *Bloody Rose* came to full power and to the same altitude as the targeted merchantman. As soon as they were in range of ship's heaviest guns, she turned to bring one side of the ship to face the Russian vessel's stern. The twelve-pound cannons fired in unison at Annika's order and then the privateer reversed direction to bring the other side of the ship square to the target's backside. The pair of heavy guns on that side fired one after the other, and then the *Bloody Rose* turned directly towards her quarry as the gunners reloaded.

The Russian was caught unawares. The first two cannonballs, primed with military-grade high-velocity gunpowder, smashed through the high stern area of the ship. Pieces of wood flew in all directions, slowly arcing down towards the ground far below. The second pair of balls slammed through the lower part of the stern, splintering one of her two propellers and tearing into her engineering area. Smoke and flame were immediately visible to Hans's vision through the spyglass he held.

The damaged ship immediately began steering a zig-zag course. At the same time, she started into a sharp but controlled dive. The *Bloody Rose* followed the fleeing ship downwards at slightly more shallow angle.

"She is heading for the cloud layer at fifteen hundred," Hans said. "If she gets into that, we will lose her, I think. It was five hundred feet of London Pea, as I recall."

"We will hit her again with the twelves and eights before she makes it there. At that point, she will be easy to track. Captain-Gunner, call the turn."

"Aye-aye, *Kaptan!*" the Russian brunette acknowledged. Hans wondered how she felt, putting the cross hairs of her very effective gun crews on a shipload of her countrymen.

Did it bother her? Did she question this? Or was it just another target; another victim amongst many?

She adjusted the sights on the range-finder, checked the result and gave the order to start another "S". The privateer heeled over, and her starboard-side guns lashed out. The ship immediately turned hard around, bringing her four port guns to bear cleanly. A ripple of thunder and iron split the air.

Pieces flew in all directions from the fleeing merchant. The *Bloody Rose* was now slightly higher than her target, meaning the incoming cannon fire was striking the target from above, digging down through the decks and into the vitals of the ship. In spite of the attempts by the merchantman to evade, almost every shot fired marked a hit.

Smoke of three different shades and thickness now poured from the merchantman's wounds. Flames were visible from the hits to the engineering area. She was visibly slowing and it was obvious to Hans that the *Bloody Rose* would have ample time to fire both broadsides before her victim disappeared into the dense layer of clouds.

"Captain-Gunner, the next volley is to be cinder balls. We will fire from point blank *en passant* and then immediately turn to cut across her stern and fire again with the other guns. Make ready," Blackheart ordered. Annika nodded and repeated the orders.

"Cinder balls?" Hans questioned.

"Hollow cannonballs packed with a mixture of tar, coal and spruce paste around an explosive core. They explode after a six second match burns down, forcefully splattering the inside of the ship with burning sludge. She will be a doomed ship after that, even if she escapes us. The crew will be forced to abandon her for want of a way to extinguish the fires," the Captain-Gunner explained while fixedly staring at the target through the range-finder.

The *Bloody Rose* raced passed the badly injured merchantman at surprisingly close range and unloaded every cannon that bore on the target. As she turned away and back, a ripple of explosions and fire could be seen. Hans shuddered in horror as he saw a deck hatch thrown open and a crewman emerged with his clothes ablaze. The burning man ran in a blind panic and stumbled as the ship lurched beneath him. He fell, flailed, and went over the side. He left a long, ugly trail of ink-coloured smoke behind him as he plummeted.

The privateer fired again as she crossed the stern of her crippled and burning victim. The merchantman's other propeller slowly spun to a stop, and her dive of escape began to look less controlled.

Blackheart lowered his spy glass and nodded. "That is it. She is finished. Captain-Gunner, record it with the Kodak box. Three exposures should do it. Port, stern and starboard, if you please. Mister Sauder, you have the navigation for that process. I will be off of the bridge for ten minutes."

Hans and Annika did as Blackheart had requested once he had departed. It was obvious to Hans that the crew was determinedly trying to save their ship, but seemed to be slowly losing the battle. By the time they had done an orbit around the slowly descending ship, over two thirds of the holes in her hull had either black smoke or white steam pouring from them.

"Steam ... I would say they are trying to put the fires out with water," Hans suggested to Annika.

"I think so, too. Not that it matters," she said with a shrug, passing Hans' spyglass back to him. "Even if they successfully put the fires out and get her to a safe port, she is effectively out of the merchant business for six months to a year while they gut her and rebuild her. Which is all our employers care about. We do not need to shoot them down, we need to take them out of business."

A few minutes later, the merchantman sank into the pea-soup cloud layer, and the privateer climbed into the clear blue sky. Hans leaned heavily against a bulkhead and took a swig from the coffee flask in his shaky grasp.

"I hate privateering," Annika said as she gave him a sympathetic smile. "It is too much like war."

*****

"Captain, they are gaining on us!" Watch Officer Doretta Tillie shouted as a fusillade of cannon fire roared past the ship.

"They are shooting at us as well, Miss Tillie," Blackheart replied bemusedly in the face of her excited statement of the obvious. They had been racing at eighty knots for the last several minutes through the valleys and passes of the Karkonosze Mountains in the south-west of Poland. High and directly behind them were two cutters and a frigate, all flying the colours of the Russian Imperial Air Navy.

The trio of ships had started with the advantage of altitude and position, and if it had not been for the doubled lookouts on the English privateer, would likely have struck by surprise. Doretta had wisely headed for the lower air and the ship was running at full power by the time Blackheart made the bridge. From that point on, it had been some sort of bizarre, armed, aeronautical drag race.

Hans reached the bridge mere moments before Annika. He had awoken to the sound of the action alarms ringing throughout the ship in the middle of the morning. The incoming cannon fire and the erratic changes of course that the *Bloody Rose* had been making suggested to him that things were not going as Blackheart normally liked. He truly knew something was afoot at the point he had seen tree-tops whizzing past the deck of the ship while on his way to the Steering House.

"Well, good of you both to join us," Blackheart commented caustically. "I know that you both were likely occupied together with something more important than the Russian Air Navy trying to blow us out of these picturesque Polish skies."

"To review the marvellous fun you have both taken your time attending to," Blackheart continued with an airy wave, "the helmsman and planesman have been given the lenience of artistic creativity in the task of flying us down this valley in as chaotic a fashion as possible."

"We have a trio of Russian ships chasing and shooting at us," he continued conversationally while gesturing behind him in the direction of their pursuers. "I was not aware the Russians equipped their airships with nose guns. The cutters each seem to have a quadruplet of fours and the frigate has a like number of eights in bow-mountings."

"As Miss Tillie has observed, they are somewhat faster than we are and are rapidly closing ground. As evidenced by the fact that the cutters are now firing their bow guns. Your suggestions?"

Hans and Annika looked at each other quizzically. They both looked back at Blackheart as a pair of four-pound balls slammed into the midships' deck. Annika answered first.

"Well, we cannot turn and fight. They outgun us and we can really only take on either the frigate or the cutters. They are unlikely to be concerned about boarding us, so they will be far more aggressive about inflicting damage than we are used to. We also cannot run forever, since they can force a fight by better speed. I suggest we arm with cinder balls on both sides, hit each cutter with a broadside and then turn and run. With a bit of luck, they will be so busy putting out fires they will leave the frigate to finish us," Annika said with a grim note.

Blackheart looked at Hans. "Your thoughts, Mister Sauder?"

"We drop a spread of four balloon mines behind us to damage the cutters and then have the Captain-Gunner's men finish them off. As the frigate closes to engage us, we use one of the ship-to-ship rockets to cripple her. Then we finish her off as amuses the Captain-Gunner," Hans replied, flinching involuntarily as another salvo of cannon fire marked hits on the fleeing privateer.

Blackheart nodded. "Make it so. Let us sample the fruits of the labours of mad military science," he chortled.

The *Bloody Rose* suddenly levelled out and then began to steeply climb. She straightened her course as she raced along. Hans closed and opened two sets of knife-switches on the recently installed panel at the back of the Steering House. Sitting on the very stern deck of the ship, four barrels went hurtling over the back guardrail.

A small drogue parachute was shot into the air from the top of each barrel by a gun-powder charge triggered by the closing electrical switch. This in turn billowed open another much larger parachute which violently grabbed the hefty device and yanked it into the air behind the ship at a relative dead stop.

A chemical candle rapidly inflated a balloon, which cancelled the mine's slow descent. It rapidly rose directly into the path of the privateer's pursuers. Just as the Russian gun-crews were about to make good on the English privateer's seeming mistake in judgement, things went ugly.

The lead cutter slammed bow-first into one mine and side-swiped a second. Each mine contained 120 pounds of gun-powder, 120 pounds of half-pound cannonballs and a time-delay fuse. The two blasts shredded the first cutter in an eye-blink. She went from being an airship to a crashing heap of wreckage in the time it took the second cutter to realize they were in similar peril.

She tried to turn hard over, but was still too close to the remaining mines when they exploded. Each blast filled the air around them with screaming violence. The second cutter took dozens of hull-splintering hits across her sides and decks.

The *Bloody Rose* wheeled around, and suddenly the battlefield was clearly in her flavor. Her broadside gutted the cutter, leaving her a funeral pyre in a single volley. The pursuing Russian frigate had to veer violently from her course to avoid fatally careening into the burning wreck that had not yet begun to plunge to the ground below.

The Russian captain was skillful and his evasive action allowed him a broadside at the English privateer. His gunners were skilled as well, and the sounds of tearing wood and screaming men filled the decks of the *Bloody Rose*. The privateer gave back as good as she got, and her guns savaged the Russian's side.

Hans pulled a handle and twisted it. A cigar shaped projectile slipped from a carrier on the stern of the *Bloody Rose* and dropped a dozen feet. A man-sized plume of white fire erupted from the tail as four pairs of stubby fins snapped open. It veered up and away and then suddenly arced over towards the Russian ship faster than anything anyone on either ship had ever seen in the air.

The rocket was controlled by Hans via wires spooling out of its tail. He had a three-by-three button pad which he was rapidly tapping to alter the weapon's course. The button pressed by Hans represented the error in course which the rocket was making. The middle button meant it was on target. The top right button meant the weapon was flying up and to the right compared to the correct course. The middle right button meant that the trajectory was at the correct vertical pitch, but veering horizontally to the right, and so on around the set of buttons.

Hans was rapidly glancing back and forth between the button pad and the Steering House windows to keep track of the flight of the rocket. In a matter of seconds, the fire-tailed monster slammed into the midships of the Russian frigate and dug its way into the hull almost its entire length.

There were three explosions in rapid succession, each one bigger than the previous. At first, the rocket's forty-plus pounds of packed explosives went off, punching a hole in the deck above and the opposite side of the ship as well. Then the liquid kerosene of the rocket's fuel tanks exploded in an orange-white conflagration that seemed to pour of out of every crevice of the ship. There was a pregnant pause and then the entire ship disappeared in a soot-black blast that tore the frigate to matchsticks and buffeted the *Bloody Rose*.

"Mother of God," Blackheart whispered. "Her powder magazine exploded."

*****

"Not hungry this evening, Mister Sauder?" Alexi asked him at supper. They were enjoying a solid meal of roasted beef, roasted potatoes, Yorkshire pudding, legumes and a rich sauce. Hans was still getting used to sitting at the table in the Captain's Mess for the main meal of the day.

This evening, however, his stomach was somewhat tight. The destruction of the three Russian ships earlier in day had left him shaken. He had eaten little at mid-day and now, in spite of the excellent repast provided by Chief Bridges and his team, everything seemed to sit heavily in his gut. He shook his head at the Doctor.

"Mister Sauder was the Shivan hand of destruction today," Blackheart stated. "I suspect he is not doing so well with the responsibility attendant to that power."

Hans was aware that everyone was looking at him as they ate. He sighed. "No, I am not," he admitted. "I am rather surprised at my reaction, in fact."

"What did you *expect* would happen when you threw a half-ton of explosives at your enemies?" Piet Adelbert chided.

Hans was about to round angrily on him when Blackheart raised his hand. Hans shifted in his chair but said nothing.

"If it makes you feel any better, Mister Sauder, I was rather taken aback as well by the effectiveness of our new toys," Blackheart said while resuming his meal.

"The frigate was a lucky kill," Annika said after she swallowed her mouthful of wine. "I have seen powder magazines touch off from the use of solid twelve-pound balls. It could have happened regardless of what we fired at them."

"From what I was told," Arietta commented as she delicately sliced some of her beef, "it was a combination of very advanced weapons and very clever tactics. You took what would have been a brutal, losing battle and used your intelligence to turn the tables. I do not think you have anything to feel guilty about."

Blackheart nodded at his Chief Engineer. "Quite right. While it might be cold comfort, Mister Sauder, do trust me when I tell you that if you had not destroyed them ... well, they would have done their very best to destroy us."

Hans nodded. He knew the Captain was right.

"Well, Mister Sauder, I for one will thank you," Doctor Koblinski said. "While I know that you are not a man of war by upbringing; your very effective actions today ensured I was not obligated to amputate anything from anyone I know."

Hans looked at him the Doctor gave a slight nod and a forced smile. He hoped he would be able to come to terms with the events of the morning soon. He expected his sleep would be poor until he did.

*****

"Well, Chief?" Blackheart asked as Arietta entered the Steering House. He and Hans were studying a chart of the local area, trying to determine where a likely place to look for new targets might be. Warsaw, it turned out, was ringed by anti-airship guns.

Some of those gun batteries were mounted on steam-powered ground walkers that could move at twelve miles an hour and fire over a mile into the air. It was impossible to guess where they might be at any time. That made operating anywhere near the city unnecessarily dangerous. Coupled with the destruction of the three Russian Imperial Air Navy ships of the day before, Blackheart had little interest in loitering around Russian cities right now.

Hans glanced over at her. Oil smudges dotted her face, and soot was smeared on her vest. Her striped pants were a uniform shade of "propulsion grunge". She was grinning from ear to ear and her brown eyes danced with the delight of having spent the morning getting messy with her beloved engines. In short, she was almost enough to make him drop his pencil. Hans never failed to be surprised at how attractive he found her when she was living within her element.

She wiped her hands together and then on her vest. "Could have been worse," she said with an amused shrug. "Both reserve tanks of lift-gas are now empty after repairing and refilling the blown bags. Two of four water tanks got emptied, so in about two weeks we either are not drinking and cooking, or we are not making steam. We had to emergency-dump one kerosene tank, as a result of damage. We were leaking like a sieve, so we transferred as much as we could to other tanks and dumped the rest. That is about a week's worth lost."

Blackheart nodded. "So we need somewhere to take on water and kerosene, as a minimum. Mechanically, how are we?"

"Two out of three propeller pods are undamaged. The port outboard lost a blade and is currently pulled in while the boys install a replacement. You are limited to seventy knots until we get that blade installed," she said. One hand naturally rested on her cocked hip, and the free hand gestured slightly as she spoke.

Blackheart grimaced. The Russian patrol cutters were already faster than the *Bloody Rose* before damages. She winked at him and grinned.

"Chin up, Michael ... Er, *Signore Captaino*," she said looking a bit embarrassed. Blackheart scowled at her as she continued. "We are still one of the most heavily armed ships in Russian airspace right now, they do not have a way to track us easily, and we still have two weeks of range in our tanks. We took a bruising, but we are still able to fight."

"*Herr Kapitän*, look-outs report two ships, far, ahead, wide to starboard and above. Estimated altitude is four thousand feet," Hans relayed. "Our altitude by last fix was twenty nine hundred over ground which corresponds to the altimeter. We have thin clouds between us and the targets," he reported.

Blackheart shook his head and muttered something about "timing". Arietta laughed in that musical tone that Hans enjoyed so much.

"Let us fill our holds off these two, *Signore Capitano*," she said with a wicked grin. "Then we can get our flag-swaddled asses back across the Scorchlands to some place we can make money and quick repairs, and then take on fuel and water."

"I know just the place. It is a quiet little town that always somehow seems to have money for a pirate's goods. Mister Sauder, make bells and whistles for action, please. Take us into the clouds and no higher. Set your course to intercept the two ships. Chief, when you get yourself back down to your hole, please bring us up to best available speed. I do not want them to escape us, injured or not."

The two merchantmen realized they were hunted ships exactly too late. Surprisingly, they each fired a barrage of blue and white smoke rockets into the air in a huge fan behind them. One ship veered to the left and the other veered to the right. The left vessel dove and the other climbed even as both tried to accelerate away.

"That makes no sense," Hans said thoughtfully. "They stand better odds by staying in formation and trying to fight us as a team. By splitting up, they are sacrificing one of their number."

"Which means," Blackheart said in a similar tone, "one of those ships has something very valuable on it. A shell game, of sorts. If we choose the high-value target, the other ship will attack us, I would guess. If we choose the dummy, then she will lead us on a merry chase."

"The high value ship will be the one climbing," Annika declared as she entered.

"Oh, how do you reason that, Captain-Gunner?" Blackheart challenged.

She shrugged. "Russians like the high air. The Allied ships favour the near-ground. So, our 'instinct' would be to chase the diving ship. Also, it means that the escorting ship would be able to approach us from our blind spot below while we were preoccupied with the chase. From high above, we would have better odds of seeing the escort returning to the fray."

"Always the cunning hunter, hmm, Miss Nadezhda?" he said with an amused chuckle. "Mister Sauder, take pursuit of the high ship. Captain-Gunner, stand by to fire two simultaneous broadsides. We will make as though we are single-minded in our pursuit and as soon as the lower ship gives chase, we will turn hard over to have each vessel on a different side and then empty all guns."

"Aye, *Kaptan*. I will load cinder to starboard and ball to port. Put the low ship to our starboard side, please," she requested and then turned to her range-finder and voicepipes.

The *Bloody Rose* chased after the fleeing ship, pretending to be oblivious to the fact that the second ship was now wheeling around and rising to the chase at her stern. She slowly closed on her fleeing prey, even as her own pursuer steadily gained on her.

Without warning, she wheeled over and fired every gun she had, having let the chasing Russian come to within range of even her lightest guns. Both Russian ships veered sharply, but the damage was done. The chasing ship began to pour smoke from every wound while the fleeing ship had taken a concentrated volley into her stern quarter, crippling her steering.

The privateer continued in her turn, holding the burning ship in the arc of her guns firing another rippled broadside of incendiary. She turned hard and away, bringing her other side guns to bear which fired *en masse* a mixture of chain shot and solid ball as a single volley. The pursuing ship was left a shredded and burning wreck with nothing but a few hastily taken photographs to mark her existence before she began a sharp, spiralling dive towards the earth below.

The *Bloody Rose* turned back towards her intended prey, only to unexpectedly have it fire a six-gun mixture of canister shot and solid ball. The armoured glass windows of the Steering House exploded inwards in a hideous, howling scream of glass, metal, wood, skin and bone. The canister shot – essentially grapeshot in a bucket – had been almost entirely targeted toward the Steering House.

The Planesman was an unrecognizably lacerated heap. The Helmsman was missing an arm and lay face down and unmoving in an expanding red pool. Blood spatter covered everything. Annika was holding up the body of the Hungarian Watch Officer, Donát Jani; she had stepped in front of Hans and then grabbed the other man about the neck to use him as literal body armour. Blackheart had reacted with surprising speed and had taken cover. He stood up to his full height, and stepped to the helm. He spun the helm over, banking the ship towards the target of his fury.

"Captain-Gunner … all guns, grapeshot, rapid fire until we board. Tear that bitch to shreds. There will be no survivors," he shouted above the sound of wind and motors. Rage was heavy in his voice.

Annika dropped the dead Hungarian at her feet and stepped over the corpse with indifference. She relayed the orders down her voicepipes with malice equal to Blackheart's. Hans stood in slack-jawed shock and horror.

The Russian guns never fired another shot. The *Bloody Rose* manoeuvred to stay to one side of her prey the entire remainder of the action and mercilessly pounded it with volley after volley of grapeshot.

The English Captain led the boarding himself, with all his officers at his side, Hans included. "They tried to kill your Captain, my lads and lasses! They tried to kill him with three cannons!" he shouted above the wind and engines as the two ships ground together. "Let us show these Russian bastards that you do not kill a legend without doing it MAN TO MAN!"

The crew roared savagely and swarmed aboard. The upper decks were empty of resistance and the fight was immediately carried below. Hans, Arietta, Annika and three other gunner-marines made their way to the engineering area while Blackheart and the other officers assaulted the bridge.

Pistol fire and the sounds of clashing swords rang out throughout the ship. Surprisingly, the "merchant" was crewed by Russian Air Navy men and women, and even carried marines. The result was a vicious collision of cold and effective training with hot-forged cunning and experience.

The battle was brutal and prolonged. Eventually, though, the Privateers won. The storm of grapeshot leading up to the boarding had killed or maimed many of the Russians. The Russian crew had fought fiercely to the last man, save for a pair of cooks and, oddly, the second officer. He had surrendered without any struggle at all and then passed Blackheart the keys to the captain's cabin door.

"You will want what is in the safe behind the painting," he had said cryptically.

In the engineering space, they had narrowly prevented two marines from rigging a sizable explosive charge to the fuel manifold for the three engines. Arietta had deduced that if it had gone off, the blast would have turned the ship into a kiln in a matter of minutes. Not one of the engineers had surrendered without a fight; something the Privateers were all too willing to give them.

"What the hell are they protecting?" Hans snarled incredulously.

Arietta wiped the gore off her cutlass and shook her head. "Even gold is not worth this sort of resistance," she said.

*****

"Well, Mister Sauder?" Blackheart asked he entered the Captain's Mess where Hans and Annika sat at the dining table. Hans was studying a large wood-and-leather bound text. Annika was thoughtfully staring at a notepad.

Hans glanced over at him, sighed and shook his head. "I am good with numbers and riddles; she speaks Russian and loves both Egyptian culture and history. Between the two of us over the past few hours, we have concluded we are no Sherlock Holmes."

Blackheart scowled. "Which means what, Mister Sauder? Badly written contemporary magazine story characters do not interest me."

"It is written in a cipher of some kind," Annika replied wearily. "We have been trying to break it for two days now – ever since our run in with those two RIAN gunned-couriers. We cannot make heads nor tails of it."

"I am aware of how much time you two have been occupying the middle of my floor, Captain-Gunner," Blackheart replied dryly. "Stop telling me what you do not know and tell me what you do know."

"As the Captain-Gunner says, it is written in a complex cipher, and in Russian. However, the book itself is very old. The way it is held together, the style in which it is made and the condition of the ink and paper reminds the two of us of old Bibles we have seen. The kind kept under glass as prized treasures," Hans explained, gesturing at the tome.

"While the bulk of the book is Russian text, there are passages written in Egyptian hieroglyphics," Annika said, holding up a sheet she had copied. "As well, there are maps and diagrams which seem to have something to do with the location of forests and farm lands in Egypt."

"That is nonsense," Blackheart scoffed. "The place is a sandbox unless you are within sight of the Nile or an oasis. I have flown over most of it and I can assure you that there is nothing resembling a forest anywhere in the entire area."

"That is what is so puzzling. Because of the cipher, we cannot determine exactly when or where the images and maps are about. That said, for it to be written in a cipher suggests to me that we should turn it over to our new friends at Whitehall when we reach London and see if it turns out to be anything interesting."

"Well," Blackheart said with a grin, "we will consider *selling* it to them, certainly. Alright, good work, both of you."

"'Good work', *Kaptan*?" Annika questioned. "We have not learned anything of value in two days of beating our heads against it."

"*Au contraire*, my Captain-Gunner. You have determined that it is worth selling to Whitehall. That is a very good thing to know. Now, get out of my Mess so I can relax and get the paperwork started before we reach our destination. We have an interesting pile of odds and sods to be prioritized for market when we arrive."

*****

It was after dark of the next day and Hans and Annika were sitting together on the flat roof of a public building, staring at the stars and talking. She downed a small glass of a clear liquid sand refilled it and passed it Hans. He sniffed at it and looked at it dubiously. He opened his mouth to question and she cut him off.

"Oh, shut up, Hans," she said, exasperatedly. "Just drink it. It will not kill you."

He chuckled and drank it as she had, in a single gulp. He made a face and spluttered. She laughed, took the glass from him and refilled it for herself.

The *Bloody Rose* had arrived that morning on the Allied side of the belt of uninhabitable terrain between Allied and Russian Europe that was dubbed "the Scorchlands". Anywhere between twelve and thirty miles wide, it was the *de-facto* border simply because crossing it on the ground was considered madness.

Once they had found a place to drop anchors and tethers, the Privateers had gotten to the task of selling the contents of their holds to the locals as well as buying needed stores and supplies. That had been the all-day job it usually was. It was made more difficult than usual since a fifth of the gunner-marines had been injured to some degree in the last boarding battle.

In addition, repairs needed to be made to mend the damages suffered from the run-ins with the Russian Imperial Air Navy. Hans had lent his efforts and expertise in the Propulsion Room and Tank Hold, since none of the engineering staff had escaped the last battle without some sort of injury. He himself had a bandage around his left bicep from a Russian swordsman's efforts to end him, but thankfully the cut was both shallow and clean, and so he was unimpeded.

A long day had eventually become evening and then night. As was usual, most of the Privateers beyond a skeleton crew had headed aground to spend at least some of their night and wealth carousing. Everyone knew that the departure in the next morning or two would be taking them back into the brutal reach of the Red Bear.

Annika had convinced him to spend at least part of the evening in her company entirely on that basis. "You never know what might happen tomorrow, Hans," she had told him. "I am sure Jani had plans for the future, but no one gets to vote on when Fate takes them."

He was fairly aware from the hungry look in her eyes as they talked for a while that she would have liked nothing more than to bed him then and there. However, she did not press or even broach the matter. They talked about a great deal of nothing for a time and then she asked him if he could name stars.

She whimsically explained that ever since she was a young girl, she had always been fascinated by the jewelled night sky, but had never had the opportunity to discuss it with another who might care. Hans, for his part, had spent some of his University studying the latest that astronomy had to offer.

He gave her a visual tour, pointing out the great constellations and the principal stars. He explained to her some of the legend behind their naming, pointing them out to her and letting her sight along his arm. He explained how to find one group by starting with others.

At some point, he realized that they were both laying down on the two fire blankets they had brought along. She was close beside him with her head on his shoulder as they talked quietly and he pointed to the heavens periodically. She asked intelligent questions and was quick to grasp the things he explained. It was a very comfortable sort of moment.

He looked at her with her slight frame curled up against him and a hand in the middle of his chest. She sensed the change in his mood and looked up at him in the pause in his speaking.

"What, Hans?" she asked quietly.

He looked at the Russian brunette cuddled against him for a long moment before he spoke. "I have one question for you, Annika. It has been bothering me for some time. Why did you not just kill me?"

"Pardon? When?" she blinked and stiffened slightly against him.

"When the *Bloody Rose* captured the passenger-merchant I was aboard. I was providing 'armed resistance'. I have seen you many times just shoot someone without comment or warning in exactly that situation. No questions or quarter. You are very consistent in how you conduct boardings."

"Yet," he said thoughtfully as he continued, "I had downed three of your crew and fought two others to a stand-still. Why did you not just shoot me in the back, instead of knocking me unconscious with the bell of your cutlass? And what possessed you to have me brought aboard the *Bloody Rose*, instead of leaving me on the deck of that ship?"

She blinked at him and for the first time which he could recall, she turned red. She opened her mouth to speak and the water tower beside the old train station at the edge of town was struck by lightning and exploded.

Both Hans and Annika reacted the same way, covering for a moment against the initial blast, in spite of its distance from them. They both sat up, looking around.

"There is something wrong," Hans said.

"What?"

"That stroke ... it was *horizontal* ..." he said. Below, people were streaming out into the street to see what the noise had been.

"Listen!" she said. "Do you hear a train?" Annika asked, concentrating over the noise of the townspeople.

"Why ... yes ... yes, I do. A bit late for a train, is it not?" Hans asked. It certainly sounded like the pulsing sound of a steam locomotive, albeit throatier than he was used to.

"The train station has been closed for years. The tracks are destroyed on both ends of town. It is not a train ..." she said and then was cut off by what sounded like a series of massive pressure tanks venting one after the other. Then, the air was filled with the unmistakable sound of incoming cannonballs.

"TAKE COVER!" she screamed with all the voice she could muster. The volley slammed into the taller buildings of the town, shattering wood and sending splinters and debris flying in all directions.

On the street below, it was easy to tell who were Privateers and who were townspeople. The Privateers had all flattened to the ground when Annika had shouted, while most of the townspeople had turned around to see who was yelling from a roof top.

"RUN FOR YOUR LIVES! DRAGON!" she shouted. As if cued, another searing arc of electrical energy cut the bell-tower off the Church. It crashed to the ground and the echoes of the bells rang cacophonously against the sounds of smashing timber and planks.

It came into view at the lighted edge of town, lumbering out of the night. The lights of the town glinted off its armoured hide as it advanced. It was easily two heights of a man to its shoulder, if not three, and double that to the top of its steel head. It was probably the length of a Pullman railway car including its tail, advancing on three pairs of legs.

Six bombard-styled cannon barrels were set along its spine, each one apparently firing at a different target. High pressure steam instead of powder propelled their payloads. Heavy cannonballs fell down upon the highest buildings, smashing them and throwing shrapnel in all directions. Metal whips, some twenty feet long, were mounted at the top of each leg, snapping back and forth in lethal arcs and shimmering in the town lights.

"Oh, Mother of God," Hans breathed, turning white. "It really *is* a Dragon ..."

Dragons were the hammer that had broken the anvil of the Crimean war for both sides. They were 90,000-pound armoured cars or ground walkers. They carried the combined firepower of an infantry company, an artillery battery and a mad-scientist's laboratory. Each one was directed by an autonomous analog differential analyzer with the intelligence and cunning of a Saint Bernard. This allowed them to problem-solve and act on their own to complete their mission.

The first ones had been used in 1855 at the Battle of Eupatoria where two were dropped via Russian airships about six miles away from the Turkish garrison at night. In spite of the fact that the the Turks were ready and waiting for the Russian attack, they were completely unable to stop the two metal monstrosities that led the assault. Long-arm fire simply bounced off and artillery could not target the rapidly advancing machines. Once the two Dragons had gotten to within half a mile, they annihilated the entire defending artillery battery with blasts of electrical energy.

The Turkish troops fought back bravely, but even with covering fire from Allied naval units – one of which was sunk by return fire from a Dragon – the Turks were forced to retreat. Russian artillery and infantry supported the attack and took the town, while the Dragons then headed off to their next planned target.

Within a year, every nation in the war was deploying Dragons as weapons of mass destruction in a technological race of one-up-manship. A year or two later, the first of the armoured monsters "went rogue" and the face of Europe changed forever.

The townspeople began to scatter like geese, with screams and shouts of fear. The Dragon stopped at the small pond caused by the toppled water tower. It lowered its head to the water and began suctioning it up. The steam-powered bombards on its spine swivelled around and fired again, shattering facades and roof tops.

Hans and Annika climbed down from the roof they were on as quickly as they could. It was obvious to both of them that the Dragon was effectively "tearing down the town", targeting the tallest buildings first with its steam cannon. At this pace, they would be standing on top of an upcoming target fairly soon.

Before Hans or Annika had a chance to fully descend, two groups of the Privateers opted to take matters into their own hands. One group started shooting with their pistols at the armoured monster. It was too big to miss and ricochet sparks flashed over it as the Privateers steadily advanced in a rather military-looking line, firing as they went.

A second group, lead by Mariana, was breaking down the door to the town Mining Store. Within moments, they were inside and then had re-emerged, each carrying two or three sticks each of Nobel's Blasting Powder. They ran towards the monster like a charging line of valiant grenadiers.

A set of sliding doors over each front shoulder opened and a brass and copper pipe bundle emerged from each opening, pointed straight up. It was on a hinged mounting at its base, much as a cannon might be set. It lowered its nose end toward the advancing pistoliers and then started spewing steam and metal at them.

Each bundle of piping was, in fact, a hundred or more steam-powered muskets all hooked together. Each barrel fired one after the other, throwing a storm of projectiles towards the Privateers in a sustained stuttered hissing-crack. The mountings were not particularly accurate and dirt and debris flew into the air on all sides around Privateers. However, much like Doctor Gatling's gun, it simply fired so many bullets so quickly that when the two barrel-banks had run dry of ammunition, not a single one of the pistoliers was standing. At least half of the impromptu grenadiers had been felled as well. The two mountings retracted into the chest of the Dragon and the sliding doors closed over top as it reloaded.

Only a few of the remainder of the Privateers which Mariana was leading kept their nerve. The others ran for their lives. Mariana and the rest of the resolute few ran forward, lit their fuses and threw their deadly charges. The night rang out with the sounds of the detonations of sticks of high explosive. The blasts tore pieces out of the Dragon's armour, but did little to slow its renewed advance.

It was the last mortal action any of them made. The Dragon suddenly rushed forward and simply crushed one of them under foot. Mariana was decapitated by a metal whip as she tried to shout a warning and retreat. The area around the metal monster was engulfed in steam and screams of scalded pain cut the night.

"Brave, brave IDIOTS," Annika hissed. "We cannot stop that thing, Hans. We have to get the townspeople and crew to safety," she said in a determined voice.

Hans looked at her in surprise. "Yes. The townspeople and the crew. Start yelling and let us get people moving the right way!"

Hans and Annika started shouting at the remaining Privateers to herd the townspeople away as the monster stopped to tear apart, crush and swallow the side of a wooden building. Bombard rounds fell down around the town smashing wood, brick and bodies with little discrimination. The multi-barrel steam-musket mechanisms raised, sprayed death and steam across the town street, and retracted.

It resumed its advance and then spat lightning in a searing blue-white arc that struck the Mining Store and the adjacent General Store, setting them both ablaze. An explosion took part of the store front apart, tossing burning material in all directions. A nearby stack of hay at the front of the horse stables caught fire.

Hans and Annika dove for cover as the ball from a bombard fell short of its target, throwing a fountain of earth into the air and in all directions for yards around. They got behind a horse cart which had been tipped on its side and continued yelling orders and directions at everyone that they could see. At the same time, they kept a wary eye on the advancing war machine. They both knew that they, too, would soon have to flee before its advance.

It was a world of steam, fire, blood and death. Hans was filled with rage at the injustice of what was happening around him. Thirty years after the end of the Crimean War, the horrifying artifacts of that time continued to cause suffering and pain to the innocents of Europe. No armies or generals or kings or tzars were here to defend the people of this little town. Instead, it was just a band of pirates-turned-privateers who were almost equally powerless before one of the most awesome pieces of technology the world had ever seen.

The *Bloody Rose* roared in, with search lights blazing. Every gun on her facing side fired, but in no particular order. Fountains of earth erupted around the Dragon, which had suddenly reversed direction in response to the airborne attack. One 8-pound ball slammed into the middle leg on the left side, crushing the internal mechanisms. The leg dragged now, instead of moving properly.

"What the furnace-fed-Hell kind of gunnery is THAT?" Annika bellowed while shaking her fist in the air, clearly displeased at the lack of hits on a target the size of the Dragon.

"Skeleton crew, Annika," Hans reminded her. "For all we know, it is Blauchuk at the helm, and Bridges and Salvador firing the guns by themselves."

The airship heeled steeply and sheets of water began pouring from her port and starboard sides. The ship ran the length of the town with the water being turned into a heavy fog by the propellers. The spray dampened the fires and obscured vision. It was at once both fire-fighting assistance and visual cover for everyone on the ground retreating from the advancing Dragon.

"Bless you, O'Raedy," Hans breathed.

The Dragon lashed out with its steam cannons and scored two solid hits on its antagonist. The heavy cannonballs tore through the bow and midships without stopping. The *Bloody Rose* snapped all its search lights off and rapidly climbed out of sight. A blast of electrical energy from the monster's mouth failed to mark a hit even as it lit the night for hundreds of yards around.

Blauchuk leapt down from some point above Hans' vision and onto a wooden over-hang with a crunch. From there, with a speed and agility that again surprised Hans, he bounded to the ground and ran out into the middle of the fog-swirled street, directly into the path of the oncoming juggernaut.

"Blauchuk! Get out of the way!" Hans shouted.

"I am thinking, Sauder! I am thinking!" Blauchuk cried back over the roaring howl of mechanized devastation. He stood his ground, watching the Dragon advancing along the main street. He stared fixedly at the right-hand multi-barrel steam-musket doors. Sauder saw blood fly from one of the Slav's arms. The doors opened and the gun-mount retracted again to reload. Blauchuk nodded furiously and ran into the burning mining store.

Hans and Annika continued shouting instructions to the fleeing townspeople while the Dragon continued its murderous advance. Its steam-powered weapons remorselessly shattered buildings, lives and structures. There was nothing that the two of them could do but try and minimize the loss of life, including their own.

The sustained hiss-crack reports of the multi-barrel gun mounts filled the air again. Steam-cannon rounds slammed into the building beside where Hans and Annika were hiding, showering them with splinters and dirt. Another shattered part of the cart with a near miss.

Over the din, Hans clearly heard Blauchuk screaming "I can do it, Sauder! I am thinking!"

Hans peered over the edge of the splintered cover he was behind. His jaw went slack in horror.

Blauchuk, with a huge sack in each arm, was running towards the Dragon. His hair was on fire, as were the legs of his pants. His shirt smoked and was blackened. The bags steamed in his arms.

"NO!" Hans screamed.

"I can stop it! I know how! Thank you, Mister Sauder! I can outsmart it!" the Slav shouted back with a huge grin on his face. He came at the monster from the side, gamely taking rib-cracking blow from a steel whip to the chest. He stumbled under the impact, but pressed on. He clambered up the damaged and dragging middle leg, dodging another pair of blows from whips. A blast of steam raised shilling-sized blisters on his skin, but he did not even break step.

"What is he doing?" Annika whispered in fascinated horror.

"Cutting Achilles' tendon," Hans said, beginning to understand what the heroic Slav was about to do. Tears began to well at his eyes, but he could not look away.

The doors opened to retract the right hand steam-musket gun-pod for reloading just as Blauchuk reached that point from behind. With a bellow of "... thirty, thirty-one, THIRTY-TWO!" he threw the bags into the opened doors. Hans realized that Blauchuk had counted the load-and-fire cycle of the gun-pod. He must have hidden in the burning store as cover, counting away even as he burned, to ensure that he would arrive at exactly the right moment.

The gun pod retracted, mashing the bags into the opening; into the chest of the mechanized monster. There was a deafening roar that eclipsed all other noise for a ground-shaking moment. The Dragon came apart at the seams, torn open by two internal explosions; one from the bags, the other from its own ruptured high-pressure steam plant. Hans and Annika were thrown to the ground in a heap together, holding each other in awed fright. Shrapnel screamed through the air in all directions, blocking everyone's vision and breaking bodies. For a moment everything was lost within showers of splinters, dirt, debris, and clouds of steam and smoke.

Silence descended on the night. It was broken only by the crackle of flames and the cries of the wounded who littered the street. Annika helped Hans to his feet and they peered from behind the wrecked remnants of the cart towards where the Dragon had been.

It was dead. It was a broken heap of metal and junk, collapsed on itself, flames and steam shooting high into the night. It did not stir in the least.

"Blauchuk," Hans breathed. He ran towards the unmoving bulk of the man, who was laying on the ground some twenty yards from where he had last been. Hans turned him over, and shouted the Slav's name. One eye was ruined, one leg was blown off, his hair and scalp burned to an ugly mess. The good eye opened and focused on Hans.

"You are alive! My God ... We ... We have to get you to the *Döktor*!"

"Of course ... I am alive ... I am not stupid anymore ... I tried to jump clear. Mister Sauder... I did it ..." the Slav said weakly.

"Yes, my good man, you did it. That was the most brave thing I have ever seen a man do, Blauchuk. Now, just you hold on, we are going to get you to the ship," Hans said as tears filling his eyes.

"Do not cry ... Mister Sauder. I'm so happy ... you... helped me ... be... smart. I ... out-smarted ... it ..." Blauchuk's voice faded to a whisper, and then silence. The big man convulsed, spat up blood and bile, and died.

"He is ... gone ..." Hans said through a choked throat.

Annika collapsed beside him, clinging to Hans and crying like a fragile little girl. Through her muffled sobs against his shoulder, all Hans could make out was "thank-you for everything, Bloo".

"Runaways"

Diary Entry for June 18th, 1888

It has been another two weeks since I updated my diary. We are finally returning to the relative safety of the skies of Allied Europe. Should I not return to Russia for a hundred years, I believe it will be too soon.

The events of the past two weeks are such a jumble of action and emotion that I hardly know where to begin or what to say. I suppose a tally of our labours is of some value.

We took prey of two merchantmen, destroyed two more and likewise destroyed two frigates. We were also chased by a 50-gun ship of the line, named the *Zheleznyĭ Molot*, but were able to escape with little damage to ourselves. We gave her a bloody nose for her troubles, courtesy of myself.

The third frigate was another matter, entirely. The *Severnyĭ Volk* was a more tragic Triomphe. When Blackheart spoke highly of the skill of the Russian airship crews, he was not overstating their prowess. She caught us out of a cloud line and before we were entirely aware, had pressed us for a boarding.

Annika was seriously injured. The good Döktor is certain she will live at this point, but the initial few hours were harrowing for both he and I.

I am somewhat discomfited at my reaction to seeing her fall to the deck. It is the first time I have ever intentionally killed anyone with my sword or my hands. I cannot resolve how I could let my anger transform to such malice that I would become such a monster. It is doubly distressing when someone like Blackheart becomes the calming voice of reason.

Alexi and I had a long talk. He is quite a philosopher, amongst other things. He understands me better than I thought anyone other than my parents might. We spoke at length about his reasons for being aboard the Bloody Rose and I now have an even greater respect for the man. At some point in our lives, we are all left at a crossroad that bears no signs. It is not just the direction we choose for ourselves, but why we choose it, that is important to who we become.

Annika and I also had a long talk. We spoke at length about who she was and what brought her to the Bloody Rose and why she intends to stay until it kills her. I am afraid that I am becoming all too caught up in my relationship with the Captain-Gunner. It reminds me entirely too much of the relationship of a moth and a candle.

*****

"Annika said I might find you here," Chief Itala said as she entered the Tank Hold. Hans glanced over at her from his perch on a low catwalk beside a water tank. "Do you mind some company?"

He shook his head and gestured for her to join him in the barely lit cavern. He was holding a wax tablet in his hands and his gaze went back to it.

She sat down a short distance from him on the catwalk. She had her back against an upright length of pipe, one leg pulled up under her chin and the other dangling off the platform they both now sat upon.

"It is not fair," he announced.

"No. It is not. But you cannot be surprised at that, Hans. If life was fair, the *Bloody Rose* would not exist, for want of men and women to crew her. Every one of us, you included, is here because life is not fair," Arietta replied softly, picking idly at a loose thread on her vest.

"I feel like I killed him," Hans said in a morose tone.

"You did not. You gave him the tools to die a hero. There is a difference. I can understand the chain of thought that might lead you to believe Blauchuk's death is on your shoulders. But it is not. He would have died eventually, and likely far more uselessly. *He* made the decision. He did something that no one else could do," she said encouragingly.

"It seems silly. I miss our daily teaching sessions. He was doing so well. We were going to start playing chess soon," Hans said as he set the tablet down beside him.

"Do not rob him of his moment of glory by wallowing in self-pity. Remember him for who he really was, which was a man that beat the odds of his origin every day just by waking up here. Remember him for the man who knew he could be more than he was and who came to you for help. Remember him as the man who saved a lot of lives, most of whom he did not even know. That is the mark of a true hero."

He thought about that for a little while and then nodded. "Thank you, Arietta. I take it Annika was concerned for me?" he asked, looking at her for the first time since she entered.

She shook her head and then paused before speaking. "Well ... yes, she is concerned, but that is not why I am here. I am here because I am concerned. You have been awfully distant and withdrawn since we began our *piccola avventura* in Russia."

"Well, in all honestly, Arietta, it has been one nightmare leading into the next since we began. I have no idea what it was that I was expecting. I can assure you that being the 'Shivan hand of destruction' or being helpless as I watched Mariana, Klaus, Sean and Blauchuk fall to a rogue Dragon was not it. I just wish I could go home."

"No you do not," the dark-skinned beauty said with a melodic laugh. "You are quite happy where you are. You wish you were less affected by the deaths of your friends. You wish you were more 'manly' like the others. You wish you were more roughened, more calloused. But then you would not be the Hans Sauder that has the Ladies of the Rose a-twitter and the men of the Rose wishing they could be more like you."

"What?" Hans said with blink.

She turned and swung her other leg over the edge of the catwalk and then let herself down to the floor in a fluid and graceful motion. She wiped her hands together and then wiped them on her vest. "Stop wishing you were a moronic cutthroat pirate and start accepting who you are and where you are. It is what makes you the man you are, Hans. You have made quite a splash since you came aboard and none of it would have been possible if you were anyone but who you are." Without another word, she turned and left the Tank Hold with an easy sashay, leaving a somewhat stunned Hans sitting on the catwalk staring after her.

*****

Hans landed flat on his back with a heavy and graceless thud. Before he had a chance to do anything, Annika's booted heel came down on his sword-side wrist and the point of her cutlass came to rest on his nose. She looked at him disdainfully from behind her goggles.

"Wake up, Hans. Nasty bitch with a sword calling. Voicepipe one. Hello? *Lyuboĭ dom*?Anyone home?" she questioned bemusedly. Her voice was muffled by the breather mask she wore.

"Fine, yes, you won," he said crossly. "You do not need to be insufferable about it."

"I did not win, Hans, so much as you failed to compete. Really, I did not take you as the sort of man who would leave a woman so unsatisfied," she teased. He rolled his eyes at her as she removed her heel and her sword point from him, and took a step or two back. "Your heart is really not into this today, is it?"

"*Herr* Koblinski has suggested I have had too much to think of late," he said irritably as he regained his footing and sheathed his scimitar.

"I would tend to agree with the diagnosis," she said as she returned her blade to its scabbard. "You keep forgetting half of the secret of happiness, Hans. You act like you have never heard it."

"Oh? And what would that be, oh great Russian Spiritual Adviser Annika?" he scoffed.

"'And Move On'," she said, refusing to rise to the offered bait. They started walking back across the deck in the sunset glow together.

"'And Move On'?" he questioned.

The Russian brunette nodded. "Yes. As in, 'Mourn, and Move On' Or 'Regret, and Move On'. Or, 'Learn, and Move On'. You are perpetually stuck, Hans. Usually in mourning or regrets, I note. You seem disinclined to 'move on'. Which, as far as I am concerned, is the secret of happiness."

"Koblinski?" he asked. She simply nodded again. He paused at the hatch leading down towards the sleeping bays. He looked at her thoughtfully for a moment, and asked "Care to meet me in the Rope Locker after the evening meal? Coffee and talk?"

She pulled her goggles up and looked at him in evident surprise. "I am not going to question this at all. I would love to. Should I bring a ..."

The rest of her question was abruptly lost in the sound of the action alarm repeater they were standing beside suddenly loudly blaring. She said something nasty sounding in Russian.

"The fun begins again. See you in the Steering House!" Hans said with a grin.

*****

"Thank Heavens for attentive look-outs," Blackheart stated as he lowered his spyglass. Annika and Hans nodded at him. One of the on-watch crew had spotted a Russian ship of the line while it was still far enough away to not yet be a danger. "Captain-Gunner, find out who that man was and make sure he gets a plate of whatever Bridges has planned for us."

"What are we going to do?" asked Hans. "We cannot think to fight that. She is four times our size."

"The good news is that she has not yet seen us. Hmm... *Zheleznyĭ Molot*; the Iron Hammer. With a name like that, I very much doubt she is a merchantman," Annika said ruefully.

"Helmsman, take left turn, fifteen degrees rudder to heading two nine five," Blackheart ordered. "Engineering, I want 80 knots. A ship that big will carry sixteen pounders, if not twenty-fours and will have twice our striking range. I do not wish to tangle with that. We have just gotten the holes from the 32-pounders patched."

The *Bloody Rose* turned forty-five degrees away from the *Zheleznyĭ Molot* and increased her speed to open the distance between them. All looked well for a few minutes until the Russian suddenly fired a series of five smoke rockets off her stern with each one being a different colour than the prior.

Hans groaned. "She's challenging us, *Herr Kapitän*."

Blackheart cursed under his breath. "Aye, and now she is turning towards us. She will have at least our speed."

"She is running out her bow guns ... um, I count six barrels," Annika said somewhat worriedly.

"Mister Sauder, do be a gentleman and convince them that pursuing us is not in their best interests," Blackheart said. Hans nodded grimly. There was no doubt in his mind that if the Russian got into firing range that the *Bloody Rose* and her crew were in a great deal of trouble.

The Sargasso balloon-mines were not going to be effective, he decided. The *Zheleznyĭ Molot* would have plenty of time to see them and a load of grapeshot would clear them from her path. He grabbed the firing handle for the Cudahawk launcher, nodded to himself, and then pulled the handle up and twisted it counter-clockwise. A light went from blue to red and they could clearly hear the sound of the rocket motor roaring to life.

A few moments later, the rocket slammed into the bow of the pursuing Russian ship. The Russians fired at least two bow guns at the incoming weapon, but scored no hits. Fire and smoke trailed from all the Russian's port side bow gun-ports. Hans put the lever back to the "Ready/ Safe" position and then rapidly flipped the switches required to reload the launcher. As soon as the status light went blue, he fired a second rocket.

The second weapon hit its target on the foredeck area. Hans had intentionally steered the rocket high over the Russian gunboat and then plunged it down at the last moment. The *Zheleznyĭ Molot* immediately veered away from the fleeing Privateer with smoke and flames now pouring out of two sizable wounds.

"Record that with the Kodak box, please, Captain-Gunner. We have certainly not hurt her badly enough to shoot her down or even force her back to a port. However, it is not every day a ship our size manages to convince a ship of the line to go do something else for a while," Blackheart said with a laugh. "Now, Mister Sauder, how many more of those do we have left?"

Hans checked a log sheet for a moment. "Nine Cudahawk rockets and sixteen Sargasso balloon-mines," he replied.

"And do you think, Mister Sauder, that the Allied governments will be inclined to allow us to keep those fine toys past the end of our Letter?"

"Not if they have any sanity about them at all," Hans laughed. "The *Bloody Rose* as a pirate armed with these would be a Holy terror over the Mediterranean. At the point we can give a sore jaw to a ship of the line, the only way they would be able to stop us is with something bigger."

"Do not think too much of us, Hans," Annika said with a smile. "The *Zheleznyĭ Molot* was likely a 4th Rate ship of the line. There are much bigger ships on both sides of the Scorchlands and they, too, will be carrying things like Cudahawks, or worse."

Hans nodded. Blackheart chuckled and then said "A very good point, Captain-Gunner. However, my point was that there is little value in being miserly with those. If they extend our Letter, we will get more. If they do not, we will likely have to surrender what we do not use. So, use them. If we are not planning on taking a ship as prey, we will save the powder and balls and instead use the mines and rockets. We are heading for London in less than two weeks and we have a lot of damage left to do."

*****

Annika passed Hans back his flask after taking a mouthful of hot coffee from it. He tipped it to his lips and had some as well. They were stretched out and cuddled together in the Rope Locker on a knee-high coil of inch-diameter rope. Annika had tossed some sail canvas over it to transform it into a reasonably comfortable spot. She leaned her head against his shoulder and gave a sound of contentment.

After they had been sure that the Russian gunboat was no longer pursuing them and they were safely away, it had been time for supper in the Captain's Mess. Supper had gone well, with much of the talk having been about the escape from the *Zheleznyĭ Molot*. There had been some verbal sparring between Hans and Piet Aldebert about whether the *Bloody Rose* should have pushed its advantage and tried to inflict more serious damage on the Russian ship.

Blackheart had ended the discussion by pointing out that while they both had interesting points, it was entirely irrelevant because they were not getting paid to harass RIAN ships. They were getting paid to damage and destroy merchant shipping. So long as he was in charge, they would remain focused on the things that made them all rich men and women, as opposed to risking getting the ship shot out from under them.

After the meal and games were done, Annika and Hans had made their way to the Rope Locker as he had suggested earlier. Annika had absconded with a bit of extra dessert for them and Hans had ensured his flask was full of fresh coffee.

"I know it is considered *gauche* to ask a lady such questions, but how old are you?" he asked her thoughtfully.

"Well, the good news, Hans, is that I am not a lady," she said with a chuckle. "And I am five."

He looked at her skeptically. "Do keep in mind, Annika, that I have been both swimming and wrestling with you in the nude. I am fairly sure I would have noticed bolts in your neck."

"Mmm, yes, that was quite an evening," she said absently with a nearly feline noise. "No, I am not saying I am a Galvanotaur. I am saying that I count my life as having started when I joined my first pirate ship, which was five years ago."

He lofted a brow at her. "And what of your life before then?"

"Unless you have a ready supply of opium, I am not interested in taking that particular trip down memory lane. I have worked very hard to put that behind me and to forget those days," she said with a fair mixture of belligerence and defiance in her voice.

"So your ... vice ... for opium is not purely recreational, then?"

"Consider it far more medicinal," she replied bitterly.

A long silence passed between them before Hans spoke. "I am impressed. You made Captain-Gunner, as a woman, in five years? That is quite an achievement."

"Thank you," she said quietly. "I am not proud of every choice I have made along the way, but I am certainly proud of where I am today. I was told it could not be done, so I chose to do it."

"You are a remarkably stubborn woman, to be sure," he said with a laugh.

She pursed her lips and scowled at him. "Yes, Hans Sauder, I am. And when I decide I want something, I *do* eventually get it. Keep that in mind."

His amused chuckle was cut short by her lips suddenly and decisively seeking his. They kissed for a few moments and then she returned to her previous position with her head on his shoulder.

"You are surprisingly good at that, Hans," she sighed contentedly.

"*Dankeschön.*"

He had another sip of the coffee and offered the flask to her. She had a bit and returned it. They sat together in the relative quiet of the ship's sounds for a few moments before Hans spoke again.

"Have you decided what it is you wish to do with yourself after you give up the life of a pirate, Annika?"

"I am not going to, Hans. I will be the Captain-Gunner of the *Bloody Rose* until the day my sword falls from my lifeless fingers," she said in a quiet yet matter-of-fact tone.

Hans looked down in shock at her nestled against his shoulder. "You cannot be serious. You will be dead within a decade."

She looked up at him, clearly offended. She sat up and shifted away from him.

"Neither Arietta or Blackheart are showing any signs of slowing down, and they are both ten years or more older than I. Gwendoline started as a pirate older than either of them. I live every day I am aboard the *Bloody Rose*, Sauder. Every day. I am not some droning house wife or *babushka* who is worried about the cut of her petticoats or if the paper upon the walls of her husband's study is of the latest fashion. Besides, what do you care, Sauder? You are leaving in two or three weeks for your cozy rich man's life. What befalls me is hardly your concern."

"That is unfair, Annika, and you know it. Of course I care. Of course I will continue to care. I will care about all of you. My stay aboard the *Bloody Rose* and getting to know her crew has changed the way I see the world as well as my understanding of it. You, Arietta and even Blackheart will be people I will always wonder about when I sit in my office in London or the smoking room at the house in the Cotswolds. But you, most of all, Annika."

"Really?" she asked cautiously.

He looked at her for a long moment and then grabbed her one-handed by the front of her shirt and pulled her to him. Her gasp of surprise was cut short by his mouth upon hers. He kissed her for a timeless moment with an intensity that surprised them both.

"Yes, really, you little Russian witch. You are the only woman aboard this ship whose lips I have tasted. That should tell you something," he whispered to her as she settled down with her head on his chest.

"Yes, well, I know you had more than a passing interest in Arietta," she teased. He spluttered a denial that resulted in peals of laughter from the Russian brunette.

"I do not care or mind, Hans" she said with a chuckle. "Arietta has that effect on almost every man she meets. Some women, too. I will warn you, however, that I would be somewhat grumpy with you if I find out you chose to bed her before me." She winked at him and poked his chest.

"You have little to fear of that, my dear. My moral compass not withstanding, she is the *Kapitän's* woman, and I have no interest in running afoul of Michael O'Raedy."

"The *Kaptan's* woman?" she asked, looking at him in clear puzzlement. He reminded her of O'Raedy and Itala's drunken arrival aboard the *Bloody Rose* in al-Myāh Wālsma, Egypt, and their subsequent retirement to the captain's cabin together.

Annika started giggling impishly for several seconds while Hans looked at her with a lofted eyebrow. "Hans ... oh, Hans. You are delightfully naive sometimes," she said, still giggling. "All the women aboard this scow have slept with the *Kaptan* a few times. Usually after we have been aground drunk with him somewhere. Except Aunt Gwen of course. So old fashioned; she only has eyes for Alexi. They are such a sweet couple."

He blinked at her in shock. "You are kidding?"

"About Michael and the Ladies of the Rose? *Nyet*. Whenever we are in some port where there is a *kaptan's* party or some official function he'll ask one of us to be his arm candy for the night. He usually asks which ever one of us is closest to the nationality of the host. He knows how to show a girl a good time, he dances well, he is quite a flatterer in public, and the parties are always fun," she said while gently tracing the line of his jaw with her index finger. "He is an average lover with an average appetite ... but really, average is better than not at all, particularly if it eases an itch and creates a bit of good will with your boss, *nyet*?"

Hans was silent for a few moments as he considered this piece of news. On one hand it seemed rather scandalous that Blackheart would use the women of his crew in such a fashion. On the other, thinking back to the stay in al-Myāh Wālsma, the "Ladies of the Rose" were just as aggressive about seeking trysts as any of the men were.

"You are offended at the notion I have slept with Blackheart, *da*?" she asked carefully.

"*Nein*, I am trying to determine why any of it bothers me at all. From what I saw between him and Arietta, he does give a choice in the matter. You have said he gives a fine evening out. From what I have seen, pirates of either gender are fairly casual about who they take to their beds and what it means," he said thoughtfully.

"But?" she prompted.

"But it still feels wrong to me," he said as he scratched at his brow. "It is just that I have always been taught that the joining of a man and a woman should be about love. Not scratching an itch, as you put it."

Annika sighed. "You are amazingly idealistic. Hans," she said gently, "there is no point falling in love with a pirate. We die tragically and without warning. Usually violently, as well. We have to keep a layer of insulation between us and those around us. We never know when someone's hammock will be empty and their clothes will be on the backs of someone new."

She shifted so she was lying atop him, looking down at him eye-to-eye. She brushed a lock of hair from his face. "You, Hans," she said quietly, "you have the luxury of love. You will not have to worry about the woman you choose being shattered by a cannonball, or scalded to death, or run through with a sword, or falling to her doom from a mile in the sky. None of that applies in your world. The worst you need to worry about is making sure you visit a credible physician and keep to a reasonable routine of exercise."

They looked at each other for a long moment and then she rose to her feet, standing on the deck beside him. "Annika," he began uncertainly.

"Oh, shut up, Hans," she said with a light smile. "We are star-crossed. I cannot afford to love you because you will leave my life all too soon, one way or the other. I cannot be a broken-hearted, weeping woman as the Captain-Gunner of the *Bloody Rose*."

She buckled on her weapons belts and picked up her mask and gauntlets. She walked to the door and opened it. She paused and then looked back at him over her shoulder.

"You cannot afford to love me because you must be able to give your heart to whoever she will be with a clean conscience. And you will not share your bed with me even for a night unless it is for love. I understand all of that. It does not make any of this any easier," she said.

"For either of us," he replied.

*****

"If it were not for bad luck," Blackheart groused as he lowered his spyglass, "we would have no luck at all. A bloody convoy."

"Take it as a compliment, *Gospodin* Blackheart. It means that we, along with whoever else the Allies have hired as privateers, are causing enough grief that they are taking us seriously," Annika replied.

Hans shielded his eyes against the mid-morning sun with a hand. "So ... do we pretend we did not see this and just carry on?"

"Under normal conditions, I would say so, *Gospodin* Sauder," Annika said as she sighted the lead ship with her range finder. "But I think we can pull this off if we are not too concerned about taking prey."

"Oh?' said Blackheart, turning to face the Russian brunette. "What is on your mind, Captain-Gunner?"

"We put him to good use," she replied while jerking a thumb towards Hans. "The biggest dangers are the two frigates. So we hit them with rockets and then finish them with guns. We then use mines and rockets to destroy two of the merchants. If the Heavens are in alignment, we board the third merchantman and take her as prey."

"Careful, young Sauder. Being put to good use by the Ladies of the Rose is not always as fine a proposition as it sounds," Blackheart gave a bawdy chortle.

"I will keep that in mind, *Herr Kapitän*. I trust you are a man of experience in these matters," Hans returned dryly.

The Planesman snorted in amusement and then clamped his mouth shut in terror while staring fixedly at his gauges. The three officers looked at him for a moment and then Blackheart broke into a grin at the other two.

"So, Mister Sauder, what do you think of the Captain-Gunner's plan?" the Englishman asked.

"Casually insane," the German replied in amusement. "However, that seems to be the daily routine aboard the *Bloody Rose*, so I will make ready for the first shot."

"That's the spirit, Mister Sauder. Captain-Gunner, make bells and whistles for action. Engineering, I want eighty knots." Blackheart began rattling off the familiar string of orders that once again took the *Bloody Rose* and her crew of pirates-turned-privateers into the fray. Routine and familiarity were important aboard a ship like this, Hans reflected. Even in moments of bone-chilling terror, there would be something you instinctively knew how to do and recognized its importance to the situation.

The *Bloody Rose* pushed as high as she dared to get into a diving position on the Russian convoy now below her. She carefully manoeuvred to set her attack from the sunward side, all too aware that surprise would be crucial. Every moment she spent jockeying for position was another opportunity for a Russian lookout to spot her.

In the end, it was almost a tie. One of the frigates turned toward the diving *Bloody Rose* and launched smoke rockets in a colour-coded challenge at the same time as the first Cudahawk went over the stern railing.   The three merchants began to turn away while the second frigate turned towards the attacking Privateer even as the rocket struck the first frigate. The blast tore apart most of the bow section and a barrage from the *Bloody Rose*'s twelves and eights finished the job. The stricken frigate began an end-over-end tumble to the earth more than three-quarters of a mile below.

The second frigate fired with all guns and marked several hits on the convoy's assailant. As the frigate manoeuvred to screen the fleeing merchants from the Privateer, the *Bloody Rose* fired another rocket which crashed into the engineering area. A second explosion spewed flames, smoke and debris in all directions around the Russian frigate. The *Bloody Rose* flew past and fired all her bearing guns, tearing lethal wounds into her victim. Two balloon-mines dropped over the stern rail finished the job as the heavily damaged frigate haplessly wheeled between them while trying to give pursuit.

A third ship-to-ship rocket blew apart a merchantman. The privateer did not even bother firing cannons at the burning wreck as they went past.

One merchant struck her colours and stopped her engines, apparently having decided there was nothing they could do about the wolf currently amongst the sheep. The other gamely tried to flee, only to have two volleys of cinder balls leave her a crippled wreck, burning and drifting in the cold air of four thousand feet above the countryside of the Russian Empire.

In the Steering House of the *Bloody Rose*, Blackheart applauded and Annika sketched a bow. "Well planned, Captain-Gunner, and well executed, Captain-Rockets. That was a thing of beauty to behold. Let us get alongside that remaining ship and pay her cargo holds a visit!"

The surrendered merchant was packed full of expensive luxuries from across Russia including fine vodkas, caviars, mink and sable furs and fine porcelains. The Russian crew surrendered without a fight and did everything they could to ensure their own safety. The Privateers could scarcely believe their luck. They took the captured ship to five thousand feet, and set about the task of transferring her cargo. If all went well, by morning, they would have their holds packed with the most lucrative haul any of them had recently seen.

*****

Dawn broke, filling the Russian sky with a luminous red fire that tinted everything with its ruby glow. The *Bloody Rose* was more than four hundred miles north and east of the Russian border with Allied Europe. She was patrolling westward about twenty-five hundred feet above the home ground of the enemy, running parallel to a cloud front on her starboard side that threatened unpleasant weather within its mass.

The burly frigate burst out of the cloud wall on the quarter of the *Bloody Rose*. Her lines were aggressively cut, her sails sharp and tight, the white, blue and red tricolour of Russia flew from her staff, and across her stern was painted in gold on black "*Severnyĭ Volk*". The "Northern Wolf" closed on her prey.

The *Bloody Rose* spotted her attacker with little time to act. She veered sharply and dove as a volley from the Russian's bow guns tore into her side even as she called her crew to defend her. A pair of Sargasso balloon-mines launched over the stern forced the Russian to veer; she cut a full circle and swept the mines aside with canister shot from a pair of her four bow guns.

The Russian dove sharply, undercutting the line the English ship was taking. She angled up smartly and fired her remaining two bow guns' worth of canister shot into the electric propeller pods of her quarry. Flame, smoke and violently surplussed parts streamed from two of the pods.

The *Severnyĭ Volk* took a broadside as she flew past and then surprisingly reversed her engines at full power, crying and shaking in every joint as she came to a halt. Grappling harpoons fired from the Russian, streaming their metal cables and slamming into the English Privateer.

The two ships struck at each other one last time with their four pounders loaded with grapeshot and then readied for the boarding action. The two crews traded pistol and rifle fire as the two ships were pulled together and then collided into each other at the gunwales.

The battle was fierce and cruel. The Privateers were at the disadvantage, having been caught unprepared at breakfast bells by the attack. They had also suffered at the skill of the Russian marksmen during the exchange of gunfire.

Blackheart was in the thick of the battle, having left no more of this fight to chance. In his hands were a pair of electrical weapons. His sword looked like a pair of rapier blades with a "Jacobs Ladder" between them. He electrocuted any swordsman whose blow he parried. In his other hand was a pistol that fired short range bolts of electricity that dropped a man as effectively as any revolver.

Hans was fighting at the top of the stairs leading to the Steering House, being pressed by a Marine and Sailor who were doing their formidable best to be rid of him. All he could do was defend himself, hoping for an ally. The door to the Steering House flew open and Watch Officer Onora Lynch stepped out with a pistol in hand and without warning or comment blew the Marine's brains out. The Russian Sailor went down the ladder hard as Hans slammed him in the chest with his boot.

Two Russian Marines hurled fire bombs at the windows of the Steering House, engulfing it in flames. Hans and two other crew worked with water from deck barrels to quench the fire before it caught into the wood of the structure. Hans and the two crew rushed the two Marines and engaged them as quickly as they could to prevent a repeat while the Steering House crew finished with the firefighting.

Steel clashed. Wind howled. Smoke swirled. Gun fire rang out. Rain began to fall. Men and women screamed and tumbled to the deck. Blood soaked into timber.

It was impossible to any science known to Hans that he could have heard Annika's next words. The cacophonous tumult of battle separated them both by more than a dozen paces. The chaos of the pitched fight filled his senses. In later years, looking back, he would never be able to understand nor adequately explain how he knew exactly where she was or what she said. And yet, as clearly as though the words were whispered in his ear, he did.

"I am... sorry... Hans..." she said.

His head instinctively snapped around to where she was, knowing with exact certainty where he would find her. The image he beheld was the stuff of nightmares.

The Russian Lieutenant's sword was driven straight through the front of her corset, having slipped between two of the armoured bones. It had stopped half way along its thrust, having fetched up on a duraluminum bone in the back. Her eyes were wide with shock and her attempt to draw an avenging pistol failed clumsily; it tumbled to the deck. Her sword fell in what felt like slow motion to Hans, landing on the deck with a sound of cannon fire.

He heard her voice clearly in his mind from just a few short days ago. *"You will not have to worry about the woman you choose being... run through with a sword... None of that applies in your world... I will be the Captain-Gunner of the Bloody Rose until the day my sword falls from my lifeless fingers..."*

"no... No... NO!!!" he screamed. The Russian sailor about to strike him died instantly as the scimitar seemed to move of its own, slicing the Russian's blade in two pieces as though it were made of *papier-mâché*. It cut through the Russian's collar bone with equal ease and did not stop until it reached his belt. Not that Hans noticed. Everything was a dull grey wash of cold rage.

Three more Russians died in the dozen charging steps he took to reach Annika and her assailant. The Russian Lieutenant was still trying to pull his trapped sword from her armour. The pirates between them simply knew to get out of his way; they had seen Sauder in action like this before, even if they did not yet know the reason or the severity.

The Russian Lieutenant grabbed Annika's sword from the deck to defend himself from the oncoming German. It did him no good. Hans swept the legs out from under him, grabbed the sword from his grip, and nailed him straight to the deck with it through his left lung. He then scooped up the Captain-Gunner's tri-barrel pistol as he came to his feet.

Hans cocked the primary hammer and fired all three barrels into the Russian's terrified face. He might have been begging for mercy. Even if Hans had been able understand Russian, he would not have given it.

It was as though the scimitar in his hand could sense his need for vengeance. Everything he swung at over the next few minutes died. Swords, bucklers, leather, flesh, bone; nothing was proof against its scything arc. He was caught rather off-guard by Blackheart stepping in from his off-side and belting him across the face with all the force the back of his ham fist could deliver. Hans reeled from the blow.

"Are you listening NOW, you damned kraut?" Blackheart roared at him. Hans hesitated, trying to find comprehension. Blackheart slapped him again. "What about NOW?"

"*Ja! Ja!*" Hans nodded while trying to clear the ringing in his ears.

"You have done enough up here, Sauder! Get her down to the Doctor before she bleeds out, ye damned fool! Leave making the Russians pay in blood for this to me, man. You have done more than enough to satisfy your account with them. Go. GO, I said!"

Hans nodded dumbfoundedly and held Annika's limp form in an arm against him. He looked around to see Cemil and MacIssac appear out of the fray beside him.

"Git yer lard arse under way, ye stupid Kraut," MacIssac said with a wink. "Nuthin' in Heaven above or Hell below will stop us from gettin' ye two te the hatch."

Hans nodded and sheathed his bloodied sword. He cradled her in his arms and said "Thank you."

"Dunnae thank me. Ye earned it. Ye fight like a man possessed when ye takes it te mind," MacIsaac said with his gap-toothed grin. "I ain't about te be accused o' fightin' weaker than ye."

*****

Hans leaned with his back and one foot against the wall, his arms crossed and his head bowed, outside of the infirmary. The battle was over and the Privateers had won, snatching victory from the jaws of defeat, if at harsh cost. Blackheart had rallied the crew to the cause of vengeance for their beloved Captain-Gunner and the crew of the *Bloody Rose* were suddenly transformed men that nothing less than an act of Armageddon could stop. He still did not have details; he had been forbidden by Koblinski from returning to the fray. He was more than welcome to send any Russian coming down the ladder packing for home, but he was not to return above decks without the Doctor's express permission.

He had assisted many members of the *Bloody Rose*'s crew down the ladder and into the Sickbay, and then back out and up. He was there; he might as well be useful. The one person that he had not seen sent to their hammock was Annika.

The door opened and Hans stood up. Gwendoline Coline looked at him sternly and then the expression on her face softened. *"Oh, vous pauvre fou.* Come in. Quickly. Come, come!"

She ushered him in. The infirmary looked like a slaughter house with bloody sheets on the floor and the three occupied beds. Annika was on the bed furthest from the door and Hans took a step towards her.

"*Pan* Sauder, if you are considering running to her side, please consider that the deck will hurt a great deal when I shoot you in the face with a jet of spray-ether." Hans stopped and looked at the bearded Pole standing beside him with a cheery grin, bloody apron, blinking surgical goggles and his pocket gas-jet in hand.

"Ah, excellent. I am glad to see *Pan* O'Raedy's enthusiasm for returning you to your senses did not damage your ability to reason cogently. To answer the question foremost in your mind, she will live. Perhaps she should not have, but she will. Now, I need to keep you from being a morose and useless bag of distress. So take this," he said putting a medical bag into Hans somewhat baffled possession, "and visit every sleeping bay. Women included. You stop at any hammock that has been tagged with a red card. One injection of the blue vial, left arm. One injection of the green vial, right arm. A single unit of each, and no more; the side of the syringe is clearly marked. Note time, pulse and respiratory rate in this journal, beside their name. Do you understand?"

"Yes. She will be fine?" Hans asked anxiously.

Alexi shook his head. "She was not 'fine' when either of us first met her, *Pan* Sauder. However, she will live to resume her duties aboard the *Bloody Rose*. Now," he said, pushing up his goggles with a sigh. "Since I notice the object of your overriding concern, please repeat to me the instructions I gave you."

Hans did so, though he had to stop mid way and think. "But, *Herr Döktor*... I am not a physician."

"Neither is he," Gwen chuckled from where she was mixing a batch of something. "However, modern medicine being what it is, injections are difficult to make a disaster of. Off you go; you will do fine," she said with a warm and encouraging voice.

Hans nodded obediently, checked the contents of the bag, and stepped out into the hallway. It was not until he had closed the door that the Head Nurse's initial comment sank in. He paused at the door, about to reopen it when he clearly heard their voices.

"Irreverent trollop! You are the only person aboard that knows that."

"*Oh, calme toi, cheri.* You were the best money could buy for pirates until I happened along. I will hold my tongue on this matter in the future. *L'homme* Sauder is very clever. He would have figured it out eventually."

******

Hans was thankful for the Doctor's assigned work, much as Alexi had implied he might be. The task of visiting all hundred or so hammocks aboard the ship and giving such mercy as he could, kept his mind and his emotions very busy. The green vial was a sedative; the blue was an advanced military-grade healing serum. A dose of each needed to be administered every hour. It took him nearly that long to reach every hammock with a red tag affixed to it.

He was shocked to find Arietta in a red-tagged hammock. She grinned weakly at him. A blow had swollen her left eye shut, her rich lips were bruised and split and heavy bandages were wrapped around her stomach. "I got two in the Propulsion Room, Hans. It was three, four and five that caused us some problems. I do not think Salvador made it ... the stupid kid took one for me. I am pretty sure that Vis is okay. I might be off my feet for a few days ... do you think you can take my watch for me?"

He wiped an eye and nodded. "I ... I think so, Chief. It will only be for a few days, as you say. Now, I have a bit of medicine for you that will help. Have a good rest and know that your beloved engines are in good hands."

She giggled at him as he injected her with the sedative. "Good Hans ... yes, that is you all right ... Very Good Hans," she giggled again, her speech starting to slur. "Sometimes Too Good Hans ..." she sighed wistfully. She nodded and drifted off to sleep. It took him a moment to still his shaking hands enough to give her the second injection.

He returned to the sickbay after his second set of medical rounds. He knew there was not enough remaining in the vials for a handful more injections. He knocked on the door, and Auntie Gwen opened it. She nodded at him, and beckoned him in.

"Ah, *Pan* Sauder. Good to see you. Your first foray into medicine has gone well, I trust?"

"*Ja*, well enough, *Herr Döktor*," he answered with a nod.

"And how do you feel then, good sir?"

"I do not know where to begin, Alexi. So much suffering ... people I know and respect ... and all I can do is administer a needle. I feel ... helpless. Weary. Done," he sighed heavily.

"*Gute Nachrichten dann mein Freund*," the Polish gentleman said in surprisingly clear German. "It means you are likely still human inside, regardless of reports I have received to the contrary. Now, take this, drink it, and go to your hammock."

"But what about ..."

"You are exhausted physically and emotionally, *Pan* Sauder," Koblinski said sternly. "Thus your options are to sleep soundly in your hammock because you did as I asked, or on my sickbay floor in a heap because you did not. Your choice, while you still have it, would be?" he trailed off expectantly, holding the gas-jet up by his face with a genial smile. Hans opted for his hammock.

*****

The *Bloody Rose* ran low and fast across the Scorchlands back into the supposed safety of Allied airspace. By the time the morning sun had risen, she had put almost six hundred miles between the battle with the *Severnyĭ Volk* and her current position. She was challenged twice by Allied warships on patrol, but the challenge-and-reply book they had been given held true and they were allowed to pass without incident.

Hans joined Blackheart in the Steering House, which still smelled sooty from the exterior fire it had suffered. Blackheart looked at him in mild surprise.

"There is no way, Mister Sauder, that you are here to relieve me of watch. You are not on until the afternoon bells, and only if the good Doctor clears you. So, what is on your mind?"

"I was told by a couple of the crew that you were dissatisfied with my skill at battle yesterday afternoon," Hans challenged.

Blackheart cast an eye over the German and nodded. "Helms and Planes. Lock your gears and go for coffee. I feel like flying the old girl myself for a while. I will send

Mister Sauder to the mess to let you know when I need you back."

The two crewmen looked at each other, looked at the Englishman, looked at the German, mumbled thanks and apologies and then tried not to sprint as they left the Steering House. Blackheart closed the yawning door behind them.

"I think you have taken insult, man."

"Should I not? *'If that weak-spleened, thin-gutted German mother's boy can fight like that for his Captain-Gunner, the least you scallywags can do is try to keep up'?'"* Hans said coldly.

Blackheart burst out laughing. "Did I say that? Damn, man. That is Saint Crispen's to this rabble. Look, Mister Sauder. I know you have gotten yourself all caught up in the Russian minx's skirts, but fighting like a madman only gets you killed. You are an excellent fighter, Sauder, but foaming at the mouth and ignoring orders makes you a rabid dog. I need men to fight for me, not dogs."

There was nothing more said between them for a long moment until the Englishman broke the silence. "If," he said casually while he checked the path ahead of the ship with his spyglass, "that twitch in your cheek and that clenched fist means you plan to take me to task over my remarks, I would ask that you get to it. Just do recall that at the least, you will be challenging my position as Captain. Thus, at the least, I will leave you in the good Doctor's sick bay with a broken wing and a concussed skull. You might want to consider that in your decision."

After a dangerous moment of silence, he turned his head to look at Sauder without lowering his spyglass. "Some day, Sauder. Some day," he said cryptically. "But not today. We both have too much to lose. Dismissed. Go report to Koblinski. I need you back in my Propulsion Room."

*****

"Speaking with *Pan* O'Raedy recently, were you, Hans?" Alexi asked him as he scribbled something down on his notepad.

"Yes. Why?" he asked stiffly as he sat on a plank set across two adjacent counters. The bloody laundry had been removed and the entire space scrubbed with something astringent smelling. The three most seriously wounded but savable crew occupied the exam beds still; Annika was among them. Nurse Coline was out on bed-side rounds.

"Elevated blood pressure, somewhat accelerated heart rate and shallowness of breath. In a word, Hans, you are quite clearly in a snit about something," he said bemusedly, waving his fountain pen as he spoke. "Generally speaking, Captain Blackheart is the source of such ills with you."

Hans scowled. "So who are you?" he demanded.

The Polish doctor lowered his pen slowly. "A very interesting question, *Pan* Sauder. One best not answered here. Shall we adjourn to the Tank Hold?"

Hans nodded and gestured for the other man to precede him. Koblinski nodded, pocketed a few items off a nearby counter-top, and scribbled a note. "So Gwendoline knows what is needed next for the patients," he explained, and then headed out into the hallway. Hans followed him and closed the door.

They made their way to the Tank Hold. It was empty of other crew, as it usually was. It seemed as though no real damage had happened here during the last battle. Hans closed the hatch door behind them with a clang, and dogged it shut.

"Again, I ask you ... who are you, '*Herr Döktor*'?"

"You always start your interrogations with the wrong question, *Pan* Sauder. To know who am *I*, you first need to know who is *she*," Alexi said with an expressive gesture that came very close to infuriating Hans.

"She? You mean the Captain-Gunner? Annika?"

"Yes," Koblinski replied, taking a seat on a catwalk and then shifting somewhat to make himself comfortable.

"Fine. Who is she, then? I know she joined her first ship five years ago. Beyond that, she would not tell me," Sauder growled impatiently, beginning to pace.

"Now, I will request that you refrain from any urge to shoot or stab me during this conversation, Hans. It would complicate our friendship somewhat. She is the runaway daughter of Yuri Ilyich Maksim," Koblinski said. "You may know him as the 'Nightmare of Nizhny Novgorod'?"

Hans' blood went cold. Yuri Maksim was the sort of bogeyman that mothers frightened their children with. Both his laboratory near the Russian city of Nizhny Novgorod and the prison that fed it with raw materials were infamous across Allied Europe. While he was an undisputed master at the creation of Galvanotaurs, he was also reputed to prefer his source of parts fresh enough to be "still screaming". Some of the other rumours that came out of that laboratory were less savoury, still.

"Are you sure about this?" Hans asked carefully.

"Very," Alexi replied.

Hans nodded. That explained a great deal about Annika's disinterest in revisiting her life before becoming a pirate, he thought. He could not imagine what having a monster like that as a father must have been like.

"So what does that have to do with you, Alexi?" Hans asked, leaning against a vertical strut, opposite where the man was seated.

"Are you familiar with an American organization called the 'Pinkerton National Detective Agency'?" the bearded

Pole asked. Hans shook his head. "Hmm. Well, as the name implies, they are a company that supplies professional detectives to anyone who wishes to hire them for an investigation. For example, a missing person's case."

Hans lofted a brow, starting to see where this might be going. "There is a similar company in Russia, called '*Ivanovich bezopasnosti i rassledovaniĭ*'. I worked for them up until two years ago," Koblinski said.

"Which was when you joined the *Bloody Rose*. You were hired by *Herr* Maksim to find Annika, I would guess?"

"Correct." The two men looked at each other for a long moment.

"I note that you are not doing much detective work these days," Hans commented dryly.

"No, not much at all. You see, when I finally caught up with Annika – Nadezhda is an assumed last name, as I am sure you now realize and for obvious reasons – there was no easy way to get close enough to her to make contact without getting my guts handed to me. I heard that the ship had no doctor and thus presented myself to Blackheart as such at a meeting aground. *Pan* O'Raedy is an intelligent man, and could see the benefits to having a physician of any stripe aboard and thus agreed."

"Clever of you. Beyond the part where you are not actually a physician of any stripe," Hans commented.

"I purchased a couple of very good illustrated books as part of establishing the sickbay on the *Bloody Rose*. I am a quick study and have always had a steady hand. The pirates knew no better. *Pan* O'Raedy has given me many opportunities to improve over the past two years."

"I see. So ... why are both of you still here? Why have you not reported your discovery to *Herr* Maksim, collected your bounty and ended this charade?" Hans asked carefully.

"It would be the wrong thing to do," Koblinski replied.

"Pardon?" Hans blinked.

"It would be the wrong thing to do," he repeated. "In the first month I was aboard the *Bloody Rose*, it was obvious that she had made a successful life for herself. It was also quite obvious she wanted no part of the life of her past. Her opiate habit is symptomatic of that. If I were to have revealed myself to her, she would quite likely have killed me to ensure her safety from her father. There was certainly no way I could even conceive of kidnapping her beyond hoping to catch her in an opiate stupor somewhere. And then what? Trying to get her back to her father without her full cooperation would have been both impossible and fatal. Even if I had been successful, I would have robbed her of everything she had achieved for herself with her own sweat, tears and blood."

Hans nodded. "Quite a fix you were in. So that explains why she is still here, but not why you are."

"Put yourself in my shoes, Hans. Do you relish the idea of having to personally deceive the 'Nightmare of Nizhny Novgorod' about the failure of your assignment, and spend the rest of your life hoping he never finds out otherwise? Being the doctor of a pirate ship is a far safer job. I have chosen to remain politely 'missing, presumed lost' to my employer and their notorious patron."

"That explains the bullet-proof corset, then," Hans said thoughtfully. "I thought it odd that you would have given such a thing to Annika as a birthday present. It implied, amongst other things, that you knew her birthday. Which you could not know, since she will not speak of her past."

"You are frighteningly perceptive at times, Hans," Alexi replied, somewhat shocked.

"Thank you. Blackheart knows the truth, of course. Who else does?"

"Annika does; she drew the same conclusion you did about the corset and confronted me about it. I was able to convince her I have every ... erm, *vested* interest in her whereabouts remaining a mystery to her father," he chuckled. "Blauchuk did, as well."

"Blauchuk?" Hans said, puzzled.

"Yes. Annika stole him when she ran away from home. He was her guardian and protector for many years."

Hans whistled. "A cunning and dangerous woman indeed. That was quite a *coup*," he said, shaking his head. Yuri Maksim must have been beside himself, he thought. He paused and then tilted his head, looking at Koblinski.

"So, she is about my age ... twenty-two ..."

"Twenty-one, actually," Alexi corrected.

"Well enough, then. So she started her life as a pirate at ..." Hans blinked and stalled as he did the math. "Sixteen? So she would have run away at fifteen? Good Heavens!"

Koblinski shook his head. "Thirteen. She was thirteen; it was her birthday present to herself."

There was dead silence between the two men for several moments as Hans digested the notion of a thirteen year old girl and her Galvanotaur making their way from Russia, somehow traversing the Scorchlands, passing into Allied Europe and eventually becoming an airship pirate. It was utterly astonishing to him.

"I heard you did not cope entirely well with Annika's injury, initially?" Koblinski asked with a wry note.

Hans hung his head and considered the toe of his boot for a moment before answering. "*Nein*," he said quietly without looking up. "Not very well at all. I ... well, I took leave of my senses. I ... have never felt such ... hatred ... before. I killed ... mercilessly. Remorselessly."

"Gave yourself quite a fright, did you?" Alexi asked sympathetically.

Hans nodded.

"You are quite caught up in *Panna* Annika, Hans. Any man reacts savagely to the fall of a friend. Any man reacts angrily to having even the most unlikely of hopes and dreams taken away. Any man reacts violently when a woman he cares for is harmed. Up there, today, was all of those things, at once. I do not think you need to worry that you are becoming some bloodthirsty monster, Hans. I do, however, think you need to accept that Annika's chosen life makes moments like today unavoidable, for both of you. And then you need to decide if that is something you can live with, as a price. Eventually, one day, she will arrive in my office beyond my skill. All that saved her today was Gwendoline's experience. It was barely enough."

Koblinski lowered himself to the deck from the spot he had been sitting. Hans looked up at him. The detective-turned-doctor dusted himself off and gave Hans a nod. "You need to decide if that is something you can live with," he repeated.

Hans nodded. "*Dankeschön, Herr Döktor*," Hans said quietly.

"*Moja przyjemność, mój przyjaciel*. Which reminds me ... do not repeat my lack of official standing, if you please? Gwendoline has a quick tongue, and while that does have its value, this is not one of those times. I doubt the rest of the crew would care that I am not really a doctor, but it is difficult to tell who might decide that they need my blood spilt at the loss of a friend who perished in my care."

Hans nodded. "A lady I once met told me that '*...we all have our secrets, and I have learned that some are best left covered*'. Yours is safe with me."

"Brussels And London; a Book And a Gun"

Diary Entry for June 23rd, 1888

Tomorrow my career as a Pirate ends. One might think that I could hardly wait. Oddly, my impending departure leaves me with mildly mixed feelings. I will miss my friends aboard the Bloody Rose. But it is time that I return to my responsibility to my family.

To the best of my knowledge, my parents are unaware I am in London. It being summer they have moved, as we always do, to the country home in the Cotswolds. It is a grand place with many fond memories and I am looking forward to showing it to Annika and Arietta.

I hope to convince the two of them to accompany me tomorrow to meet my family and to see the country estate. To part ways with me in my world, as it were.

I realize that I am getting rather ahead of myself. Allow me to retrace my path from Russia to London.

The battle with the Russian Frigate, the Severnyĭ Volk, was five days ago. While Kapitän O'Raedy claims a victory, I cast our circumstances to be more in the vein of "we lost less" than the Russians did. This is not the same as a victory, in my eyes.

One man in ten died. Another three in ten was injured sufficiently that they were unable to stand some of their watches. When you combine our losses with the fifteen crew who died as a result of the Dragon and the eleven others who perished in Russian airspace prior to that, we are barely a functioning crew any more.

I have been essentially running the Propulsion Room with Aaron Visivald during our flight home. We have been working in 8 hour shifts around the clock, as Arietta was only allowed to return to her duties the night before we arrived in London.

We ran from Russia straight to the commercial airship docks of Brussels, where we spent a day unloading cargo. As crippled as we were for man power, Kapitän O'Raedy opted to pay for local stevedores to unload the ship, which Andre Dubé tells me is highly unusual. Normally, if you are not either a Pirate or a prisoner, you do not cross the gunwale of the Bloody Rose. Other than a night aground with a few of my crewmates, the visit to Brussels was both quick and quiet.

From there we made way straight for London, England. Anyone who was still lying injured in their hammock was transferred aground to a private hospital for paid expert care. Fortunately, that was only a handful. Almost everyone who survived was back on their feet, including Arietta and Annika. The healing serum that we have possession of is amazing. I sincerely hope that wherever Alexi found it, he has ready access to more in the future.

I contacted Camilla Williams, of British Intelligence, at the Kapitän's request. She was rather pleased to see me again and our rendezvous in a local restaurant was very pleasant. She was very interested in the encrypted book we found and agreed to arrange a handsome payment to be delivered to the Bloody Rose. She was good to her word, and given the sum we were received, I would say that the book has some very interesting things to say. I must admit to some disappointment in knowing I will never find out what that was all about.

I "Paid My Respects" to both Chief Arietta and to Kapitän O'Raedy as is part of the Traditions. A full third of my final shares to each of them. It felt rather odd to do so, and yet, it was also a sort of a closure.

Annika bought me a ridiculous revolver. Leave it to the Americans to confuse a carbine with a pistol. It is a beast of a gun with a pistol barrel mounted over a small shotgun barrel. She taught me how to use it, as well. She commented she very much doubted I would ever have cause to fire it in anger, but I would have something distinct to remember her by. I very much doubt I will ever need help in remembering the Captain-Gunner of the Bloody Rose.

It is time I closed this entry and this Diary. As of tomorrow, this text will simply serve as a reminder of an education unlike any other I could imagine to receive.

*****

Both the sun and the *Bloody Rose* were descending from the sky over the city of Brussels. She was running only on her port-side propeller pod. The centre-line pod was lowered for apparent use as well, but that was only because the retraction mechanism was heavily damaged. Neither it nor the pod's motor functioned any longer.

Her approach was not as clean or as decisive as it normally was. It took two tries to get the first line to the dock. Her decks were thinly crewed and it was longer than usual before she was fully secured fore and aft, with the gangway extended from the platform to her quarter deck.

In the Propulsion Room, Hans looked over from the Watch Keeper's chair and nodded at Aaron Visivald, his Norwegian crew mate. "That is it, Vis. Put the EMIPALE to stand-by, and let us get started with shutting everything down. We will be here at least for a full day, so with some luck we can make some more progress on the repairs. I would love to have things in better shape than this by the time the Chief can make it back down the ladder."

"Aye-aye, sir," the other man replied with a nod and began stepping through the process of safely shutting down the electromagnetic lift engine.

"You know, it almost bothers me to have you call me 'Sir'," Hans commented as he moved to a set of valves and began closing them.

"So you have said, Sir. However, it comes with the territory. You accepted a Commission. That makes you an Officer whether you are shooting rockets or running the Propulsion Room. In the strictest of terms, you out-rank Chief Itala but I would sincerely recommend against challenging her authority between this deck and deck-head," the big Norwegian said with a chuckle.

Hans laughed aloud. "She would string me up off the Number Five riser with my own guts as a noose. No, no, I am hardly that courageous or foolhardy."

"How is she doing, anyway, Sir?"

Hans frowned before he answered. "She is getting stronger every day. She lost a lot of blood, but her wounds did not get infected, thankfully. Another day or two and I expect *Döktor* Koblinski will clear her for duty again."

"Let her know that I said you are doing a lousy job as the In Charge for the Propulsion Room and I cannot wait for her to get back down here, if you please, Sir?" Visivald chortled.

Hans grinned at him. "I will."

*****

Even with half the injured now to the status of either whole or at least walking wounded, everything took longer. The Mediterranean Menace and her crew had been harshly mauled in their confrontation with the Red Bear of Russia, and the effects were being felt everywhere.

Once the Propulsion Room had been squared away and secured for the stay alongside the dock, Hans and Visivald went to the weather deck to lend a hand to the various jobs that the Gunner-Marines were working on. There was much to do, and not nearly enough able hands to do it.

"*Bonsoir*, André ," Hans said with a smile.

"*Oh, allo*, Hans ... *comment ca-va*?" the Franco-Brit replied.

Hans thought for a moment and gave up. "I know what you said ... I just cannot find the words in French to answer. I am well, thank-you. Do you and your men need help with anything?"

"I am impressed you are trying to learn French at all, *mon ami. Oui*, if you can lend a hand, we have a lot to do. *Le Capitaine* has told me he is hiring stevedores to unload, so we need to clear the working path from the hold to the hoists. That whole area over there needs to be rearranged."

"Stevedores? Really?"

"*Vraiment, mon ami*. I cannot think of a time before he has not insisted we bring our own goods aground. But ..." Dubé paused and then shrugged. "I also cannot think of us being ever so short on crew, either. So, we will watch their every move and let the locals do the lugging. It will be odd to have someone neither pirate nor *prisonniers* aboard. I will need to watch the Pirates as much as the Stevedores."

The objective was clearly to ensure there was nothing that the hired help could either hurt, hurt themselves on, or make off with. A guard rotation was established, the access route that the workers on the deck would be allowed to use planned and cleared and then ropes were run to mark the boundaries. Once the work began, the stevedores had clearly been told exactly who their clients were, because they kept to themselves, worked hard and said little.

*****

While the apparent cost of the month in Russia had been harsh, the numbers were a very different story for Hans. Uncharacteristically, there was no great announcement on the upper decks about crew shares. The word was passed around to go talk to Chief Bridges for pay.

Hans nearly choked when Bridges passed him the stack of money. "Are you sure this is right, Chief?"

Bridges nodded amiably. "Aye, sir. Being an officer, I can explain the numbers to you. We were paid four thousand up front. Half that was paid out to the crew before the little to-do with the Dragon. So we had a baseline equal to about a solid month of raiding before we fired a shot. Now, that is all getting eaten up in repairs, refit and what-not. However, it meant that the cargo hold of Russian luxury goods and the like was all profit. We do not have to sell that load through back channels because it was all stolen legally. That means we made more money than we normally would have on a full set of holds. Do you follow?"

Hans nodded and gestured for him to continue. He was rather amused at the comment about "stolen legally" and it showed.

"Now, we are missing about forty of the lads and lasses. The Devil's Shares, as they say, Sir. That means they are not here to collect their shares, so that money goes back into paying everyone else. So, a share winds up being seven and three-quarters Pounds Stirling after all the paper is pushed and the ink is dried. You get one share for being here less than six months, Sir; another share is for being an engineer. On top of that, you are now an officer, so that earns you five more. That makes your total seven shares which is a Prince's wage of fifty-four Pounds and a few guineas. If you are thinking that is a lot of money, Sir, you are damned right but you earned it." Bridges grinned at him.

"Thank you, Chief. This is a bit of a dazzle pile."

"Well, Sir, if you are worried about how to spend it, I would be pleased to pass an evening assisting you with the task," the Chief Steward laughed.

*****

Hans made his way along the gas-lamp-lit thoroughfare, somewhat lost in his thoughts. He was supposed to be meeting a few of the other crew at a popular public house for a bit of relaxed carousing. "Laughing at the Devil" the Gunner-Marines called it. Spending an evening living well, just to tell the Devil – or God, or the Fates, or the Cosmos, whatever guiding force that it was that chose when one man died in a fight yet his two bunk-bay mates lived – that they had made it to port once again, and were laughing.

It was also a way of coming to terms with losses that, because of the way ships and men work, had been put aside until now. Say the names, tell the stories, drink the Oblivion, and convince yourself that you had some control over what happened and that you would not make the same sort of lethal mistake they had. Hans looked up at the thin veil of clouds covering the night sky and shook his head at some of the faces that played through his mind. They had been people he lived with for only a few weeks. Yet, he felt their loss keenly at some inscrutable level of comradeship that now dogged him.

Pirates, all of them. It did not matter, really, what the lawyers and newspapers called them because of who was paying and who was targeted. They were Pirates, every last one. Yet, as trite as it sounded, it seemed that he had been irreparably tainted by the knowledge that "Pirates were people, too".

"*If life was fair,*" Arietta had told him, "*the Bloody Rose would not exist for want of men and women to crew her. Every one of us, you included, are here because life is not fair.*" While perhaps there were other roads they all could have chosen, they had not.

His mind drifted to the notion of Annika's extraordinary flight as a 13 year-old girl and the life she had led to the point that she was now the Captain-Gunner of the *Bloody Rose*. Unbidden, the image of her 21 year-old athletic body dotted with tiny jewels of lake water and bathed in a glow of moonlight came to his mind. His breath caught with the memory of that moment and he realized his heart had quickened. He shook his head silently as he walked past a couple leading a brace of hounds for an evening walk

His lips pursed and he winced at the image of her in the sickbay, with the technologic paraphernalia of the most modern of available medicine protruding from various places in her arms, legs and chest in an attempt to keep her from being counted amongst the Devil's Shares for the cruise. He realized his fist was involuntarily clenched at the notion of her possible demise.

He understood that for some reason he could not identify, it was very important to him to be able to believe that Annika was alive, well and free. Of the two of them, he might be held by duty and responsibility, but Annika needed to be free.

He crossed a busy street, waiting for a bevy of horse carts, steam carriages and electric cars to pass in either direction. He kicked an empty can laying on the walk, watching as it bounced along and then rolled out into the street where it was flattened by a passing steam carriage. For some reason that darkly amused him.

He paused for a moment, suddenly feeling lost. He looked around, intellectually knowing full well where he was relative to the pub and the docks. He missed Annika, he realized. What he really wanted right now was to be perched on a rooftop somewhere with the "little Russian witch" curled up against him, drinking some of that fire-water she called vodka and discussing the Universe, debating ethics or talking about Life as Pirates.

"Bloody hell," he breathed, eliciting an arched eyebrow from a passing gentleman. He scratched at the back of his neck and then shook his head irritably. He set off again at a somewhat faster pace towards the Public House where he was meeting his shipmates.

This was, he thought in an exasperated tone, the exact circumstance he had been trying to avoid. Now what?

*****

It was a single night's trip at forty knots between Brussels and London. The *Bloody Rose* had departed the airship docks in the commercial district late in the afternoon, and got underway. She cruised at an uncharacteristically low altitude of 500 feet, and left her masts and sails furled. While things were quiet aboard, her look-outs kept steady watch on the space around them. Blackheart had wryly noted that challenge and authentication books only work if the other ship asks before shooting.

In the Propulsion Room, Hans turned at the sound of the upper deck hatch opening. To his pleasant shock, Arietta was slowly making her way down the ladder.

"Chief! *Willkommen zu Hause!*" he said with a broad grin.

She made her way over to him and hugged him much to his surprise. "It is good to be home, Hans. How's the old girl doing?"

"She is in good health, given what she has been through. Here, take a seat," he told her as he vacated the Watch Keeper's Chair. She smiled and slipped up into the chair, visibly relaxing.

She had lost some of her mass during her recovery, leaving her looking thin in the cheeks. The normally bright sparkle in her eyes seemed dim. Hans guessed that Alexi had cleared her to return to her beloved Propulsion Room as much to ease her boredom and frustration as anything else.

"Do not look at me like that, Hans," she said irritably. "I am fine."

"I did not ..."

"No, you did not say anything ... aloud. Your features did more than well enough. I am fine," she said firmly.

Hans nodded. "Well, then, I suppose you will be standing the whole watch with me. If that is the case, you can run the Station, and I will take a look at the General Exchange Manifold."

They spent most of the next few hours chatting as though they had not seen each other in a year. This was in spite of the fact that he had stopped in to visit her at her hammock at least every other day and the past two nights she had been at the table for the evening meal with rest of the officers. They talked about the ship, the crew, the last pay, the party in Brussels, the repairs to the Propulsion Room, and innumerable other things. She insisted on doing the upper deck rounds herself and he gave only cursory argument to that.

When she came back down, she took over the repairs list for the evening and he kept the Watch Keeper's Chair.

They continued talking in a mixture of engineering-related discussion and teasing banter.

Eventually, she was leaning against a pipe not far from the Chair, with both of them sipping from their coffee flasks in a companionable silence.

"So you are leaving in London, *sì*?" she asked as though they had just been discussing it.

"*Ja*," he nodded. "It is time."

"Have you told Annika yet?"

"*Nein*," he shook his head. "Well, not of late. She knew that I was only aboard until the end of the Russian adventure. That adventure is at its end, and thus, so is my time aboard the *Bloody Rose*."

There was another pause. "I heard that you had saved her life," she said after a sip from her flask.

"The *Döktor* did that. I simply carried her to the sick bay."

"*Di ringraziamento* ... thank-you. While I am given the impression you have more than a passing interest in her good health, it does not change that you saved a friend of mine. Doctor Koblinski is a gifted saver of lives, but he can do nothing for those lying in a pool on a deck somewhere else."

The voicepipe from the Steering House barked. They were coming up on London, and it was time to prepare. Arietta gave his shoulder a squeeze, favoured him with a smile and then moved to start with her part of the tasks associated with bringing the ship into port.

*****

While Paris was officially the "City of Lights", the view of London at night from the air was a challenger for the title, Hans thought. They had increased altitude over the hour prior to crossing the English Channel to 1500 feet to avoid over-zealous anti-airship guns at the coast. Once they had reached the North Sea, they had turned to steer down the border between England and France, leading into the Channel. Then, they had turned north, taking a lead mark to the Thames River and followed it to the inland side of the great city, which was where the airship docks were.

Hans was doing the last set of upper deck engineering rounds prior to docking to ensure everything was "ship-shape and Bristol-fashion" as O'Raedy liked to say. He paused at a railing, looking out over the lights of the city sprawling out around the ship in all directions.

"Beautiful, *nyet*?"

Hans turned, startled, to find Annika standing beside him in the dark. She put a finger to his lips gently and winked.

"I am cleared for duties, Hans," she said as quietly as could be managed over the sounds of the ship, the wind, and the city. "So do not fret. And if you grab me, hug me and kiss me in relief, I will cry and that will just make a scene in front of the crew, so please spare me that."

He blinked at her for a moment, and then burst out laughing. It was a laughter born out of tension, worry, and relief. She started grinning and within a few moments was consumed with the same laughter as he was. It took them a few moments to calm enough to speak again. Passing crew pointedly did not notice the outburst.

She had been at supper last evening, seeming somewhat frail and excused herself before dessert. Thus, Hans had not expected to see her either on her feet or on deck tonight. Even now, behind her goggles, he could see that a certain amount of being here was raw willpower.

"I cannot afford to not be here, *Gospodin* Sauder," she said as though reading his mind. "It is my job as the Captain-Gunner. There is much to do coming into a place like London. I have been uselessly on my back long enough." She gave him a bawdy wink from behind her goggles and he shook his head and chuckled.

"Yes, I see you are definitely in good health," he said with a laugh.

"Tomorrow will be very busy, and likewise tomorrow night," she said. "The night after, I would like an evening of your time, one last time, *Gospodin* Sauder. If you please, of course."

He nodded without hesitation. "I had planned on asking you," he replied.

She smiled and nodded. "Well, there is work to be done. I will speak to you later, Captain-Rockets."

"Likewise, Captain-Gunner," he replied.

*****

The *Bloody Rose* made secure her first line to the dock just before the witching hour. Since her holds had been emptied in Brussels, there was little to be organized beyond getting the ship properly secured alongside the dock and getting the gangplank run out and secured. By half-past, the few crew heading aground right away were stepping off, and the balance were arranging themselves for a quiet night.

The next morning, the eight members of the crew that were still sufficiently wounded that they could not stand watches were taken off the ship on litters. Hans learned from Alexi Koblinski that they were being sent to a very good private hospital in London. The ship had pre-paid the hospital the sum of thirty pounds Stirling per patient against the costs of their stay. If their care ran more than that, they would have to pay out of their own shares.

The *Bloody Rose* would likely be sailing again without them. Blackheart had said that they would be in town for five days. If they were able to make it back up the gangplank under their own steam, they were welcome.

Otherwise, if they wished to return as crew, they would have to catch up with her at one of her usual haunts. No wonder, Hans mused, that Arietta and Annika had been so adamant to return to duties before they arrived in London.

Jimeno Salvador, the Spanish engineer who had nearly gotten himself killed trying to save Arietta in the Propulsion Room, was one of the eight. He had lost part of his left arm just below the elbow as well as his left eye. Hans had made sure an envelope was tucked into the young man's belongings.

The envelope contained a ten-pound note and his contact information at his Father's London office. As well, it had a personal recommendation signed by Hans that the young Spaniard be hired as a service and repairs mechanic at the Southampton airship manufacturing and maintenance dock that the Sauder Industries owned.

It was the least Hans felt he could do.

*****

"Mister Sauder, my good man. Do you have any easy way of contacting your pretty English spy?" Blackheart asked him over cigars after the meal that evening.

Hans considered his answer for a moment and then nodded. "*Ja*, I have a telegraph exchange number for her," he said as he slowly exhaled the spiced smoke of his cigar.

Annika glanced at him with a flash of jealousy on her face. "You must have been in fine form, *Gospodin* Sauder, if she gave you her number after your first meeting with her," she said sweetly.

Blackheart and Aldebert both chuckled at Sauder's discomfiture. Arietta finished a sip of her port and spoke up while she set the glass down on the table before her.

"Oh, go easy on him, Annika. All he had to do was smile at you and you were happy to take him to breakfast," she teased.

Annika spluttered for a moment, Hans turned scarlet and the rest of the officers enjoyed a round of laughter at their expense. Before Annika had a chance to mount a defence or reply, O'Raedy quelled things with a raised hand.

"Tomorrow, Mister Sauder, I want you to make use of that telegraph exchange number. Get a hold of your pretty widow-spy and make arrangements to sell that Mystery Book to Whitehall through her. Start at six hundred pounds Stirling, but take any counter-offer above three hundred. If she balks, tell her we can always sell it back to the Russians."

"Aye-aye, *Herr Kapitän*. I will head into the city immediately after breakfast."

*****

He walked along the cobblestone streets in the morning fog of London. While warm, the air was laden with a moisture that coated everything, bringing with it an unpleasant chill. He turned up the collar of his coat and adjusted his gloves. He had left his sword belt aboard the ship. Some things would not go over well in London, no matter whose son he was. One of Annika's men had provided him with a secretive type of holster that went under the arm and he had borrowed Itala's air pistol. He carried a portmanteau in his left hand as he strode along the street.

Passers-by glanced at him curiously. It was unusual to see an airshipman in the business district of Westminster, London. However, he needed a public call booth, and the only of those to be found in London for money of any kind were here in Westminster.

It felt rather strange to be once again back in the sights, sounds and smells of "jolly old London". He had schemed and struggled for two months to return here. Then, at the call of his country and the request of a woman, he had delayed his return by another month. Now, here he was, wearing the attire of an airshipman and on a secret mission from an infamous Pirate Captain to sell an encrypted stolen text to a beautiful spy that worked for British Intelligence.

It occurred to him that the way that entire notion seemed perfectly normal to him should likely have suggested he retire for a week or more to Bedlam until he was somewhat more firmly grounded in the real world again. He wondered if his sister Valeria would accuse him of making the entire thing up. Of course, he had to admit, it did sound rather like a bad piece of fiction writing in one of those monthly magazines that his brother Karl loved so much.

He found a battery of call booths in the lobby of a business building. He paid the operator a few shillings for the call. He entered an unoccupied booth, pulled the door closed and then hung his coat on a brass hook. An electric light came on when the door was about half-closed, and remained on. He took the the cream-coloured calling card with gold script from his inside vest pocket. Upon it was written her name, an address in the Holborn district of London and a telegraph exchange number.

He momentarily considered simply going to her door and knocking, but Blauchuk had told him about the beating she had put upon a few louts in the town where he met her. He also distinctly recalled speed with which she drew that nasty little silver pistol. Discretion was, he decided, the better part of valour.

Since he had no idea who else might be able to listen to the call, he thought carefully about his words before he called. He needed to convey a message of urgency without telling any eavesdropper what this might be about. The other question, of course, was if she would even remember him.

He took the ear piece off the hook and adjusted the mouth piece to his level and tapped the "attention" button. The pleasant voice of the operator requested the number he wished to be connected to, and he gave it to her. There was a word of thanks, a brief pause, and a very mechanical ringing noise was heard.

He had never had occasion to use a telephone before and when Camilla's warm voice answered the call he was rather surprised at how clear she was. It occurred to him that the *Bloody Rose* could benefit from this sort of technology, instead of voicepipes.

"Hello?" Camilla repeated.

"Oh! My apologies, *Frau* Williams. It is Hans Sauder, if you recall me. I am the airship crewman that you met for a glass of wine outside of Brussels a month ago. I am in London and ..."

"Hans! My favourite Pirate! How wonderful to hear from you, darling! I most certainly do recall you," she said with a bawdy chuckle. "You are entirely too modest given your ... talents," she cooed.

Hans was taken aback at her words until he concluded she was likely just as concerned about eavesdroppers as he was. A phone call about a couple of lovers getting together was likely to be of little interest to anyone.

"I am very glad I left an impression, Camilla," he said smoothly. "I very much enjoyed the presents you left with me after our evening together. So I brought you something in return. It is not free though. I am sure you can come up with some way to repay me."

"Oh, Hans ... I am sure we can come to some agreement. Mmm, yes ... yes, indeed. Do you want to meet me for brunch, perhaps? We can move on from there?"

"That sounds delightful, Camilla. Where do you have in mind?"

She gave him the name and address of a restaurant and closed the conversation with a spicy *double entente* about "getting together". After she had hung up, he eyed the ear piece suspiciously. His logical mind told him that she was unlikely to have a wit's interest in him at all and was likely excellent at playing any role she chose.

"Merry widow, indeed," he muttered and returned the receiver to its clip on the side of the phone. He grabbed his coat, his case and left. Once he had reached the street he hailed a Berseys "Hummingbird" electric motor cab and gave the driver the address to the restaurant.

He stepped out of the cab in Holborn, and paid the driver well. He looked around, got his bearings, and set off the short distance to the restaurant. The district was a busy place, bustling with people even on a foggy midweek morning. Of course, there were nearly thirty inns and taverns alone in the district, plus two "Molly" houses and a handful of brothels. Just the patron traffic for these businesses would have made for a busy street.

He was a handful of doors down and across the street from Staple Inn when he found the restaurant. It was a moderately upscale-looking place. He gave an amused smirk as he glanced at himself and retraced his steps to a quiet alley he had passed on the way.

When he emerged from the alley a handful of minutes later, he had changed his shirt and coat. He now wore a modest quality burgundy frock coat and a sharp white shirt. A burgundy cravat which matched the colour of the coat was at his neck. He had thought ahead and gone to a clothier before he had gone looking for a call booth.

He enquired with the *Maitre de Salon* of the restaurant about Camilla, to find that she was already seated and waiting for him. He noted her attire as a travelling widow had been foregone for a motif which was very in tune with the suffrage movement. A black lace fan lay folded on the table beside her right hand. A rich, satin-like fabric in deep amethyst tones was used for her jacket and skirt and flowed flatteringly over her curves. A plum hat with an assortment of subdued plumage was perched on her blonde coif.

Her pale blue eyes sparkled in delight as he approached the table. "Oh, well, Hans ... my, my ..." she said appreciatively. She flipped her fan open to modestly cover her features, but obvious appreciation was still evident to him. "You look quite the part of a proper English gentleman. I think that looks smashing on you."

He smiled at her and gestured to the empty seat across from her. She nodded with a flutter of her eyelashes and he seated himself. "Such a pleasure to see you again, *Fräulein*. I am glad you approve of my new look. I must say, your choice of attire is so much more alive than the last time I saw you."

She smiled demurely behind her fan and then favoured him a moment with a glance before folding it and setting it down again. "One dresses as their fortunes permit and their situations demand. I am sure you completely understand."

"Oh, yes, indeed," he said with a nod. The waiter appeared and they each ordered a glass of fruit juices and ice to sip while they perused the morning menu.

"So, how has my adventuresome airshipman fared since we last parted ways?" she queried pleasantly.

"It was a most trying voyage," he replied in a cheerful tone, choosing his words carefully. "We had numerous instances of poor 'weather' along the way," he said and then sipped at his just-arrived glass. "It made for some unfortunate times for the crew. However, we were ultimately successful at what our patron had requested of us on the voyage."

"That is so good to hear. I am very sorry to hear about the poor weather. I have heard from friends that a few other Allied ships that were up in that area were lost in storms of one kind or another. I am so glad you made it to London safe and in one handsome piece," she said, eyeing him over the top over her juice-filled wine glass.

"Your concern is touching, *Fräulein*," he said with a smile.

They chatted together about current events in London and Europe for a while, with her filling him in on many things. The unsteady truce between the Allied and Russian Empires seemed to be holding once again, but there was a significant amount of finger pointing and strong talk going back and forth in diplomatic folders. While no one expected a shooting war to resume any time soon, it had to be noted that the Russian Empire was launching four new classes of combat-airship designs in the next year and had enough keels and bags bought to keep every yard in Russia humming for the next three years.

"You do not need that big an Air Navy just for parades," Camilla observed bemusedly.

In addition, the German and French Empires were quarrelling about borders and trade practices, which was a development the Allies certainly did not need. While internal sabre rattling had not yet begun, shuttle diplomacy within the Allied Empires was at an all time high.

To complicate matters, the Americans seemed to be just as content to sell arms and raw materials to either side of the Scorchlands, regardless of who they infuriated. With the Americans supplying the Russian building binge, there were many in Europe who were less than impressed with Yankee profiteering, since they were also selling potential war materials to Britain and France. Rumour had it that the American war merchants were the ones responsible for the latest round of tensions, so as to improve their profits.

Between the two of them, they demolished a surprisingly good breakfast of freshly prepared porridge, fried eggs and bacon, kippers and toast. She flirted lightly with him as they chatted and ate, but it was in the fashion of most English women that Hans had known over the years; they might be dangling bait, but there was no hook or line present.

Eventually, the talk turned to the Book. He passed her the cloth-wrapped tome, and her eyes went wide with surprise when she saw it.

"Hans, darling ... where did you get this?" she asked sweetly and with an appreciative flutter of her eye lashes.

"I am guessing you or your patron are likely devout book collectors," he said, choosing not to answer her question. "So, for a sum of six hundred pounds, you can add that to your collection."

She pursed her lips in the first visible evidence of displeasure he had yet seen on her lovely face. "It cannot possibly be worth that much," she said, still carefully flipping through its pages.

"Well, if you do not care to purchase it, I am sure someone north of the Scorchlands would pay for it," he said levelly in a low voice.

"You ... Pirate," she said with her eyes narrowing. "You would not dare."

"Oh, *I* would not. *Mein Kapitän*, on the other hand, would not blink. And we still have two weeks of viable code books," he reminded her.

She drummed the perfectly manicured nails on the elegantly shaped fingers of her left hand upon the table while looking at him. "You, Mister Sauder, are an amusingly difficult man to deal with," she whispered. "I cannot decide if I wish to praise your cunning, blow your brains out in frustration, or offer you the chance to court me."

"I would happily accept the first, would rather avoid the second, and my sweetheart aboard ship would disapprove of the third," he replied dryly. "So? Six hundred?"

"Three hundred and not a bent penny more," she countered.

"Bloody hell," he sighed. "I was really hoping to avoid ever seeing Russian airspace again."

"Four-fifty," she said crossly.

"Sold," he said, raising his juice-glass to her with a smile.

*****

"Good afternoon, Annika. I got your message when I came aboard. You wished to see me?" he asked her. They were each standing on opposites sides of the threshold of the barely opened door to her Sleeping Bay.

She nodded at him. "Rope Locker in ten minutes?" she suggested.

"Certainly. I will meet you there," he replied.

He made his way up, his mind alternating between wondering what was on Annika's mind and what Camilla had told her bosses. His boss had been visibly surprised at the sum the book had fetched. Annika entered the Rope Locker dressed her in casual shipboard attire and carrying a hefty bundle of some kind.

She suddenly looked rather uncomfortable, which was an entirely new demeanour in Hans' experience with the feisty Russian brunette thus far.

"Here," she said, thrusting the bundle at him. "This is for you. I bought you a present. I ... I wanted you to have something unique to remember me by."

"Annika, you did not need to ..."

"Oh, shut up, Hans," she said with a sigh and roll of her eyes. "It does not matter what I did or did not need to do. I did it because I wanted to. Please accept it."

He grinned at her. "Always a shy and retiring flower, Annika?" he asked with a laugh. The bundle was a tote sack two sizes too large for what it contained. The telltale smell of gun oil caught his nose as he undid the mouth of the tote sack. He reached into the bag and pulled out what had to be the biggest revolver he had ever seen. He blinked at it.

"There is more in the bag," she prompted. He set the revolver down beside him on a crate and rummaged in the bag. A beautifully tooled and stained leather holster and shell-belt was also in the bag. There was a box of small shotgun shells, and another of regular pistol bullets. He held up the box of shotgun shells and looked at it curiously.

Abruptly, she was all business. She hefted up the huge handgun and pointed at its rather distinctive barrel profile. "It is a Belgian Lemat Revolver," she explained. "It is European bored at twelve millimetres for the centerfire cartridges. You see how there are two barrels?"

He nodded, being a bit shocked at the notion of a fifty calibre revolver.

"It is a twenty-four gauge shotgun barrel. The cartridge cylinder revolves around the shotgun barrel, as you can see. You move this lever up or down to choose between the revolver bullets, or the shotgun load. The American

Dragoons called it a 'Grape Shot Revolver'. It is a very good gun for either on horseback, or in a brawl. With a moment of notice, I could probably drop a man at forty yards with the revolver, and you could not miss a man at twenty yards with the shotgun."

As she spoke, she easily showed him the various points she talked about, as well as showed him how to load both the cylinder and the shotgun. She passed it to him and he took it, rather surprised at how heavy the thing was.

"Good lord, this thing must be half a stone!" he exclaimed in disbelief.

"Not quite," she chuckled. "A bit more than a quarter stone, fully loaded. It is a big gun, though, no doubt. It is nearly fourteen inches long, and holds nine shells. The Americans have such a romance with big and heavy guns," she chuckled.

"Lemat is a French name, and you said it was made in Belgium," he commented absently, inspecting it.

"It was designed in New Orleans, by an American there," she answered. "What do you think?"

"I think that New Orleans must bear a shocking similarity to the Scorchlands for it to have inspired this sort of artillery," he said with a laugh. "A very respect-inspiring sort of profile, I must say. However did you find one in London?"

"I did not," she said with a shrug. "I asked Michael to find one for me in Brussels. I could not yet leave my hammock, but he was willing to run the errand for me."

"But why?" he asked as he slid the hefty handgun into its holster.

"It is a very rare gun. There were perhaps four or five thousand made, most of which were shipped to the south of the United States. These are modern times, Hans ... swords are good for Piracy, but a pistol is even better. So now you have your very good sword from Egypt, and a very good American pistol from Belgium given to you by a Russian. You can hang that on your wall in your office or your smoking room and think of me."

He set the gun in its belt down on the crate atop the tote bag, reached to her with his hand, slid his fingers along her cheek and into her hair, and pulled her to him. She did not even pretend at resistance as the first and then several more kisses came easily to them.

"Thank you, Annika" he said to her as he held her against him. "I somehow doubt I will need an *aide memoir* to conjure you in my mind. However, it will be an interesting object of conversation, of that I have no doubt."

"Care to go for a picnic with me, and I will teach you how to shoot it?" she asked, looking up at him.

"That sounds rather intriguing. Yes, let us."

*****

They rented a self-propelled carriage and left the city together. They had taken a few minutes to impinge upon Chief Bridges' good nature by making off with a few things out of the galley. On the way, Hans drove and Annika directed. Yet again, she knew of a secluded spot outside the city's limits where they could go and do as they pleased with little risk of seeing anyone else.

The sun was bright, and the sky was clear save for the odd white cotton-ball cloud. It felt very good to both of them to be sitting side by side on the bench seat, motoring along through the tree-branch tunnel that was the country road they were on. After about twenty minutes of distance along the lane, Annika pointed out a turn off that led them for a few minutes more until they reached an ages-old cherry grove sitting beside a meadow. A beautiful pond that fed a babbling brook made its way out of sight through the meadow.

Hans looked around and then shook his head in amazement. "How is it," he asked incredulously, "that you manage to find out about these places?"

She smiled at him. "I have my sources," she said with a laugh.

"Do tell. Picnic first?"

She nodded at him and together they took the basket, wine bottle and two fire blankets down to the shaded area of the trees, but still with a clear view of the water. Sandwiches, cheese and wine composed the menu.

They re-corked the bottle at half, Annika commenting that until she was sure he could shoot straight sober, there was no way he was firing the Lemat half drunk. They both had a good laugh at the mutual mental image that sprang to mind. They talked for a brief while, stretched out on the blanket together, enjoying the warm breeze and sun. The breeze was rich with the smells of meadow, grove, and pond while the air was alive with the sounds of early summer in the country. Their lips met and their hands sought each other. After a few fiery moments, Annika pulled back.

She was sitting astride his hips, still fully clothed, less her corset which had been tossed aside a few moments earlier. She bit her bottom lip in concentration before she spoke.

"I cannot believe I am about to say this," she said through gritted teeth. "Be sure this is what you want, because in a few more minutes you are going to have me so wound up I will not be happy if you change your mind."

He blinked at her and then closed his eyes and hung his head. "Sorry," he said.

"I want you," she said simply. "This would make a wonderful memory, sharing our pleasure here like this ... but apparently I actually give a damn about your feelings, because I do not wish it to be a wonderful memory only for me."

"I want you too, Annika. In a way I am unfamiliar with and that I have not known with any other woman. But I cannot. I am ... sorry."

She nodded with a pout playing at her lips. "I am sorry too. I cannot say I entirely understand, but I know how important this point of honour is to you." She moved off of him with a sigh of regret. She sat wordlessly, cross-legged, a short distance away. There was an uncomfortable silence between the two of them.

"So, in the absence of being able to teach you something about blanket-play, shall we get to the task of teaching you something about gun-play?" she asked with a slightly forced humour. He nodded and relaxed slightly.

"I will put the basket back in the carriage and get the tote-bag," he told her and then got about the job of setting words to actions.

"Well enough. While you do that, I am going to go see if I can find a couple of things of serviceable value to us at the abandoned steading over in the meadow. I will likely be five minutes." So saying, she set off at an easy jog through the tall grass and wild flowers that covered the distance to the dilapidated structure she had indicated.

She came back with three fence posts in dubious condition over a shoulder and a similar quality stump under an arm. She dropped them on the ground and then started jogging back over to the old steading. He followed her, and together they each did two more trips. She lashed the first trio of fence posts together to make a tripod, and sat a stump upon it. Seeing what she was about, Hans copied her efforts, and within a half-hour they had five targets set up.

"As with most things, Hans, there is a sufficient way to do this, and a more effective way. At anything less than forty yards, sufficient is that you point the gun at the centre of mass and pull the trigger. The bullet is so fast that unless your target is on horseback riding a traverse compared to you, you will hit your man somewhere," she said as she dropped three cartridges into the breech of one of her tri-barrel pistols. She snapped the pistol closed and cocked the hammer. He nodded at her words.

Without really looking at the target she fired upon, she pointed her pistol at a stump and fired one of the barrels. The rapport of the shot filled the air, and a piece of wood flew off the stump. She shrugged. "Pistols make soldiers out of idiots, and Gods out of soldiers," she said.

He nodded. "They are very effective, yes."

"However, if you run out of bullets before opponents," she said with a laugh, "you had best know something about a sword. You are unlikely to be given time to reload. So, missing your man, or hitting him without dropping him, are just going to cause you problems. If you shoot a man, shoot him in the face. If you draw a 'T' described by the lines of the eye-brows and the nose, you will kill your man almost instantly every time with a bullet in that area."

Hans nodded, but said nothing.

"Now, fire one shot at each of the targets," she instructed. He did so, the big gun booming in the warm summer air. He scored two hits and three misses. She nodded.

"Not bad," she said. "First, do not be so tense throughout your body. Second, leave the elbow slightly bent. When you aim, do not swivel the arm and head. Instead, leave them facing directly ahead, and twist at the waist, like so. It gives you a more consistent way to aim. Next, always raise the gun to the height of your shoulder when you fire. There, yes, that looks better," she said as he changed his firing stance.

For the next two hours, the two of them worked together to improve his technique with the big gun. She taught him how to use his peripheral vision to fire at a target while looking at something else. She demonstrated how to tuck, shoulder-roll, emerge into a crouch and fire in a single fluid action; useful, she said, for crossing doorways or similar areas. She explained to him how to clean and maintain the gun so that sooting in the barrel would not affect the accuracy.

She taught him how to do a line-of-advance with another pistoleer, where the left-hand person only fired on targets to their left. The right-hand side person of the pair only fired on targets to their right. Neither shooter looked at a specific target, instead only using their peripheral vision to sense a target and fire at it. At the call of "miss" or "empty", the other person would step ahead and take over the full area ahead. Then the person behind would step back into place and they would resume.

"It is a very effective way for two or three pistoleers with a pair of guns each to potentially kill five to ten times their number with minimal risk to themselves," she concluded. Hans nodded, rather impressed at her technical knowledge in the art of war as practised by handgunners.

By this time, there was not much left of their make-shift targets. In addition, he was feeling positively sore from holding the four-pound gun at arm's length, in addition to everything else. He holstered the Lemat.

"Enough and done?" she asked.

"Aye," he said with a stretch and roll of his shoulders. He blatantly eyed her up and down. "Care for a swim with me for a quarter hour or so before the ride back into town?"

"Just a swim?" she asked carefully, trying not to look surprised.

"Just a swim," he said and then paused. "Perhaps a kiss or two, but nothing more. Acceptable rules of engagement, Captain-Gunner?"

"Hardly, Captain-Rockets, it leaves you with the advantage of position. But I have never shied away from any offer of engagement," she said, pulling her shirts off over her head and tossing them onto the blanket beside the earlier-removed corset.

*****

Hans brought Annika back to the ship, and had then cleared out his hammock, locker and deck box. As he stowed what little he had in the back seat of the rented carriage, he found himself saddened. This is what he wanted, and he had finally achieved it. For some reason, it felt hollow.

He had then gone to the London family home. It was essentially empty beyond a trio of the family servants whose singular job was to keep the place in perfect condition until the family's return in fall. There was a tremendous amount of excitement at his return, and he swore the group to secrecy so that he might still be able to surprise his parents.

He had spent some time exploring the old house with new eyes. He asked every one of the servants their names, twice, to be sure he would remember them. He quietly pushed open the door to the room he and his brother shared, marvelling at the luxury of it. Aboard the *Bloody Rose*, that space was big enough for the three hammocks and work desk of an Officer's Sleeping Bay, with ample room left over. He remembered the countless quarrels between he and his brother while growing up over whose stuff was taking up whose space. It all seemed so silly now.

He bathed and shaved, and put on fresh clothes. He carefully folded and stowed his airshipman's attire. He likely would never wear it again, he mused. On the other hand, as evidenced by his small detour on the way to school, one could never tell what the future might bring. Either way, discarding it was beyond his capacity right now.

He relaxed in the Study for a while, or at least tried to. The servants were constantly hovering around him in case he might need something and nearly panicked when they discovered he had gotten his own coffee. To preserve the nerves of everyone involved, including his own, he gave them all the rest of the day off with each a pound of spending money out of his own pocket. While Hans was given of the impression that they thought he might well have taken leave of his senses, they did not question and shortly he had the house to himself.

It was a very large, and now very empty, house. Hans was alone with his thoughts, in the Study. He scowled at his coffee cup, went up to his room and got his flask. He then went to the kitchen and transferred the contents of the cup, plus a bit more from the pot, into the flask. He left the cup in the kitchen and returned to the Study with his flask, and sat down in his favourite chair again. He took a sip from the flask and nodded; much better.

He picked up a copy of the South London Press; no matter that the family was not here, his father continued to have it delivered. At the end of the day, it would be "cleaned away". That was to say the servants would take it to their quarters and it would be theirs to read. Hans began reading the sections he used to love; World News, South City Social, and Business Events.

Not terribly long afterwards, he abruptly closed the paper, folded it, and irritably cast it aside. For some reason it held no interest for him. He went across the room and pulled the "European Airship Design and Innovation Annual Journal" from the shelf. He returned to his chair, adjusted the lamp three times and opened the text. He flipped past the awards and praise for his family's company to the technical sheets and "brag pages".

He went and got a pad of paper and a pen from a desk and returned to his chair. He started reviewing the designs from the major manufacturers with a very different metric than he ever had considered before — the likely outcome of an encounter with the *Bloody Rose*. How would he improve the Dornier 129-B? Or the Sauder Industries SI-747H? Or the ageing SI-213J that he had been aboard when he had been captured at the start of all of this?

He spent an hour at the task and set the Journal and his notepad down. Something was wrong. Even the latest "Bernoulli Barge" designs from Sopwith or Francospatial were incapable of defending themselves against any modest pirate, let alone a uniquely capable crew like those aboard the *Bloody Rose*.

The clock on the mantel piece chimed in a harmony of doom, announcing the hour to be much later than anticipated. Hans cursed under his breath.

"She will kill me if I am late," he muttered anxiously. A few minutes later he was stepping out to the street, hailing a cab, even as he was still pulling his frock coat on.

*****

Hans and Annika regarded each other quietly over their port glasses. The silence between them was heavy. Neither wanted to be the one to say the words they both knew were between them.

Annika had been somewhat frosty when he had met her at the airship dockyard gates; he had been nearly forty minutes late. She was dressed in about as feminine a style as she managed, which is to say she was dressed in a man's frock coat, a man's pants, and a man's ruff shirt. The shirt was buttoned one stay higher than scandalous for a woman in London. She wore an airship officer's tricorne hat upon her head, and her flight gloves were hung over her belt.

Hans had chosen the restaurant as an old favourite and the owner recognized him when he arrived with Annika. There had been a moderately raised eyebrow at his company, but nothing was said. They were given an excellent table and a bottle of wine had shown up unbidden, compliments of the owner.

The meal had been a very good medley of pork, fish, and chicken with a selection of vegetables. The dessert was a white cake with diced brandied fruits poured over top and then crowned with a liberal dollop of whipped English cream. It was terribly tasty but, as Annika casually stated, "Chief Bridges does better". Hans could not disagree.

They had been talking through most of the meal, but there was very little substance to it. Her features were guarded the whole time and she spent just as much time looking around the restaurant as looking at him.

He sat his port glass down. "What is on your mind, Annika?" he asked, breaking the silence of the past few moments.

"So this is the 'real' you, is it?" she asked. He could tell by her tone she was looking for a fight.

"*Ja*, it is. Or was."

"Is," she said firmly. "I do not want you to come back to the ship," she stated, equally firmly. "Write a letter each to Chief Itala and Captain O'Raedy, and give me the funds to pass on to them to Pay Your Respects. I swear to you it will arrive."

Hans blinked at her, surprise clear on his features.

"Pardon?"

"You heard me, Hans. I do not want you to come back to the ship. When we part ways tonight, stay away from *Bloody Rose*," Annika said quietly, with a determined mask of resolve upon her face.

"But why?"

"If you go back, you will have second thoughts. I was wrong. You are no pirate, Hans. You are an English gentleman that happens to have a keen intellect and be a quick study. You belong aboard the *Bloody Rose* about as much as I belong in a Bank Boardroom."

Hans stared at her in agape silence, clearly taken aback by her pronouncement.

"And do not argue the point, Hans," she continued after a sip of her port wine. "It is self evident. I was selfish when I delayed your return to your real life by begging you like a stupid school girl to come to Privateering. I never should have done that. All it did was cause you pain and force you to do things you had no stomach for."

"That is more than enough, Annika," Hans said sharply, trying not to raise his voice. "You did not beg. You were emotional and perhaps far more honest about your heart than before, but you did not beg. You are not to blame for my decision to head into Russian airspace. I am. I *wanted* to go. Your arrangement of the facts as they were just made it a more self-evident decision."

"But ..."

"Oh, shut up, Annika," Hans said crossly in a quiet voice. As much as he felt like shouting, they were in a restaurant, after all. The last thing he needed was his father to read in the social pages about him having a spat in a restaurant owned by a family friend with a woman dressed in a man's aeronautical attire. "I might have gotten more than I bargained for on that trip, but Aldebert was right. What did I expect would happen when I fired those weapons?

Candy floss and confetti? We went to war, and those are weapons of war, and I knew that."

Annika watched him carefully but said nothing as he continued.

"And the truth of the matter is that my educated, self-righteous guilt aside, the entire experience aboard the *Bloody Rose* has been some of the most exciting moments of my life. Telling me that I have no place or fit there is an insult to me and everything I learned and did." He was fairly glaring at her as he tapped a finger on the handle of his tea spoon.

"You are deluding yourself, Hans," she replied stiffly. "I have spent five years working with Pirates from ten different countries and three continents. It takes one to know one. I am and you are not."

The conversation paused for a moment as the waiter returned to refill their port glasses and enquire about whether they would prefer tea, American coffee or Turkish coffee. They both ordered Turkish coffee.

"I think perhaps," Hans hissed at her, "that the good Captain-Gunner is forgetting which one of us took three years to become an officer aboard a pirate airship, and which one took two months. I also think that the good Captain-Gunner forgets which one of us it is that the infamous Blackheart considers a threat to his authority, and which one he does not. If you do not recognize me as a Pirate, Annika, it is because you choose not to."

It was quite clear she was debating throwing her port glass at him. She was visibly biting her lower lip in an attempt to keep her temper in check.

"You are a One-Eyed Man in the Land of the Blind, Captain-Rockets. Of course Blackheart is worried you might be stupid enough to try to be King. I can take you with one arm behind my back and I do not test the

Captain's resolve for a reason. That he worries you might try is a testament to your foolhardiness, not to your status as a Pirate."

He opened his mouth to reply, but she cut him off. "You wound up an officer because he needed a Mathematician, not a Pirate. Do not kid yourself about having 'earned' your promotion. He used you and you happily went along with it, thinking you were on some big story book adventure."

"You are very close to earning another slap, Annika. Mind your mouth," Hans said in a low-toned snarl.

"Proper English Gentlemen do not strike members of the weaker sex," she reminded him sweetly, gave him a coy look and had a sip of her port.

The return of the waiter forestalled any comment or action Hans might have been considering. The waiter placed the glass coffee carafe, associated cups and service items on the table, and cleared away a few other things. He looked back and forth between them for a moment before he left, but said nothing.

Hans resumed tapping the handle of his teaspoon while he watched her pour herself some of the coffee and have a sip from the porcelain cup.

"Pirate," he suggested with a forcedly amiable tone.

She shook her head. "Gentleman," she countered bemusedly.

"What makes you so sure, Annika?"

"Supper."

"Supper?"

"Mmm-hmm. We are not off at some sea-side gambling house both snogging and drinking together like a couple of truant teenagers. You did not ask me where I might want to go; you told me we were going here. You even went so far as to tell me what sort of attire might be *apropos*. If you were a Pirate, you would not give a motorwell bat's ass how we were dressed."

"Really?" he said, obviously unmoved by her analysis.

"Really. Pirates live for freedom, Hans. I have said it before; I shall say it to you again, now ... you are fleeing from freedom into servitude from what I can see."

"Your sight is somewhat limited," he suggested dryly after a sip of the strong coffee he had just poured.

"Really?" she said, mimicking his earlier tone.

"Really. I did not choose the life I was given, Annika. My grandfather built a family fortune from rags. He taught his son how to run and improve the business. Now it is my turn. You call it freedom, while I call it hurting the members of my family that are counting on me. If I had any reason — any reason at all — to believe that my family would prosper and be under able stewardship with someone who wants the job done well if I went back to the *Bloody Rose* and spent the rest of my days living a pirate's life, then I would do so."

He paused, sighed and sipped at his coffee, enjoying the sweetness and the hint of vanilla in it. Annika watched him but said nothing.

"It is sort of a cruel joke, really. I have discovered I love living the life I have aboard the *Bloody Rose*. So many challenges. You may insist that I do not meet your criteria for a Pirate, Annika, but I know that if it were an option that would not haunt me, I'd be aboard her when she sails from London. Something has awoken in my heart, in my blood, and in my spirit."

He paused with a chuckle and shook his head. "I thought Aunt Gwen was a madwoman when she Jumped the Gunwale. And now, I find myself repeating Jimeno's words; *'quiero ser un pirata también'* -- I want to be a pirate, too." He paused again and once more shook his head as if to dismiss the notion. "Unfortunately, I am not prepared to pay the cost of abandoning my family to continue on this path."

"Really? You would continue on this path if you could, knowing eventually you would die long before your time?"

"Really. We all die eventually. I have seen enough evidence of that of late. For some reason old, grey, infirm and bed ridden now sounds less noble than with a sword in my hand and blood in my mouth."

There was another long pause as they both sipped their coffee.

"Will you take me home to your house and make love to me once in your favourite chair, before we part ways, Hans? So that I do not have to spend the rest of my life wondering?" she asked quietly. Hans nearly snorted his coffee.

He set his *demitasse* down and looked at her. He sighed and shook his head. "I am sorry, Annika, but no. That would have far more of an impact on my resolve than any visit to the *Bloody Rose* might."

She nodded, visibly disappointed. "I expected you to say no. But I had to ask." She gave a forcedly cheerful look and shrugged. "Care to go find some place with me that serves rum, vodka, cigars and cigarettes?"

He chuckled. "Yes, you Pirate. Let me pay the bill and we can get out of here."

*****

Hans carefully climbed down the nearly vertical ladder into the Propulsion Room of the *Bloody Rose*. He had spent the last little while of the morning walking the ship one last time, trying to memorize her layout. It was nearly saddening; he had come to know the *Bloody Rose*'s 110 feet of length with a genuine respect for her capabilities as both a fighting ship and a home to the men and women who lived aboard her.

He rubbed at his forehead slightly as he turned. He had stayed out far too late last night with Annika, and while a great deal of fun, he was somewhat worse for wear today. He was convinced that he would never understand how a culture that drank vodka as a national pastime were capable of getting out of bed the next day to wage war.

Chief Itala looked over at him as he covered the distance from the ladder to where she was currently on one knee, working on part of the Watch Keeper's Station. She stood up, wiping her hands on a rag which she then cast onto a tool bag.

"You are not here to work, are you, Hans?" she asked.

He shook his head. "No, Chief, I am not," he said. This was suddenly much harder to say than he had expected and he looked away from her for a moment. "I am sorry, Chief. I am here to Pay My Respects. It ... is time for me to go. I ... here, take this, please," he said awkwardly. He was equally awkward in how he passed her a small velvet sack. "Thank you for everything, Chief."

"So that's it, Hans? A mitt-full of Marks, 'so long and thanks for all the fun', and good-bye?" Arietta said, disappointed.

"No, Arietta," he said with a heavy and frustrated sigh. "That is far from it. But its all I can do. I wish there was some way that I could hire you as a Trials Engineer for my Father's airships. I wish there was some way I could adequately explain in a few words how much I have learned from you, both about airship engines and about living life. I am going to very much miss our o'dark-thirty in the morning talks."

He rubbed at his forehead as he continued, sounding almost weary as he spoke. "I wish I had met you at a similar age with either both of us in our twenties or both of us in our thirties. I wish I could throw common sense to the wind and kiss you right now just so I would have the memory of your taste on my lips for my future years."

Arietta smiled softly but said nothing.

"I wish there was some way," he said, looking around as though the answer to his wish might be hanging on a sign nearby, "that I could stay aboard the *Bloody Rose* and have both you and Annika in my life, and not feel as though I was selfishly abandoning my family. But, if wishes were shillings, I would be the Baron of a Caribbean Island by now. In any case, Arietta, I cannot imagine that I will ever forget you to the end of my days."

Arietta smiled warmly and nodded. "Thank you, Hans. I think that is one of the nicer compliments I have been paid in a long time. Good luck. While I am sure *Signore Capitano* will say something similar, please know that you always have a place in any Propulsion Room or Steam Deck that I run."

*****

Hans paused before the door to the Captain's cabin, his knuckles poised to rap upon its scored hardwood surface. This, as it were, was it. In a few moments, his grand adventure of a lifetime would come to an end. He shook his head one last time against the irresponsible notion of changing his mind.

"Come in, Mister Sauder," came Blackheart's voice from the other side of the as-yet un-knocked door. Hans blinked in surprised, and pushed the door open. He stepped into the Captain's Mess to find Blackheart sitting at his desk, setting down his pen.

"How did you ..."

"The boot mat in front of the door has an electric switch under it, Mister Sauder," Blackheart explained as he set aside a few papers on his desk. "As long as someone is standing on it, a small buzzer rings in here. It prevents anyone from surprising me. I could not think of anyone else among the crew that would take that long to apply knuckles to timber. Do not just stand there looking like you have met the Pope in his underpants; come in, man."

Hans chuckled and closed the door behind him and walked over to where Captain O'Raedy sat. "I have come to Pay My Respects, *Herr Kapitän*," he said simply.

The Englishman looked at the German for a moment and nodded. "Not entirely unexpected, Mister Sauder; I am still a bit surprised, I must admit. I was starting to think that the good Captain-Gunner had managed to charm you into hanging around for a while longer."

Hans shook his head slightly. "*Nein*. She has tried, to be sure. However, I have my duty and responsibility to my family. Thus, my career as a Pirate of the *Bloody Rose* must end today."

"Well, Mister Sauder, I cannot say that you have not left your mark on this ship, and I cannot claim that you will not be missed," O'Raedy said as he rose from his chair and slowly made his way around the desk to where Hans stood. "You have been a fine engineer for me, a fine officer, and a constant source of challenge and surprise."

"You are very kind, *Herr Kapitän*," Hans replied with a gracious nod. "I am compelled to admit that the 'education' I have received while a member of your crew cannot be matched. As much as it pains me to say it, I will likely consider having met you a very positive turn of events in my life."

There was a brief pause of silence as Blackheart blinked at Sauder and then he roared with laughter. He clapped Hans on the shoulder almost hard enough to knock him off balance for a moment. "Well, damn, man..." O'Raedy chortled, "I will have to work at keeping your compliment a secret. We both have professional reputations to protect, after all."

Hans laughed aloud and nodded. "Indeed we do, *Herr Kapitän*, indeed we do. Please, take this. It is my honour to thank you by the Traditions for teaching me what I needed to learn to be a successful member of your crew."

Hans held out a small velvet sack like the one he had given earlier to Chief Itala. Captain O'Raedy took it with a nod and set it down on the desk they stood in front of without a second glance. He picked up a sealed envelope and passed it to Hans. Hans lofted a brow as he took it.

"Open it," O'Raedy ordered.

Hans did, and took out the single sheet of paper, scanned it and then both eyes went wide with surprise.

"This is a full performance and technical sheet of the *Bloody Rose* ... why?"

"That sheet will be wrong in about a month. The old girl will have all three of the electric motors replaced with slightly more powerful versions, and the two Spitz 656's will be replaced by Motorenfabrik 790's. That should increase her top speed to 88 knots. The four pounders are all being removed and she'll replace them with an equivalent number of eight pounders. All the eights will be the new high pressure, super-velocity ones coming out of Vickers. They will have the same range as the twelves," Blackheart paused and looked at Hans. "What is your question, man?"

"Why are you telling me all this?" Hans asked, clearly baffled.

"So you can build better, you twit," O'Raedy said with the same exasperated tone that a fireman might use to explain that fire is hot to bystanders. "We are heading to Persia from London, Mister Sauder. The *Bloody Rose* will spend two months in a ground cradle being refitted. You, sir, are being given the most valuable thing any man in your position or your father's could wish for."

"The information to design the ship that can escape the *Bloody Rose*," Hans replied with a dawning look of understanding.

"Correct. Amongst other things, Mister Sauder, it will keep us lot on our toes. It is getting too easy. Even that fancy Dornier we ran into was not really that big a challenge," Blackheart said, gesturing dismissively. "A challenge is what keeps a man from getting complacent, Mister Sauder, or old before his time. I leave it to you in your future career to ensure I remain challenged."

The two men shook hands, and then Sauder stood at what he thought a proper military stance of attention might look like. He gave his best approximation of a salute. Blackheart smiled, and returned the courtesy.

"Good luck, Mister Sauder. There is always a bunk aboard the *Bloody Rose* for you, should you need it for something, even just temporarily. You know where to find us."

"Very Different Circumstances"
(Morning, June 24th, 1888)

Big Ben had struck eight bells some time ago as the sun worked to burn away the fog of the late June morning. A flock of pigeons, disturbed from their roost on an airship dock platform by a morning engine test, swirled and darted above. On the damp street, lorries and steam carts, as well as dock workers and airship crews streamed through the airship dockyard's black wrought-iron gates. The air was full of the smells of steam, coal smoke, scorched rubber, spilled fuel, and innumerable other odours that came from a city that sustained the lives of four million souls.

Across the street from the yard gates, Hans sat alone with his thoughts in a rented steam carriage. He periodically glanced over at the gate, keeping watch for his two friends.

If he had grown up under very different circumstances, he mused, it was entirely likely he would never have laid eyes upon the *Bloody Rose* let alone sailed aboard her. Yet, in some bizarre twist of surreal reasoning, those very circumstances that allowed the past three months to unfold as they had, were the very same forces now pressing him to leave. He had made remarkable friends, found an improbable love, fought, killed, saved lives, wept and laughed all over a half-a-mile in the sky for three remarkable months. He knew what it was he had been missing his entire life.

"But I cannot stay," he said quietly to himself.

He glanced over towards the gates to see Annika and Arietta crossing their threshold. He disembarked and waved at them. Arietta waved at him and he could see her smile from where he was. Annika looked rather cross.

"This should be interesting," he said to himself with a sigh. He adjusted his cravat absently as the two women crossed the busy street to where he was.

As he waited, he noted that the two of them were dressed as twins for some reason. They were both wearing rather snug pants with a bold red and black stripe pattern, knee-high aviator boots, black sashes and crossed leather belts at the waist, blue and white checkered "slops" shirts that were immodestly buttoned, and tricorne hats. Given that Arietta was tall, statuesque and dark-skinned, while Annika was shorter, athletic and fashionably pale, the effect they had on local traffic as they traversed the street was rather amusing.

"Hans!" Arietta said as she gave him a hug. "Well, well ... you were right, Annika. He does clean up rather handsomely, indeed." She grinned at him and gave Annika a nudge.

"Gossiping like milk-maids after you got back to the ship, were you?" Hans laughed.

"Cat's Call," Arietta gave a bawdy chortle that turned into a laugh when Hans flushed red. The laughter turned into a lean-against-the carriage-and-stomp-a-boot sort of moment for her when she saw that Annika had gone scarlet as well.

"Are you quite done yet, Arietta?" Annika scowled.

"Almost," she said impishly with her musical giggle. "Oh, you just have your knickers in a twist because of Hans' idea," she teased. "Come on, Annika. It will be fun."

Annika planted her fists on her hips and looked thoroughly unconvinced.

"Explain it yourself, Hans. I am sure it will sound like a better idea to her if it is in your voice," Arietta grinned.

"I see you are in a fine mood this morning, Arietta," Hans said, trying to suppress the urge to join her in laughing at Annika's visible displeasure and discomfiture. Beyond the fact that getting knocked on his backside by a short Russian brunette in front of an Airship Dockyard would be difficult to live down, he also knew full well that if he laughed that she would just become more stubborn.

"Oh please, Hans," Arietta laughed again. "I get to go shopping, play dress-up with an attractive man, get treated to lunch, have you pay for it all, and then pull the wool over a total stranger's eyes for an evening at an English manor. Why would I not be in a great mood?"

"When you say it that way, it does not sound nearly so bad," Annika admitted grudgingly.

"It is all a matter of perception, Little Sister," Arietta grinned.

"'Little Sister'?" Hans questioned in a rather sceptical tone.

"Well, yes," Annika said brightly. "Can you not see the family resemblance?" she asked in mock seriousness. The two of them struck "show-girl finale" poses just long enough to result in a distracted gentleman bicycling into a lamp post. Hans clamped his hand over his face and the two women hung onto each other in laughter. The rather embarrassed fellow said something disparaging about the probable nature of their employment as he remounted his bicycle.

"Thanks for the praise! Leave a tip! Come back tomorrow! They are here all week!" Hans called after him, further prolonging their collective mirth. "Okay, let us get out of here before you two beauties start resulting in property damage and loss of life with your antics."

*****

"All joking temporarily aside, Hans, please do explain what it is you desire to achieve. The envelope you sent aboard for me was a bit thin on details," Arietta said.

Hans sipped at his cup of coffee and thought for a moment before answering. They were sitting in a *kaffehaus* he knew well, having coffee and pastries before they truly embarked on their outing.

"I have spent the past three months living in your world, as it were. I want you to come to see what an evening in my world looks like," he said. "The problem is that my Father and my Uncle Orel are very German, my mother is very English, and my brother Karl, and my sister Valeria are suitably confused. So I really cannot stroll in the front door after a three month absence and introduce you both as the Pirate women that kidnapped me and took me all over the skies of Russia, Allied Europe and Egypt. I doubt that would go very well," Hans said dryly.

"Do tell," Annika snorted as she sipped her coffee.

Arietta nibbled at her scone and nodded. "I see your point," she said. "As a minimum, there would be some question about your virtue having remained intact with such company," she teased.

Hans rolled his eyes. "I was more concerned with them having you sent off to Dartmoor."

"Not my idea of a retirement venue," Annika commented.

"Nor mine," Arietta agreed. "All right, so what exactly are we going to do?"

"Go shopping," Hans replied.

"One of my preferred answers, I must admit," Arietta responded. "For what?"

"You, my dear Arietta are going to be Annika's hired bodyguard ... and Annika will be a Russian Heiress I met on my way back to London."

"*Nyet*," Annika said immediately and sharply set her coffee cup down. "*Nyet*."

"Pardon?" Hans asked, caught aback by the intensity in her voice. Arietta lofted a puzzled eyebrow at the younger woman.

"You heard me quite clearly, Sauder. No."

"Annika, please," Hans began carefully.

"Do not 'Annika, please' me and then try and steamroller me with your logic and reason," she hissed at him across the table. "I will not play pretend at being something I do not wish to be."

"This is about your father, correct?" he asked her quietly. She nearly dropped her coffee cup which she had just once again picked up.

"What? What do you mean?" she demanded. A couple of patrons glanced over at the noisy trio at the table.

Arietta sat back in her chair, and took a mouthful of her coffee, watching the other two intently. Hans had no clue what she might be thinking.

"I know who your father is," Hans said with a sympathetic tone. "I can understand not wanting to return to those memories, though I cannot imagine what it must have been like for you."

Annika's eyes went wide for a moment and then she regained her composure. "Who told you?" she asked crossly. Woe was clearly in future of whomever Hans named.

Hans only hesitated for a moment. "Blauchuk," he lied. "He wanted me to know so that I would be able to understand you more clearly." There was a pause and then he continued. "I find your story rather spectacular. But I am not asking you to ..."

"Oh yes, you are," she said sharply.

"Oh, grow up, Annika," Arietta said wearily. "That your father is one of the most notorious mad scientists to come out of the War has no reflection on you. You did the right thing when you fled him and declined your birthright. However, you have been trying to hold yourself to some impervious, super-human standard ever since. The sins of the father are not those of the daughter."

Annika blinked, slack-jawed at Arietta. "You ... You knew, too?" Arietta nodded and took another bite of her rapidly diminishing scone. "How?"

"Michael told me. That man cannot keep his mouth closed in bed," Arietta said with a chuckle.

Hans tried to not to look too shocked at the notion that Blackheart had a loose tongue with his crew's secrets after a tumble into bed. This was the sort of thing that could get a man killed with the wrong person. The image of Camilla pointing her little silver pistol at him across a table sprang to his mind.

Annika bit her lip for a moment. "Then you of all people should understand, Arietta. This is the same as Michael asking you to put on your Habit again!"

"No so loud, dear," Arietta admonished. "And no, it is not. Trust me, if you were to put on a hoop skirt and bustle, and I was to put on my Habit, I expect you would be far more welcome almost anywhere in London than I," the Italian-Ethiope said pointedly. "Besides," she said with a wave of her hand, "I do put it on when asked for good reason. I do not allow myself to be reduced to a squalling brat by worries about the boogeyman leaping out of my clothing box."

"Look, you ..."

"Ladies, please," Hans said patiently. The last thing he was interested in right now was trying to break-up a cat-fight in a *kaffehaus* between two of the most dangerous women currently in London. "Annika, your father has no candy-coated clue where you are. The evidence to this fact would be that as soon as the ship was seen north of the Scorchlands, we were not dogged at every turn by Russian mercenary vessels. It was made painfully obvious by the *Severnyĭ Volk* that as soon as they decided to start hunting back, the RIAN had the means to find us. Allowing yourself to dress like the beautiful woman you are will not reveal your existence to your father, nor will it instantaneously transport you back to the horrors of your youth." Hans paused for a moment.

"... And if he does suddenly show up, I will kill him myself. You do not need to live in fear of him, Annika," he said with a measured intensity which the two women clearly found surprising.

"I could be wrong," Arietta said slowly, "but I very much expect that Michael would be more than prepared to reduce your father's castle and compound to rubble in order to rescue you. He expects fierce loyalty from his officers, but he gives back equally. I think Hans is right. You have nothing to fear, Annika."

Annika sat back in her chair and folded her arms across her chest. She was quite clearly unhappy with the entire notion.

An amused thought curled the corner of Hans' mouth. "What exactly are you afraid of, Annika?" he questioned.

*****

Hans and Annika disembarked from the carriage as Arietta held the door for them. Arietta had suggested that they all get used to their roles and stories as soon as possible before they drove out to the manor. As such, Arietta decided that in her role as the bodyguard, she should do all the driving.

"You confound me, Arietta," Hans said, adjusting his cravat.

"Oh?"

"Aye ... I know you can land a steam-powered glider in an area the size of a postage stamp. But somehow, that skill does not seem to translate to your abilities as a carriage driver."

The Italian-Ethiope glared at him, even as Annika covered her mouth with a hand to suppress a laugh. "At least she is a more skilled navigator than you are, Hans. We are at the right address first try."

It was the German's turn to glare as the two women laughed at him. They were in the east-end of the city on a quiet side street. The storefronts and buildings here were older and more weathered than other places Hans had seen in London. The trio entered the store, known to Annika to be owned by a tailor who clandestinely produced armoured garments to order. Arietta wanted something that would make her look the part of a bodyguard, but would also give her something else to wear in combat aboard the *Bloody Rose* other than the very distinctive armour of the Sanguine Sisterhood.

"I am looking for Leopold," Hans stated to the shop keeper.

The older gentleman lofted a brow and shook his head. "Leopold no longer works here. He quit last winter."

"He left his scissors downstairs. Can I get them?" Hans replied.

The shop keeper nodded and went over to the door and turned the sign from "open" to "closed". The three phrases the two men had exchanged were a sign and counter-sign to identify themselves to the proprietor as potential clients for the less reputable part of the store's business. Annika had coached him on exactly what to say during the ride to the store.

The shop keeper walked towards the back of the store and beckoned the trio to follow him. He opened a door to what looked to be a closet. A flick of a switch set a clockwork mechanism spinning, lowering the back of the closet into a staircase. He then led them down.

"So what are you looking for?" he asked once they were all down the stairs. The room was dimly lit and dominated by a large leather-topped pinning and cutting table. A couple of very industrial-looking needle machines were to one side. One wall was entirely loaded with shelves of fabrics, leathers, threads and the like. Another wall was bins of what looked like completed garments of various kinds.

The merchant was a chestnut and silver-haired fellow, stout of build with a slight limp to his left leg. He had a very relaxed air about him, but at the same time, Hans was left with the impression of a keen sense of assessment and perception about the man.

Hans looked at the two women blankly. Annika smiled and pointed at Arietta. "Emerald *baejab*, six, six and one, plus tacking and details in brass, for her. Chest and legs."

The shop keeper blinked and then looked up at Arietta, who was as broad at the shoulder as he was, but more than half a foot taller. She smiled pleasantly down at him.

"You have cash on you?" he asked.

"Lots," said Hans. "And much less time."

The shop keeper grunted and headed over to grab his note pad and measuring tape from the cutting table.

"Six, six and one?" Hans asked.

"Six layers of cotton sandwiched inside six layers of silk, with one layer of leather in the middle. It is a modification of a twenty-year-old Korean design that they made to stop French bullets when France tried to invade. Done this way, it will stop just about anything from a pistol under forty-five calibre and as well as most slashes from cutlasses or lighter."

"A straight thrust and I am still in trouble," Arietta said with a shrug. "Nothing is invulnerable."

Annika nodded. "As evidenced by the scar over my left lung," she said grimly. She rubbed absently at the spot where she had been run through.

The merchant returned with a foot-high step-stool and started systematically taking all of Arietta's measurements. "Emerald, you said?" he asked.

Annika nodded. "With her skin colour, she'll look glorious in it."

"And we must look fashionable when standing to battle, you know," Arietta chuckled in her musical tone.

"Is this going to be covered up all the time, or should it be wearable as a stand-alone garment?" he asked gruffly, apparently ignoring the humour.

Annika and Arietta looked at each other and then at Hans.

Hans shrugged. "If you can build it so that it looks like an attractive silk garment in and of itself, do so."

"After the French style, or the English?"

"French," Hans replied.

The merchant nodded, grabbed his scissors and headed to the shelves of fabric.

"French?" the two women asked Hans simultaneously.

"Not terribly certain. However, I do know that when it comes to dressing up women attractively, the French do a much better job," he grinned.

*****

"Um ... Yes, French was a good choice," Hans said, rubbing at his chin.

"Stop that ... actually, do not, but still Hans ... this is supposed to be armour for me, not evening wear for

Montremart," Arietta chuckled, examining herself in the full length mirror.

The armour was an absolutely beautiful moss-green silk done as a shoulder-to-floor fitted dress. It had been shaped to fit flatteringly over Arietta's lush curves, but its lack of inherent flow betrayed its true purpose. It was open — "strategically" as the tailor had described it — from floor to mid-thigh on the outside of each leg, and then rather scandalously over an oval patch of her midriff and again the same way from the base of the neck down to expose part of her cleavage.

"You are quite well protected, Madam," the tailor said, looking rather proud of his work. "You simply undo the clips at the back for the bustle, thusly ... and then hook them to the opposite shoulder. So from the left back hip to the right shoulder," he said showing her what to do, "and then the right back hip to the left shoulder. *Et Voila*, as the French say, you are completely covered. In addition, because the fabric is not under tension, it makes it more able to slow heavier calibres and sword points."

As soon as the *faux*-bustle was redeployed as the tailor had demonstrated, she was completely covered. Diamond-shaped brass plates, two or three inches in size, dotted the open expanses of the fabric in a dazzling counter-point. Likewise, brass strips and rivets decoratively reinforced a few seams.

Arietta nodded and flashed one of her dazzling smiles. "Very ingenious ... and even done this way, it still winds up looking rather attractive. Almost a Moorish feeling in its cut."

"I heard you chatting with your companions about your Ethiopian origins, and I have a passing familiarity with the region, so the drape is intended to resemble a pair of crossed *neTela*. I hope you approve."

Arietta blinked at him, her jaw agape. She turned to the left and then the right and then back again looking at herself in the mirror. "Oh my. I had not noticed, but yes, now that you say it ... you have it very close. This is positively amazing."

He bowed. "Now, instead of hooking to the points of the shoulders," he said, "you can also hook to points at the wrist, thusly." He undid and moved the corners from the opposite shoulder to the same-side wrist. "While it may look as though you are intended to dance in the Arabian style, this actually allows you to cast protection over someone simply by pulling them against you and enveloping them in the two sections of suspended cloth. For light calibres, at least, it will offer plenty of protection. Of course, for a blade fight, it allows you to use the fabric away from the body to both block and obfuscate."

Arietta took a few long-paced strides with it, and nodded. "I will not be kicking anyone in the teeth wearing this, but I can certainly move as I please otherwise." She paused and thought. "Can you do this sort of thing again as a riding coat and pants, without the cut-outs, in a London pea-soup fog grey? This is a glorious outfit for cities and socials, but it is impractical for airships. I could pick it up tomorrow."

The tailor made a few scribbles on a piece of paper, and nodded. "Come by around four o'clock tomorrow and it should be ready," he said with a nod.

*****

(Afternoon, June 24th, 1888)

"I look ridiculous," Annika said from the other side of the dressing room door.

"You look smashing, Annika," Arietta countered. "Every part the fashionable lady."

"Which is exactly what I said; I look ridiculous," she groused. Hans covered his mouth to stifle a laugh as he sat and waited. They had gone from the armourer's store — with Arietta wearing her new attire — to the centre-west area of the city. Once in Soho, they had tried three stores before they found one that was willing to speak to Arietta at all. She was upset at the treatment, but remained calm about the entire matter.

Hans remembered his first reaction to the statuesque Negro woman and sighed. While he had been given his comeuppance on the point of gender and colour, most of the rest of Queen Victoria's London had not. He found it rather amazing how Arietta could deal with that sort of prejudice every day and not be bitter about it. Then again, she had chosen to spend her life in one of the most egalitarian and meritocratic of communities. Pirates had little care who you were, who your parents were, and where you came from as long as you were not "walking ballast". Gender and colour had nothing to do with it, as evidenced by the Chief Engineer and Captain-Gunner of the *Bloody Rose*, he thought.

Blackheart had once philosophized to him at the end of an evening meal that the life of piracy was akin to what happens when the French Foreign Legion buys airships and embraces American Capitalism. He still was not entirely sure he agreed with that, but it was an interesting point of view on the matter.

Once they had found a store that was willing to answer her enquiries about fitting and tailoring, she had come out to get Hans and Annika who were waiting in the carriage. She caused a bit of a stir to passers-by, dressed as she was with her figure. Annika had complained she felt like everyone had been disappointed the Italian-Ethiope had not been opening the carriage door for the Duke of the Danube Basin and his lover.

At the point that a six-foot Abyssinian in a Montremart-styled silken floor gown had entered the store to enquire about a fitting for a head-to-toe ensemble for a visiting Russian heiress in needed of dinner-attire, the store owner met the trio at the door to find out what his staff were all a-twitter about. He looked at the trio in a moment of obvious confusion and then recovered with a remarkable amount of poise. Within minutes, Hans was seated comfortably with cup of tea and the store owner's copy of the London Times to read, and the ladies were behind a privacy door.

Annika was obviously out of her element, and the store owner apparently found that rather odd. Hans had explained she was Cossack by birth, but as a result of a most peculiar set of events starting in Egypt, was going to be meeting his parents for dinner this evening in the Cotswolds. The shop owner thought about that for a moment, and opted to go ensure a fabric display was properly arranged. Hans had smirked and gone back to reading the paper.

The privacy door had opened several times over the past hour as one of the two women outfitting Annika had emerged to grab some item, accessory or the like and then again wordlessly disappeared behind the re-closed door.

Hans had nearly emptied his tea cup for the second time when the door opened and Arietta stepped out, followed by Annika. Hans stared and his mouth went dry.

"Based on the bedazzled expression on his face and the vacuous look in his eyes, Lady Nadezhda, I would say you look just fine," Arietta commented dryly.

It was a stunning gown in pale lavender silk, with a hint of jewel or metallic in the threads. It was off the shoulder with a daring neckline. The darker tone of the neckline's mantle was reprised in the long gloves she wore. A translucent shawl of silk and metallic threads draped over her shoulders and pulled together in the middle gave a shallow nod towards maintaining modesty. She was obviously corseted under the gown, giving her a slightly bustier appearance and the bustle also added to her modest curves.

Annika fidgeted slightly, unfolding a sandalwood fan and reflexively trying to hide behind it. "Do you like?" she asked Hans.

"Yes," he said with a slow nod. "I am very close to speechless."

"Very good news then, Master Sauder," Arietta commented. "I will not have to listen to your complaints about my driving so long as Lady Nadezhda is so dressed."

Hans shot her a foul look and Annika snickered behind her fan. "I think, Lady Nadezhda, that it would be time for us to make for the road. We have a good sixty miles to cover," he suggested. She beckoned him over with a gesture of her fan, and he obliged her.

She stood on her toes and whispered to him. "I hope you are going to be in a mood to undress me later," she said quietly and with a slight wink. "I do not think I can get out of this by myself for bed." She then gave him a demure look of coy innocence and strolled off, leaving Hans blinking with a slight flush to his cheeks.

*****

"So how much is this little play going to cost you in props?" Annika asked as they drove along. She sat close beside him, her head on his shoulder.

"About a third of an irrelevant fortune," Hans replied, looking at her with a smile. "The money I made aboard the *Bloody Rose* is paying for this. I really do not need it, and this will be a memorable way to spend some of it. Arietta is so happy with that armoured social dress that she is insisting on paying for it out of her own pocket. Between that thing and the other set she ordered, I think our tailor will be living very well for this month."

"He is not cheap, but it does stop bullets. That is worth paying for," she said with an amused smile.

"Indeed it is. As for you, my dear ... I would have paid twice that sum to see you in this. The only attire you look better in is water drops with moonlight accents."

Annika smiled slightly and then hesitated. "Really?"

"Really. So the next time Blackheart asks you to be arm candy for a Captain's Ball or a Governor's Dinner, you can be the *belle du soiree* without contest," he said softly.

She pouted. "I would rather wear it for you."

"I cannot go, and you cannot stay," he said.

"I know," she replied with a disgruntled sigh. "You may assure me that I look lovely, but I feel like an alley cat in a silk sack," she scowled. She shifted against him slightly, and he put his arm around her shoulders. She sighed. "Even when I was younger ... I always hated this sort of clothing. I always thought that the boys' clothes were so much more practical - particularly those of the ever-present soldiers. The only time *Ahtyets* ever insisted I dress like a girl was about once a month for the social parties he used to host. Once I turned nine he expected me to dress pretty and at least be seen at the beginning of the evening."

"Ahteeyets?" he asked.

"*Ahtyets*," she corrected. "Um ... *Pahpa* ... 'Father' in English," she said. "I was talking about my father."

Hans nodded.

She frowned in silence for a moment, lost in her thoughts before she resumed speaking. "The rest of Europe may hate him, but to those in power in the Russian Empire — the Tzar, the Generals, and many of the wealthy

— *Ahtyets* is a respected man. He spends a certain amount of his wealth very carefully to cultivate good social relations with the town's elite and those in the power in the ruling class. Or at least, he did back then. So, part of that was throwing lavish parties with impressive guest lists about once a month."

She looked up at him suddenly, looking rather afraid of something for a tense moment before she spoke.

"You do not think ill of me because of who *Ahtyets* is, do you?"

"No. While who he is pushed you to become who you a re... Well, really, how else would we be here, right now? You have worked very hard to be your own person, to have your own life, to control your own destiny. You, at a young age, made decisions that I still cannot make now. How could I possibly think ill of you, my lo-- ..." he stopped, leaving the word unfinished.

They looked at each other uncomfortably for a moment before Annika spoke "Hans, for both our sakes ... Please do not call me that again."

*****

(Evening, June 24th, 1888)

The self-propelled carriage rolled to a stop outside the front door of the beautiful country home near Chipping Norton, in the English Cotswolds. An improbably tall woman descended from the driver's perch, dressed in brass-adorned green silk. She had left a driver's duster coat in the cab. She walked up the steps with a clear surety in her motions. She rang the bell and waited.

The door opened a few moments later. A somewhat short and youthful man, still in the process of managing the door, began speaking even before it was fully open. "I am very sorry, the family is currently making ready for the evening meal. Solicitations and..." he trailed off with the dawning realization this was not the sort of evening door-caller he was used to.

"Please inform Mister and Missus Sauder that their eldest son has returned. He has dinner company with him," Arietta said, looking down at the servant.

The servant looked up at Arietta with wide eyes in a moment of awe before the message sank in. "Master Hans? He is back! He is safe?"

"Yes, Master Hans is back. He is in the carriage. In good health, beyond a bit of hunger from the travel. Go tell the Master and Lady of the house that their son has returned."

The young man excitedly ran off to deliver the momentous news, leaving a somewhat bemused Arietta standing by herself at the still-open doorway. Inside the carriage, Hans and Annika were laughing to the point of tears.

In short order, Hans, Annika and Arietta were surrounded by the entire living contents of the home, including the trio of excited Yorkshire terriers.

Hans' surprise at the rough embrace he was given by both his father and then again by his uncle Orel was evident upon his features. His mother wept with happiness at the sight of her son, and hugged him tightly while at the same time scolding him for having worried her so badly. Valeria, the youngest of the children was plainly overjoyed to see Hans again, but also quite clearly curious about the two impressive women in his company. His brother Karl, the middle child of the trio, shook his hand, welcomed him back politely and seemed rather reserved.

"Everyone, please ...   if I may introduce my companions?" Hans asked.

"Bring them inside, my son. We will adjourn this to the drawing room, and I will inform the kitchen to set another two places at the table and ensure that your driver is fed as well," Hans' father said, sounding very grand. Hans winced inside, but thankfully Arietta did not seem fazed.

They made their way down the central hall that was so familiar to Hans and yet now felt so alien. The paintings, the small statues on shelves, the rich woodwork; he was again assailed by the feeling of having new eyes.

Shortly they were all seated in the drawing room. A servant had brought in a couple of more chairs, resulting in a number one less than those to be seated. Arietta silently stood by the door, her arms folded across her chest with the points of the *faux* bustle clipped to her wrists. There was an uncomfortable moment of silence when it was clear that everyone was waiting for Arietta to leave, as a servant-driver might be expected to.

Annika flipped her fan open and then snapped it shut again, drawing attention to herself. "She is my bodyguard and does not let me out of her sight. You may speak freely in front of her," she said rather imperiously. She reopened the fan and lightly waved it towards herself.

The notion that whoever the lady Hans was travelling with had both cause and means to have a bodyguard obviously was rather impressive to everyone in the room. Hans' father nodded and asked if Arietta would like a chair. Arietta declined with a shake of her head.

"Everyone," Hans began slowly, "this is Lady Nadezhda. Her bodyguard is Arietta of Abyssinia. Lady Nadezhda, please allow me to introduce my family. This is my father, my mother, my Uncle, my brother Karl, and my sister Valeria."

Hans' father gave a semi-bow as Hans gestured to him. "Please, Lady Nadezhda, call me Friedrich. This is my wife Emmeline and my brother Orel."

"Such a pleasure to meet you," Emmeline said with genuine smile. That was something Hans had always liked about his mother. While his father might well be difficult to fathom at times, his mother was always both genuine and straightforward. She meant what she said, and said what she meant. While she was never cruel, she was always very firm.

"A pleasure to meet you all," Annika said with a polite grace. "Please, call me Annika." There was a murmur of polite nods and acknowledgements from everyone around the room, save Karl who remained somewhat distant.

"So ... what have you heard?" Hans asked.

"Pirates," Karl said stiffly.

Friedrich nodded at his son's statement. *"Ja,* we received word from the company which owned the ship you were a passenger upon that it had been attacked over France. We had been told that there had been some loss of life, that you had fought bravely to defend the crew, and had been taken as a prisoner."

He paused for a moment while Emmeline fussed for a moment, wringing a handkerchief. He took her hand and patted it gently and continued speaking. "I made some enquiries with friends in the Admiralty and discovered you had been taken by the *HMAFS Bloody Rose.* We heard nothing else."

Orel spoke up. "With the reputation of the ship in question and that of her *Kupitän,* we feared the worst. The silence of the past three months has been rather disheartening," he concluded in a rather pointed tone. Hans noticed Annika bristling somewhat.

Hans nodded. "I apologize for the silence. I was actually aboard the ship in question until a few days ago. They are somewhat reluctant to allow letters home detailing their exploits," he said dryly.

Friedrich and Orel both chuckled in understanding, while Karl forced a smile of acknowledgment. Hans glanced at him, wondering what was keeping his usually outgoing brother so dour.

A servant entered the room and announced that supper was ready. Hans knew he had seen the young woman before, but had no idea who she was. He resolved to ask tomorrow morning. Friedrich led everyone to the dining room and insisted that Arietta sit with them at the table and had a place rapidly set for her. It would be too difficult for her to eat standing up and would be ridiculous to set another table for just one person elsewhere in the room. Arietta conceded the point graciously and agreed.

*****

Over the meal, Hans explained in moderate details what had happened to him since he had awoken to the sounds of cannon fire and panicked crewmen aboard the *A.S. Windy Maid*. He did not use anyone's names, instead, referring to them by their jobs or their nationalities. Only Blackheart did he call by just his *nom de guerre*, but that was as much for dramatic effect. He carefully left out any reference to his complicated relationship with the Captain-Gunner, or his infatuation with the Chief-Engineer ... or the Wench in that bar in Egypt.

He carefully kept his focus on how very different things were in the day-to-day life aboard than he had imagined them as a boy. Or how ferocious the battles were, and the frightening cost they exacted.

As he had expected, it had taken two tries to convince his father that a pirate ship could mount an EMIPALE. Both Friedrich and Orel had peppered him with questions about it and the other engineering systems of the ship. Hans noticed Arietta twitching slightly, but she kept her tongue still.

His sister Valeria was thrilled to squeals when, in his narrative concerning the stay in Egypt, he passed her the two alabaster statues he had bought for her. His mother Emmeline had looked positively aghast when he described the shoot-out in the engine room of the Spanish merchant. His Uncle Orel bombarded him with questions about the underground economy when he described the hidden airship tower outside the town near Brussels. His father Friedrich was openly surprised when he explained the *Bloody Rose* had been approached to be a Privateer by the British Government.

Both Orel and Friedrich applauded him when he explained his decision to voluntarily stay on for the month foray into Russian airspace. Both looked impressed at the revelation that in doing so, Hans was now considered a Commissioned Officer within the Empire. Valeria scoffed at the notion that the spy who was their contact was a woman. Hans assured her it was very much the case, but she did not seem entirely convinced. The entire room fell to horrified silence as Hans described the battle at the Allied border town against the Dragon, and of the valiant sacrifice that one man made to save them all.

Eventually, the dishes were cleared away and the group retired to the smoking room for tea, coffee and dessert. They all sat around in a loose circle of chairs as Hans continued his story. He described the battles over the Russian Empire, the cunning and skill of the Russian airship crews and the vicious battles that were fought, including the near defeat at the hands of the RIAN Northern Wolf. He then explained the flight from the dangers of Russian airspace to the safety of Brussels.

"And it was there that you took your leave of the Privateer?" Orel asked.

"Essentially, yes," Hans nodded. "Which reminds me ... Father, you may find this interesting. Consider it a personal request from *Kapitän* Blackheart to make his stock-and-trade more difficult." Orel muttered something uncharitable in German about the Pirate Captain in question, even as Friedrich took the offered envelope. He read it over and looked at Hans.

"*Du musst scherzen*, Hans?" Friedrich asked in clear disbelief at what he was reading.

"*Nein, mein Vater.* I was specifically given that sheet by the *Kapitän* to give to you so that we might be able to build your next generation designs to out-perform the *Bloody Rose*. I know little else about it; I am merely the messenger," Hans chuckled.

Emmeline had a sip of her tea and then looked curiously at the Russian woman sitting with them, who had said precious little so far through the story. "So how do you know Hans, Annika?" she asked curiously.

Annika had a sip from her cup and flicked her glance at Hans for a moment. "He ensured my safety during the battle in the town with the Dragon," she said. "He is quite a brave man, and rather charming. We fell to talking and then we parted ways. I met him again in Brussels — such a coincidence, you know — and he mentioned he was travelling to London. It is a city I love dearly, and so I suggested we travel together," she said demurely. "We have gotten to know each other quite well in our travels. If I may be so bold, I think you have raised quite a dashing and courageous gentleman."

Hans flushed slightly, as much because of the unspoken text of her praise as what she said. He noticed his Uncle Orel giving him a knowing and approving look. It was a pity, Hans thought, that none of the trio were who they appeared to be.

"What are your plans now, Brother? Home to stay? Or leaving on another grand adventure?" Karl asked somewhat sharply. Emmeline looked rather shocked, and Friedrich lofted a brow.

Hans eyed him carefully. Something was wrong. Karl was usually far more easy-going and gregarious than this. If the truth were to be told, he had rather expected to be competing with Karl for Annika's attention most of the evening. Instead, Karl had been dour, withdrawn and becoming progressively more hostile.

"Karl, may I please speak to you in the Green Room? Alone?" Hans said, rising from his chair. Arietta lofted a brow at him, recognizing the clear bearing of challenge in both of the brothers.

"I thought you might never ask," Karl responded coolly.

Annika looked between them and it was rather obvious she was itching to come along. Valeria shorted that circuit with a series of questions about Annika's travels and her Russian homeland. Hans and Karl went to the other room and closed the oaken door behind them.

*****

"So, are you going to explain this intolerable attitude of yours without my having to resort to either brandy or cudgel?" Hans asked casually as the two brothers stood in the middle of the room looking at each other.

"Brandy? A cudgel? I see you have adopted a few vices during your travels as a Pirate, Brother," Karl remarked caustically, folding his arms over his chest. Karl was the same height as Hans but, having been the athlete of the pair, he was always a stone or two heavier in muscle. He was subtly broader at the shoulder than Hans, as well. Where Hans was dark haired, Karl was blonde. Both had their father's sharp blue eyes.

"All of them social, and worthy of the company I have been keeping," Hans countered. "What is the problem, Karl? Do not play games with me, as I have no time for them. I have spent the past three months weathering worse storms than your spoiled temper tantrums."

"I apologize for troubling the great and mighty First Son of the Sauders," Karl snapped back.

Hans blinked with a stunned realization. "You ... You did not want me to come back, did you, Karl?"

There was an ugly pause where Hans became convinced Karl might well swing at him. Then, suddenly, his brother's face was transformed into a mask of guilt and grief. It was also clear the younger brother was trying not to shed tears.

"Have you any idea how useless and diminutive I feel next to you, Brother?" Karl asked between clenched teeth. "Do you? I have lived for twenty years in your shadow, knowing that I am simply the back-up plan. Only if the mighty and gilded first son, Hans, should somehow pass on prematurely do I get to be of any value! Do you know how GUILTY I have felt, torn between wanting a chance to shine and knowing that it would only happen if my beloved older brother DIED?"

Hans stared at him, stunned to silence.

"It was like some cursed Lovelace-logic for an infernal Babbage-Engine of Fate ... IF Hans THEN NOT Karl ... Can you imagine how that must feel, dear Brother?" Karl continued in a whisper, trying to remain with some dignity, even as a tear traced his cheek.

"And then ... you go get captured by pirates!" he exploded, throwing his hands in the air. "And not just any pirates! Oh no, only the best for Hans!" Karl said with a bitter laugh. "Taken prisoner aboard the *Bloody Rose*! The Mediterranean Menace, herself! We get that news and then a terrible silence ... No letters, no messages ... You were gone! Vanished into the skies of France! Mother was a wreck, Father was a brooding beast, our poor sister was beside herself, our Uncle encouraging us all to cling to hope and suddenly, I MATTER! Suddenly, I am a man of the

Sauder house! I felt horrible, Hans ... I did not know if I should weep, laugh, be miserable or jump for joy."

Karl began to pace back and forth in front of him. Each step was short, tense and percussive as Karl continued speaking.

"Weeks and then months had passed! Just when Father and I have come to terms, and Mother has all but given up hope, you stride in here with an Abyssinian goddess in silk as a bodyguard, a beautiful Russian heiress on your arm — whom you met while fighting a *Dragon* for Peter's sake — and announce yourself as a prized crew member and Commissioned Officer of the now Chartered *Bloody Rose*! Four Russian Imperial Air Navy ships to your count. A bloody HERO!"

Karl stopped suddenly and turned on his heel to face Hans, folding his arms across his chest again and tapping a foot agitatedly. "You might as well just shoot me, Brother!" he shouted, pantomiming shooting himself in the temple. "I am sick to heart of only being of worth in your absence! If you are back to stay ... Then where does that leave me? What am I?"

Karl fell silent, his arms dropped and his shoulders caved forwards in near despair. "Part of me," he said in a low and shaky voice, "wants to chain you to mother's wrist so she never weeps so despondently again, and part of me wants to kill you so that I can live ... And you have the gall to ask about my 'intolerable attitude'? To ask what is WRONG?" Karl looked him squarely in the face and shook his head in disgust.

A long silence passed between the two brothers. "Thank you, Karl. You have no idea how important that was to both of our lives for you to say. Leave it to you to yet again have the answers to both our problems," Hans said quietly.

If there was a reaction that Karl had been expecting, that clearly was not it. His entire demeanour collapsed, like sails in doldrums. "What do you mean, Brother?"

"I mean that you should have a sword. Come with me."

*****

"Father, I have issue," Hans announced as they returned together to the drawing room where everyone waited for the brothers to conclude their private conversation. Everyone looked surprised at this declaration, particularly Hans' father. Hans walked to Arietta who tilted her head as he whispered to her. She nodded wordlessly and strode out of the room.

"What exactly do you find issue with, my son?" Friedrich asked as he carefully packed his pipe with a sweet-smelling tobacco.

"Karl has no blade to defend the family with. When I was four years younger than he is now, I was given a sword so that I could defend my honour and that of the Sauder name."

Friedrich considered that for a moment. He nodded. "You are correct. An omission, to be sure. I will see to it that it is addressed."

"With your permission Father, I would like to address that matter myself. Now," Hans said in a tone that made it clear there was little actual choice in the matter.

"Well, by all means, if you are in a position to do so," Friedrich said with an airy wave of his pipe. He lit the bowl and drew deeply. His exhale filled the air with the smell of apricots, brandy and wine.

"I am. But a moment, if you please," Hans said and walked out into the hallway. He unhooked his smallsword belt from the peg where he had left it with his coat as they had come into the house. He looked at it, nodded to himself and took a deep breath. He returned to where everyone waited for him. Hans moved to stand in front of Karl, who opened his mouth to protest.

"Please, Brother," Hans said cutting him off. He held out the sword and its belt to his younger brother. "Take it. Fate has made it clear to me it should have been yours all along. It will only hang idle where I am going."

Karl nodded slowly, realizing what Hans had just told him. He took the sword belt and buckled it on, adjusting its fit as Arietta strode into the room and passed Hans his scimitar. Hans buckled the blade of a Sultan's son about his waist, with his eyes on his fingers as he did. He looked up at Karl.

"Care to play a brother's game, Karl?"

"A game?" Karl said, surprise evident in his voice.

"You, sir, are a man of the Sauder House. I, sir, am a Pirate, within reach of your mother and sister. I suggest, sir, you remove me from your house. A Pirate, sir, is not to be trusted." The scimitar slid like liquid metal from the sheath and Hans' mother gasped.

"Hans! No, you cannot..."

"Leave them *play*, Emmeline," Friedrich said firmly. "This is important for both of them."

Hans glanced at Arietta and Annika. "You two stay out of this. No matter what happens," he warned them. Arietta gave a wordless and curt nod. Annika snapped her fan open and glanced away from him as she shielded her mouth. Valeria glanced from Arietta to Annika, clearly wondering how the Russian could conceivably interfere in a sword fight between two men.

Hans turned to Karl, who nodded and slowly drew the smallsword. They took guards, regarded each other for a long moment, and struck. The clash of steel rang throughout the English country home. They paused, eyeing each other warily, taking both time and measure of the man opposite. How could it be, Hans wondered, that for all the years spent as his brother, he could have mistaken Karl so badly?

The swords rang together again, and Karl pressed the attack, steering Hans away from the family. Hans gave ground and his brother pursued, his lighter and faster blade feinting and probing Hans' defences.

Hans had always been the intellectual, the thinker, the reserved one of the two. Karl was the physical, the doer, the bolder of the brothers. While certainly the deadly experience Hans had gained aboard the *Bloody Rose* had changed his style somewhat, it was obvious to the onlookers that Karl was slowly gaining the upper hand. A leg sweep missed, only to be replied to with a closed fist to the gut and a forceful shove that nearly cost Hans his footing. A clash of steel missed its mark on Karl, but left a sleeve slashed open on Hans.

Emmeline and Valeria were clutching their kerchiefs, unsure who to cheer for and becoming more and more convinced that this was not an innocent game. Orel looked as though he was quietly prepared to put a forceful end to the match with the walking stick he now held. Friedrich watched impassively from behind a thin blue cloud of pipe smoke.

The brothers rallied up and back down the hallway; a keen-minded servant opened the outside sets of doors and the fight spilled out into the front yard. Swords glinted in the gas lamps and moonlight, and rang like discordant bells.

Hans pressed Karl who stumbled a moment as he retreated. Suddenly, Karl sprang forward and turned, slamming his back against Hans' chest. Karl's left hand struck back over his left shoulder squaring Hans in the face and then his right elbow drove hard in to his brother's gut. There was a shriek of steel and the scimitar flew through the air to land a distance away, even as Hans marked his length on the ground.

The two brothers stared at each other, chests heaving and sweat dripping from their faces. The tip of his brother's smallsword hovered in front of Hans' face. "Swear it!" Karl hissed at him.

"Dolt," Hans spat back, propping himself up on his elbows in the grass. "I always play to win. When have I ever let you win at anything?" They stared at each other for another long moment and Karl nodded. The sword tip did not yet retreat.

"Do it, Karl," Hans growled. "We are both men of Heidelberg and we carry our scars proudly. Do we not?" Hans asked, setting his jaw.

Karl nodded and stared at his grounded brother for a long moment, their gazes unwavering. With a barked cry of tumultuous emotion, he sharply whipped the tip of the smallsword. Hans cursed and clapped a hand over the fresh red line from his chin to his ear. Both Emmeline and Valeria gasped and recoiled. Behind her fan, Annika gritted her teeth. Arietta looked darkly amused.

"My Brother is welcome home any time, Sir. A Pirate is not. Are we clear?"

"We are clear, *Herr* Sauder," Hans replied calmly as Karl sheathed the sword.

*****

Hans looked out the window at the moon-lit English countryside scrolling past. He had been silent since they had left, shortly after the end of the duel. His father's parting words still rang in his ears and he tried to hold onto them; "*No matter what ship you crew, what life you lead, Hans ... You will always be my son. You will always be welcome home*". He had no idea when he might speak to his family again.

"You let him win, did you not?" Annika asked quietly, brushing the back of his hand with her fan.

He looked over at her and smiled. "Of course I did. I could have cut that sword I gave him into two pieces before the first had hit the floor. But he does not know that. He needed to beat me, in front of Father and Uncle. There is no question whether he is the man of the house now." He paused for a moment and then gave a wry smile. "Besides, I never would have heard the end of it from Mother if I had spilled his blood. Always picking on Karl, I am, you know," he said with a laugh.

"Are you sure that this is what you want, Hans?" she asked softly. "You just gave up everything you have been struggling to return to since I met you."

"I will explain some other time, Annika. But my priorities have changed for the foreseeable future," he answered quietly.

"What now?" she asked.

He looked out the window for a long moment and then back at Annika. "I understand there is a ship called the *Bloody Rose* at the docks in need of an Engineer," he said with a thoughtful look. "I think I shall see if they will take me aboard as crew."

"EPILOGUE"

(Morning, June 25th, 1888)

Camilla Williams moved swiftly through the crowded oak and mahogany halls of the Admiralty of the British Air Navy. She was dressed as an officer and clearly wore a Lieutenant's rank. She drew a few surprised glances from the men she passed, but if she noticed she gave no sign. She knocked on a door and entered when she was given permission. She doffed her cap as she entered.

"I came as quickly as I could, sir," she said, somewhat out of breath.

"At ease, Mister Williams," the grey-haired and jowled officer sitting at the desk before her said. "Do you have a way of contacting that pirate that sold you the Serpentis Combine's lost Book of Min?"

Camilla blinked for a moment. "I believe so, sir. They are scheduled to sail tomorrow or the day after. I am sure I can reach my contact before then."

"Do so. Our man in Egypt has reported that the Russians have been sniffing around. We have reason to believe that they may have partially decoded the Book."

"What do I tell my contact?"

"The British Government would like to extend their Letter, but not for Privateering. We want them to do some snooping around of our own, without a Union Jack hanging over it," he said. He picked up a sealed tube and passed it to her. "Have that get to Blackheart's hands. I am sure he will find the compensation for a month of doing something other than shooting up Allied shipping worth his detour."

"But, Sir, why do you just not leave it to the Foreign Office to ..."

"Do pay attention, Mister Williams. We do not want the Russians to know the game is yet afoot. If anyone at the Office starts mucking about in this, we might as well send a letter to the Tzar himself on the matter. No, we will leave this to our new expendable best friends aboard the *Bloody Rose.*"

###

Author's closing:

I hope you've enjoyed visiting the Steampunk world of Hans, Annika, Blackheart and the rest of the scoundrels of the *Bloody Rose*. If you'd like to stay in touch to hear about upcoming books, connect with other fans or let me know what you think, here are some useful links:

Facebook Sauder Diaries Community Page:
https://www.facebook.com/the.sauder.diaries

Twitter: http://twitter.com/MichelV69

KindleGraph Signatures:
http://www.kindlegraph.com/authors/MichelV69

GoodReads Author Page
http://www.goodreads.com/michelv69

My blog: http://michelrvaillancourt.com/

I hope you enjoyed the story...

Welcome to the world of The Sauder Diaries!

Thanks so much for reading!

Regards,

Michel R. Vaillancourt, Author